UNFINISHED BUSINESS

UNFINISHED BUSINESS

The Cases of Walter Anchor Ghost Detective

ROBERT J. MCCARTER

Little Hummingbird Publishing

Walter Anchor, Ghost Detective Stories

Preface

First off, this book is the complete (as of now) collection of *Walter Anchor Ghost Detective Stories*, all six cases. It contains:

- Detecting Haley
- The Ghost Bride's Gift
- A Long Hard Fall
- Death of a Dentist
- A Hollywood Kind of Murder
- The Red Arrow Murders

If you've been reading them individually, there is nothing new besides this preface and an afterword.

Now that we are clear on that, on to the fun part. Walter Anchor and a little bit about his origins.

There are two elements that conspired to create this character:

- After my first novel, *Shuffled Off*, and the other first-person ghost novels I wrote, I knew there was room for other voices in this ghost world.

And I wanted it to be a different voice and a different genre. I mean, if ghosts can write their own stories there must be so many stories to tell, right?

- I was at a writing conference featuring Kevin J. Anderson in 2012 and he was introducing his *Dan Shambles. Zombi PI* series. Since he had created a zombie detective, why not a ghost detective?

Those two things combined and off my crazy creative brain went. And not just a ghost detective, a ghost detective trying to solve his own murder!

While each of Walter's cases are stand-alone there is a larger story arc that goes through them all and the preferred reading order is as they are presented here.

Ready to find out how a ghost solves murders and what happens when he tries to solve his own?

Enjoy!

Robert J. McCarter
October 2020
Flagstaff, Arizona

DETECTING HALEY

A WALTER ANCHOR
GHOST DETECTIVE STORY

ROBERT J. MCCARTER
AUTHOR OF *SHUFFLED OFF*

Chapter One

I HATE BEING A GHOST. DON'T GET ME WRONG, I'M GLAD to have consciousness and all that, but it's the little things I miss. Like the taste of a tender, juicy steak and a cold beer. The sound of an audience clapping for me. The feel of a pair of dice in my hands. The rough texture of a cat's tongue. The searing heat of the Tucson sun.

But so what? I'm a ghost and I've got a murder to solve. *Mine.*

We ghosts usually have unfinished business, and since I haven't heard the "call," I figure my unfinished business is my murder—that's what's keeping me earthbound. The "call" is that glorious event when a ghost moves on to the next stage of their afterlife. Opinions on exactly what this is varies, but I'm ready to be out of here.

Not that I'm qualified to solve murders or anything. I was a dentist by trade and before that an out-of-work actor.

These thoughts rumbled through my mind as I stared at the dead body on the grimy carpet below me.

"Well?" Emily asked. She looked at me with her

ancient green eyes that inhabited her round baby face. She has short, curly blonde hair that reminds me of Shirley Temple when she was a kid. Emily died when she was four years old, but now she's eighty years dead. There is a lot of wisdom packed in that adorable little body. But I gotta tell you, it's more than a little disconcerting.

"What?" I shrugged, looking at the dead body and her ghost. She was in her late twenties with long brown hair. Her blood had pooled and congealed on the light-blue carpet. Her ghost was gape jawed and clearly in distress, the thin silver cord that attached her soul to her body still intact, going from belly button to belly button.

"You've got to do something," Emily insisted. She has an adorable lisp, so it was "You've got to do *thomething*." I won't write it that way so you don't go crazy reading my little story, but you get the idea.

"Why?" I asked.

"The poor thing is suffering," she said, pointing at the wispy mess of a ghost, its mouth open wide, a pitiful moan escaping from its throat.

"You do something," I said.

"I am. My plan is to whine until you do something." Emily may be eighty years dead, but there was still a lot of four-year-old left in her.

I sighed. "This is a distraction, Emily. We are here tracking a clue to my murder."

"Yeah, and that clue took us here. To her. I think we need to investigate."

I nodded, stooping down and looking at the body. "Maybe we can snoop around and get Banquo to come take care of the bardo-brain." The bardo is a place we ghosts often find ourselves when things don't go so well and this ghost had all the signs.

"Should I go get him?" Emily asked, her voice going all

4

high when she said "him." The girl has a great big crush on Banquo. He's kind of the ringleader of our graveyard community, and Emily has had a thing for him since he first came there around ten years ago. He is an expert, as much as anyone is, in helping these distressed ghosts.

I looked closer at the corpse, getting down low so I could clearly see her face. I felt a tingle of shock flow through my ghostly form. I knew this woman. She temped at my dental practice the month before I was murdered. And now she lay here also murdered.

Even though I wasn't experienced at the detective thing at the time, the knife sticking out of her back gave away the "murder" part of the equation.

My name is Walter Anchor. I solve murders. This is my first case.

Chapter Two

"YEAH," I SAID TO EMILY, "GO GET HIM." WITH A girlish squeal and a "pop" she was gone, and I was left there with the dead dental assistant.

I looked around the grubby little Tucson apartment. A small bedroom, a kitchen with dirty dishes everywhere, a cracked LCD TV in the living room. I then looked at the victim again. Tall, slender, dressed in designer jeans and a pastel blue blouse stained with her own blood. Her nails were well manicured and the makeup on her face expertly applied.

This was not her apartment.

Being a ghost detective is all about observation. It's not like you can question witnesses, or root through their garbage, or run a background check. What you can do is watch and observe, twenty-four hours a day, seven days a week.

The ghost groaned and I got up and looked at it. Her ghostly appearance was nothing like her physical appearance. She had a diffuse vapor-like form, her eyes wide, her limbs vague stubs. She was lost, trapped in her own personal hell, a place known as the bardo. This torturous state is not uncommon for us earthbound spirits, and even less uncommon for the murdered.

I have never been in that state. I have Emily to thank for that.

The ghost moaned again and I listened carefully. The one great advantage of being a ghost detective is that you can sometimes talk to the dead.

"Haley," I said, remembering her name. "It's me, Doctor Anchor. Can you tell me what happened?"

"Blaaa," she hissed, her eyes meeting mine briefly. "Blaaaack Shooooes."

"Black Shoes?" I asked.

"Blaaaack Shooooes," she moaned again. In fact, the need to listen carefully was overkill. Haley just kept saying it over and over again, the moan of it becoming a kind of eerie mantra as I went back to examining the body.

The knife was thin and long, buried to the hilt between two of the vertebrosternal ribs. It had pierced her heart, she hadn't been alive long; the person wielding the knife had known what they were doing.

I made a slow sweep of the apartment and found out several things. Someone named Roger Coptic lived there, he was a slob, a drug addict (the used needles in the trash can were a dead giveaway), and hadn't been home in quite some time (the wilted marijuana plants in the bathtub helped with that).

Which led to the question, what was a nice girl like her doing in a place like this? And, what did this Roger Coptic have to do with my own murder?

Chapter Three

MAYBE I SHOULD PAUSE AND GIVE YOU A LAY OF THE land. Like when I was alive and a patient would come in for a procedure. It seemed to always help for me to sit down with them and tell them what to expect, warn them of the difficult parts, and make sure they understood both the risks and the rewards. Especially the unpleasant procedures like a root canal or an extraction or root planing. Ah, hell, who am I kidding? I was a dentist, most of the "procedures" were unpleasant.

I would put on my deep actorly voice and tell them the toughest pieces in the calmest, most reassuring voice possible.

So here goes.

The world thinks I committed suicide, which I frankly find depressing. I know, suicide is pretty high in my line of work, but I was a happy dentist. Seriously, I was. I loved my job, I loved my staff, I loved my patients. My life wasn't perfect, I had been divorced for several years and found myself a bit phobic about relationships (could explain why my best friend as a ghost appears to be a four-year-old), I had a bit of a gambling problem (okay, okay, by a "bit," I meant "massive"), and I hadn't talked to any family members for a few years.

So yeah, there was the good in my life and the not so good. Just like any other human on the planet, you peel back the layers you're going to find some nasty stuff. Me, I was lonely. I worked too long because I didn't have much else to do, except for gambling. It's hard to feel alone when you're throwing the dice at the craps table and people are cheering you on.

Anyway, where was I? Oh yeah... lay of the land. So about six months before finding Haley murdered, I had been working late, finishing my charting, avoiding going back to my crappy apartment, when I was murdered. It wasn't anything spectacular, I had just sat down in one of the dental chairs and closed my eyes for a moment—I must have fallen asleep. Next thing I knew I was a ghost hovering over my own body.

It was a shock, to say the least. Looking at my body, a hypodermic still sticking out of my arm, a drop of blood at the injection site. It looked like a suicide, but I know it wasn't.

I spent several months in the dental office—and not by choice, I must say—watching. I guess you could say I was haunting the place. I didn't really "do" much of anything but creep people out occasionally, but I watched and waited and listened.

My partner in the practice, Doctor Wheeler, kept things going and soon people started talking about me. Specifically, talking about me like I wasn't there.

Let me give you a piece of advice. If you find yourself a ghost, get away from the people you knew if you can. This shouldn't come as a surprise, but folks don't see you the same way you see yourself. There are misunderstandings and your intent is not always apparent. The experi-ence can be disturbing to say the least.

I could give you lots of examples, but let's just say that some of my employee's feelings about me were rather surprising, some liking me way more than I thought proper and others disliking me more than I thought possible. Which makes sense, no one sees you like you see yourself. It just isn't comfortable.

So, I was stuck in my dental office, and as the picture of the events of that day became clear, I decided I needed to find my own murderer. One clue at a time, one step at a time.

It's not like I had anything else to do.

Chapter Four

WHEN I HEARD TWO POPS, I LOOKED UP FROM HALEY'S body and saw Emily and Banquo. Emily was beaming and looking up at the big-bellied man. Banquo stepped forward, his eyes on me and then the ghost.

"Good evening, Walter," he said.

"Banquo," I replied. Look, I give the guy his props. He knows a lot and does a lot for our little community, but I just ain't in the fan club. Not one of his students.

Now it could be that he is also the leader of the Midnight Circle—the nightly gathering of the ghosts at the graveyard—and that irks me a bit. Sure the guy's an English Lit professor, knows a lot of Shakespeare and other plays by heart that he leads the circle in. But maybe they should give someone with acting experience a chance every now and then. Someone like—

"Have you tried to reach her?" he asked.

I snorted in response. I knew he knew the answer. He just wanted to hear me say I couldn't be bothered.

"I know you can help her," Emily said to Banquo, her little lispy voice higher than usual. She's one of the reasons

I don't feel the need to faun over Banquo—she does it more than enough for both of us.

"My boy," Banquo said to me, "you really should take the time to help those in need."

I straightened up and met Banquo's gaze. "I am," I said, pointing at myself with both my thumbs. "Who else is going to solve my murder?" I moved away into the bedroom to see what I could see there. I left Banquo, Haley's ghost, and Emily to do their thing.

ALL THAT TIME I spent haunting my dental practice I learned many things, but most of them not useful to solving my murder.

Mostly what I learned watching and listening was the messy reality of humanity: unhappiness, affairs, depression, petty bickering, addiction, and the like. I also saw the good stuff (kindness, love, and generosity), which I had known was there too. But, it was the quantity of the not so good stuff that surprised me.

Ultimately I did find a clue to my murder. There was something off about Midge, my office manager. It was the guilty look she kept getting on her round Midwestern face when no one was looking. She knew something.

When I could finally leave the dental office (that's a whole 'nother story), I started following her everywhere and eventually came the day when the letter arrived. It was a plain white envelope with her address shakily written in blue ink. She had rushed into the bathroom with it, avoiding her husband and daughter, and opened it.

It said, "If you need to reach me again about your financial problems, drop a note at this address." It was followed by the address of the gross apartment Haley died in.

Midge's hands shook as she slowly tore up the letter and flushed it down the toilet. At first when I saw that guilt on her face I had been angry; seeing her scared like that softened that feeling. She knew something, but whatever she had done, she had been coerced.

I shook right next to Midge, my ghostly form turning diffuse, my vision tunneling in, a crushing depression descending on me.

Conspiracy... had there been a conspiracy to kill me? Was Midge part of it? It looked like my death was part of something larger. I was nobody, just a failed actor turned dentist. Who would want me dead?

I would have fallen into the bardo right then and there if it hadn't been for the little voice that said, "Not cool, let the lady go to the bathroom in private. What kind of sicko are you?"

I saw the little ghostly form of Emily, her hands on her hips, her mouth a sneer.

Seeing her shocked me back to myself. "Who are you?" I asked.

Chapter Five

As I looked around Roger Coptic's bedroom with its unmade bed, its piles of dirty laundry and unopened mail, I tried to tune out Emily and Banquo. Her voice was an octave higher than usual as she said things like, "Oh, I so know you can help her," or "Did anyone ever tell you you look like Lawrence Olivier from when he played King Lear at the West End in London?" or "What are you doing later tonight?"

Banquo's replies were curt but courteous. And then at some point things got quiet out there, which was fine by me.

"I had a thought," Banquo said to me, from the door of the bedroom.

I looked up from the grease-stained pile of mail, not answering, but giving him my best "can't you see I'm busy doing important things" look.

"I think you should try to pull her from the bardo. She might have some information for you about her murder and that might help you along."

Emily stood behind him and to his left, her eyes all

doey as she stared up at him. "Walter," she gasped. "Isn't that a brilliant idea? That was brilliant, Banquo."

And it was a good thought, but I certainly didn't want to say that in front of Emily. "I guess," I replied. "But, I have no idea how to—"

Banquo's face lit up like a kid on Christmas morning. "I'll be happy to show you what I know, my boy." Banquo loves to teach, it's really his thing. And while I appreciated the thought, I can't stand it when he calls me "my boy." I'm not his boy.

BANQUO IS CHUBBY, bald, sixtyish, and grey haired. He slowly paced around Haley as he lectured, his hands clasped behind his back. Very much the professor.

He started by explaining the bardo—I know what the bardo is. It's that place ghosts often get stuck where they are reliving the worst of their past, stuck in their regrets. It's hell, quite literally. Haley was there, no doubt. Her eyes were wide, her mouth slack, B-movie-ghost groans coming out of her mouth. And I felt for her, I did, but it's not like there's an easy foolproof five-step plan to get someone out of the bardo.

"The essence of it," Banquo said, "is finding something more important to her than her suffering."

"Oh," I said in my best dry sarcastic tone. "That's all."

Banquo stopped and looked at me. He has this penetrating gaze that, if the rumors around the graveyard are to be believed, can see directly into your soul.

"People like to suffer," I said by way of explanation, his eyes focusing on mine. I really didn't want him looking into my soul. That grunge and disorder that has its home there is mine, all mine. Emily looked at me too, her little brow furrowed. "Really, they do," I continued. "Look at anyone you knew when they were alive. How many ways did they make their life harder, how many things couldn't they let go of that would have made them happier? How much—" I cut myself off when I saw Emily's face, her lower lip was quivering and she looked like she was about to cry. I knelt down in front of her and said, "What is it, honey?"

As little girl tears rolled down her ghostly face, she said, "My mom, after I died. She couldn't let it go, she suffered so much. I…"

I carefully modulated my ghostly form (a must for a ghost to touch another ghost) and pulled Emily in for a hug and let her cry. She was in the past, and when she was like that she was much more the four-year-old girl and much less the eighty-year-old ghost. I caught Banquo giving me a "look what you've done now" look.

After she was done crying, she growled, "Get your mitts off me, you perv."

I didn't take it personally. It was Emily's way of telling me she was all right.

"Now," Banquo said, clearly about to resume his lecture, "you knew her, what might be more important to her than her suffering?"

"Knew her?" I said. "She temped for me for a month. We weren't exactly bosom buddies." I mean, yeah, there a little more to it than that, a moment where I stupidly thought she might like me and I didn't actually hate the idea, but I wasn't going to tell Banquo that.

"Nevertheless, you knew her best. What might be more important to her?"

And thus began my first lesson with Banquo. And I will admit he was smart, knew his way around the ghostly world, and was generous with his time. But, that doesn't mean I suddenly became one of his disciples, hanging on his every word, kowtowing to him. I listened and I learned.

We tried everything, it took hours and hours. I kept hoping someone would discover the body so we could, at least, get out of that disgusting apartment. But no such luck. The sun set, night passed, and the sun rose before I finally stumbled onto something. It came from fatigue, not thinking.

"Hey, Haley," I said. "You look good today. You know I really appreciate you coming in and helping us out, but I'm kind of torn. I have a policy of not dating any of my staff, and if you weren't... well I would... you know." I used to be an actor, so I sold it. Being all shy and coy, my ghostly cheeks flushing red. I am not sure what possessed me to try it beyond fatigue and what I had learned haunting the office—more than one of the girls and at least one of the boys had had a crush on me.

There was a sharp snap, as the silver cord connecting her spirit to her body broke, her eyes came into focus and a smile formed on her lips. "Doctor Anchor, why, I had no idea." She blinked rapidly a few times, her eyes widening, her mouth opening, her form firming up a bit, looking a little less bardo-ish.

"I couldn't tell you then, Haley," I said, fighting to keep her present. Out of the corner of my eye I saw Banquo beckoning me towards the door, out of the apartment. Yeah, that made sense. Not a good idea for Haley to see her body with the knife sticking out the back and her dried blood looking like reddish-brown cottage cheese. "But now... you know... maybe we can spend some time together."

Her eyes stayed focused on me as we walked through the wall and out of the apartment into the Tucson morning, the sun just peaking over the horizon. "I think I would like that, Doctor Anchor."

Inside I was freaking out—I had no desire for a ghost girlfriend, but I just smiled and held my character. "Haley, it's not Doctor Anchor. It's time you called me Walter."

Chapter Six

THAT DAY I MET EMILY, IN MIDGE'S BATHROOM, THE bardo so very close, she wore what she calls her "summer outfit." Blue shorts and a white T-shirt with a drawing of a red lollipop on it. I stared at her. I hadn't seen a well-formed ghost before. She looked like a person, just a bit transparent. The only other ghosts I had run into at the dental office had been vaporous presences like me.

"You heard me," Emily said. "Leave the lady alone. I mean it."

My shock and curiosity at seeing her chased the bardo away. "I… What?" I stammered.

"Christ on a stick, are you a bardo-brained perv or what?"

"Huh?" I said, not understanding what she was talking about.

"Did you die in here?" she asked. "Are you going to spend the rest of eternity haunting people trying to relieve themselves?"

"No," I said, coming more into myself. "Of course not.

I… I was murdered. She knows something, that letter she just read is a clue."

"Well then, prove it," she said, turned on her heel, and walked through the bathroom door. Something made me follow her. Part of it was that she was a different kind of ghost, part of it was how articulate she was and how young she looked. She spoke with a bit of a lisp making her sound young, yet her words were anything but.

"So," she continued once we were out of the bathroom, "are you trying to be a gumshoe or something?"

I blinked. I knew she was asking if I was a detective, the archaic slang adding to the mystery of her. "I just want to find out who killed me."

"And then what?" she asked, crossing her arms.

"I… well…" I hadn't thought that far.

She shook her head slowly, giving me a most disapproving look. "You don't know anything, do you?" She looked up and added, "Lord, why me? This fellow is so wet behind the ears he's about to drown." She sighed and looked back at me. "Come along. I guess you've won the lottery, big boy, because ole Emily here is going to show you the ropes."

"I need to stay here," I said. "I need to follow Midge. I need to find out who killed me."

She sighed again. "One track mind. Can't say I mind that in a man, as long as the track his mind is on is one I like." She gave me a leering grin that was completely out of place on her young face. "Look… What's your name?"

"Walter."

"Look, Walter. You stay here you will end up in the bardo, a lost cause, a waste of an afterlife. But if you really want to find your killer, come with me now. I'll teach you enough so you can be a proper ghost." With that she walked away. I followed.

Chapter Seven

I KNOW THERE ARE MANY METHODS TO ACTING, BUT there is only one way I know to make my face do what I want it to do: feel the feelings. So if I am playing a part and my character is scared, I do my best to scare myself. It's not the same as a "real" scare—like someone pulling back the shower curtain and lunging at you with a knife— but it's the memory or shadow of the emotion. That's enough.

So my method for acting is… well… Method Acting. I draw on my own past and emotions for the role I am play- ing. And with Haley, right outside the boring two-story apartment she was murdered in, I was playing the part of suitor. As painful as it was, I summoned the memories of when I courted my ex-wife, that giddy time of being young and falling in love.

Haley was pretty enough—if much too young for me —with high cheek bones, a constellation of freckles perched there, and pale blue eyes. As I talked, her ghostly form came into better focus, but it wasn't great.

I had kept up a patter of flattering talk and gotten her away from the apartment complex and into a little park across the street. It was early morning and except for us ghosts the place was deserted.

"Do you remember?" I asked. The question was intentionally non-specific. I needed info about her murder, but didn't want to push her off the edge back into the bardo.

"What?" she asked, her ghostly form becoming more diffuse.

"It was your eyes, you know," I said, backpedaling. "That light powder blue, they remind me of the sky after a good rainstorm. So lovely."

Her form solidified a bit and her cheeks flushed. "Oh, Doctor Anchor." She saw my stern, but cute, look and added, "I'm sorry… Walter."

"I know," I said, putting a bright smile on my face. "Tell me about your day, tell me everything."

Her eyebrows furrowed, I suspect no man had ever said that to her with such enthusiasm. But I held the expression (and yes, I was acting) and her eyebrows rose and a smile bloomed on her face. She began telling me about her day, every little thing, in exhaustive detail. The girl was obviously starved for attention.

I "um-hummed" in all the right places, asked questions and encouraged details, long before I knew I would need them, and did an Oscar worthy performance hanging on her every word.

It took a while, but when we came to the important information, what she was doing at Roger Coptic's apartment, she had such momentum talking that she didn't seem to notice the bardo-rific territory we had strayed into.

It took everything I had to keep the look of rapt attention on my face when she told me what happened. I wanted to run (or rather, fly) away and give up this whole quest to find my murderer. But I didn't, I held my character and got it all.

Chapter Eight

WHEN EMILY RESCUED ME FROM MIDGE'S BATHROOM, a fact she insisted on telling everyone in the graveyard when I met them, I was a green, wet-behind-the-ears ghost. Emily took me in, kept me out of the bardo, and taught me the basics.

You might think it's easy being a ghost, but you would be wrong, *dead* wrong.

(And if you'd like to laugh, or even clap at the clever use of "dead" in the previous sentence, I won't mind. Actor, remember. I get off on that kind of stuff.)

It is nice to be able to fly, go through walls, not have to eat or bathe. But you trade all that regular human overhead for crushing boredom and the waiting bardo. So as a fresh ghost you have time on your hands (boredom) and way too much time to think about all the mistakes you made in your life, all your regrets, and (in my case) who the hell killed you (that would be the waiting bardo part).

Emily was no gentle teacher, but with eighty years of being a ghost she knew her way around all of that. She taught me and kept me in and around the graveyard for a few months until the day she got tired of me whining (see, I did learn some things from her) and went with me to that apartment where we found Haley with a knife in her back.

———

HALEY HAD FINALLY LANDED a full-time position at a dental office, so the day she told me about was a day familiar to me. Getting up, doing the mundane activities required to maintain biological life—you know, bathing, eating, eliminating, getting ready to go. It made me nostalgic, because the girl talked about these activities in great detail.

BUT IT WAS HARD FOR ME TO LISTEN TO. DENTISTRY WAS my fallback career but it was still one I enjoyed. And that was fine, but Haley's fulltime job was at Wheeler Dental. As in Doctor Wheeler. As in my former practice partner. As in Haley was working at *my* newly renamed dental office.

Stuff I knew but had effectively repressed after Emily saved me and started helping me be a proper ghost.

I hated the thought, but I smiled and nodded and congratulated her. She had been a fine dental assistant and deserved a full-time gig. Except she wasn't working anywhere anymore, was she? Because she was dead just like me.

And then we got to the good—as in "holy crap"—part.

"Doctor Wheeler asked me to do an errand for him," she said. "As I think back on it now, he seemed a little nervous. He gave me a small package, one of those bubble wrap mailers. It was real light, so it couldn't have had much in it. An address was written on a sticky note, not on the package."

"Did he tell you what was in it?" I asked.

She shrugged her shoulders. "He said I would get paid for the errand, that he would pay overtime. I had done the same thing for Midge a few times before and I needed the money. So…"

So, she didn't care, didn't think to ask.

Now that my memory was coming into clearer focus, I had known that something odd was going on at my office. On my last night alive, Midge had told me she wanted to keep Haley on, which was a surprise. And when I was haunting the office, I had witnessed some of the handling of these packages.

But what does this have to do with my murder? Or Haley's?

"I can see his face so clearly," she continued. "His smile was so big, his teeth so white, but I noticed a bead of sweat on his forehead. And Midge was always a little strange about it too. Super nervous. Sometimes mumbling to herself." She paused, her eyes focusing on me. "It's funny that I can remember things so clearly. My memory has always been a little poor, but not today. I can remember my first day of high school as clear as a bell. Want to hear about it?"

"I would love to hear about it," I said, making sure the smile on my face was not too big. "But, let's finish up with the day you are telling me about already. Okay?"

She nodded.

"What was the address on the package?"

She kind-of walked towards the swing set as she rattled off the address to Roger Coptic's apartment. Her walk was most definitely a "kind-of." While her form was better than it previously was, she still looked positively ghostly with a vague movement of her legs as she floated over the green grass towards the little swing set. It takes practice, a lot of it, to look fully human.

"Do you remember what happened when you delivered it?" I knew she did. She was clearly experiencing the enhanced memory that we ghosts have. Funny, we are all literally brainless and yet have a nearly eidetic memory.

"The little man that answered the door scared me. He hadn't shaved in a few days and his teeth were stained yellow. I handed him the package and he smiled at me. He had a missing tooth." She pointed to her mouth, tooth number ten, the right lateral incisor. It was really bad form for her to be so vague, considering our former business. "He invited me in. I didn't want to go in, but he insisted, saying he had to get something for me to return to Doctor Wheeler. I stood there holding the package, smelling the rotting garbage smell of the place when..." She stopped, her form going diffuse, her eyes getting wide.

"What?" I asked.

"I... My..." she stammered, her right arm vaguely pointing towards her back where she had been stabbed. "Pain. It hurt so much. I cried out. I fell. Someone took the package out of my hand."

"Did you see him?" I asked.

She shook her head. "But he had nice shoes. All black and polished and old fashioned. Like the dads wear in those movies about the fifties."

Well, that explained the chanting of "Blaaaack Shooooes" when we found her. "What happened then, Haley?" I knew she was on a one-way ticket to bardo-land, but kept pushing. I needed to know what she knew.

"Then I saw that man's face, the one that answered the door, with his scraggly beard and his horrible breath. It smelled like old cigarettes and rotten cheese. He was freaking out, cursing, and then I was alone. It got so cold… it hurt so much…"

The girl was definitely losing it. I caught Banquo looking at me, his little nod and widening eyes making it clear he wanted me to do something about it, that he didn't want to see her bardoed again.

"What happened to me? So cold…" she muttered.

Emily was staring at me too, her arms crossed, her little hip cocked. Her body language said, "I helped you, you've got to help her."

So I did the only thing I could think of. I fell back into the role I had been playing and I kissed her.

Chapter Nine

BEING A GHOST, THE RULES ARE DIFFERENT. EVERY ONCE in a while things happen that remind me just how different they are. Like when I kissed Haley in that little park across from where she was killed.

Touching as a ghost takes a lot of skill. Emily had taught it to me when she was showing me the ropes. She thought it essential to my survival (and even though ghostly touching is a shadow of what it is like when you're alive, imagine an existence without it). And besides, Emily likes to high-five. Well, with us it's more of a high five for her and a low five for me.

Okay, so ghosts can walk through walls and, really, walk through anything—even other ghosts. So there are two components to ghostly touching: matching frequency and intent. The frequency part is about making your ghostly form the same as the ghost you want to touch. In this case that meant me becoming a diffuse almost-bardoed mess. I was trying to make what passed for our lips come together.

Back at the graveyard, Jim and Jane are a couple, but

they don't seem to be into public displays of affection, so I was going in blind.

When our lips met, what happened was not what I expected. I felt our lips touch, the numb sense of ghostly touch, but then...

I felt my body, weak and cold, with the hard floor underneath me. I smelled the musty, grimy carpet. I saw the slick, old-fashioned black shoes, a well-manicured hand taking the package, and the person leaving. I saw the gap-toothed grin of Roger Coptic and smelled his rotten breath. And then I was alone and so cold. I couldn't move, I couldn't speak. I realized that I was dying, that the pain in my back was killing me. I worried about my mother, we were supposed to go to the movies tonight. I worried about my cat, who was going to feed him? I thought of a man I had once loved. But then, even my thoughts became less coherent. I felt confused and upset and knew death was close, ready to take me.

The sequence of senses and thoughts restarted and played over and over again. I was stuck in Haley's death, feeling what she felt, thinking what she thought.

"All right, all right," a high-pitched voice said. "Break it up kids. I mean, really, get a room." I heard it dimly as if it was coming from a great distance. But it distracted me from the death scene I was reliving. "Seriously, you two. Break it up or I'm going to get physical with you."

I couldn't do anything about what was happening. I was lost, stuck, sliding into the bardo with Haley.

"Okay, don't say I didn't warn you," Emily said. I felt this sharp sensation in my foot. I can't call it pain, but it got my attention, and then I was standing right in front of Haley, her eyes wide.

"Doctor Anchor," Haley whispered, her hand going to

her face. Her form looked better, less ghost-ish and more human-ish, actually much better than it had.

I looked down at my own form and I was the diffuse mess. Emily was standing right next to me shaking her head. "Kids these days," she said, and marched back to Banquo who had a bemused look on his face. I concentrated on my own form until it came into focus. I was wearing my usual post-death outfit. Actually it was my usual pre-death outfit: scrubs. As a dentist I had practically lived in them, it is what came naturally.

"Are you okay, Haley?" I asked.

She nodded and gave me a smile. It is the kind of smile Emily would call "come hither." It was clear that my experience kissing her had been different than hers. When I talked about ghosts touching, I mentioned intent. Well, my intent had been to keep her out of the bardo, and somehow I had taken on part of her death burden and done that, but nearly went to bardo-land myself.

"Are you okay, Doctor Anchor?" she asked. I was most definitely out of character. I am sure the wide variety of emotions I had been feeling had been all over my face.

"Please, Haley," I said, pulling the tatters of my role back on, just as I had pulled my ghostly form together. "You must call me Walter. I think we are far past the point where you need to call me Doctor." I offered her my arm, modulating it for touch and having a clear intent to *just* touch. She took it and we walked away from the park and towards the graveyard.

It would take us most of the day to walk there, but it gave me time. Time to get her oriented. Time to help her understand that she was dead. Time for me to find out if Haley knew anything else that might lead to her murderer and mine.

Chapter Ten

DOCTOR ELIAS WHEELER AND I BECAME VERY CLOSE after that. Haley, as it turns out, didn't know anything else. Doctor Wheeler had had her deliver a package to Roger Coptic. She was murdered. Someone took the package. Roger fled.

Wheeler—I am going to drop the "Doctor"; it's a sign of respect, something I no longer have for him—was under our surveillance. And by "our" I mean me, Emily, and Haley.

For the first few weeks it was either Emily or myself watching him, while the other stayed with Haley at the graveyard, helping her adjust to being a ghost. After that it was all three of us. Once Haley started getting comfortable as a ghost, she got mad.

"Haley's gone comet," Emily whispered to me. I had come back to the graveyard for our shift change. Emily was on her way into the mortuary, a ritual where the ghosts check out the newly dead that is called the "greeting committee." Wheeler was asleep and it was a safe time to do it.

"What?" I asked.

"You know, Haley's Comet. The girl is on fire, lit up, burning across the sky—"

"Emily, can you please just tell me what's going on and stop with the metaphors."

Emily rolled her eyes and stuck her tongue out at me. "Spoil sport. The girl is pissed. She's angry. She's ready to rip Wheeler's heart out and eat it for breakfast. She is the proverbial woman scorned. She—"

"Okay, okay," I said, cutting her off and holding my hands up. "I get it. She wants revenge."

A wicked smile crept onto Emily's lips. "Which brings us to your planned breakup."

I had continued on with my "relationship" with Haley. It wasn't that big of a deal. We spent time together, held hands, and kissed here and there. When she got into troubling territory, kissing seemed to calm her down, ground her, and I had gotten better at not taking too much on from her. I had told Emily that I planned to break it off as soon as she got stabilized. I liked the girl, had grown quite fond of her—I just didn't want to carry on a relationship that I had started out of desperation.

"You think..." I began.

"Didn't you hear what I said about 'woman scorned'?" Emily asked.

"Where is she?"

"She's talking with Banquo," Emily said, her voice rising half an octave when she said his name. "I refused to give her any haunting tips, so she sought him out."

"As if he'll help her with that," I said with a chuckle.

"As if I was going to tell her *that* in the mood she was in," Emily shot back.

We stood there silently. I was lost in my thoughts, frankly dismayed at what I had gotten myself into. "I'm sure she'll understand," I finally said. "I mean, I kissed her to save her from the bardo."

Emily snorted and shook her head. "Look, Walter, you kissed her so you could get what you wanted and just happened to save her from the bardo. I may have died when I was four, but even I know you don't mess with a woman's heart." She chuckled softly. "Especially not a woman like that."

I really do hate being dead sometimes.

Emily walked away and left me there to stew. I looked around. Ghosts were rising out of the ground, flying, or popping in, gathering in small groups around gravestones. Midnight was approaching, we all could feel it. Midnight is our time, when we ghosts feel most "alive."

I didn't stay long. That night the surveillance became the three of us. And let me tell you, you've never been surveilled until you've been surveilled by ghosts. There is nothing you can do, nothing you can say, nowhere you can go that we can't follow you, can't hear you, can't know what you are doing.

We were brutal—the man got no privacy at all. Emily even insisted that we follow him into the bathroom, and that is where things got interesting.

Chapter Eleven

ELIAS WHEELER IS A YOUNG, COCKY DENTIST, WITH A shaved head, overly bleached white teeth, and a chubby face. He is also much more of a salesman than I ever was. It's one of the reasons I had brought him into the practice three years ago. He was eager to get out there and bring new clients in, he had energy for that. I didn't anymore.

I have never trusted people in sales. They have an ulterior motive—their own profit—so how can you trust what they are saying? They are worse than actors in my book. At least sometimes us actors aren't playing a role.

"I don't want to watch him take another dump," I complained to Emily. Wheeler had just gone into his bathroom in his lovely ranch-style home, in what would likely be another long session. He's got IBS or some other kind of issue, because he spends a lot of time in there.

"Too bad," Emily said. "I am young and innocent and shouldn't be subject to such indignities, and you wouldn't make your girlfriend watch another man defecate."

I sighed and nodded, heading for the bathroom,

pondering how Emily had found me in a bathroom but refused to watch Wheeler there.

"And who said chivalry is dead?" Emily offered as I walked through the bathroom door.

I can't tell you how sick of Elias Wheeler I was. His every little habit annoyed the hell out of me. Singing in the shower, checking all the locks on the doors two times before going to bed, the three girlfriends he was stringing along while setting up several more on online dating sites. But while he seemed to be a contemptible human being, we hadn't turned up a single clue in the ten days we had been haunting—I mean surveilling—him.

As he sat on his porcelain throne, his jeans down to his ankles, playing some stupid game on his iPhone, it rang. And horror of horrors, he answered. That's right, in the middle of an extensive toileting event, he answered his phone. No class whatsoever.

I didn't see the caller ID, I wasn't positioned correctly—and I should have been. It only rang once and he put it to his ear.

"Wheeler," he said.

He bit his lip as he listened and nodded his head a few times, the color draining from his face. "Look, we had a deal. I've orchestrated your deliveries. I don't—"

Belatedly I maneuvered my ghostly head right next to Wheeler's fleshy one so I could hear both sides of the conversation. I normally did better than this, but I think time and the whole "bathroom" part of this had thrown me off my game.

"…release the photos, but I will," a female voice said. "You are in deep, my friend, and the only way out is through."

"Look," he said, licking his lips and sitting up straighter on the toilet. "Someone died last time I had a package delivered for you. That wasn't what was supposed to happen."

"I told you, we weren't expecting the intensity of our competitor's interest. We've taken precautions. It won't happen again."

Wheeler sighed. "This has got to end," he said.

"It will," the voice on the phone said. "I promise, it will end soon." There was a brief pause and then she added, "The package will be at drop point three. See that it is delivered promptly."

⸻

WHEN WHEELER and I finally got out of the bathroom, the last thing I thought I'd be feeling was empathy for the fellow. After that phone call, he appeared to be a victim too.

As we all stood in the kitchen watching him nervously eat some cereal, I brought Emily and Haley up to speed.

"He... he wasn't trying to hurt me?" Haley asked.

"No, darling," I replied, still playing the role of the dutiful detective-boyfriend. "He appears to be a pawn in this thing."

She nodded mutely, staring at Wheeler.

"Don't get all misty-eyed there, Haley-Bopp," Emily said. "This still doesn't make him a shining example of the human race. He's done things he's ashamed of; the blackmailers are using that against him."

"Right," I interjected, trying to get things back on track. "We'll follow him to the drop point. Emily, you will stay there and see if the blackmailers come back. Haley and I will stick with Wheeler and follow him to the delivery and track the package from there."

And that is what we did. On the way to work, Wheeler stopped by Freedom Park north of the air force base and pulled a package from under a park bench. Emily stayed there and we followed Wheeler who went to the office and talked another young girl into delivering a package for him. Her name was Rachel, she was even younger and more innocent-looking than Haley.

"I don't have a good feeling about this," Haley said.

I nodded. At this point I never had a good feeling in the dental offices. It reminded me too much of the life I once had, the life I had lost. I mean, it hadn't been much, but it had been mine. I looked at Haley and wondered if she would kiss me if I started to lose it and go bardo.

"Stay with Rachel," I told Haley. I really didn't want to split us up, but I didn't think we were done with Wheeler yet.

She nodded, her eyes wide. We had hardly been apart since I had gotten her out of the bardo.

"It's okay, Haley. I won't leave the office without you. If you run into trouble, just come find me."

She bit her lip, her eyes lingering on me for a moment before she turned and followed Rachel.

I stayed with Wheeler. I was sure there was something else to be learned from him.

Chapter Twelve

In some ways the kind of scrutiny we were giving Wheeler wasn't fair. No human that is watched that much turns out looking pretty. People have their oddities, their addictions, their weaknesses. Wheeler was no exception. He picked his nose, stared at ladies' asses when they weren't looking, and liked to look at himself in the mirror.

But that is all I found out about him as I watched him go about his job, my former job, doing dental exams, fillings, root planing—all the joys of dentistry. It was a hard day for me. As much as I have grown to dislike Wheeler, I was jealous of him that he was alive.

Just after 5:00 p.m., Haley came and got me. Rachel was leaving. I looked back at Wheeler as we left. There was something else there, something important. I just knew it.

Rachel was skinny and tall, with short blonde hair and a quick walk. She left with the package Wheeler had picked up in the morning, got in her little red Hyundai, and drove to the Park Mall on Broadway. She did a lot of window shopping as she darted from store to store.

"Is she shopping?" Haley asked. "What the hell is she doing?"

I shrugged and we kept following her. She stopped at every clothing store in the mall and finally went into Spencer's. You know, the place with all the goofy stuff like drinking and sex games, odd clothing, and kinkier stuff. Haley gave me a look. I shrugged and we followed her in.

Rachel went right to the counter and asked for George. The overly perky checkout girl went into the back and out came George. He was thirtyish, overweight, and (I would wager) under-dated. He had greasy brown hair and wire-rimmed glasses.

"Are you George?" Rachel asked.

The big guy just nodded.

"This is for you," she said handing over the package and walking out of the store. George grunted and went into the back of the store, we followed.

The back room was what you would expect. Small and crowded with boxes, cleaning supplies, and a cramped desk. George sat at the desk and ripped opened the package, licking his lips like he hadn't eaten for days and this was a juicy steak he was tearing into.

He pulled out a small rectangular piece of plastic.

"That's a micro SD card," Haley said.

I looked at her. "A what?"

She rolled her eyes, looking back at George. "A memory chip for your computer. There's data on it."

Post-divorce, I had dated a few younger women, and even though Haley and I were both dead, she had just managed to make me feel old. It is not a pleasant feeling, a twisting in your guts. The young don't understand—as you get older, sure your body feels different, but no matter your age you feel like *you*. In my experience, it's the world that makes you feel old. The changing times, changing activities, and the attitude like Haley had just had.

The youth do not treat older people like we treat them. Think of children, people older than them are patient and understanding of their ignorance. The young do not tend to show the same tolerance for ignorance in people older than them.

I didn't say a thing, though. I kept my mouth shut and watched as George plugged the card into his computer and tapped on the keyboard.

Haley narrated what he was doing—she made an assumption that because I hadn't recognized a micro SD card without any labeling that I didn't know anything about computers. Which wasn't exactly true, but close enough. I was, though, grateful that the eye rolling had ended.

"The data is compressed and encrypted," she said. "He's entering the encrypting key..." She watched him carefully as he typed, he had to do it a couple of times to get it right. "The password is 'GetRichGeorge**$$.' Okay, he's got it unpacked. It's a bunch of files... there's some source code. He's compiling it. Now he's running it. Oh..."

She trailed off, I could see for myself as the screen lit up with a still of tanks and soldiers and explosions, with "Warmonger II" emblazoned on it.

Haley went diffuse as she watched as George briefly played the game. I didn't say anything.

"Holy shit," George said to himself. "This is the real goddam deal. I'm gonna be rich!"

Haley was sliding towards the bardo. "A video game?" she said, looking at me. "I was killed for a video game? What the hell kind of world is this?"

I had a brief, stabbing moment of empathy. What if I had been killed over something mundane or trivial? Did I really want to know? What kind of difference would it make?

"Walter?" she said, her voice cracking, her powder blue eyes way too wide. "Why?" She looked back at George as he continued to tap away at the computer.

I thought of kissing her again, the first time I had seemed to take on some of her fear and stabilized her. But that wasn't the right thing to do for her long-term, she needed to learn to calm herself. I modulated my form to match hers and took her face in my hands.

"Look at me," I said, her eyes reluctantly leaving George. They were still too wide, but she stopped getting more diffuse. "Listen to me, Haley. Focus on my voice. You are strong enough to do this. It doesn't matter why you were killed, but I promise you, I will find who did it and find a way to make them pay."

I was a bit taken aback by my tone. I sounded fierce and protective. I sounded strong and sure of myself. I sounded like I cared about her. And, actually, I wasn't acting. Something changed in that moment. I wasn't off farting around trying to do something for myself. I now had a mission, a purpose beyond my own needs.

Haley blinked, her form coming back into focus. I kept my hands on her face, matching them to her form as she changed. Tears rolled down her cheeks and she slowly nodded and licked her lips.

"I need you, Haley," I said. Her eyes grew wide again, but for a different reason. "I need you to be strong. I need your help. I can't do this without you."

She leaned in and kissed me. It wasn't like a flesh kiss, we didn't have "lips" per se. It wasn't about a physical sensation. It was what was left over. Passion. Communication. Communion.

I lost myself to that kiss and gave her back everything I

could. It was like we spoke volumes to each other in those moments. It was like falling off a cliff, or riding a rocket, or losing your mind. With the flesh aspects gone, the spiritual aspects of it were multiplied.

I don't know how long it lasted, it's like time didn't matter there, but when it was done I was changed. No more acting. Haley *was* my girlfriend. I felt this relief well up in me—all those lonely years I had experienced when I was alive were over.

Our faces only inches apart, she smiled broadly and I smiled back.

She looked around, her eyes growing wide again. "Oh shit," she said. "Where did he go?"

Chapter Thirteen

WE COULDN'T FIND HIM. THAT BREAK IN OUR FOCUS had given George enough time to get away from us. We searched the mall. We searched the parking lot. We searched and searched until night came and midnight approached.

The search after the first hour had been useless. I had known it, but Haley was upset and seemed to need to keep looking.

"He'll be back," I said. "We can just go back to the store and wait for him."

She sighed and nodded.

"But, I don't think it matters. We should go back to the graveyard, catch the Midnight Circle, and then rest."

"What?" She shook her head, looking confused. Now that the whole "you died for a video game" thing was known, she was holding on even tighter to finding her killer.

"George doesn't matter. He didn't kill you. I've been thinking about it. We've got a seller, the one blackmailing Wheeler, a buyer, George, and a third party—your killer."

She was staring at me now, her blue eyes flashing. I was glad to see anger instead of despair. We floated just above the parking lot of the mall, a bland expanse of pavement mostly devoid of cars at this hour.

"We need to find the third party. George can't help with that. The seller might be able to."

She nodded. I was glad I was making sense, because I was just working it out as I spoke.

"We left Emily at the package drop-off. Let's go see if she found something out."

Haley nodded slowly and then came close to me. "Thank you," she whispered and she kissed me again.

I have to say, we were getting better at this, and once again, no acting. I was falling for this girl and hard.

Chapter Fourteen

"YOU'RE DISGUSTING," EMILY SAID TO THE HOMELESS man sleeping on the bench we had left her at. "Don't you care? Thank God we ghosts can't smell, because I'm sure your scent would make me vomit. Look, I know life is hard. I know it can just mow you down. But, really, wake up. Get your act together. Do something worth doing. You are alive, for God's sake. Do you know what kind of gift that is? And here you are passed out drunk on a park bench with your dirty clothes and your scraggly beard. You're wasting that gift. Don't you have family? A mother, a father, a child, someone that cares for you, someone that needs you?" Emily paused, taking a deep breath. "Find the strength to make something of your life. Please. You've got one. I never did, I..."

Haley and I had taken our time getting back to the park. We had talked and held hands and kissed—and in general acted like people falling in love. When we entered Freedom Park and saw Emily, we both stopped without a word and listened. As her soliloquy went on, I began to feel guilty, but I couldn't bring myself to do anything about it.

She eventually noticed us, and stopped mid-sentence, a blush of red springing to her chubby cheeks.

"What the hell are you looking at?" she yelled.

"I... We..." I stammered. In our relationship, Emily had been the strong one (expect for the occasional four-year-old fit). Her being jealous of a drunk, homeless man wasn't something I had been expecting.

"Useless damn day," she said, looking down at her little feet. "Nothing happened here. I..." Emily's face clouded up and she took a few steps towards us. "I was just..." she began, looking back at the homeless man. "I think sometimes we can get through. You know, be the 'still small voice' that helps people turn it around. Be..."

Tears started to roll down her face. I let go of Haley's hand and went to her. I modulated my form to hers and took her in my arms. She held me tightly and cried for the longest time. This was no four-year-old fit, this was a ghost's grief. We all feel it. We aren't "alive" anymore. We barely exist in this world. The only thing we really have is each other.

I forgot Haley and gave Emily my full attention. I held her and whispered to her and let her get it all out. For the first time in our relationship, she really needed me.

When it was all over, I looked around and Haley was gone.

Chapter Fifteen

IT DIDN'T TAKE LONG TO FIND HALEY. SHE STOOD IN Roger Coptic's apartment staring at a reddish-brown stain on the floor. The place she had died. They had finally taken the body away and there had been yellow crime scene tape over the door.

"Haley..." I said softly. Her form wasn't in very good shape, and I was afraid she was lost to the bardo.

"What kind of life is this?" she asked.

I didn't know if she was referring to her murder and her physical life or her ghostly afterlife. "The only one we've got," I answered, covering both possibilities.

She looked up at me pursing her lips and nodding. "It doesn't seem like enough."

I approached her, leaving Emily by the door. I extended my hand to her and said, "Please. Come."

She ignored my gesture, her gaze returning to the blood stain. "I didn't do anything wrong. I didn't deserve this."

"No, you didn't," I said, putting my hand on her shoulder. She let my hand stay there, not moving, not speaking, just staring at the stain.

Finally she looked up at me, her eyes hard and unwavering. "We are going to find who did this. I don't care how long it takes. And then I'm going to make his life a living hell."

I stepped back, my hand leaving her shoulder. I was scared. Emily had been silent this whole time, but I heard her gasp as I backed away. Haley wasn't close to going bardo. She was somewhere else, somewhere very different.

"Okay," I said. It sounded empty next to her fierceness.

"What's our next lead?" she asked.

"I don't know," I answered.

"That's not good enough."

"I know." My answer sounded hollow, like I was whispering into a hurricane. Haley now seemed like a force of nature. You don't let down a force of nature. I racked my brain trying to think.

A gaming black market. Buyers and sellers. A third party that killed Haley and stole the product. We found one of the buyers, but that's it.

I looked around the grubby apartment of Roger Coptic. I ignored Haley as best I could, but I could feel her eyes on me as I studied the place. A sink full of dirty dishes. Overflowing garbage. Dirty clothing all over the bedroom. A cracked flat-screen TV. No computer in sight.

"Whoever Roger Coptic is, he wasn't the buyer," I said, desperate to fill the silence.

"Who was he, then?" Emily asked. I was so glad she had stepped in. Emily is as tough as they come, but Haley's shift from scared love interest to avenging ghost had shocked even her.

"I am guessing he was a middleman," I said. I thought

it all over, trying to connect the clues we had found. "I don't think this is just about video games."

"What? Why?" Haley asked.

"Both Doctor Wheeler and Midge are involved. Midge for money and they have something on Wheeler. They've done this before, moving things. It can't always be video games." I paused, thinking it over again. "I think this is about industrial espionage. Trade secrets."

Haley nodded. "That SD card had the source code to the video game. That's valuable, and using the old-fashioned sneaker-net may be more secure these days than the Internet."

"Great," Emily said. "So what the hell do we do now?"

"I'm guessing that since a murder occurred here, Roger is not coming back. He's probably on the run. He must know something."

"Then we find him," Haley said.

"How?" I asked.

Emily caught my eye and then pointedly looked at Haley. I gave Emily a nod and sighed. It was the only way.

"You're a ghost," Emily began, walking over to Haley and looking up at her. "You saw him. If you really want to find him, nothing in this world can stop you."

"I don't know what you mean," Haley said.

"It's generally called 'popping,'" I said, "because of the sound a ghost makes when they appear or disappear. You can travel from point to point at will."

"Like this," Emily said. She was standing next to me, her face going blank, and then she was gone with a soft "pop." A moment later there was another "pop" and she was standing next to Haley.

"How..." Haley began.

"It's kind of an advanced skill," I said. "Not one that

I've acquired yet, but Emily here is very good at it. She can teach you."

Emily nodded. "But not here. Let's get back to the graveyard. This is going to take some time."

As Emily and I floated towards the door, Haley said, "Wait." We both turned and looked at her. "If I can do this, then why don't I just 'pop' to my murderer? I saw those old-fashioned shoes."

"That's not enough," Emily said. "You'd probably end up in a shoe store or shoe factory or someone's closet. A face, though. That is unique. That will work."

EMILY TRIED to get Banquo to help teach us how to pop. Since the teaching was going to happen, I was determined to learn too. But Banquo would have nothing of it once he learned what Haley intended. And it's not like Haley was keeping it to herself. She came right out and told him when he asked her why she wanted to learn. The phrase "make his life a living hell" put a most sour expression on Banquo's face.

Haley was different and I missed her. My affection had become real, and then she became this avenging spirit. No more displays of affection, no more long talks, just a single-minded focus. Find Roger Coptic.

I did, though, find a use for my acting skills. I spent the next several weeks while Emily taught us acting like it didn't bother me that things had changed.

But they had and it did.

Eventually Haley "popped" and we found Roger Coptic. He was dead, and that turned out to be our big break in the case.

Chapter Sixteen

THE SAYING "DEAD MEN DON'T TALK" NEEDS TO BE
rethought. Roger Coptic sang, he sang like a bird.

When Haley finally popped, both Emily and I were
surprised. It had been days of frustrating, never ending
attempts. And then, finally, she was gone. Emily grabbed
my hand and popped us to her. And there we found Roger
Coptic.

His body was on the ground next to a dumpster behind
a Denny's, the head at an unnatural angle. Roger's spirit
was hovering above it, a thin silver cord snaking from the
body to the spirit.

He hadn't been dead long—usually ghosts figure out
how to sever the cord pretty quickly. This is the first initia-
tion into the ghostly afterlife.

"Who killed me?" Haley asked Roger, her voice loud
and strident.

First recognition bloomed on Roger's face and then
confusion. "What? You... you're dead."

"Who killed me?" Haley repeated.

Roger's eyes darted around, he still looked confused.

"I'm angry," she said. "I'm sure you can see that. You help me, I walk away. You don't help me and I take out my anger on you."

Both Emily and I took a step back; Haley's form was flickering red along the edges. I looked down at her and saw fear on Emily's face. Ghosts can go bad just like people.

"Yeah… yeah… sure," Roger began, his eyes wide, his hands up. He backed up until his body was halfway into the brick wall of the Denny's. "What the…" His head swiveled around and his diffuse limbs flayed. He didn't know he was dead. He didn't understand he was a ghost. Such confusion is very common.

"Talk. Now," Haley said. "Or it will only get worse."

"Right… yeah… The dude's name is Halifax. He's the one that stole the delivery. He hurt me too. Said he was tying up loose ends. He…" Roger looked down and saw his body, his mouth going wide and his form diffusing even more.

"Where can I find this Halifax?" Haley yelled at Roger, getting his attention.

"He's here," Roger said, his head nodding towards the restaurant. "After we talked, he said he was hungry."

Haley gave him a sharp nod and began flying around the building. She was still a new ghost, a practiced one would have just flown through the wall. I looked at Emily.

"You stop her," she said, "before she does…" Emily sighed. "If she does what I'm afraid she'll do, you know where it will end up for her. I'll handle the little guy, see what else he knows."

I nodded and flew after Haley. I got in front of her before she got to the door.

"What are you going to do, Haley?" I asked.

"Out of my way, Walter," she said.

"This won't end well."

"No it won't," she said, a grim look on her face. "But it will end."

I kept myself in front of her, blocking the door. This went on for a minute or so before she sighed and walked right through me.

It was early afternoon and the Denny's wasn't very crowded. It didn't take long to find the man with the black shoes; they were pointy, cap toe Oxfords. He was eating waffles and drinking coffee.

He was meticulously groomed and wore a shirt, jacket, and tie. He ate with a slow precision. Cutting a piece of the waffle. Putting down his knife. Using the fork to put the food in his mouth. Putting down his fork. Chewing slowly and thoroughly. Taking a sip of coffee and resuming the process.

He seemed to take great pleasure in it.

Haley stood staring at him, her hands shaking, tears running down her cheeks. The red flickering along her form had turned to crimson, making her rage abundantly clear. She kept looking at his shoes. They were indeed the same as the ones I saw when I first kissed her and experienced her death. There was no doubt that this was her killer.

"Let's follow him and get his name and address," I said softly. "We can then go to the SECI chamber and let someone know. They can tell the police." SECI stands for the Search for Extracorporeal Intelligence. A project started at the University of Arizona to allow the dead to communicate with the living. This is what JJ Lynch used to write his memoir. It is what I am using now to write this story. Haley knew about it, I was just reminding her.

She shook her head slowly, her nostrils flaring. "That's not enough." She turned and looked at me. The look on her face made me want to take a step back, but I held my ground, keeping my face passive. "He's a killer. He has to die. He deserves to die."

I didn't tell her, but in principle I agreed, although I preferred someone locking him up and throwing away the key. Killing him didn't sit well with me, but then again I wasn't the one he murdered. If I was looking at my own killer I would probably want the same thing. "If you kill him," I said, "he could become one of us."

"And then I'll find ways to make his afterlife a living hell," she said, turning back to him.

Can a ghost kill a person? It's not easy, but it is possible. If the stories are to be believed, JJ Lynch did it. There are whispers that if you have the right focus and modulate your form correctly, you might be able to make someone trip or look away at the wrong moment when they are driving. There is even darker talk of possession.

"You might not want to stay around for this," she said.

"Sorry, you can't get rid of me that easily."

She glanced at me and shrugged and began her haunting. She went at it like she had a plan, like she knew what she was doing, like she knew that it would work. This puzzled me. How could she know what to do? I didn't and I had been dead a lot longer than her.

They say that "hell hath no fury like a woman scorned." Well, try a ghost confronting her murderer. Haley got her head close to Halifax, who was seated comfortably at a booth table, and started speaking to him. Her tone low, she spoke quickly, and didn't stop. She kept up a nonstop diatribe against him. "You are worthless. You would be better off dead. How can you stand yourself? Do the world a favor and stab yourself in the throat with that fork. You don't deserve to be alive." And on it went. It was as if she was playing the part of that negative voice we all have in our heads. The one that doubts us. The one that wonders whether we are worth the space we take up.

"What the hell is she doing?" Emily asked. The man had finished his breakfast and paid. Emily found us in the parking lot as he got into his vintage Cadillac.

"I think she's trying to talk him to death." I said it with a grin, but my attempt at humor fell flat. "I think she's trying to get into his head. Get him to do something to himself."

Emily sighed as we flew into the car with Haley and the man. "She's been talking to some of the ghosts over by the crypts."

"What?" I asked.

"I spotted her there a few days back. I didn't say anything... I was hopeful she wouldn't go this way."

At our graveyard some of the more disturbed and dangerous ghosts live by and in the crypts. Most of them are in the bardo, but kind of violent—they'll lash out at any ghost (or person) that comes too close to them. And there are other ghosts that choose to stay there that are into the darker aspects of what you can do as a ghost.

"Why didn't you tell me?" I asked.

"I could see you were getting attached... I..." Tears welled up in Emily's eyes. She was going all four-year-old on me and I couldn't be mad at her. "I'm sorry, Walter. Can you ever forgive me?"

I gave her a hug and said, "Of course. We'll get through this." I sounded confident, but I was far from it.

Chapter Seventeen

AS FAR AS HAUNTINGS GO, THINGS THAT GO BUMP IN THE night are no big deal. Furious murder victims that unleash an unending soul sucking tirade on you... well, that's a whole 'nother story.

We tried everything (short of touching her) to get Haley's attention. She was oblivious to us. And we didn't try touching because of what I had learned when I kissed her the first time. It's possible to take on some of the emotional content of another ghost with that kind of intimacy, and I didn't want to take on what she was giving.

Haley's technique seemed to refine. She floated behind her victim, her furious face recognizable and her arms visible, but the rest of her diffuse and vaporous. She ended up with her fingers stuck into the guy's temples and slowly refined her screed.

"You are a worthless human being. You should do the world a favor and kill yourself. Right now. What do you have to live for? Your life is an unending torment. Pick up the knife, go ahead. Look how sharp that blade is. Just pull it across your throat and this will all be over."

It was starting to get to me, and Emily had this pinched look on her round face. But we stayed with Haley and followed them as the man drove to a beautiful little house that bordered the Catalina Mountains north of Tucson. As he went about his day, checking his email, typing on the computer, paying bills, swimming in the pool, dusting and vacuuming.

Haley's diatribe seemed to be having an effect. He started rubbing at his temples and stretching his neck. He took some Advil and he tried to take a nap.

The man's name is Edgar Halifax, and as far as solving Haley's murder, and many others, we had him. That typing he did on his computer? He documented, in exacting detail, the murder of Roger Coptic. He had a diary of everyone he had killed, whether it was contract or personal and how much he was paid. Roger's murder was on contract, part of the one that involved him stealing what Haley was carrying.

The man was meticulous in his dress, how he kept his home, and in documenting his work. We also watched closely as he typed his password. It's "GardenState32#!." My guess is he's from New Jersey.

I didn't feel good about it, though—solving the murder, that is. Haley was unreachable, inconsolable, incoherent, and raging. Emily's jokes earlier about Haley's Comet and Haley-Bopp now seemed unnerving and prescient.

"This is no 'small still voice.' This is…" Emily said after about five hours of this, her face pained. We were in his kitchen, all gleaming steel and granite countertops, watching him prepare his dinner in his ultra-meticulous fashion.

"We're in over our heads," I said. "Go get Banquo."

Her eyes got wide and she nodded her head quickly a few times and with a "pop" was gone.

"Haley," I said, trying one more time to reach her. "Please stop this. Please. Can't we go back a few steps? I... I thought maybe we had something there. I thought maybe this life had gotten less lonely for me. I thought maybe, just maybe, I had found something that had eluded me when I was alive."

You may be wondering if I was acting. I wasn't. Her eyes found mine and her diatribe stopped.

"Please, Haley. Can we just talk? I just want to have a conversation."

Her brows furrowed and she blinked, her eyes holding mine. The look on her face tore my heart out. Her bottom lip quivered as if she was trying to speak. Her eyes spoke clearly of pain and regret. A single tear ran down her cheek. She then turned back to Edgar and resumed her soliloquy.

I turned away. Not because I didn't want her to see me cry, but because I knew part of her wanted me and that part was not in charge. She wasn't the Haley I had grown fond of. She knew exactly what she was doing and the terrible price she would have to pay.

I turned away because I didn't know how to stop her... or rather didn't have the courage to try the only thing left to try.

Chapter Eighteen

BANQUO CAN BE ARROGANT AND DEMANDING. HE CAN BE short with people and doesn't suffer fools. When Emily finally came back with him, he was none of these things.

The night had passed and Edgar was having breakfast. Meticulous little bites of his poached eggs and toast. He sat at the little breakfast nook in his kitchen that overlooked the formal Zen garden in his backyard. But he looked different. He was harried, black circles under his eyes.

"Thank God you're here," I said when I saw Banquo.

Banquo nodded and gave me a small compassionate smile. He strode over to Haley and Edgar and stood for a long time staring at them.

"Sorry," Emily whispered. "He was otherwise engaged. I had to wait."

I looked at Emily and nodded. I caught a view of my own form and found that I had gone pretty diffuse myself. Edgar was not the only one getting worn down by this. "Did he say anything?"

"Not much. He's worried." Emily's awe for Banquo

was still fully intact, but the girlish crush was gone. He was our best hope and we both knew it.

Banquo paced around the two of them, walking right through the little table. His eyes had this faraway look to them as he stared at Haley and Edgar. Banquo kept walking and then holding still and then walking again. At one point he most tentatively touched Haley's form, but quickly removed his finger like it stung.

Finally he moved to Emily and me and said, "This way." He flew straight up and out of the house.

I would have told him I didn't want to leave Haley. But he was gone and then Emily, so I followed.

"How long has she been like this?" he asked once we were atop the ceramic shingled roof.

"About twenty hours," I said. He was looking at me, not at Emily.

"And how invested are you in her recovery?"

I blinked and looked to Emily. Her green eyes were wide and kind, but not helpful. "Umm... very. I'm very invested in her recovery."

He nodded. "Then you know what to do and you know how risky it is."

"How..." I began.

He shook his head, moving it a minute distance to the left and the right. "Not a useful question."

Here he was: terse, teaching, demanding Banquo. One of the reasons I wasn't a big fan of his, but I needed him.

"Can you explain the risk? I'm not sure I completely understand."

He nodded once and began pacing along the peak of the roof, his hands clasped behind his back. "If you do not act you will lose her. That is the risk here. Whether or not she succeeds with this man, she will be lost."

"To the bardo?" I asked.

Banquo stopped pacing. "Best case."

I blinked. There was a worse case than the bardo? What the hell was that about?

"And if I try to reach her?"

"At its best, you will pay... you will have to take on much of her burden. At its worst, you will both be lost."

"Bardo?" Emily asked, her voice quiet and small.

"For him, yes. We might be able to pull him out. For her... I'm not sure."

I took a deep breath and looked at Emily and then back at Banquo. "I... It's... it's too much. I just met her. I..." I couldn't stand the empathy showing on their faces, so I sunk back into the house, back down to Haley and Edgar.

Edgar was now washing his dishes. Slowly, meticulously, carefully. Haley's hands were buried in his temples, the remnant of her form floating behind him in that classic ghostly look.

"I'm sorry," I said. "I can't. I... we..."

I felt a deep fatigue descend on me. I needed to rest—all ghosts need to rest. It's this dreamless nothingness called "fading." A faded ghost is just gone—where, no one really knows (and I don't think "where" is even the right way to think about it). They are gone and unreachable and don't come back until they are rested.

I could sense Emily and Banquo coming after me. I couldn't fly faster than them and they could both pop, so I gave into the fatigue and faded. Haley's words were the last thing I heard. "You will kill yourself, believe me, you will. This, right now, this will be your life until you do. I will give you no rest I will give..."

Chapter Nineteen

I WAS FADED FOR ABOUT TWELVE HOURS AND CAME TO IN
the sweet darkness of my grave. Some ghosts, like me, rest
with their bones, down in the ground where our remains
are. I know it sounds weird, but there I feel calm and
connected.

As I rose out of the ground, I lingered, looking at my
gravestone. "Walter George Anchor, 1971–2011." That's
all it said. No "Beloved Husband," I was divorced. No
"Devoted Father," I had never had children. No "Cherished Son," my parents were gone when I died. Just my
name and a couple of years.

"It's okay, you know," Emily said.

Her little voice shocked me.

"I don't blame you for not trying. Even Banquo
doesn't. Some things are just too much." She was still
wearing her shorts and her T-shirt with a lollipop on it.
Today the lollipop was blue. She had very good control of
her ghostly form and could change it easily. A blue lollipop
generally meant that she was sad. And judging from what
she was telling me, she was sad for Haley, sad for me.

"Thanks," I said.

"What now?" Emily asked. "Maybe we should go do something fun today. That house over by Fairview Avenue, they've probably got *Law and Order* on."

When Emily had been tutoring me in ghostly matters and my resolve to find my killer became clear, we had fallen into the habit of watching legal or detective shows. I wouldn't call it good training, but it was something to do.

I shook my head. "Nope. Off to the SECI chambers. Time to get in line. Time to tell this story so…" I faltered, unable to articulate what I wanted to say. Something about justice being served. Something about a wrong being righted. But it didn't feel like justice would be served for Haley or Roger or any of this man's victims. But it would prevent him taking more lives. And that was something.

Emily took my hand and smiled up at me. Her hand was so small, her face so young. We've spent a lot of time together now, but it is still disconcerting. The world jolted suddenly and then with a "pop" we stood in front of a nondescript industrial building in front of a door that said, "Afterlife Communications, Inc."

JJ Lynch is something of a legend around the grave-yard. Banquo tutored him and a Mexican guy named Jesus after they died. JJ dove into his afterlife and did the unthinkable. He reached his loved ones, stopped his best friend from killing himself, and killed a man in the process. He documented all of this in a memoir that he wrote in the SECI chamber.

I've never met JJ. He's been in the bardo for months, having gone in intentionally to try to rescue someone else.

He's a legend, all right, and something of a cautionary tale. Emily tells me that Banquo is shorter than usual because he worries about JJ.

So, JJ did all this writing, the people behind the SECI chamber published his memoir as a book called *Shuffled Off* (there is lots of Shakespeare at the Midnight Circle in case you recognize that phrase from Hamlet). Some of the living read the book before they died. Some of them find the SECI chambers.

That's not what this story is about, but I mention it because the wait for a SECI chamber was about five days. Lots of ghosts were in line waiting for their chance. And that gave me five days to think about what had happened since I died. To think about Haley and what she was attempting to do to her murderer. To think about my life and my afterlife.

The SECI chambers, there are three now, sit in a bland industrial space with a cement floor and a high ceiling. The ghosts waiting spiral out from those three structures. The chambers are about four feet on a side and about seven feet tall, made out of some fancy new electromagnetic (EM) shielding. They have sensors inside that detect ghostly EM emissions in very specific patterns and turn them into letters. It's complicated and I know JJ explained it thoroughly in *Shuffled Off*, so suffice it to say that it allows ghosts to type.

As we waited, Emily was great and supportive, doing her best to distract me. Teaching me how to play jacks—which is anything but easy. The jacks and the ball have to be an extension of your ghostly form, so it was quite the advanced lesson.

We got to know the other ghosts in line with us, and in general it was a pretty good time, but the closer we got to the SECI chambers, the more agitated I got. I kept thinking about Haley. What would happen to her? What fate could be worse than the bardo? Could I actually help?

There were only two ghosts in line in front of us when it became too much. "Emily…" I began.

"What is it, Walter?"

"I… Haley… I have to…"

Emily gave me the gentlest smile and grabbed my hand. "Is it time to go to her?" she asked.

My jaw dropped. Sometimes I think Emily is the wisest person I have ever known. At those moments, the wisdom of the four-year-old she was when she died and her eighty years dead come together. She is wise like a child and wise like an old person at the same time. How could she have the patience to give me this much time? How could she know to seize the moment when I gave her the smallest of openings?

"Yes," I said. "Please."

With a "pop" we were with Haley. It was not what I expected.

Chapter Twenty

"YOU ARE AS GOOD AS DEAD NOW, SO WHY NOT FINISH it? You know you don't want to live anymore. You know you are worthless. No one loves you and no one will ever love you…"

Haley's diatribe was intact but everything else had changed.

I would not have recognized her except for her voice. Haley didn't look like Haley and barely looked like a person. Her face had elongated and gone was any detail but the vaguest notion of eyes, mouth, and hair. Her form was dark grey like some great storm cloud. What passed for her arms were still attached to Edgar's head.

Edgar's transformation wasn't as dramatic, but it was significant. He sat slumped in a wheelchair, his eyes vacant, his skin pale, his jaw slack.

I looked around. We were in a plain institutional-looking room with quite a few other people. Some sat still and quiet. Others rocked and mumbled. Others looked pretty normal and sat around playing checkers or cards.

"Oh, shit," I said.

"We're in a loony bin," Emily said.

"This is bad."

"Should I go get Banquo?" Emily asked.

I shook my head. "He said I knew what to do. I don't think that has changed."

"But…" Emily began. "But this is worse, much worse than before."

I looked down at her. The worried look on her face almost stopped me. I squatted down to her level. "I have to do this, you know." She nodded. "If I don't, I won't be able to live with myself."

"But…"

"If this goes wrong, then go get Banquo." I stood up and went to Haley. She was stretched out horizontally behind Edgar's head. I carefully positioned myself in the circle of her arms. I was facing her strange-looking face and away from Edgar.

"Come back to me, Haley," I said. I then matched my form to hers—which was not easy and felt dangerous— and kissed her.

Chapter Twenty-One

IT BEGAN WITH INTENT. TO HELP HER, TO BRING HER into balance, to demonstrate my caring for her. That intent translated into action. Haley was doing what she was doing because of the feelings in her, because of the pain in her, because she had to. Those emotions flowed from her into me. I took in her anger and her pain. I took in her fear and her doubt. I took it all in.

Maybe you've experienced something like this. You spend time with a good friend who is sad or upset. You talk to them, you try to help them, and when you leave, they are better off than when you started, but you are worse. It's as if you took some of their burden from them. This was like that, but without the intervening flesh, much more rapid, much more intense, and ironically, much more real.

It just poured into me until I didn't think I could take it anymore and then it just kept coming and coming and coming.

I felt like destroying something, killing someone, making the world as miserable as I was at that moment. I needed to let some of this go, let some of it out. I wasn't aware of Haley anymore and only vaguely aware of the room, but I was aware of Edgar. He was this dark void sucking all the light out of the world. He was cruel and evil and deserved to die. He was all that was wrong with the world. I would be doing everyone a favor by ending him. It was what I could do to help.

But a patter of words, as Haley had done, was not good enough. I reached my hands—they looked like smoke —into his mind. I wasn't going to talk to him. I was going to destroy him. I could do it. If I poured all the rage I felt into his mind, it would break even further. His mind would cease to operate. He would die.

I poured all that rage and hate into him and soon I heard a sickening snap, like a bone breaking. I knew it was a piece of his mind crumbling under my attack, taking him one step closer to death.

"Walter!" I heard the voice as if from a great distance. It was a child's voice, high and light. The child was scared, terrified. Time had passed, but I had no idea how much. "Walter," she said, choking the word out amidst a storm of tears. "Please, Walter. Don't do it. I need you, Walter, I need you."

I paused and pulled my hands out of Edgar's head. She needed me? Someone needed me? I saw Emily. She looked so vulnerable in her shorts and her lollipop T-shirt. "Emily?" I said, her name coming to me. I had become something else, I wasn't Walter, I was something much more primal, but Emily, I knew Emily.

"Please, Walter, come with me." She extended her hand towards me. I didn't take it. I knew that somehow that would be bad for her. I didn't want to hurt her. She slowly moved back and I followed. She needed me, someone needed me.

It seemed impossible to leave. I wanted to return to my

revenge, but I could not deny this little girl. I could not turn my back on her.

I was vaguely aware as we flew over Tucson, the full moon illuming the city below. We came to a grassy area surrounded by trees, filled with the glow of spirits and stones of smooth granite.

"Here, Walter. Here is your place. Here are your bones. You need to rest, Walter. You'll feel better after you rest."

"I don't want to rest, I want to——"

"Please!" Emily shouted, tears running down her cheeks. "Please, Walter, you must rest. Sink into the ground, find your bones. You are tired. So tired, I know you are."

"But he deserves to die. He must..." My mind was starting to come back to me. "Haley... where is Haley?"

"She is with Banquo. You saved her. You did good, Walter. But now you must rest, you must find your bones."

I blinked and looked around. I was in the graveyard. Emily was there and many other ghosts had circled us, kind of like it was the Midnight Circle. "You saved her," Jim the cowboy said. "Rest now," his companion Jane added. "You deserve it," another ghost said with a broad smile. Many more of them spoke to me saying kind things.

I looked down at the granite stone. "Walter Anchor 1960–2011." It was a plain gravestone, but I could feel its weight. Like it was my anchor point. My bones were down there. I loved to rest with my bones. It felt so calming, so much like home.

"Justice, Emily," I said. "Justice must be served."

"It has been," Emily said quietly, the tears still running down her cheeks. "He will never hurt anyone again. You made sure of that."

"Okay," I said, feeling slightly more like myself. "I *am* tired."

"Just sink into the ground. Rest. I'll be here waiting for you. I'll always be here for you, Walter."

As I slowly sunk into the ground, I smiled. I knew Emily was there for me, she had been ever since she found me. I wasn't alone anymore. I wasn't alone.

As the earth surrounded me, I felt myself slowly calm and then I knew nothing.

Chapter Twenty-Two

EDGAR HALIFAX IS STILL ALIVE, BUT THERE IS NOT MUCH of his mind left and he won't hurt anyone ever again. First Haley, and then I, saw to that. I can't say I feel that bad about it—he was a psychotic murderer and he had it coming. What I do feel bad about is the price we had to pay. Doing something like that changes you. Doing that changed the "us" that was forming between Haley and me.

"I have to go," Haley said, her face tight, her arms crossed. Her form was back to normal, she was no longer an avenging spirit, but the cost of what had happened was clear in her haunted blue eyes. They looked much paler than I remembered.

The sun was setting over our graveyard, the thin layers of clouds and Tucson pollution putting on a good show to the west.

"Where?" I asked. I had been faded for a long time—I think about a week had passed.

"Utah," she said, her head bobbing to the north. "There is a small graveyard there in a ghost town called Silver Reef. Not too many ghosts and they've all been dead for a long time, they're all stable." She shrugged, her shoulders seeming very thin. "Banquo seems to think it will be good for me."

I nodded, but didn't know what else to say. I didn't want her to go, but after what had happened, I didn't really want her to stay either.

"I've been waiting for you to come back so I could say good-bye. I... You..."

I smiled at her. "You're welcome, Haley. I am glad I could help you. I hope things go well for you."

She leaned in and carefully kissed me on the cheek. She did it right so I could feel just the barest brush of her lips, like a feather or a rose petal. Banquo walked over and gave me a nod and took Haley by the arm. They walked a few yards away and with a "pop" were gone.

In truth, I will miss her.

"I've been thinking," Emily said. She had found me standing alone in the graveyard after Haley and Banquo had left. "I think it's time for you to upgrade your outfit."

"What?" I asked, looking down at my blue scrubs.

"You're not a dentist anymore, Walter. You are a detective. You solved Haley's murder and brought a terrible man to justice."

I shrugged. It didn't feel much like a victory. We found out about these strange happenings in my old dental office but didn't get anywhere with my own murder. I suspected there was more to learn from Wheeler, but couldn't imagine surveilling him again. We had no leads. I looked at Emily, her lollipop was a pale yellow. She was worried.

"We didn't find out who was behind the corporate espionage," I said.

She snorted and crossed her arms in front of her chest. "Let the cops chase that down once you write the story. White-collar crime is for wimps. We solve murders."

I nodded and smiled. "It was a team effort, Emily. It wouldn't have happened without you."

She put up her hand and we did a high five, our ghostly hands slapping together, a big smile on her face. The smile melted into something coy and she said, "Really? Because... well... I've heard rumor of a murder at the University that happened just last night. Maybe..."

I laughed. "You want to go investigate?"

She nodded vigorously, her blonde curls bobbing around her face. "But first you need to look the part. I'm thinking a long brown trench coat and fedora. Like Humphrey Bogart in *Casablanca*." I must have looked dubious, because she added a high-pitched "please."

I could not deny her enthusiasm, or really anything she wants, after what she has done for me. We spent the next hour working on my new form. It wasn't great—a bit vaguely shaped—but it would do, and I knew I would get better at holding it as time went by.

"There he is," she said once I was done. "Walter Anchor, ghost detective! Let's go."

I kneeled down and stared into her youthful face that hid her many years of experience. "Can I say one thing before we go?" She nodded, her eyes getting wide. "Thank you for stopping me... for what you did for me." She nodded again, her brow furrowed. "I can't do this without you." I wasn't referring to being a detective, but to "being" in general. I saw her blinking back tears, so I think she got it.

"Emily, can you give me a few minutes? I've got something I've got to do."

She looked me up and down, nodded gravely, and let go of my hand.

"This won't take long," I said, giving her my best, most reassuring smile.

THE GHOST HAD AN UNSAVORY LOOK, with small eyes and crooked teeth, dressed all in black. He leaned, in a display of faux nonchalance, against the grey stone of the crypt. I had been doing some independent investigation, there were some loose ends in regards to what had happened to Haley.

He gave me a derisive snort as a greeting. "Nice outfit," he said, the sarcasm way overdone.

"You called Galt?" I asked.

He nodded.

"You the one that taught Haley how to mess with the living?"

He nodded again. I heard some moans and the sound of metal scraping against stone. Emily had always told me to stay away from the crypts, but this was important.

"Then you and I have a problem," I said.

He shrugged and pushed himself away from the stone wall. This was all artifice. He was a ghost, the wall could not support him, and he couldn't push himself away from it. It looked real, it was well done, which led me to believe he was a mature ghost. "The girl asked nice," he said with a thin grin and a shrug. "How could I turn her down?"

I crossed my arms and shook my head. "You should have turned her down. What happened is on you."

He chuckled, it was dry and thin and sounded danger-ous. "The girl had a choice. She chose to come to me. She chose to do what she did."

"That may be, but if I ever see you so much as speaking to Emily, or any of my other friends, I will destroy you."

He slowly smiled, showing his crooked teeth off. "First off, that old witch Emily can take care of herself. Secondly, I see why you and Haley got along so well."

"What?"

"What she did to her killer, is that how you would 'destroy' me? You're just like Haley—you'll do what it takes to settle a score."

"I... No, that's not what I meant."

He held his hands up. "Relax, I appreciate the senti-ment. You are willing to defend what is yours. I understand that. Maybe you and I aren't so different. Maybe you and I could be friends. Maybe I could show you a few things Emily and Banquo won't show you."

His words rattled around my head. What did he know? Would I act differently than Haley if I found my killer?

"Look," I finally said, "just stay away from Emily. Got it?"

He smiled and slumped back against the crypt wall. "Yeah, I got it. No problem. I do favors for my friends all the time."

As I walked away from him, I knew Galt and I weren't done, but Emily was waiting and there was another murder to solve.

THE GHOST BRIDE'S GIFT

A WALTER ANCHOR GHOST DETECTIVE STORY

ROBERT J. MCCARTER

AUTHOR OF *SHUFFLED OFF*

Prologue

THE EMPTY BASEBALL FIELD WAS EERIE IN THE SILVERY moonlight, fast moving clouds taking turns blocking the nearly full moon. But maybe it was Helen Kim and the fear engraved on her face that made the scene creepy.

Helen was beautiful, of Korean ancestry, her features exotic to an Arizona boy like me. Long, black hair, a delicate upturned nose, beautiful brown eyes. She looked just like my ex-wife Sun when I had married her, and that was the problem. I kept getting distracted. I kept failing Helen, my mind going back to Sun over and over.

Helen's furrowed brow, wide eyes, and open mouth turned her features from exotic to frightening. She looked like she wanted to scream but was too scared for that, only a low moan escaping her.

She had on a silky, white gown, a wedding dress, her shaking index finger pointed at me, a tear leaking from her left eye. "You did this to me, Adam. This is your fault. Why did you..."

I wasn't Adam, I wasn't her fiancé, the man that had hurt her, maybe murdered her. "Stay with me, Helen," I said. "Look into my eyes. We're going to get through this. We're going to find out who killed you."

Her eyes focused on me briefly, her brow furrowing, and then it was too late. Her moan increased in pitch and turned into a wail and then a scream, her eyes and mouth getting wider, but the rest of her features relaxing. Her white dress and face softened, like she was just a little bit out of focus, and her scream rose up into the moonlit Tucson night.

I kept talking, kept pleading, but it was too late. The bardo—that place many ghosts get stuck in where they are consumed by their fears and regrets—had claimed her and I had failed her.

I didn't know Helen, she had only died hours ago. A murdered ghost has a tough path in front of them. If they know who their killer is, they can fall into the trap of rage and revenge. If they don't know, the uncertainty can ruin their afterlife. I should know. I was murdered. I'm a ghost too.

My name is Walter Anchor. I was a dentist and before that an out-of-work actor. I fell into this detective thing trying to solve my own murder. And while I've helped out a few ghosts, I've failed to find my own murderer, or Helen's, for that matter.

Chapter One

EARLIER THAT AFTERNOON, I WAS FLOATING ABOVE THE fifty-yard line watching the Cardinals square off against the Cowboys. To me, this is what a ghost should be doing with his afterlife. Phoenix, and the Cardinals' stadium, is a short flight from Tucson for a ghost, and during the fall, what could be better?

I was rooting for the Cardinals, they are an Arizona team, after all. Think about it. I can hover over the huddle and listen in on the play. Float behind the quarterback as the football is hiked to him. Soar with the ball as it flies over the field.

No traffic. No expensive tickets. Unfortunately, though, I can't have any overpriced beer.

It was the end of the first quarter and I was floating about two hundred feet up with a good view of the action. I'm not the only ghost to have this idea, so there were about fifty of us floating up there in a queue to take our turn down in the action. Two at a time, one with each team.

There's a burly ghost everyone calls Coach acting as traffic director. "OK, Hughes, you're down with the Cards," he barked. "Ortega, you got the Cowboys." He's dressed like a referee in black and white vertical stripes with an NFL ball cap on and a whistle around his neck. "Anchor and Lee, you're up next."

That's me, so I get into position next to Jeff Lee, a former programmer and fantasy football freak. He nods and smiles. It's all very exciting and very collegial. There have been some ghosts who don't want to play by the rules, but Coach and a few other ghosts will always chase them off.

Below us the football soars in a long pass as the Cardinals try for a first down on their third down with fifteen yards to go.

The audience screams, rising to their feet, a good number of the ghosts behind us let out a yell too. The ball soars twenty yards to the outstretched hands of the Cardinal's receiver, but at the last moment a Cowboy leaps and both men reach for the ball. It's a real nail biter; time seems to slow as the spiraling ball bounces between the men's outstretched fingers. The audience hushes in a collective in-breath. This could change the tide of the game for the Cardinals. And then—

Pop! "We've got to go. Now!"

I tear my gaze away—sounds painful because it is—and see Emily. She's my best friend in the afterlife and my detective partner. She died when she was four years old—and looks like it with her tiny body and Shirley Temple curls—but has been dead for eighty years and often acts it.

"What?" I point down to the field to a pileup in process. I missed what happened, I didn't know who had possession of the ball. "Damn it, Emily!" Second-guessing referees was another great pastime. We had lots of eyes on the play and usually got it right.

"Language, young man," she said in her little girl voice. She grabbed my arm, and with a "pop" we were gone.

Chapter Two

───────────

AT FIRST THE BRIDE LOOKED TO BE IN REPOSE, A beautiful look on her face, her strapless Vera Wang silk gown perfect and unwrinkled. Like she had just laid down for a moment on the bridal suite's couch. Her face was serene, her red lips slightly parted as if a contented sigh had just escaped her lips.

"You're welcome," Emily said with a grin.

I nodded, dumbly. Emily knew everything about me, including my predilection for Asian woman. My wife had been a Korean-American, but we didn't talk about her, considering the disaster the divorce had been and the downward spiral it had thrown my life into. And normally this would have been a fine distraction, but the wedding dress and the beautiful face reminded me too much of her, of Sun, of our wedding. I was still young, still hopeful that despite having started dental school that an acting gig would come along and take me away from it. I still thought it was possible to follow my bliss, live the life of my dreams.

I felt things stir in me, dangerous things. I wanted to fly away to the nearest casino and watch people gamble all night. I wanted to be alive so I could break something. I wanted to—

The dead woman stirred. Well, it looked like she did. She briefly looked a bit out of focus and then her spirit started separating from her body.

"How?" I mumbled to Emily. How could she find out about this murder and get me here before the spirit had even separated from the body?

She shrugged her little shoulders and smiled. She had on her usual lollipop T-shirt and shorts. "Her name is Helen Kim, she died less than an hour ago. So, what do we do now, Walter?"

Emily still has a lisp, despite all her years dead and it reinforces the youthful vibe she gives off. I won't write it this way, but what she said sounded more like, "*Tho*, what do you want to do now, Walter?"

The lollipop on her T-shirt acts something like a mood ring, the color changing with her mood. It was a cheery red, she still thought this was a fabulous thing for me. I had been fairly depressed since our first case when I had fallen for Haley, a former dental assistant at my practice that had been murdered as part of a strange smuggling operation. Haley had gone a bit crazy, attacking her murderer. I had gone a little bit crazy, too. That relationship hadn't ended very well.

I had started back at the casinos, trying to get that gambling thrill vicariously. Not that it worked worth a damn, but it was better than stewing in my own despair. Emily would pull me away to work cases, trying to pull me out of my funk.

"This isn't a good idea," I said to her as the woman's ghostly form slowly separated from her body. "I don't think I can—"

"Where's Adam?" the new ghost said, looking around. "Where am I?"

Chapter Three

DEATH CAN BE A RUDE AWAKENING. I "WOKE" IN A dental chair in my own office after I died. Someone had overdosed me with propofol, made it look like a suicide, and left me there to die. I was just a lonely dentist with a bit of a gambling problem and some history with the recreational use of propofol, both of these issues behind me. No debts to loan sharks, no enemies, who would want to kill me?

I was alone those first few hours as a ghost. It was a terribly disorienting time. I floated around my office, trying to touch things, my hand going right through them. I can't tell you how many times I tried to open the door, my hand going right through the handle.

I didn't see my own body at first. I had wandered off, so disoriented. When I did see the body, my body, that's when the darkness came. I could feel it. This black hole of despair that promised me escape from my situation, that whispered in my ear like the need to play craps or the promise of forgetting—or at least not caring—that is propofol.

Around here they call it the "bardo." The word comes from the Buddhist tradition. For them it's the dark passageway between lives. For the ghosts around here it's the place those clichéd, slack-jawed, moaning ghosts get caught in, a hell of their own making, where they confront their fear and their doubts.

When I saw my body, it's the bardo that called to me.

All of this is to say that I had empathy for the newly dead bride, I really did. But she reminded me too much of Sun.

"Who... who are you? Where am I?" she asked, her face stricken.

I turned to Emily, my own version of stricken on my face. Her eyes widened and her mouth formed an "O." I think she finally got how hard this was for me.

I turned away from the dead bride and Emily. I flew through the suite door and then up and out the ceiling of the hotel. I couldn't deal with this.

Chapter Four

OLIVES. FAT, JUICY OLIVES. PITTED BLACK OLIVES, green pimento-filled olives, clay-colored Kalamata olives. They sat there in the buffet taunting me. I stared at them like a teenage dweeb stares at the head cheerleader in high school. I wanted them so badly, but knew I never would.

And I hate olives. With a passion. They are, frankly, disgusting to me. But still I floated above the buffet as the living shuffled by and scooped food on their trays. They would, I know, go back to their tables, stare at their phones, and shovel the food in, hardly tasting it.

If I had the chance I would take one of those olives and let its oval, salty form roll around in my mouth, letting the briny juice hit my tongue first. I would then bite down, letting more of the intense, earthy flavor escape before slowly chewing and swallowing. I then would let the flavor subside before taking a different kind of olive.

I would cherish each bite, each flavor, each sensation. Even with the olive, which I hate. What I would give for the chance to eat food I don't like, much less something I love—like a medium-rare steak.

I snorted out a laugh as I floated there staring at the olives, these thoughts roiling around my mind. It's because I don't believe my own bullshit. I would be like that dweeb if he actually got a chance with the cheerleader. I wouldn't be slow and thoughtful, I would gobble, shoving food into my mouth and swallowing as fast as I could. The kind of desperation I felt towards that food (and the dweeb towards that cheerleader) doesn't lead to thoughtful, controlled action.

"I believe you're having an existential crisis," a resonate male voice said.

It was Banquo. I hadn't heard him pop in, but there was no mistaking that voice. It belonged on stage, a voice that could carry the weight of Shakespeare with ease. A voice that could easily project to the back of the theater. A voice much more suited to the theater than mine. One of the many reasons I wasn't that fond of the man.

I shrugged and continued to stare at the glorious olives.

"That woman needs your help."

I shrugged again, trying to keep my mind on olives, not on beautiful brides that reminded me of the happiest times of my life which soured into the worst, all facilitated by my ex-wife, Sun.

"Emily needs you," he said, his voice quiet and gentle.

I looked up at the big-bellied, balding, older man. He was standing in the buffet staring at me. "What do you want, Banquo?"

"She was worried enough to find me." He was referring to Emily. She must have popped to Banquo, told him to find me, and popped back to the newly dead bride. While little Emily could be saltier than those olives, she had a good heart. While I was here wasting time, she was there trying to help the new ghost, just like she helped me when she found me haunting my dental practice's office manager. I had followed her to the bathroom, I was following her everywhere, desperate for a clue as to why I was murdered. Despite that first impression of finding me in the toilet with the woman I was haunting, Emily helped me.

I flew up through the roof of the restaurant onto the boring, flat, air-conditioning-unit-filled roof. There wasn't much to see—we were in downtown Tucson, just a few high-rises jutting up to the east as dusk settled down on the city. Banquo followed. It was clear I would have to have a conversation with him, and I didn't want to do it amongst the food and the living. It's weird, but roofs and ghosts kind of go together.

There is a lot missing from a ghost's "life." A sense of smell for one, and not much of a sense of touch either. What we can do is see and hear, maybe rooftops are part of that. We still feel in touch with our surroundings, but can see farther. Or maybe it's just a place to be that lets you feel a little connected to humanity without being surrounded by the living.

Banquo stood on the roof staring at me, his arms folded across his chest, highlighting his large stomach. He didn't speak. He just stood there, his ghostly form was crisp, sharp, and only a little bit transparent.

Mine, not so much. Maintaining a human-looking form as a ghost takes effort and discipline. It's one of Banquo's lessons—if you will sit at his feet and be his student. But he's right. The more you look like a wispy, freaked-out ghost, the more you feel like one. I tightened my form up. I "wear" a long trench coat these days and a fedora, making me look like a 1940's detective. Something Emily suggested. I do it for her.

"You don't understand," I offered.

Banquo shrugged, just like I had been doing. "So, explain it to me."

But I didn't want to explain. Not to Banquo. I didn't even want to speak the words. I folded my arms across my chest, mimicking Banquo's pose and just stood there.

The minutes crawled past as we stared at each other. Finally, Banquo sighed and shook his head. "Do you have any idea how long most ghosts struggle to find something useful to do? How few find a friend like you have in Emily?"

I shrugged. "Explain it to me."

That did it. His cheeks flushed red and he took a few steps toward me before stopping. "You don't deserve her," he said, his usually calm voice charged with emotion.

I blinked several times—a very conscious act for a ghost—and that did it for me. My shoulders sagged and I let out a long sigh. "You're right about that." I didn't deserve Emily. And if I was being honest, I don't know if I had deserved Sun either.

Color flared on the horizon, like a match being lit, as the sun slid behind some clouds. "I couldn't tell you why she sticks with me," I said, staring at the sunset, my voice low, the defiance gone.

"Me neither," Banquo said with a chuckle, his gaze on the evening spectacle.

We stood there until the sun disappeared below the horizon and darkness began to settle on the city. We were silent, but it was a companionable silence now.

"You need to deal with this," Banquo said. He was speaking of my issues with Sun, of my recent abandonment of Emily.

"Yeah," I said. "Haven't the foggiest clue how."

Banquo laughed, the sound of it deep and booming,

his face jolly as our eyes connected. "You're a detective, isn't finding clues kind of your thing?"

I smiled. "I guess it is."

Banquo nodded and walked a few steps away from me. "Emily is special, take care of her."

Before I had a chance to reply, he was gone with a "pop."

Chapter Five

Sun-mi Parker stood there, her hip cocked, a smile on her red lips, her hands carefully holding a carton of orange juice. A slight breeze played with her long, silky black hair. She wore a frilly blue blouse and black pants, her body thin and athletic. She did this under bright lights with a green screen behind her, but for me it was like she stood on a perfect white-sand beach with the sun slowly sinking into the ocean behind her.

She was twenty-one at the time, and I was twenty-eight.

This was 1999 in Los Angeles. Sun was filming a screen test for her first commercial, having easily made it further in acting in her first few months than I did in my first few years. I was working as a grip, rigging lighting and schlepping equipment. Nothing wrong with the job of a grip, except a lot of us wish we were on the other side of the camera.

It was all an accident. I shouldn't have been there. I had been called in because of a sick coworker and was late for the shoot. The key grip, Bobby, was rattling on about the lighting setup and a problem with the skateboard dolly that was going to be used. But I just stood there. Staring.

Sun smiling, bright lights illuminating her black hair, the breeze playing with her bangs. The director said something and she laughed, and I felt something stir in my chest. I hadn't been in a relationship for a while and they had never lasted long—the quest for success always came first.

"Anchor, did you get all that?" Bobby asked.

"Yeah," I mumbled. I hadn't heard a word he had said, and I just didn't care.

Chapter Six

WHEN I GOT BACK TO THE BRIDAL SUITE IT WAS A LOT more crowded.

The corpse was still reclined on the couch, a peaceful look on her face, but she was now attended by two people in lab coats, with two uniformed police officers manning the open door to the suite. A man and a woman in suits were looking through the room—detectives, I presumed. And the bride's ghost was there, her eyes wide, her mouth open, floating above it all, staring down. Her silk dress looked like it was turning to smoke at the edges as she floated there, making her look way too much like a movie ghost. She was in trouble.

"Can you just look at me, Helen?" Emily said, her little girl voice higher than usual. She stood on the arm of the couch, one hand reaching toward the bride. The lollipop on her T-shirt was a bland yellow showing her worry. "Just turn away from them. Take my hand."

Emily could have flown up to her, but she had a thing about it. Not that she wasn't capable, all ghosts can fly, it's actually a lot easier than walking—or looking like you're walking when you have no body and no gravity to affect it. Ghosts that don't end up in the bardo each do things that help them stay grounded. For Emily it was literally keeping her feet on the ground—or in this case, the couch, whenever she could.

All of this took place in the sitting room of the bridal suite, the curtains opened to a starry Tucson night. I stood there taking it in. Feeling a heavy lump of guilt sitting in my gut. The bride was close to going bardo. Emily was desperate to save her. I had abandoned both of them.

I took a deep "breath" and centered myself. I didn't exactly push aside all those feelings, I just ignored them. I had work to do here. A role to play. I wasn't sure exactly what it was, but it came into my mind as I strode forward.

"There you are, Helen!" I said. "I have been searching for you near and wide. I can't tell you how relieved I am to see you up here resting, just like I asked."

The ghost, Helen, looked at me, her Sun-like eyes locking with mine. I almost lost it right there. She wasn't Sun, she had thinner lips, an upturned nose, and her face wasn't quite as symmetrical. But all beautiful Asian woman are Sun to me. Not proud of this, but there it is.

My clothing had shifted along with the role I was playing. Instead of a detective's trench coat and fedora, I was wearing an expensive black Armani suit, with a white carnation at the lapel. This was an ability that had come about in the last few months as Emily and I worked cases. I could look the part of whatever role I was playing—no costume change required. Today I was the harried wedding planner.

"Oh my, darling. We do need to touch up your makeup, don't we? I mean, you are beautiful, any dummy could see that, but we must have you absolutely radiant for your big moment."

Helen's eyes stayed fixed on me as I babbled on, and she slowly floated towards me. She was confused, but that was an improvement from the terror of watching her body be poked and prodded.

I caught a look of relief on Emily's face, but kept up my patter as I slowly walked backwards. "I mean, this is your big day. Your day, my dear. Take it in. All eyes will be on you, and rightfully so. Has there ever been a bride this beautiful?"

We were just outside of the suite. Helen was still a mess, her dress trailing into what looked like smoke, but she was listening. Emily was behind me now, guiding me through several turns in the hallway. "And who did your makeup? Using autumn colors on you is just a sin. I mean, really, you are a winter if ever there was one." Helen nodded.

And so it went until Emily guided us into an empty room. I was worried about the door, it was closed and we all had to go right through it, but I kept the patter up and she kept following. By some miracle, or because Emily was a well-advanced ghost and was aware of much, the room had its lights on, and once in the bathroom we got Helen sitting down while I did her makeup.

Let me explain. Ghosts have something of a body, their ghostly form, and that is all we have. We alter how we appear through concentration and long practice. In the bathroom, Emily had a small makeup kit and started handing me brushes and lipstick and rouge. But there was no makeup kit. All of these things were a part of Emily's form. I didn't have time, but if I had looked closely, I would have seen a small thread running from Emily to the makeup kit and from the kit to each of the implements she handed me. It was all a charade. I was playing a part and she was providing the props, our ghostly state allowing us to manipulate our forms enough to pull it off.

"Nervous?" I asked as I brushed at her cheeks. She pulled back as if startled. She had felt something. Not much of a sense of feeling in the ghostly world, but if two ghosts have their forms at the same "frequency" (more complicated than that, but that works as an analogy) they can feel just a whisper of a touch. Emily, no doubt, had modulated the frequency of her own form, and thus the makeup kit, to match Helen's.

"Don't be nervous, darling. It's perfectly natural, but not really necessary."

She nodded, just a little, her face still very confused.

"Where is Adam?" she asked.

"Oh, I don't know," I said. "You are my focus today, Helen. What does a groom need, but a shave and a splash of aftershave?"

"Something happened..." she began. "I remember his face, so sad when he came to talk to me."

I didn't speak immediately, worked on her lips, and then asked, "When was this?"

She shook her head. "I... Was that today? I... I don't know. So sad... He..."

I stopped. Because I didn't want to miss a word, and because something wasn't right. Where was Adam? Where was the grieving family? I glanced at Emily and she shrugged. Something was most definitely not right here.

Chapter Seven

TURBULENCE HIT AND JOSTLED ME JUST AS I TRIED TO sit, turning what I hoped would be a smooth sliding into the seat next to Sun into an awkward fall with my head bouncing off her chest.

"Sorry," I mumbled, my cheeks turning beet red—quite a feat with my Italian heritage and olive skin tone.

This was in 1999, two weeks after I first met Sun in a Hollywood soundstage, all the lights and attention on her. I had stared, trying to not look like I was staring, of course. I fixed the dolly, did my job, and developed a full-on crush. I didn't speak a word to her, though.

That day had been a screen test and we were now in a small jet flying to Tucson to film the commercial for real in an orange grove.

"So sorry, I..." I began. And I was, but I breathed in deep of her flowery scent. Replayed the feel of my head touching her chest while my heart thumped out a Caribbean rhythm in my chest. "I... well... I just wanted to introduce myself."

Sun looked at me, a smile playing on her lips. The jet

was small, four seats across with an aisle in the middle. No one had sat next to her the whole trip, except for the director—a sleazy fellow who didn't even know my name. I figured she was one of these women that didn't get hit on very much because they were so beautiful that most men were too intimidated. And I was—intimidated—but I was also obsessed. Like a teenager with his first crush.

"Well?" she asked after some long seconds ticked by as I sat there, lost in the depths of her brown eyes.

"Umm... what?" I had no idea what she was talking about.

"You were going to introduce yourself."

"Oh! Yeah. I... umm..." I extended my hand. "My name is Walter, Walter Anchor."

She delicately took my hand and shook it. "I'm Sun-mi Parker, but everyone calls me Sun."

And then silence. A courteous greeting and then me staring at the seatback in front of me and her going back to her *Vogue* magazine. After an uncomfortable—for me— minute, she asked, "Is that your stage name?"

"What?" My brain was too busy insulting my substandard intelligence and my poor social skills to follow her.

"Anchor."

"Oh... Yeah. Right... My name." I smiled at her and was sure I looked like an idiot. I certainly felt like one. "Anchor is my legal name, but I was born Anello."

She nodded as if it had been the most obvious thing in the world and went back to reading *Vogue.*

LA to Tucson is not a long flight and I was wasting it sitting there saying nothing, getting lost in her flowery scent.

"I was in *Buffy the Vampire Slayer,*" I finally said after the plane landed and while we taxied to the airport. The words sounded silly out there on their own. A blatant brag. An obvious last-ditch, desperate attempt to—

"What? Really?" Her face lit up and those lovely brown eyes really looked at me, her *Vogue* magazine forgotten. "Did you meet Sarah Michelle Geller? I just love her."

I sat there mute, basking in the warmth of her attention.

She elbowed me in the ribs. "Well, come on, spill."

Chapter Eight

A WEDDING IS A BIG AFFAIR, ESPECIALLY ONE THAT CAN afford the kind of dress Helen wore and the kind of suite she died in. Where was her family? Her groom? Why had room service been the one to find her body? Who was Adam and why hadn't we seen him yet?

"So beautiful, just exquisite," I cooed over Helen as I drew out putting her "makeup" on. I turned to Emily, my tone low and words fast. "We are going to need the irregulars. Get the hotel searched. Have someone stick with the medical examiner. Go!"

Emily going meant no more makeup kit. While I had proved to have a knack for character-oriented costume changes, I couldn't do the "pop" thing like Emily could. "Let me see, my dear," I said, keeping Helen's gaze on me while Emily walked out the room and with a "pop" was gone. Just like Sherlock Holmes's had his Baker Street Irregulars, street boys that helped him out on occasion, Emily and I had some ghosts that could be trusted when we needed them and were eager for something different to do.

"Anchor's Irregulars" is what they were called. The name was not of my choosing, Banquo had coined the term the first time Emily and I had recruited a few ghosts to help on a case. While there is no better tail than a ghost, Emily and I could only cover so much—we needed help.

But what to do with Helen? New ghosts are not my specialty—that's Emily—but I had reached her with my wedding planner role.

As I pondered this, her face relaxed and her eyes grew wide. She was staring at me. I looked down and my form had reverted back to its trench coat and fedora mode. My default form these days.

"I'm going to level with you," I told her, not knowing what else to do.

She nodded, looking scared.

"I'm a ghost."

She bit her lip.

"But I'm going to help you."

She looked surprised.

"Because you're a ghost too."

She just stared at me, almost through me. We were still in the hotel bathroom, the fan whirring above us. Her form going diffuse at the edges and a look of terror began to transform her beautiful face into something disturbing. She was falling into the bardo. I had to do something.

I swept forward, my form properly modulated to Helen's, grabbed her, and flew her out of the building.

This was instinct. I didn't have time to think it through. I guess part of me thought getting away from the location of her murder would help. I held Helen as she screamed, the traffic on Broadway Boulevard below us, the moon above.

"What is happening?" she said between tears and gulping breaths. "Why... Why am I like this? Why am I here?" She dissolved into incoherent mumbling as I flew her away from the hotel.

I had no answers for her and I wasn't the right ghost for this. I could never stand it when Sun cried, I always felt stupid and powerless. And with Sun, that is exactly what I was.

Chapter Nine

ON THE FLIGHT BACK FROM TUCSON TO LA, SUN sought me out. She flopped into the seat next to me with a heavy sigh. The shoot had been exhausting. We had boarded the plane to come to Tucson predawn and it was close to midnight now. I had an anatomy book out and was studying.

"What's that?" she said, a whiff of vodka floating over from her exhale. I had kind of tuned the plane out, but now I could hear the sounds of laughter and loud voices coming from the front of the chartered flight. I was in the last row, my midterm in Anatomy and Physiology in two days.

"Class," I said with a smile. While I did need to study, it was hard not to stare at Sun. She had been distant during the shoot, and I thought maybe I had done something wrong.

"What kind of class?" She drew the "s" in class out and giggled.

"Not an acting class," I said, closing the book and holding it up, a skull on the cover.

"Ewww." She wrinkled her nose. "Why?"

I sighed. "My father."

"That's your father?" she said, her finger poking at the skull, another giggle escaping her.

"No. I promised my father that I would give acting ten years. That during those years, I would go to night school and get a degree while I tried to act." I ended with a shrug. It sounded lame on this plane of celebrants. These people, at least right now, were living the dream. It may have been a cheesy orange juice commercial, but they were getting paid.

"And what happens after the ten years?" Her brow furrowed and she looked very serious, leaning close to me. I could smell that flowery scent again, along with sweat and alcohol.

"Dental school in the spring."

I held my breath. I thought she would bolt, not want to be around me if I wasn't going to try to be an actor anymore. Truth be told, I hadn't acted in a couple of years. The grip jobs kept me busy and I earned enough to go to school.

A smile slowly blossomed on her beautiful face. "My dad's a dentist."

"Yeah?"

She leaned her head against my shoulder and I felt her nod. Her scent, sweat, alcohol, and the lingering floral note of her perfume, overwhelmed me. Had I found the perfect woman? She was beautiful, wanted to be an actress, and actually liked dentists.

Butterflies rioted in my stomach and I tasted fear, but I said, "We should go out, Sun."

She nodded again, "Mmmm hmmmm," her voice quiet.

She promptly fell asleep and began snoring like an

overweight sailor at the end of a three-day leave. I didn't move, not an inch, until we landed and she woke up.

Chapter Ten

IT WOULD HAVE BEEN SO USEFUL TO TAKE HELEN TO THE graveyard. There I could get help, but she was far too delicate. Realizing you are dead and coming to grips with that can be quite the rite of passage. JJ Lynch, one of the ghosts at our Tucson graveyard, has written several books about his time as a ghost. He writes his books the same way I write these missives, using this device called a SECI chamber, that is essentially a keyboard for ghosts.

She sobbed, her ghostly head pressed to my shoulder, reminding me in a twisted way of Sun passing out with her head on my shoulder on that plane. Part of me liked the intimacy of Helen in my arms as we flew above Tucson. Part of me was terrified of it, and part of me was repelled. She was too much like Sun for my feelings to be simple.

Helen's wedding dress was smokier now, elongating into a wispy, silky trail as we flew—she was still on the edge of going bardo.

"Helen," I said, my voice quiet and gentle. "Helen, can you tell me what happened?"

She didn't speak, but her sobs quieted, so I knew she heard me.

"I just want to help you. What were you and Adam doing at the hotel today?"

She stopped sobbing completely as she stiffened up.

"I can't help you unless I know what happened."

I landed us in the middle of a baseball field east of the hotel a ways. It wasn't much. Part of me, an instinct I hated, thought I should have found a more romantic local, like El Presidio Park. In any case, I thought getting her grounded might help.

I untangled myself from her and stepped back. "Please, Helen. Talk to me."

She stood for the longest time, just staring at me, her face stricken. "Adam, I can't believe he... I... I just... I..."

"What about Adam?"

She sniffed and nodded, looking around. "Where are we?"

I shrugged, it didn't matter.

"Who are you?" She looked down at her ghostly form, her dress like smoke flowing around her. "What happened?"

"Honey, you're dead." This kind of disorientation is fairly common to the newly dead.

Her eyes widened and she stared at me. I had called her "honey." I hadn't meant to do that. My cheeks felt hot and I must have blushed—even though we are ghosts, our forms will often mock biological reactions.

This wasn't Sun. This wasn't my bride or my life. My "life" was over. I was stuck as an incorporeal consciousness trying to find some semblance of peace or balance—something that had thoroughly eluded me when I was corporeal. Hell, peace and balance eludes everyone. What was I doing anyway? Solving murders for something to do.

Going to the SECI chamber and banging out the stories on that "keyboard for ghosts" so that the police can follow up and the murderers can be brought to justice.

It's not a bad existence, I guess. But it doesn't seem like a life. A life would have been Sun and I having kids. Acting together. Growing old together. Loving each other until "death do us part."

But the accident had happened, and then things with Sun had gone to shit and my life had followed. I had no right to be here, no right to—

"...understand why he would do that. What makes a person, someone you trust, suddenly..." Helen, her head down as she stared at the moonlit grass, had been talking, had been telling me important things, and I had been lost in the desolate land of "Sun left me and ruined my life."

"What!? What did you say?" I stepped forward and reached for her. She looked up, fear blossoming on her face.

"You..." she said, pointing at me, her hand shaking as she backed away. "You're just like him. You're just like all of them. You're... You're..."

Chapter Eleven

SUN-MI PARKER FELL IN LOVE WITH ME. AT LEAST, IT looked like that. I still don't really know. After that orange juice commercial, we started going out. I regaled her with tales of 1997, my "good year" in acting, when I did a lot of guest spots on TV shows. I died in the tender embrace of Jane Seymour's Dr. Quinn, I was a vampire slayed by Sarah Michelle Gellar on *Buffy the Vampire Slayer*, and I was a paramedic on *ER*. In 1997 I thought I was going to make it in acting. I thought I had broken through. I was a decent actor, I always showed up on time, knew my lines, hit my marks, but the roles just dried up and the grip job took over.

And school. To make it in Hollywood you have to be good, but you also have to be lucky. And you have to have the right "look." I guess I would call myself handsome, but in a "small-town, boy-next-door" kind of way. I didn't have the kind of face that could lead a show. In 1998 I had a few roles as corpses, and quite a bit of extra work, but found that being a grip put me in the action, paid better, and was reliable work. It kind of happened without me deciding it.

I remember a dinner Sun and I had that fall. We had been dating for several months, but with our crazy schedules, that didn't turn into as many dates as you would think—and not nearly as many as I wanted. The restaurant had a patio overlooking Manhattan Beach. Seagulls spun in the breeze dodging kites as people walked in the cool evening. The sun slowly sank as the waitress brought our wine and then an artichoke dip appetizer. The warm light made Sun look even more beautiful than usual. The dinner was kind of a celebration. Sun had just completed another orange juice commercial, and I had just finished finals and was assured my bachelor's degree in premed.

"Do you miss it?" she asked, her eyes down as she knifed some dip onto her bread.

There was no easy answer. I mean, I was on set often, I was making a living in Hollywood, but it didn't feel quite right. I was on the wrong end of the camera. I sighed and watched some kids on boogie boards flying into shore. "Sure. I miss it."

She bit her lip, her eyes shyly finding mine. "I could never quit."

There was a look there, for just a moment, that made my belly tighten and sweat pop out on my forehead. She looked at me like I spoke another language or was an alien from another planet. For just a moment, that look said that she didn't understand me, that she didn't like me.

And then it was gone. She laughed and smiled and raised her wine glass. "To Walter the graduate and soon to be dentist."

I raised my glass, catching a whiff of the appley white wine. "Only four more years and I'll be spending my day with my hands in strangers' mouths."

The glasses clinked and dinner was lovely, but that sick feeling in my belly didn't quite go away.

Chapter Twelve

HELEN'S HAND SHOOK AS SHE STARED AT ME WITH WIDE eyes. "You did this to me, Adam. This is your fault. Why did you..." Her face went from fear to sadness to anger as her form became more diffuse. She thought I was Adam. I was losing her. "If you hadn't..." Her words trailed off into a low moan.

I never knew what I was doing with Sun, and I sure didn't know what I was doing with Helen. Emily had started this, Emily had found her dead and thought it might be a fun little case, not considering Sun and all the memories it would bring flooding back. It was the four-year-old Emily, the innocent little girl, who thought it would be a delight to distract me with a dead Asian woman. Her intent was good.

It was also the four-year-old Emily that wanted to save this ghost, who kept me chasing her when what I wanted to do was run away and find Sun.

"Stay with me, Helen," I said. "Look into my eyes. We're going to get through this. We're going to find out who killed you."

And then she focused on me, for just a moment, her face looking puzzled, and then her moan turned into a wail and then a scream as the bardo took her. She slowly started floating, like a balloon in the breeze, back the way we had come, the smoky white of her wedding dress trailing behind. I started flying after her, talking to her, pleading with her, but then stopped. What could I do that would help her now? What good had I done for this dead bride that looked just like my Sun?

It had been years since I'd seen Sun. I was a ghost now. I could find her. I could be with her. I could love her. I could... be the biggest, creepiest ghost in the land stalking my ex-wife because of my unresolved feelings and trauma.

I shook my head, trying to expel both sides of that. The creepy, stalky, needy me, and the judgmental me.

But there was some truth there. Maybe I did need to find Sun and try to resolve what had happened to us.

I saw her in my mind's eye. She would be thirty-five now, the years adding a bit of character to her beauty, but not lessening it one bit. No grey in her jet-black hair, though. She would have eradicated any that dared make their presence known. Her laugh lines would be a bit deeper, but her smile would be as dazzling as ever.

Sun was Hollywood beautiful with her symmetrical features, her silky, long hair, her expressive eyes, her beautiful lips.

Hovering over Tucson, my mission forgotten, I folded myself into my memories of Sun. After our divorce, after I came to Tucson and opened my dental practice, I had withdrawn from anything that might remind me of Sun. I didn't watch TV or go to the movies—she might get a part and could be in anything—only old shows on Netflix for me. I stopped reading *Variety* and Hollywood gossip websites. I immersed myself into being a dentist and using my acting skills to keep my patients calm and relaxed as I drilled on their teeth.

That only lasted a few years until Sun got her big break and her TV show. I had to watch that, to celebrate the success, but it was like torture and I came to separate Sun from the role she played. I tuned in to *Detectives: LA* to watch Melissa Lee every week, who just happened to look like the love of my life. It was this weird compartmentalization, something I had to do to deal with it.

But floating there, I let myself really remember Sun. How she was, how the years would have made her more beautiful. I remembered her ever-present floral scent, her long, lithe limbs, her bright smile, her laughter, how she snored at night after drinking too much. I remembered the feel of her hand in mine, somehow both strong and delicate at the same time. I remembered the feel of her body next to mine and how I could never, ever get enough of her.

I was an addict and Sun was my drug, and I had just fallen off the wagon. With a loud popping sound, Tucson disappeared and Sun stood in front of me.

Chapter Thirteen

AT FIRST I DIDN'T RECOGNIZE HER. IT WASN'T ANYTHING specific, really. Long black hair with bangs, slim, lithe body, beautiful face. Except she was pacing in a large living room dressed in sweats and a T-shirt, her hair up, a glass of wine in her hand, and a frown on her face. Jazz played softly in the background as she paced on a plush, off-white carpet in front of floor-to-ceiling windows that overlooked the lights of Los Angeles.

"Sun?" I said. She couldn't, of course, hear me.

She stopped her pacing and looked right at me, and if I had had a heart it would have been thumping hard. She chewed on her lip and quietly cursed in Korean under her breath. She resumed her pacing, taking small sips of her white wine from time to time.

I didn't think about the fact that I had "popped" for the first time. I didn't think about Helen, lost and newly a ghost. I didn't think about Emily and how disappointed she would be in me. I actually didn't think. I just stared at Sun.

"What's wrong?" I asked.

She stopped pacing and stared at me again, her face

more full of worry than I had ever seen. The only thing that had ever seemed to worry her was whether she would get a part or not and I knew her detectives show was still on the air. She had a part. A good one. A leading role. One that afforded her this house and appearances on talk shows and occasional movie parts.

She didn't stay still long, cursed again, and resumed her pacing.

I couldn't stand it. I started walking with her, talking to her. "Honey, I'm here. I'm finally here. I'm so sorry I was away for so long. I can't imagine how my death must have affected you. But don't worry. Whatever this is, I'll help you figure this out. Ghosts can communicate with the world now. I'll go and write you a letter so you know I'm here. So you know I'll never leave you again. So you——"

The words tumbled out like I had been mute all my life and finally found my voice. Tears ran down my cheeks and I felt happy, so happy, to be with my Sun. But I stopped talking when she stopped again and stared at where I used to be standing. My elation crashed as I followed her stare. She hadn't been looking at me, she had been looking at the wall. At a picture on the wall. A picture of Sun with a huge smile on her face. She was on a beach with her arm around a boy. A boy with crooked teeth and curly black hair. A boy that looked like a cross between Sun and me.

Chapter Fourteen

My love for Sun was all encompassing. I went to dental school, I worked as a grip, but it was my moments with Sun that made the long days worth living. A quick lunch on the Paramount Studio lots when we were both there. A phone call while she drove between auditions and I took a break from studying. Sunday afternoons watching football with her.

Snatches of time here and there that felt stolen and precious. We were both so very busy and it didn't feel like enough. I wanted every day to be as full of Sun as possible. I wanted to see her face, hold her hand, kiss her lips as many times as I could. It was like my life had new meaning and the world without her seemed to be covered with a grey film, like it was a movie being shot with a dirty lens.

Three months into our time as a couple and we were past "I love you" and I was longing for more.

"You could move in, you know." I said it quietly. We sat on my overstuffed couch late on a Sunday night, the credits rolling on some romcom starring Jennifer Aniston that I had crewed on. I slipped my hand into hers and squeezed it.

Sun blinked and studied my face while butterflies put on steel-toed boots and marched around my stomach. My brain went into overdrive, worrying that I had asked too soon, that she wasn't ready, that this would send her running away, that I was the dumbest guy ever and I should be happy with what I had.

She had said something, but I didn't hear it, so loud was my brain. "It's just that we don't get to spend enough time together," I said. "We are so damn busy, at least this way we would always wake up in the same place. You know, breakfast and coffee—you like my eggs. If we both have a day off we'll already be in the same place, no getting on the damn highway and dealing with traffic. My place is closer to the studio anyway. I just think—"

She pressed her finger to my lips. "Shut up, Walter. I said okay." And then she was in my arms, her lips finding mine, and my brain finally quieting as my heart swelled. I was sure this was perfect. That we were perfect, that this would go on and on.

And it did go on for a while. Eight months later, I proposed. A year after that we got married. And then we tried to have a baby and things changed, and just like in Chaucer's "Troilus and Criseyde," all good things must come to an end.

Chapter Fifteen

I SEARCHED SUN'S HOUSE FRANTICALLY WHILE SHE continued pacing her living room, framed by the nighttime view of LA. Three bedrooms, the master was a mess, clothes everywhere, and clearly her room. There were two other bedrooms, both neat and clean and generic—obviously for guests. A garage with a nice Lexus sedan, a backyard with a koi pond. The hallway had family photos, her parents, siblings, nieces and nephews—all people I know— and an eight-by-ten from our wedding. Not one single sign of a child. Her child. Our child. I was frantic and kept going from room to room to room, flying quickly and then stopping to look. It wasn't a big house—if there was a kid here I would have found it.

"Who is that, Sun? Who is it!?" She was slumped on the couch, her glass of wine empty, her eyes unfocused and staring out at the lights of the city.

I flew over to the picture and studied it. Sun was younger in this picture, maybe thirty, they were in a park, with an expanse of green behind them filled with people and the ocean in the distance. No landmarks. Nothing to place it.

The boy was six or seven years old and looked happy. It looked like they knew each other well. His hair was curly, just like mine, and he had pale blue eyes.

My mind was grasping at something. It didn't all go together. Sun would have been twenty-four when the child was born, and we were together then. There was something else too.

A pop interrupted me and Emily was there.

"Walter! Where have you been?" Emily's voice was a high-pitched four-year-old squeak, her lisp thicker than usual. "You left our client alone, she's in the bardo. Why would you... Hey! Where are we?"

I didn't want to stop looking at the picture. There was a mystery here, one I needed to understand, but I knew Emily would be relentless. She's been dead eighty years and can have the wisdom of age, but she can often be as impatient as the four-year-old she was when she died.

"That's Sun," I said, pointing to the woman slumped on the couch.

Emily's mouth was open to fire more words at me, but she looked at Sun and then back at me, her jaw silently moving. She knew I hadn't seen Sun for many years, had never sought her out as a ghost. She was my best friend and knew how difficult the divorce had been—she had often told me she thought Sun was the reason I was a ghost and my purpose as a ghost was to reconcile what happened with her. I would always insist I was here to solve my murder, and up until today I had believed it.

Her face softened and she looked me straight in the eye. "What do you need, Walter?"

Chapter Sixteen

LOW MOTILITY. THAT WAS WHAT THE DOCTORS HAD told us. My swimmers didn't swim so well. In other words, it was all my fault.

Sun wanted a baby, really wanted a baby, in fact it was the only thing she wanted more than an acting career. Which seemed odd at first. She brought it up on our honeymoon—a few days in Cancun lounging on the beach.

"Honey," she said, her hand brushing mine as we reclined on lounge chairs, the sounds of the ocean and children playing having nearly lulled me to sleep.

"Yes, Mrs. Anchor," I said. I liked the sound of it, although she had kept the name Parker, not wanting a name change to affect her career.

"What do you think of children?"

"I think they're undisciplined, unskilled, and rather short." I smiled and glanced at her, but couldn't see anything past her movie star sunglasses.

"Seriously, Walter."

I sat up and took a deep breath. "Yeah. Someday. After

you're a star and after my practice is doing well. Sure. I'd love to have a baby or two with you."

She frowned and crossed her arms over her chest like she was cold under the beating sun. I woke up quick. "What's going on, Sun?"

She wasn't looking at me, but staring at two kids, maybe four or five, playing along the edges of the water as it lapped up onto the beach. "I stopped taking the pill," she said, her voice quiet, almost a whisper.

I was fully awake then. "What!? Why would you do that? Why would you do that without talking with me first?"

"I want to be a mother."

"That doesn't explain anything. We're married. We have to make these kinds of decisions together."

We argued. People stared. The rest of our time there was tainted. She told me she started taking her pill again, but could I trust her? It disturbed me that the moment we got married she seemed to have changed. Sun was still a driven actress, but now she was driven to be a mother, and she had never mentioned kids to me before. Something wasn't right.

Chapter Seventeen

A BREEZE BRUSHED AT THE PALM TREES AND CREATED ripples in Sun's pool. I stared at the water and the distorted reflection of the moon there. It seemed like everything around me was distorted in some way. A newly dead ghost of a bride that wasn't really a bride. My Sun pensively staring at the picture of a child that could be ours, except it couldn't be.

I had let Emily coax me out of the house and it felt wrong to be away from Sun. After so many years apart, the attraction I felt for her had not diminished one bit.

"Can you just stay here?" Emily asked, her voice unusually gentle.

I nodded.

"We need some help. I'm going to get it."

I nodded again, but I wasn't really listening. With a "pop" Emily was gone so I floated back into the house and found Sun still slumped on the couch. With a concerted effort, I focused on my ghostly form, firming it up. I was having trouble thinking, my thoughts wispy and diffuse just like my form. It took a few minutes, but I was pacing in front of Sun in my trench coat, taking realistic steps.

Sun and I met in 1999 when she was twenty-one and I was twenty-eight. We married in 2001 and divorced in 2004. Five years together. I went back to the picture of Sun looking to be around thirty with a six-year-old boy. That would put her at twenty-four when the boy was born, when we were still together. But what if I was wrong about their ages? What if he was five and she was thirty-two? What if she got pregnant right at the end of our relationship, right before we split for good? That could be my son.

I walked over and squatted down in front of Sun. Her brown eyes were half lidded and moist. Sun could cry on cue for a camera but was never much of a crier in her life. This, for her, was crying.

"What happened, Sun?" I asked. "Is that our boy? Why didn't you ever tell me?"

She didn't answer, of course. I'm a ghost, she's alive, and while I could type her a message in the SECI chamber, we couldn't talk.

Her phone buzzed but she didn't even look at it, another unusual behavior. I looked at the smartphone's screen, the message was from Taylor, an actress she had known since the beginning. "So sorry, hon," it said. "I know this is a bad day for you. Should I come over?"

"Dammit!" I shouted. I needed to know what was going on, what had happened. Taylor knew and she was probably talking about it right now. If I was with her, I would know.

I turned away from Sun and looked over the Los Angeles Valley, strings of light arrayed as far as I could see. I had popped to Sun because I was thinking so strongly about her, so I started to think about Taylor. She had green eyes and long, straight, blond hair. She loved sushi and hated football. She had been Sun's maid of honor and had given me hell the week before the wedding telling me that if I hurt Sun, she would kill me. At first I thought she was joking, but the flash in those green eyes made me rethink it. She hadn't been as successful as Sun, but made a living doing guest spots on a myriad of shows. She favored musky scents in her perfume choices and liked Jimmy Choo high heels. She had two boys and was married to a real estate broker.

I filled my mind with Taylor, but nothing happened. Traffic crawled on the highway while the moon watched from above. And then I remembered that I had done a series of crowns on Taylor. It had been after Sun and I split and so very awkward, but I did it just to get some news on Sun. I remembered Taylor's mouth well, the missing molar, the scar tissue on the inside of her right cheek—she was a clencher—and the way her tongue always seemed to be in the wrong place. No two mouths are the same, each tells its history, has its own personality.

That did it. With a "pop" I left Sun and found myself staring into the open mouth of Taylor Oldsman as she belted out "And I... I will always love you."

Chapter Eighteen

SUN HATED NEEDLES, BUT ONLY SLIGHTLY MORE THAN I did. Yeah, I know, a needle-hating dental student. I hate receiving injections myself so I hate giving them. Shoving a thin metal tube through your skin somehow seems wrong, doesn't it?

"Don't look," I said, as I pinched her at the waist poised with the needle, an FSH shot to stimulate follicle growth in the ovaries which would in turn result in more eggs. We were gearing up for in vitro fertilization to give my lazy sperm a fighting chance.

"Screw you," she said, taking a deep breath and holding it.

She stared at the needle as I did the injection. While she was willing to let me make the injection, she wasn't willing to turn away. The fear was like a challenge for her and she wasn't one for turning away from a challenge.

And that "screw you" might have been about the hormonal fluctuations the meds produced, it might have been directed at her fear, or it might have been for me, since it was my substandard contribution to this process that made this necessary. Or, maybe all of the above.

She exhaled, her breath rank. It was midday on a Sunday, but she had just woken up. Her latest gig was as an extra on a vampire movie that shot nights. Not good enough for her, by far, but she was working.

"Coffee?" I asked, as cheerfully as I could, sitting on our bed in our tiny bedroom. I had opened the curtains letting in the California sunshine. "Orange juice?"

"Screw you!" she said, but this time with a tiny bit of a smile. She had gotten very tired of orange juice while doing that series of commercials. "Coffee," she said with a big sigh. "Please."

I walked to the kitchen and brought her back a cup of black coffee—no cream, no sugar, she didn't want to hide from the bitter bite of the beverage.

"I ran into Taylor on the way home yesterday," I said.

She mmmed around the first sip of her coffee sitting up in bed, her black hair wild and a light blue tank top on. I stared for a moment and marveled that this beautiful creature was in my bed. A moment I had experienced so many times with her, but it never did grow old.

"She was wondering if you might want to go to the farmer's market today."

Sun rolled her eyes and sighed. "And hear about all the preparations for little Tony's second birthday? See her smug pregnant lady waddle of joy?"

I shrugged to hide my worry. She had pulled away from Taylor after our troubles getting pregnant. It was the unusual thing that she didn't want to face head on, and I had learned to worry about those things.

"Toast? Cantaloupe?" I asked.

She shook her head and took another sip of her coffee.

"Maybe we should wait, you know," I began, the words

feeling sharp as they came out, as if they would cut me, cut her. "You're young, what's the rush?" I ended in a weak shrug.

She took a deep breath, her nostrils flaring slightly, but didn't speak. I should have shut up, changed the subject, but the words had to escape.

"You know, wait until I have a practice up and running. Wait until your career is back on track, wait until—"

"I have to go to the bathroom." She set her coffee down hard enough for some of it to slosh onto the bed stand as she swept into the bathroom.

I stood there, shifting from one foot to another for five minutes and then ten. She didn't come out.

"You okay, babe?" I asked from the door.

"Leave me alone, Walter."

At the time, I blamed it on the hormones. In retrospect, part of me knew something else was going on.

Chapter Nineteen

THE KARAOKE BAR WAS A PRETENTIOUS AFFAIR. A RAISED
stage with spotlights, a fog machine belching grey smoke, a
wall of sixty-inch LCDs behind Taylor that showed scenes
from the movie "The Bodyguard" as she belted out "I Will
Always Love You" ala Whitney Houston.

And Taylor can sing. She's no Whitney, but she did a
fair job with the song, hitting the notes, injecting gobs of
emotion, holding the mic and stalking the stage like she did
this every night. She was better than 99 percent of the
folks there and she knew it. The audience was rapt as they
watched. Taylor didn't have a very robust acting career, but
on the karaoke stage she ruled.

When I first met Taylor, she would do this every
chance she got. It was a balm to the audition blues. After
she started having kids, that had to change.

All of this was a brief spark in my mind. I didn't care
about Taylor and her singing, I just had to know about
what was going on with Sun, with that boy in that picture,
and that made this the longest rendition of the song I had
ever heard. It seemed to go on for days, giving me entirely

too much time to think. When it finally ended, she smiled and did a small bow. The audience clapped, and it wasn't just polite, they had loved it. She hopped off the stage and wiped sweat from her brow—she had worked hard up there. I flew right above her so I could hear everything.

Normally I would walk, a conscious effort, and look as alive as I could. Right then I didn't really care about all that, but mostly I didn't want to collide with any of the living in the crowded bar. To be frank, it creeps me out, that tingling sensation that occurs when the dead collide with the living. Many don't mind it—hell, some ghosts seek it out, but I hate it. It puts the reality of my biology-free life in too sharp a contrast.

"Fabulous, darling," a well-dressed, middle-aged man said at the small table she went back to. He wore a lavender dress shirt with a white tie, his hair was short and his goatee well-trimmed.

Taylor smiled and nodded but went right to her phone. She pursed her lips and then put on a smile for her companion.

I didn't know who he was. Not her husband, not her brother.

"No word?" the man asked.

Taylor shook her head. "I was hoping this would take my mind off of it, but..." she trailed off, glancing at the stage where a nervous, and clearly inebriated, young man was getting ready to follow Taylor's performance. She looked at her phone again.

The man put his hand on Taylor's. "Just go over there, Taylor. Bang on her door until she answers."

Taylor gave him a weak smile and shook her head. "Not today. It can't be the normal Sun-Taylor thing today. She has to ask."

They continued to talk, but the conversation didn't get

back to Sun. I was going mad. Couldn't she just say it? "Such a shame that Sun had that child and hid it from Walter and now the kid is dead after a long bout with..."

It was too silly. Sun wouldn't have hidden our child from me, would she? And if she did have a child, how could there be no evidence of him in her house?

What was going on?

"What's going on, Walter?" Emily asked. She had popped in and stood on an empty table behind Taylor and her companion.

I turned towards her and I told her who Taylor was and why I was there.

She listened, her little face scrunched up into an expression of concern that no four-year-old could muster. After I finished, she sniffed and her face took on a more common four-year-old configuration as big tears ran down her cheeks. "I... I'm so sorry, Walter. I... I just thought... I didn't mean... I..."

I came down onto the floor and modulated my form properly and embraced Emily as she stood on the table. She is an enigma of a ghost with her four-year-old body and her eighty years dead, but she's my best friend. I can't do my afterlife without her and I can't stand to see her cry. It jolted me out of my own head. "It's okay, honey. This was long overdue."

"No," she said through the tears, I could feel her shake her head which was buried in my chest. "It's not. You were just getting back to normal after Haley. I should have thought this through."

"You couldn't know." While Emily was a wise ghost, she had only had four years of biological life experience.

"I should have."

She cried. I comforted her.

"Don't get too handsy, you perv," she said when the tears had run their course.

I chuckled and let her go, looking around and seeing that Taylor had left. I sighed. I didn't know if I had the patience to follow Taylor long enough for her to say something about Sun. I didn't think I could be away from Sun that long.

"I need to get back to Sun."

Emily nodded, grabbed my hand and popped us to Sun.

Chapter Twenty

I CHALKED UP SUN'S BABY MADNESS TO SOMETHING mysteriously female. Something I couldn't in my maleness ever hope to understand, the biological imperative of the survival of the species spurring her on, or some such mysterious force.

They harvested her eggs. I donated my sperm, and given how much easier my part of this was, I didn't really question why Sun always seemed to be upset with me. They injected my lackadaisical swimmers into her eggs and fertilized them. A few matured and they were implanted in Sun's uterus. All the while I kept going to school. I kept working. I kept hoping that things would get better.

"I'm pregnant!" Sun yelled, hitting me like a linebacker as I shuffled into our apartment after a fourteen-hour day of work and school. She pulled away and waved the pregnancy test with the pink plus in front of my nose.

"Oh babe, that's great!" I grabbed her and twirled her about the living room, my fatigue forgotten.

We celebrated that night, going out to eat, curling up on the couch when we got home and talking about the patter of little feet that would soon grace our home. We made love in a tender moment where it was as if she was being impregnated right then.

Then as we dozed, her head on my chest, as I slowly stroked her silky hair, it hit me.

"We're pregnant," I said.

"Hmmmm?" she said, taking a deep breath and pushing herself up.

"Earlier you said, 'I'm pregnant.' It's 'we,' 'we're pregnant.'"

She lay back down on her side of the bed facing away from me and pulled the comforter up high. "Of course. Good night, Walter," she mumbled and was soon snoring gently as I lay there wondering if she meant it. I mean, clearly, she was the one with the fetus in her, but this was something we were doing together, wasn't it?

Chapter Twenty-One

SUN WAS IN HER BED, JUST HER NOSE STICKING OUT OF her comforter, a wine glass and bottle on her nightstand as she snored loudly.

"She's pretty drunk," Banquo said as I stood there staring at her.

"She got into bed fully clothed," Emily added, her face scrunched up.

I nodded and tried to smile a thank you to them, but probably looked like I had just eaten an olive or something else terrible.

Emily had gone to get help. That help, quite predictably, was in the form of Banquo. She had a massive crush on him.

"Can you tell me what's going on, Walter?" Banquo asked.

I nodded again and we walked out to the living room and I showed him the picture, told him that I thought it could be our child, except that it couldn't be our child.

His face was full of concern, he asked questions and listened well. I'm not a big fan of Banquo's, but right then he was what I needed. A good ear and logical questions. We didn't have any insights and we all ended up standing there staring at the picture.

Minutes ticked by as the moon set and Sun snored in the bedroom. Ghosts can do this for a while. We don't get hungry, we don't get physically tired. Personally, my mind had slipped into neutral, had given up for the moment on the mystery. And then it hit me, this night had brought more than one mystery.

"The bride," Emily said, before I could. "I almost forgot about the bride."

I nodded, my mind still in neutral.

"You guys go," Banquo said. "I'll stay with Sun. I don't think anything else will be happening tonight."

I opened my mouth to speak, to protest, but before I could, Emily grabbed my hand and popped us out of there.

Chapter Twenty-Two

THE DAY HAD STARTED OUT SO PROMISING. SUN HAD woken up happy and affectionate. We had breakfast together, the window open, the sun cheerful in a clear blue sky—it had rained the previous night, scrubbing the grunge out of the Southern California air. We held hands as we walked to the car and I took big gulps of that clean air. It felt like a new day.

I had laid aside my worries about "I'm pregnant" versus "we're pregnant." There had been little time between work and school and trying to keep up with Sun's baby obsession. We had cleared out the second bedroom which had been where I studied for school and had housed Sun's treadmill—that was all crammed in the living room. Sun had exhaustively researched cribs and strollers and everything else. We had both read several books on babies.

Three months had passed and it was a different life for us. We were both focused on the same thing. I loved it.

"Nervous?" I asked as I drove us down the highway towards the obstetrician's office. It was time for the first ultrasound.

"No," she said putting her hand to her stomach, which was still flat—she wasn't showing yet. "I can feel her in there." Sun was sure it was a girl.

The morning traffic was thick, but nothing I didn't deal with nearly every day, just the whirling, barely controlled chaos of a modern American highway at rush hour. Everyone hurrying as if each person in each car had the most urgent of tasks. I was ferrying my beloved wife to the doctor in my trusty, if a bit old, Honda Civic. What could be more urgent or more precious?

I took a sip of my coffee, inhaling deeply of the heavy scent, enjoying the beauty of the day and the hum of the wheels on still wet pavement. I saw a red sports car coming up fast in my left mirror.

"You know," I said with a grin, glancing at her in the passenger's seat, her intense brown eyes meeting mine. "It could be a boy. I mean—"

I caught a flash of red in my peripheral vision, that sports car was cutting in in front of me. It was going to hit us. I swerved to the right, the Honda almost colliding with a semi there. I swerved back to the left, past my lane and a bit into the next, horns blaring. The oil on the wet roads was making my Honda a lot less trusty and a lot less responsive.

"Close call," I said, glancing at Sun, whose eyes were wide and mouth open.

"Look out!"

I looked ahead to a wall of red taillights and slammed on the brakes, but the water on the roads combined with the oil from the months since we last had a good rain made the road slick. The Honda couldn't stop fast enough. Sun screamed.

Chapter Twenty-Three

HELEN, HER MOUTH OPEN, A LOW WAIL ESCAPING HER, was back in the bridal suite, her empty eyes staring at the couch where we had found her body. Fredrick was there watching her, he's one of Anchor's Irregulars. He's an old ghost, he died in 1929 and was the original mortician of the graveyard we all call home. He was dressed formally, as always, in a period three-piece-suit with a starched collar and a pocket watch.

He walked over, his form crisp, his hands clasped behind his back. "She's been like this for a while. The undertaker had already taken her body by the time we got back. We've tried to pull her out of the bardo, but absolutely no luck."

"And the police?" I asked.

He shrugged, making the mundane gesture look somehow elegant. "Blinky has been shadowing the detectives."

I groaned. Blinky was a new ghost who was obsessed with Pac-Man. He started out chasing other ghosts around the graveyard as the red Blinky Pac-Man character, and he had been trying to convince enough of us to turn our ghostly forms into Pac-Man characters and recreate the game.

Emily joined us, a smile on her face. "Hey, Pac-Man," she said to me. "You know Blinky, he loves helping. He'll stick with the detectives 24/7. We need him."

I nodded, still lost in the horror of having to become Pac-Man.

"The preliminary cause of death is poisoning," Fredrick continued. "There is a lot of DNA contamination in the room, so they are not sure what happened. No pills or bottles found. They think maybe..."

He kept talking, but I wasn't listening anymore. The pieces fell into place and I knew what had happened, how this bride had died all alone here. I knew how to help Helen. I could only see Helen from behind. From this perspective, she looked exactly as Sun had on our wedding day.

Part of me knew what I was doing, but another part of me was lost in the Sun-ness of her. I think the last few hours had been too much, my mind kind of lost itself and the bride standing in front of me wasn't Sun—a part of me still knew that—but it wasn't just Helen either. She was Sun and Helen.

"I'm sorry, honey," I said to Sun/Helen, standing next to her, "this is all my fault." I licked my lips and took a deep breath. I was vaguely aware that I wasn't dressed in a trench coat anymore, but in a tux. I knew that I looked different too, with shoulder-length blond hair and a surfer's physique. "I shouldn't have called it off, I'm so sorry."

Helen looked up at me from the couch, her eyes focusing. She was so desperate to see her fiancé that my impersonation was working, she was coming out of the bardo. She whispered, "Adam?"

I nodded, losing myself in those eyes. I kept speaking, my words those of Adam to Helen and at the same time Walter to Sun. It all fit together.

"It was a mistake, honey. I didn't mean to hurt you so badly. I never wanted this to happen. I love you, you know that, but you were not easy. I loved you, I worshiped you, but I don't think I understood you. Not really. Not until tonight."

I walked over to the window and looked out at the Tucson night, the lights laid out in the desert in an orderly grid, not that dissimilar to the view Sun had been pacing in front of in LA.

Sun/Helen followed me to the window, her furrowed brow an anomaly on her smooth, young face.

A small part of me knew that Helen was out of the bardo, that my Adam trick had worked, but I was then lost to my own need and spoke to Helen the words I needed to say to Sun.

"I wanted a baby, our baby, I did, but I didn't understand your obsession. Your driving need. And I now know there was something behind it, something about that boy in the picture."

I looked down and I was holding that picture in my hands and I showed it to Sun/Helen. It was a trick of my ghostly form, so intense was my state that I had created the picture.

"This is not my baby. This can't be my baby. On that highway that day, with the road wet and slick, we lost our baby and you never forgave me. We didn't try again. Why didn't you forgive me?"

I was crying, tears running down my face. I was vaguely aware that Helen's form had crisped up, her dress elegant, smooth silk and no longer smoke.

"You told me that the accident wasn't my fault, that

you were just grieving, that you just needed a little time, that if I would just move out and give you that space, you were sure it would be all right.

"But it wasn't all right. The divorce papers came the day I graduated from dental school. You were there, in the audience, I saw you as I got my diploma, but you left before I could say hello, and then the papers came. I..."

Sun/Helen was crying, she took my hand and I could feel it. By some instinct, she had done it just right. Later, I realized that what Helen needed at that moment was to be needed, to be indispensable. My desperate need for her to be my Sun helped her find the strength to not just leave the bardo, but to help me. "I'm sorry," she said.

I looked into her beautiful brown eyes and could tell she meant it. And then she put her arms around me and held me.

Chapter Twenty-Four

WHEN THE MADNESS CLEARED, I WAS LEFT WITH SHAME.

"Thank you," I mumbled, trying to pull away from Helen's embrace, but she didn't let me go. It was early in the morning, the eastern horizon starting to lighten.

"This Sun," she whispered, "should not have let you go."

"I'm sorry," I added. Sorry for my madness, for the need that spilled out of me that I directed at her just because of the way she looked. As if that meant anything about her beyond genetics. She wasn't Sun. There was no Sun for me.

She let me go, and as soon as she did, I missed that ghostly touch. "What will you do now?" she asked.

I shrugged, looking around. We were alone, Emily and Fredrick must have left sometime in the night.

Her eyes strayed from me to the couch where she had died not that many hours ago.

"Actually," I said quietly. "I'd like to help you, Helen. I'd like to help you adjust to this, to accept what happened."

She smiled, her eyes meeting mine briefly before looking back to the couch. Her face rearranged itself, gone was the compassionate look she had given me, and in its place was a look I knew very well right then. Shame.

"You know how you died," I said.

She nodded, but did not meet my eyes.

It all made sense now, the bride without a wedding, her fixation on Adam, her reactions to some of my questions. The emotions hit me hard. The shame of a lover rejecting you. The terror of standing in front of a church in a beautiful silk dress while hundreds of people stared at you. Your life no longer what you thought it would be. Feeling worthless and unloved...

This wasn't a murder, but a suicide. She couldn't take the shame of her Adam leaving her at the altar. After it was all over, when she knew she couldn't live with it, she had booked the bridal suite again, put on her wedding gown, and poisoned herself.

"It was... I... I did this," she said.

"Adam wasn't good enough for you," I told her.

She still couldn't look at me, but I saw tears forming in her eyes, her dress going from silky to smoky again as she edged towards the bardo.

I held her then as she had held me. I let her cry. She had a long road in front of her, being a ghost, staying out of the bardo, coming to grips with her life and how it ended. But then again, so did all of us ghosts. We could help her through it.

And then it came to me in a flash—there was a way to solve the mystery of Sun and the boy. I would need the SECI chamber and a little time, but that was about it.

But not yet. It was time to take Helen back to the graveyard, introduce her to the ghosts there, get her talking to other ghosts that had taken their own lives and could help her now. I smiled at her and took her hand, flying us into the new morning.

Epilogue

TAMARA WATSON STOOD LOOKING OVER THE DAYTIME view of LA out Sun's window. She was tense, her shoulders high, her back straight. Tamara is the inventor of the SECI chamber, a lovely young woman with shoulder-length brown hair dressed in a black skirt with a blue blouse.

Sun sat on her couch reading the letter I had written her using the SECI chamber. She was in sweats, her bare feet folded underneath her, her lips were pursed as she quickly read, her eyes snapping back and forth. On several occasions, she went back to a previous page and reread a section before moving on.

Tamara had done more than I asked. She had read what I had written, printed it out, flown to LA and delivered it herself. I was not sure why she did it. We had brought several murderers to justice—Emily and I would solve the crime, I would go write about it, and Tamara would get the information to the authorities. But this... It was above and beyond the call of duty.

Emily held my hand as we watched. My form kept

going diffuse. If I had had a stomach it would have been rioting, I was so nervous. In the letter, I told her everything. I asked her to forgive me for the accident. I asked her to tell me who the boy in the picture was.

"This is real?" Sun asked, her voice low, like she was afraid someone might overhear.

Tamara turned from the view and gave Sun a small smile. "It's real. Walter has been solving crimes, one of them was a woman, a bride, who reminded him of you, and that..." She trailed off, gesturing at the papers. I had explained all that in the letter.

Sun looked around, her eyes a bit too wide. "And he's here?"

Tamara smiled wider this time. "Yes. He knew when we were meeting."

Sun's brow furrowed and she looked around the room. It's a difficult thing to accept, that there are conscious beings among us that the living can't see or hear, that were once alive. How does it change your life knowing that this might happen to you? How does it change how you treat others knowing they could still come back to you even when they are dead?

Sun's eyes grew moist, the guilty look that plagued her face stealing away her beauty. She bit her lip and stood.

"Just talk to him," Tamara said, picking up her purse and leaving the room.

Emily let go of my hand and walked out after Tamara. As I watched Sun pace and try to find her voice I wanted to run. I didn't want to know the truth anymore. I bared my soul in that letter, but did I want to hear Sun's side? Learn about the boy. About why she wouldn't forgive me for the accident. Could I handle what she had to say?

"I do love you, Walter," she began, wiping at her eyes. "But it's just not that simple."

I stood there, unmoving, until she was done, until she had told me everything.

"It wasn't much of a case," I said to Emily as we walked the graveyard. I have come to find it relaxing. The green grass, tall trees, and granite tombstones have become home to me.

The day was one of those hot Tucson days you see even in the fall, with a washed-out blue sky and a bit of a shimmer over the roads from the heat flowing up off the pavement. We were ghosts, though, so the heat didn't matter.

"I don't know about that," Emily said with a smile. "You figured out Helen killed herself, pulled her out of the bardo, and you tangoed with your past." She shrugged her little shoulders. "There's no one to put in jail, but not bad."

The hard part was that I missed Sun all over again, and I wanted nothing more than to fold myself into that addiction and go be with her. The boy in the picture was Sun's son, but not mine. She got pregnant at seventeen and had given him up for adoption. That picture was taken shortly after the accident and miscarriage, right after I was out of the picture. She had tracked him down and met him. His adopted family was kind enough to allow the meeting, but the boy didn't know Sun was his biological mother. She was younger than I thought when I saw the picture, I think it was the stress of the time that made her look older.

All these years later, I now understand Sun's drive to have a child, and how it was even harder on her losing our baby. I even understood how that made her push me away —she didn't have it in her to try to have another child and

I would just remind her of that. I just wish she had told me all of this at the time. Things might have been different.

And the night I went to see Sun was the anniversary of our miscarriage, which is why I found her drinking too much and staring at the picture of the son she had given up. And Helen, who looked so much like Sun, had died that night, and Emily had known and taken me to her and started this whole crazy thing. How it all happened was way too much for me to figure out.

I still loved Sun, but I knew being the kind of ghost that had no other purpose than following around a loved one would send me to the bardo and quick. I have purpose here. I have Emily. I still have my own murder to solve.

"I'm really sorry about all of this," Emily said.

"No, honey, you did good. So good."

Her face lit up and she got a mischievous look in her eye and I saw the lollipop on her t-shirt edge towards a deeper red. "Well... I just happen to know about a murder that happened early this morning. A juicy one, sure to be a crime of passion! What do you say, Walter?" She reached out her hand, a knowing and wicked smile on her four-year-old face.

I laughed and nodded and took her hand.

A LONG HARD FALL

A WALTER ANCHOR
GHOST DETECTIVE STORY

ROBERT J. MCCARTER
AUTHOR OF *SHUFFLED OFF*

Chapter One

EMILY WAS IN A GOOD MOOD AND I DIDN'T WANT TO disappoint her, but I really wasn't up for solving another murder, especially one without a fresh ghost to tell me what had happened.

"Fascinating, right, Walter?" Emily asked, her four-year-old face sporting a big smile, her head nodding and shaking her tight blond curls. But that twinkle in her ancient green eyes spoke of a lust that no four-year-old ever experienced. Emily was four when she died, but she's been a ghost for eighty years and has seen a lot of life... well, afterlife.

I nodded and paced around the body. His manner of death was interesting—his left leg was twisted in a sickening way, the left half of his face caved in, and his torso was too damn flat. It looked like he had fallen from a great height and died on impact. But instead of being on the street, this body, dressed in a boring business suit, was on the flat white roof of one of Tucson's high-rises. There was blood here too, making it seem like this is where the death had happened, but how?

I stared up into the washed-out blue of the Tucson sky and wondered how big a drop it took to make a body look like this. It was midday, the sun right above and the air hot —not that any of us could feel it, ghosts or dead guy. And if you wanted to kill somebody this way, it would be much easier to just throw them off of a building, not drop them onto the roof of a forty-story high-rise.

"Yeah, fascinating," I said, pointing at the body, "but I don't know where we come in. Are you sure this is a fresh one?"

Emily nodded and pointed to the head where some blood was still oozing out.

"And why no ghost? A death like this, you'd think there'd be a ghost." I know if I had been dropped to my death, I'd have unresolved issues. Hell, I died from a propofol overdose—I didn't do it, it was made to look like a suicide—in my own dental office. Not a bad way to go, but enough to leave me a ghost and shove me into this whole ghost detective thing trying to solve my own murder. But we are out of clues on that, and Emily just loves doing this, and maybe the practice will help if we ever do get any leads on my death.

Emily pursed her lips and shrugged. "But fascinating, right?" The young-looking, ancient ghost has a nose for death and found us a lot of fascinating cases. But today, she was trying too hard. A recent case had veered into very personal territory and resulted in me confronting my past in the form of my ex-wife Sun. I got some closure, but it left me depressed. Emily has kept us busy with nonstop cases since then. Depression is not a good thing for a ghost. You know those cliched, gape-jawed, moaning ghosts? Get too depressed as a ghost and you just might end up like that.

"Hon," I said, squatting down in front of her. "No

ghost here. This really isn't our kind of case. We don't even know his name, and the forensics on this one are going to be important. What can a couple of ghosts do?"

Her smooth brow furrowed and she looked down, a pout on her young face. Emily was still very much a four-year-old at times.

I took her hand and was about to fly us away when the door to the roof opened with a clang. "Sweet-pea," a woman called in a singsong voice. We peered over and saw that she was in her mid-twenties with auburn hair and brown eyes dressed in a tan skirt, heels, and a white blouse. "I've been thinking about this all day, baby." She was quite attractive, I must say, with a beautiful face, generous curves, and a lilting southern accent.

The main part of the building has a high wall—no suicides from up here—but the center of the building went up another ten feet, probably for the elevator machinery, and had a higher roof that has a nice view of Tucson. It's here where we found the body. Not far from it were two lounge chairs, a big beach umbrella, and a cooler.

"I hate these stairs, my God, really I do," the woman said as she slowly climbed the metal stairs to this roof. "With all these holes, I mean, they were not designed for heels."

She had a smile on her red lips when she got to the upper roof and she hoisted a brown bag in her left hand. "For lunch, we've got fettuccine Alfredo, and for dessert…" she trailed off into a chuckle and I glanced at Emily and saw her blushing.

"Sweet-pea, why are you on the ground?" From her angle, the blood wasn't visible yet. She took two more steps, dropped the bag and screamed.

Emily leaned in and looked at the body and then at the woman. "He's got a wedding ring, she doesn't." She paused, a wicked smile on her face, now more the eighty-year-old ghost than the four-year-old kid. Except for her lisp. That is always there. It came out more like "thee doethn't" instead of "she doesn't."

She was watching my face like a hawk and knew she had me. "So, Walter… Fascinating?" she asked.

I had to smile. Not because of the gruesome death or the lascivious details, but because of Emily. Every ghost needed a purpose in their afterlife, and I was lucky that Emily's purpose was me. I nodded. "I guess we've got a case."

She clapped her hands and squealed with joy like only a four-year-old can.

Chapter Two

"FOLLOW HER," I SAID TO EMILY AS SHE LOOKED AT THE retreating woman with the auburn hair. "And call out the Irregulars when you get a chance. We're going to need help."

She nodded, but didn't move right away, her green eyes locking with mine. She stood there, her hands on her hips as she chewed on her lip. She wore her usual shorts and lollipop T-shirt, which were a bit of a mystery in their own right. A ghost, with a little practice, can wear anything they want. Why does Emily always have on those blue shorts and white T-shirt with a colorful lollipop on it? Did she die in that outfit? Was it her favorite? Me, I wear a trench coat and fedora, something Emily had encouraged—with four-year-old vigor—after our first case.

But her outfit was plain, but also advanced. The color of the lollipop was something of an indicator of her mood. It was a pale yellow, reflecting her worry about me.

She didn't talk, she just stared, and I finally noticed the pale-yellow lollipop and figured out what she was waiting for. "I'm fine, Emily," I said, nodding in the direction the woman had fled, the metal door to the roof clanging shut, her sobbing finally out of earshot.

Emily kept chewing on her lip.

"Seriously. A dead body is just my speed right now. And like you said, this is a fascinating case." I ended in the best smile I could, but knew it was a bit strained. "And the sobbing," I added. "I'm just not up for the sobbing."

She nodded, her eyes suddenly sad. Emily knew everything about me and how hard touching back in on Sun's life had been. It had dragged me back through the accident and the fallout from it that had led to our divorce. "I'm worried about you, Walter," she said with a sniff.

"And I'm worried about this case." I squatted down in front of her, modulated my ghostly form just right so I could touch her, and took her hand. "I'll make you a deal. Follow our grieving mistress until she gets to where she's going. Go get the Irregulars and then come back. We'll stick together for this one."

She smiled and nodded and with a "pop" was gone.

After she left, I flew to the edge of the roof and watched the cars crawl below me for a time, wondering at the living. They are going about their days down there, so caught up in the little things, pretending they might not be like me one day.

That didn't last long, though. I quickly got tired of my own moody ghost crap and went to examine the crime scene.

Chapter Three

"THANKS FOR COMING," I SAID TO THE GHOSTS ARRAYED in front of me on the roof of the Tucson high-rise. They go by "Anchor's Irregulars," a homage to Sherlock Holmes and his Baker Street Irregulars. The Anchor part being my last name.

They were a motley collection of ghosts. Fredrick, a natty gentleman who died in 1929 and was the first mortician at our graveyard. Blinky, an overweight geek dressed in a Led Zeppelin T-shirt with glasses, a beer belly, an obsessive love for the game Pac Man, and an insatiable desire for forensics. Anna-Maria, a hot-headed young Hispanic woman on her first case with us. She was dressed in a leather jacket and had recently died after a fall rock climbing up in Flagstaff. And Emily, of course.

Boredom is a serious issue for the dead, so we rarely have trouble finding help when we need it.

"We've got a body," I said, pointing down to the corpse, "a mistress, and a mystery. Blinky, I assume you're good sticking with the body."

He grinned and shook his head enthusiastically. "Absolutely, as long as we get another game of Pac Man in soon." I nodded although I hated it. He would turn the graveyard into a big game of Pac Man and a number of us ghosts would transform our ghostly selves into characters from the game. He was, of course, the red ghost Blinky. My role was Pac Man, and I felt like a fool being chased around the graveyard looking like a huge cheese wheel with a slice cut out of it for a mouth. But I needed him, so I did it.

"Fredrick and Anna-Maria, can you two stay with the mistress? Emily can take you. And one of you break off if another player enters the picture?"

They smiled and nodded.

"Emily and I will stay with the body for now and float around as needed. Let's meet back here at midnight."

Everyone went about their tasks and I was left on the roof with Blinky. I really didn't know much about him beyond his love of video games and geek culture.

"So whatta we got, Boss?" he said, walking over and looking at the body.

"Male, Caucasian, about forty years of age. Married and I am assuming he is an executive since he has access to the roof and set up this little oasis." I nodded to the lounge chairs, umbrella, and cooler. "He's got a cat, he dyes his hair black, presumably to hide the grey, and he appears to have been dropped on the roof from a high enough distance to do this to him."

Blinky nodded and got his face up close and examined minute details of the body, just as I had done. "Some minor scrapes on his fingers," he said, pointing at his right hand.

I nodded. "Maybe sign of a struggle." I let Blinky examine the body while I slowly went over the roof. Ghosts are good at this kind of thing. We see without eyes—something for you philosophy buffs to ponder—but we all see really well. Blinky's round, wire-frame glasses were part of his ghostly form, not real. We could look at things very closely and we weren't subject to the heat of the day or assaulted by the smells I'm sure were starting to emanate from the body.

I didn't find anything interesting on the roof and Blinky didn't see anything else on the body. "So how the hell did he get here?" he asked, looking up.

I shrugged. "Helicopter? Hot air balloon? Drones?"

He shook his head. "Too heavy for drones."

"That part doesn't really matter," I said.

"What? Why?"

"The murder was elaborate, difficult to pull off. The murderer wanted this death to be all over the papers, wanted to embarrass our stiff here."

Blinky rubbed at his stubbly face. "The wife?"

I shrugged my shoulders. "Until we know who these people are, there's not much more to do."

I heard sirens below, the police were here. I went about examining the scene one more time before they started tromping all over it.

Chapter Four

WHEN EMILY CAME BACK FROM TAKING FREDRICK AND Anna-Maria to the mistress, we left Blinky with the corpse and started roaming the office building. A strange murder on their roof was bound to be talked about.

As ghosts, we can't interview the living—the dead, that's another story—but we can listen and observe. And if we are tailing someone, forget about it. We will never leave you no matter where you go. You can't lose us, it's just not possible. If you're hiding something, we will find it.

One of these days, I keep thinking the Tucson PD will wise up and start partnering with us in a formal way. Emily and I, we've solved a bunch of murders now. When it's all over, I go to the SECI chamber—that typewriter for ghosts Tamara Watson and Jin Shi invented while PhD students at the University of Arizona—bang out these stories and Tamara gets them to a detective that's open to getting leads from ghosts. It's been a few years now that ghosts have been using the SECI chamber for everything from telling their wife where the latest will is, to little stories like mine, to full blown memoirs. The SECI chamber has changed the world. The dead know it; the living haven't quite figured it out yet.

As we walked the cubes, conference rooms, and swank offices on the top floor, we kept hearing the name Andrew and it didn't take long to figure out he was the boss up here. Andrew Verner of Verner and Associates. A law firm.

"Awwww," Emily said pointing at his portrait in the glitzy waiting area. "He's quite handsome without his face mushed in."

And I guess he was. Ice-blue eyes, short black hair, a cleft chin.

"The mistress is Elizabeth Sills," Fredrick said, walking up to us with Anna-Maria by his side. And yes, we can all fly, but we walk when we can. Acting more like the living helps keep us out of that gape-jawed ghostly hell called the bardo. "She's from Georgia, been in Tucson for four years and worked as Verner's executive assistant. Not much there yet," he added. "She's absolutely inconsolable."

I thanked Fredrick for the update and he went back to Elizabeth just as the police came streaming in. Two detectives and a bunch of uniforms. I guess they were taking this murder seriously.

"Oh my. *Bello*," Anna-Maria said, eyeing Detective Alvarez—Tamara Watson's contact in the Tucson PD—with obvious hunger. "Can I have him, Walter? Please!" Her brown eyes lit up and she had a big smile on her face.

"Knock yourself out, kid," I said, and Anna-Maria glued herself to the handsome detective.

Emily rolled her eyes. "She's still so young."

I nodded. Emily meant young as a ghost, still entranced by the physical which tends to fade with time. I looked back at the portrait of Andrew Verner and his tight smile and sighed. "He's a lawyer, and you know what that means…"

"Anyone could have done it!" Emily finished with her eyes bright.

Chapter Five

"IT'S NOT HER," I SAID THE MOMENT I LAID EYES ON Victoria Hall-Verner. She was older than her husband, over fifty, with an elegant, cultured air to her. She wore a dark skirt, a mauve blouse, and a strand of pearls around her neck. She came from money, that was clear.

We were in her expansive living room with white leather couches, a gas fireplace, and big windows looking out onto the cactus-covered Catalina Mountains. There was a baby grand piano there with family portraits on it. Nothing remarkable except it appeared the Verners didn't have any children.

Detective Alvarez had just given her the news flanked by Detective Jones. He is medium height and muscular with short cropped hair and a black mustache. She's petite with dark skin and her curly black hair barely contained in a ponytail.

Victoria's hands shook as they sat clasped in her lap and she sucked in a deep breath and held it for too long, but she stayed steady, asked questions, remained focused.

"He's so kind," Anna-Maria said, referring to Alvarez's quiet, calm delivery. Emily rolled her eyes.

The interview was short and I was sure she was innocent, but we waited until *the* question got asked.

Alvarez cleared his throat and swallowed hard. "Mrs. Verner, do you know Elizabeth Sills?"

She gave him a dismissing look. "His *personal* assistant. Yes, of course." Alvarez took a breath to ask another question, but she held up her hand. "I know about the affair, and while it didn't have my blessing, I did nothing to stop it. Andy needed to… wander from time to time. It never lasted long, he always came back to me." The look on her face was pure confidence, the kind of look no one has ever seen on my face unless it was for an acting role.

"You called it, Walter," Emily said.

"Do you know anyone that would have wanted to hurt your husband?" Jones asked as she adjusted her glasses. "Anyone that would have wanted to do so in such a"—she pursed her full lips, searching for an adjective delicate and yet forceful enough to describe what had happened—"in such an *unusual* way?"

Mrs. Hall-Verner took a deep breath and bit her lower lip, the first break in her tight demeanor. "I suspect it was me they wanted to hurt, not him. They must want the affair in the tabloids, which will be a terrible embarrassment to me. Most of the money is mine, you see." She ended in a sniff.

Emily elbowed me, her smile big and her eyes sparkling. This had gone from bizarre to lascivious, straight to money and power. It really didn't get much better than this.

Chapter Six

We gathered at midnight on the roof of the Tucson high-rise, the site of the murder. Ghosts love their graveyards, and our time is midnight. We are more awake, a bit more powerful. We feel it coming, we naturally tend to gather. Our graveyard has the "Midnight Circle" which is kind of like an old-fashioned campfire gathering where we share stories, put on plays—mostly Shakespeare—and socialize. The living are asleep, the dead are awake. It's a good time of day for us.

We met at the crime scene partially to avoid the distractions of the Midnight Circle and partially because it just seemed like the right place. The area was cordoned off with yellow "Crime Scene" tape and a few numbered yellow markers on the roof and the outline of where Andrew Verner's body had been found.

"Emily, if you don't mind," I said. She loved this "sum it all up" detective thing. She paced in front of the Irregulars, her hands clasped behind her back, a serious look on her young face.

"We're deep into the rich upper crust of Tucson

society here, my friends, maybe even treading into the US military. Our working theory is that the murder was aimed at destabilizing Victoria Hall-Verner, a major shareholder in Raytheon Missile Systems and the owner of the local ABC television station. We know it took money to pull this off." She pointed to the outline of Verner's body and then poked her thumb upwards. "The cops are going to have a hell of a time with this one, so it's up to us. We've got to go where they can't and figure this thing out."

I smiled as I watched her. Maybe as a younger ghost she hung out in theatres for most of the forties, watching *The Maltese Falcon*, *The Big Sleep*, the Thin Man movies, and the like. Whatever it was, she just loved this stuff, and it was a good distraction for me.

And she thankfully wasn't shy about her lisp. Not a bit. Taking on phrases like "Raytheon Missile Systems" even though it came out as "Raytheon Mithile Thythem." The "System" was pretty mangled and even as well as I know her made it even harder to not think of her as an adorable little girl.

"Blinky, what do we know about the death?" she asked.

Blinky nodded. "This is a little twisted, guys. Someone wanted Verner to suffer. He was dropped from a height of fifty to a hundred feet, but likely no more than that. He didn't die right away. They found traces of a sedative in his bloodstream and the coroner believes it wore off before he died a slow, painful death. The time of death is approximately 10:30 a.m., but the coroner believes that the fall occurred some hours before that between 5 a.m. and 9 a.m."

Emily looked thoughtful. "So that means the drop could have occurred under the cover of darkness, making the mechanics of this much simpler." She turned to Anna-

Maria. "When was the last time Mrs. Verner saw her husband?"

Anna-Maria didn't hesitate, rolling out the details as if she had an eidetic memory—one of the benefits of being a ghost. Without our bodies, our memories are very sharp. "He left the house at 5:30 a.m., the time he normally heads to the gym, but he never arrived. No one saw him in the office that morning either. After the gym, he was scheduled for a breakfast meeting and then an early round of golf with a client. He did not attend any of those." Emily nodded, turning towards Fredrick, but Anna-Maria added, "Can I get back to Sebastián... I mean, Detective Alvarez? You know... just in case something happens in the night?"

Emily looked at me and I nodded and Anna-Maria flew off into the night. "That girl..." she said, shaking her head.

"She'll learn," I said. I was fond of Anna-Maria's newly dead enthusiasm. She hadn't found out why she was a ghost and if there was any unfinished business for her to attend to. It made her rather refreshing compared to the likes of me.

"And Ms. Sills, the mistress?" Emily asked, turning to Fredrick.

"She is grieving, deeply, poor dear, and is certainly not the murderer, but..."

He took a step closer. Fredrick was fairly central in the graveyard not only because he had started it back in the thirties, but because he was a well-seasoned, dependable ghost and was very perceptive when it came to human behavior.

And this is another area where ghosts have an edge over the living. Without all the dense flesh, we have a well-developed intuition, and in some instances, something a bit more. I don't want to say we're psychic, let's just say that as spirits without bodies we are more sensitive to what is going on around us. Banquo, a ghost back at the graveyard that helps new ghosts acclimate, calls this "awareness."

Fredrick took a deep breath, not that ghosts breathe, but flesh equivalents still hold power for us. He was gathering his thoughts. "I believe we can leave young Elizabeth Sills to her grief, but I think we need to take a closer look at her former lover, a man named William Costa. Elizabeth called him earlier and..." he shook his head. "He's married too. She called him 'Sweet-Pea.' Poor girl seems to have a thing for married men. They hadn't talked in a while and she still feels something for him. Well, I don't see a clear motive, but there was something about his tone. He didn't seem that surprised."

Chapter Seven

"HE DID IT," EMILY SAID, POINTING AT WILLIAM COSTA as he teed off at the Tucson Country Club, a bright green golf course backed by the cactus-covered Santa Catalina Mountains. "He hated Verner for stealing his mistress, was desperate to get her back." This was something of a game Emily and I played as we tried to hone our instincts, our awareness as ghost detectives. "That's why the elaborate setup and bizarre conditions of the murder."

He was tall and thin, handsome with dark hair and too-white teeth, and at least ten years older than Elizabeth Sills. He wore brand-name apparel and swung expensive clubs, and he was a skilled golfer.

It was just Emily and me. Fredrick was helping to acclimate a new ghost back at the graveyard—always a difficult transition. Anna-Maria was still haunting Detective Alvarez—and let's be honest, that's what it was at this point, but at least it was a kind haunting, but something we would have to keep an eye on. Blinky was still with the medical examiner as the formal autopsy was continuing today.

I nodded. I felt it too. This was our guy, but I wasn't buying the jealousy motivation. There was something else going on here.

And so began our 24/7 tail of William Costa. No matter what he did and where he went, we were with him. Listening to his phone conversations, reading his texts, watching what he ate, watching him while he slept, we were even with him in the bathroom or when he made love to his wife or one of his mistresses. Those last two duties were strictly my territory. Unpleasant, yes, but I would not ask a woman to watch a man go to the toilet, and with Emily having died at four, watching human biological reproductive urges in action was out of the question. I've been dead long enough, and am sufficiently distanced from my biology, that I don't find the latter either titillating or even interesting.

William Costa owned a series of car dealerships, and while he was wealthy, it was not nearly on the scale of the Verners. Although, he did have enough to rent a helicopter with ease.

The first day was golf, lunch with his mistress, including a recreational trip to the bathroom during which Emily excused herself and checked in with the other Irregulars, a few hours at the office, and then dinner with his wife.

The next day he worked most of the day and had dinner with a different mistress. The day after that he flew to Las Vegas for a business meeting, lost about $10,000 playing craps, and flew home.

I was so sick of this guy. He was shallow, narcissistic, and totally annoying. I was beginning to wonder if we had the right guy, and really wondering about Elizabeth's taste in men. Anna-Maria had kept us in the loop on the official investigation, and they were looking into business rivals and associates of Victoria Hall-Verner, but it was progressing slowly. The tabloids, in the meantime, had caught wind of the story and it had gone national with the kind of headlines you would expect. "Mystery Death on top of Tucson Skyscraper," "It's Raining Men," a gem from one of the tabloids, and "Gruesome Death in one of Tucson's Richest Families."

"I don't know, kid," I said to Emily as we followed William down the hallway of a Toyota dealership. He had been meeting with his manager and had excused himself to go to the bathroom.

But he didn't stop at the bathroom. He strolled back to the garage and did what he called one of his pop inspections. We had seen this a few times before; it's his way of keeping all his employees on their toes.

But this one didn't look right. He went up to a mechanic, a young man with a brown ponytail and tuft of beard under his lip, walked under the lift holding up a Tundra pickup, and started asking questions about the oil change he was doing. His words were stilted and forced. Before he had only done a quick walkthrough, not actually having a conversation with any other employees.

"You were saying..." Emily said with a grin. The lollipop on her shirt was back to its usual cherry red. It had turned red and stayed this way since the case got good. The girl does love murder.

We watched closely and we caught the exchange. When Costa went to leave, he pressed a small key into the young man's hand and headed out of the garage.

"Looks like we gotta split up, Emily. Who do you want?"

She nodded to the young man. "I can't stand Costa, sorry, Walter, but he's all yours."

I shook my head and followed William Costa to the

toilet and watched him text his two mistresses while he took a dump, once again glad ghosts can't smell.

Chapter Eight

A FEW HOURS LATER, EMILY POPPED IN—SOMETHING I still couldn't do reliably. "Anything going on here?" she asked. We were in a swank restaurant with William and mistress number two.

I shook my head.

"Good," she said, grabbing my hand, and with a "pop" we were at the airport. It used to be disorienting, the whole jump from one spot to another, but I'm used to it now. Emily is very good at it, it doesn't seem to be difficult at all for her. I did it recently, but it was almost by accident and revolved around my desperate need to see my ex-wife Sun.

"There," she said, pointing at a helicopter. "Scene of the crime."

There was a middle-aged, blond-haired man who was in the pilot's seat with his headset on and looked like he was doing a preflight check. The helicopter had a big nine on it and the ABC logo.

"This is Victoria Hall-Verner's station," I said.

"Yup. I followed the money, boss. Our boy from the garage took that key to the greyhound bus station and

179

opened a locker. There was an envelope and a small bag in there. He pocketed the envelope and carried the bag to El Presidio Park, stuffed it in a trash can, and fifteen minutes later this bozo came and picked it up. Bing, bam, boom. We got 'em!"

She raised her hand for a high five and I slapped her hand and nodded, but we didn't have all the pieces yet. We had the players, and knew in broad strokes what had happened, but it wasn't enough; we didn't know why. "Any physical evidence in the chopper?" I asked. The rotors were starting to spin, the helicopter probably headed up for a rush hour traffic report.

Emily shook her head, her Shirley Temple curls bouncing in the most adorable way. "Can't you go write it up, get Tamara to reach out to Alvarez?"

I bit my lip and thought about it. There wasn't any real motive. William Costa hadn't had contact with Elizabeth Sills for months. Did he even know about her affair with Andrew Verner? And this helicopter put the focus on Victoria Hall-Verner who did know about her husband's affair, and jealousy there was a real possibility, although she certainly didn't present that way. The cops might be able to get a confession out of the helicopter pilot, but they might not. My guess is that the helicopter was clean and there wouldn't be any physical evidence.

"Not quite," I told her, sad to see the smile melt from her face. "Stick with him a while longer and meet us at the murder site at midnight. I've got an idea."

Chapter Nine

ON THE ROOF, THE NIGHTTIME LIGHTS OF TUCSON arrayed before us, I let Emily bring the Irregulars up to speed while I stared at the lights. They were so orderly, so calm, they hid the seething stew of human frailty and weakness below. We were this team of ghosts, not a one with any formal training, whiling away their afterlives solving murders. I had been a dentist and before that an actor. Fredrick, who I was glad to see back, was a mortician. Anna-Maria had been a student up north at NAU. And Blinky, I didn't even know what he did. But yet here we were working as a team orchestrated by the ancient Emily who looked like a four-year-old, innocent-as-can-be little girl.

"So we know William Costa is behind the murder and the easy bet is he did it because Verner's mistress, Elizabeth Sills, is his former mistress," I said. "But I don't buy it. The elaborate murder is a misdirect towards Victoria Hall-Verner, even down to the helicopter used. We are missing a piece of this and I want to try something a little different, so new assignments." Anna-Maria looked sad, but the others nodded.

"Don't worry, Anna-Maria, you get to stick with Alvarez, but I need you to come up with three facts about him that aren't common knowledge, and this is important, aren't embarrassing. Emily will be around in an hour to get them from you."

She nodded and flew off.

"Fredrick, can you go find Elizabeth Sills and stick with her? I've got a hunch there is something else going on there, maybe something at the office. She's..." I shrugged my shoulders not having the words, but something wasn't right there. He nodded and popped away.

"And Blinky, I need you in the law office. Go there tonight, read every piece of paper you can see, listen to every conversation in the morning." He opened his mouth up to speak, but I held my hand up. This wasn't his area, he only wanted to hang with cops or coroners. "I know this means more Pac Man time for me. Trust me, it's important."

He nodded and sunk down into the building—the Verner and Associates offices were below us.

That left Emily and me alone on the roof and I stared back out at the lights. This wasn't a bad afterlife, we were doing some good, but I was starting to understand why all the movie detectives seemed to be rather world weary.

"Hey, Boss?" Emily asked.

"What?"

"Why'd you tell Anna-Maria to not give us any embarrassing information on Alvarez?"

I shook my head and smiled. "Because I don't want to know if he has a mole on his right butt cheek."

Emily's jaw dropped and I laughed. "You don't think... she wouldn't..."

"Honey, she was twenty when she died, and that was only a few weeks ago. Of course she's seen him in the shower."

She shook her head. "She's a pistol, that one." She watched the lights with me for a while and then asked, "What about us?"

"It's time to wake Tamara Watson up."

Chapter Ten

THERE ARE THREE SECI CHAMBERS IN THE AFTERLIFE Communications building that Tamara and her partner Jin started after they got their PhDs. They are crowded now, a line of ghosts a week long all waiting to try their hand at the ghost keyboard to get their messages out. That works for a normal case; it wouldn't work here. We needed real-time communication to pull this off.

Tamara had told me of the next generation SECI chamber they were building and told me to use it in an emergency. This was an emergency. The SECI chamber is a bit larger than a phone booth and is made out of this high-tech material that shields all electromagnetic radiation. We ghosts, you guessed it, emanate electromagnetic energy at an extremely high frequency. The old SECI chamber required ghosts to do some bizarre contortions of their forms—not nearly as bizarre as becoming Pac Man—and not all ghosts can do it. The 2.0 SECI chamber has a huge keyboard that you place your fingers through the keys and it detects the EM radiation and your words appear on the monitor above. This one is, literally, a keyboard for ghosts.

When we got there, I wrote a short message, "911." This would wake up Tamara, who could monitor all the SECI chambers from her house, and we could, essentially, text each other.

"We need Detective Alvarez now," I said to Emily. "We need the helicopter pilot and the mechanic arrested and interrogated. We need the forensics team going over the helicopter. We need him to start looking at William Costa's financial records for the pilot payoff."

Emily looked puzzled. In the past, we had solved the case and then told the police.

"Look, Costa was smart," I continued. "He was very careful. The pilot probably doesn't know who hired him to dump Verner's body on that building. We need the smoking gun, kid."

Emily nodded. "Now go get me those three facts from Anna-Maria. I need Alvarez to really believe in ghosts." She walked out of the chamber; popping was not possible inside.

Text appeared on the monitor. "Walter is that you? What's going on."

"Sorry to wake you, Tamara," I typed back. "We need you to help us catch a murderer."

"What can I do?"

"Wake Detective Alvarez up. First we are going to prove that ghosts are real and then we are going to work directly with him to catch a murderer."

There was a pause of fifteen minutes and I was getting worried. Was this too much for her? I knew that not everyone was happy about ghosts communicating from beyond the pale and that Tamara was getting hate mail and worse.

"Sorry for the delay," she typed back. "I had to fiddle with my gear. I've routed your messages to my phone and can reply too. Heading over to Alvarez's house right now. Let's do this!"

Chapter Eleven

"DO YOU KNOW THIS MAN?" DETECTIVE ALVAREZ ASKED
Elizabeth Sills in the cramped interrogation room. The
picture was a mugshot of a young man with a brown ponytail and a tuft of facial hair under his lip, the mechanic that
William Costa had passed the key to.

She dabbed at her eyes, swollen and red from crying,
and shook her head. Even in this state she was beautiful. It
kind of helped make all of this make sense. She used her
beauty to get what she wanted.

We had worked all night and most of the day. I typed
to Tamara, she relayed to Detectives Alvarez and Jones,
and she texted me back. Emily popped to all the Irregulars,
giving them assignments and coordinating the activities
and then updating me, and I would pass on the
information.

We had been a part of the arrest of Vince Smith, the
helicopter pilot, and Ian Stoltz, the garage mechanic. Both
were sitting in nearby interrogation rooms. We had
searched their residences—a ghost doesn't need a search
warrant—helped the police find them. We applied our

intuitive senses, our ghostly awareness, to help guide the questioning. It had been magnificent.

All of us were here watching, except for Blinky who was still at the Verner and Associates offices.

"That's odd," Detective Jones said, leaning back in her metal chair. "We pulled GPS data from his phone. He's been at your condo four times in the last month, but only for a few minutes each time." She leaned forward. "Long enough to hand something off. Like a note, maybe?"

Her smooth brow wrinkled and she looked indignant, her southern lilt becoming more clipped. "I do not know what you are implying here. I do not know that man."

Alvarez smiled. "Oh, but he knows you." He slid forward a picture of the two of them mugging for a selfie, and Elizabeth's cheeks flushed red. "You see, I think you and Mr. Costa are smart. No cell phones. No digital trail. Just notes passed and then destroyed like two kids in class." He showed her a plastic bag with the remnants of a burnt note that had a few letters still visible: "Verne," "rooft," and "$100,." Fredrick had witnessed Elizabeth cleaning out her condo and noticed the burned notes. The police hadn't even needed a warrant to get at her trash, but it did provide what they needed for the warrant they used to search her condo.

Her nostrils flared and she crossed her arms over her chest and suddenly she didn't look like she was grieving anymore; she looked furious. I was impressed. This girl was a fine actress, she could have gone far in Hollywood with those looks and that talent. Well... before she conspired to commit murder, that is.

"She fooled me," Fredrick said, shaking his head.

"With a dreamboat like that," Emily said, "how could you help yourself?"

"Verner couldn't," I added. "Or Costa."

"Here's what bugs me," Alvarez said. "Costa is not a nice guy. He's married. He has two, count them two, mistresses. Seems to be that Verner was an upgrade for you. Why did you guys kill him?"

Elizabeth Sills sat there fuming, her red lips clamped tight. I had no idea why they had done it. This was the one piece of the puzzle we were lacking.

"We've got Vince Smith, the helicopter pilot," Alvarez said. "Found Verner's hairs in the helicopter and some threads from the seats on Verner. Smith is talking, he made a deal, maybe you should too."

That last part was a lie. Smith didn't know who hired him, he picked up Verner unconscious in the trunk of a car in a parking garage. Everything was anonymous handoffs. The car had been stolen and was a dead end.

"I think I'll be executing my constitutional right to representation at this time," Elizabeth said.

Chapter Twelve

"IT'S QUITE SIMPLE, REALLY," BLINKY SAID, A PROUD look on his round face. We were in Andrew Verner's swank office while the detectives pulled the contents out of his wall safe.

"Our Ms. Sills was looking to upgrade from mistress to wife, but Verner would not leave his wife, and the more she pressured him, the more distant he became and the more time he'd spend with his wife. Although, he couldn't quite let go of the lovely Elizabeth Sills."

I gave him a questioning look and he gestured around the office. "You should hear the gossip around this place." There was a crowd outside the window-lined wall staring at the proceedings.

I nodded for him to continue.

"The 'marry me thing' was going on about three months ago. A few weeks ago, she started having a bit of an upset stomach every morning," Blinky said, his eyebrows wagging above his glasses.

"Preggers!" Emily shouted and then put her hand to

her mouth and looked around embarrassed as if the people in the office could hear her.

"I've seen her stomach problems, too," Fredrick offered. "I just thought it was from the trauma."

"Verner set up a trust for his child," Blinky continued, "a multimillion-dollar trust with Ms. Sills in control of it. She was set."

I shrugged. "Sounds like she got most of what she wanted. Why pull Costa in, why kill Verner?"

Blinky shrugged. "No clue, just know that this is the next layer of the onion and they needed to know about it." He pointed at the detectives.

"This is interesting," Detective Jones said, opening a manila folder. "Ms. Sills didn't mention this. Verner set up a trust in her name, for... for their child."

Alvarez grabbed the folder, his eyes snapping back and forth as he read it. "I think we need to have another conversation with Ms. Sills and Mrs. Hall-Verner."

Chapter Thirteen

A CAREER MISTRESS UPGRADING TO RICHER AND RICHER men. When she thinks she's gone as high as she can, she tries to become the wife. When that doesn't work she gets pregnant and secures a fat trust fund. And then she... kills the father? Why? Because she's nuts and still loves the last man down the totem pole and he helps her kill the father?

We were missing something.

I was pacing the roof in front of my team on the high-rise at midnight. The interviews with Elizabeth Sills and Victoria Hall-Verner hadn't yielded anything useful. Sills had admitted to the trust and the pregnancy, but she had been correct when she had said, "That ain't no crime."

Mrs. Hall-Verner had been shocked to hear of the pregnancy and the trust, but it didn't change anything. She had provided evidence—text messages, restaurant dates, gifts—that confirmed that Verner was spending more time with her and winding down his affair. She claimed to not care about the child.

"We got Costa, they arrested him today," Emily said.

"We got the pilot, too. This is good, Walter, this is really good."

I shook my head; it wasn't enough. I wanted to see our southern belle, Elizabeth Sills, in jail too. We had the burned notes from Costa, but that wasn't enough.

"Perhaps if we took a night off," Fredrick suggested, ever with the level head.

I ignored them all and kept pacing. Two love triangles with Sills a part of both, four people, and one baby.

One baby!

It hit me in a flash. "I got it!" I said. "Time to wake everyone up again."

Chapter Fourteen

THE INTERROGATION ROOM WAS TOO SMALL FOR THE crowd, so this was happening in the plain precinct conference room. A scarred wooden table, creaky chairs, a whiteboard and a coffee machine. There were the two detectives, William Costa, Elizabeth Sills, and Victoria Hall-Verner, as well as three different lawyers. Emily and I had gone back to the SECI chamber, woken Tamara up, typed up what I had figured out, and Tamara had facilitated a conversation between me and Detective Alvarez. It was time to watch the detectives execute our plan.

"Mr. Costa, you are going to jail," Alvarez said, starting the ball rolling. "We can link you directly to the murder via Ian Stoltz. He made himself a nice deal and we know all the little errands he ran for you." Costa looked great in his grey prison jumpsuit, a sour look on his face.

"Including," Detective Jones began, licking her lips, "his deliveries from Mrs. Hall-Verner to you."

Victoria's face was hard and she was dressed elegantly in a silk blouse and cashmere sweater even at this early 6:00 a.m. hour.

"You see, you all had the same problem," Alvarez said, sliding out the portrait of Andrew Verner. "Mr. Costa, you wanted her back," he said pointing at Sills.

Jones looked at Sills. "And your baby-daddy was about to dissolve the trust, so you had a problem." She slid a manila envelope halfway across the table. Elizabeth Sill's eyes got wide. This was a wild guess we had, but Verner's lawyer had confirmed it.

"And you," Alvarez said, looking at Mrs. Hall-Verner, "got rid of your embarrassing little problem—a bastard heir to the Hall fortune."

I smiled. That was the piece that had come to me up on the roof. Andrew and Victoria didn't have any children, and while she could tolerate an affair, she couldn't tolerate an heir by another woman.

Victoria's face stayed stony as she stared at Alvarez.

"The pilot, Vince Smith," Alvarez said, "is cooperating. He's got a nice deal, too." He looked at Victoria, and here is where he had to bluff. Smith didn't know anything, but the other two didn't know that. "You see, you made a mistake. You used Smith before, he knows all about—"

"There is no financial trail leading to me," Costa said, rising from his seat, his handcuffed wrists in front of him. His lawyer gave him the don't-say-anything-else look, but he continued, his hand stabbing out at Victoria. "It was her money, her plan. I have proof!"

"He's right," Elizabeth said, her face red. "She promised me ten million if I helped, if we put William on the birth certificate. Played nice with Andrew for a while longer. Arranged our rooftop reunion. You didn't think anyone could unravel a murder this bizarre."

And then they were all shouting at each other, the three conspirators laying it all out in front of two detectives despite their lawyers' attempts to keep them quiet.

I smiled. We got them, we got them all.

Chapter Fifteen

IT WAS A VERY SPECIAL MIDNIGHT CIRCLE AND I watched proudly as the Irregulars took center stage among the gravestones under a gibbous moon surrounded by ghosts and told the lascivious, decidedly human details of our case.

Emily wasn't here, but I don't worry about her. She knows her way around the afterlife.

They asked me to join them, but I demurred. I used to be an actor, was even in an episode of *Buffy the Vampire Slayer*, but I wanted this to be their moment.

Fredrick narrated and Blinky and Anna-Maria played the parts of the characters in this little tragic play. Anna-Maria even going so far as flying up into the night sky and slamming her ghostly body into the ground to illustrate how the victim died.

The ghosts went wild. A gruesome murder and tragic human failings are like candy to us who have lost our lives and are earthbound spirits. It's one of the reasons Shakespeare goes over so well.

Banquo was there. He's a bald, big-bellied guy who is

more or less the leader around here. He created the Midnight Circle, directs all the plays, and he's helped out most of the ghosts that have died since he came here. I, though, am not a big fan. He and his chosen few are kind of like the varsity team, and my Irregulars and I are definitely not the cool kids. That, and Emily. She has a massive crush on him and I know if he ever asked her to help him, she would leave me in a second.

Banquo caught my eye at the end of the performance as the ghosts hooted, hollered, and whistled—we aren't much for clapping given our incorporeal nature. He smiled and nodded as if to say good job. I probably would have gone over to receive his praise, but then the Irregulars were there and I was congratulating them and celebrating our victory.

It was a new step for us working directly with Detectives Alvarez and Jones, the living and the dead doing what neither could have done alone.

After the circle dissipated, I asked Anna-Maria to walk with me. "You did good on your first outing with us," I said.

Her brown eyes were bright. "Thanks for giving me a chance, Boss."

I nodded. "And I'd like to bring you on permanently as one of Anchor's Irregulars, but…"

Her face fell and her eyes widened.

"You've got to stop haunting Detective Alvarez."

"I… He… You know, I just…"

I laughed and stopped walking. "Look, I get it. He's a handsome guy, you're a young woman, but it's not good for you. The flesh is gone. It's not coming back. The sooner you understand that the better this will be."

She bit her lip and nodded.

I was opening my mouth to speak again when there

was a sharp "pop" and Emily was there, panting as if she had just run a long ways, her cheeks red.

"Walter. You're... You're not going to believe what I found. Holy mackerel, this one, it's... it's..."

"A fascinating murder?" I offered.

Her eyes widened and her lisp was thick. "It's a double murder and... well... you just have to see it. Right now, before the cops get there." She reached her hand out to me, so eager for the next case, and how could I resist?

I looked at Anna-Maria. "Do we have a deal?"

She hesitated, for just a moment, and then smiled and nodded. "Yes, no more haunting Detective Alvarez."

"Let's go," I said, taking both of their hands, and with a "pop" we were off to our next case.

DEATH OF A
DENTIST

A WALTER ANCHOR
GHOST DETECTIVE STORY

ROBERT J. MCCARTER
AUTHOR OF *SHUFFLED OFF*

Prologue

I LOVE EMILY. SHE'S MY BEST FRIEND IN THIS STRANGE earth-bound afterlife. I love her in ways that are obvious and in ways that are not.

I love how she seems to be the most optimistic ghost that I know, channeling the full happiness that you would expect from the four-year-old she looks like. How it can bubble up and just take her over, her cheeks flushing red and her blond Shirly Temple curls bouncing around her round face, the ever-present lollipop on her T-shirt a shining red, communicating her mood to any who cares to look.

And I love the grouchy, world-weary and wise eighty-year-old ghost that Emily is. She was four when she died of dysentery in 1927, and still looks it, but has been dead longer than any of the other ghosts in our Tucson grave-yard. At times her voice will get gravelly, and she will say things that belie her appearance that are either wise or just plain grumpy and sound wise... or sometimes scandalous, saying words a four-year-old shouldn't even know.

I love Emily for saving my afterlife and teaching me

how to be a ghost. For pulling me along like that innocent four-year-old and for shoving me into the things I didn't want to face like that wise old ghost.

But it doesn't mean that I've always liked it. I often haven't. Especially that day.

I was pacing under the washed-out winter Tucson sky, when she came and found me on the roof of the casino. It was a day when my grumpy defenses were operating at full and the plan her old/young self came up with was one I hated.

I didn't want to solve a murder. I didn't want to be a ghost detective. I didn't want to talk to anyone. I wanted to be alone and miserable.

I was pacing the casino roof, on top of the large metal air ducts, mumbling to myself. "You don't need this, Walter. You don't need this."

Below was the home of one of my addictions when I was living. Gambling. For me it was craps and Texas Hold-em. That afternoon, I had flown aimlessly over the sprawl of Tucson and "somehow" ended up there. On that roof. Pacing. Arguing with what was left of that addiction. The thrill of winning. The ache of losing. The escape into something besides my troubles, besides thinking about my past, about how I was murdered and I couldn't crack the case.

When I was alive, I used to do the exact same thing in the parking lot, on the hot asphalt among the cars. My problems were, admittedly, different now, but my actions were the same. Pacing. Mumbling. Trying to resist the lure of senseless escape.

Emily and I had had some tough cases, one recently that dragged me through my past life in Hollywood where I was an actor and married to a beautiful actress. It dragged me through the guilt I felt and forced me to reconcile with my ex-wife, as much as a ghost can. A ghost, that is, with this ghostly typewriter so I could actually communicate with her directly.

I had been fairly content (okay, fairly grumpy) in this strange afterlife trying to find clues to my own murder and stumbling into solving other murders. It was something to do, and it was clearly worth doing. Justice and all of that. But I hadn't wanted to go delving into my past, and when Emily found a bride dead alone in a bridal suite who happened to look very much like my ex-wife, it had let loose that past and sent me examining it, which I hated.

The past should be left in the past.

We had solved some other murders, but because of the case of the Ghost Bride, my past just wouldn't stay where it belonged.

And I think that's what brought me to the casino and the remnants of that old addiction. Something else to lose myself in, and this time I couldn't lose any actual money or put my dental practice at risk.

Yeah. I was a practicing dentist when I died. And yes, before that I had been an actor. And now I'm a ghost and a detective.

Don't ask me. My life and afterlife have taken some strange turns, and it hasn't been boring. But that day, pacing at the casino, I wanted boring. I wanted escape. I wanted anything but what happened.

With a "pop," Emily stood in front of me, her green eyes wide, the lollipop on her T-shirt a bright yellow.

I guess I should explain that shirt. The color of the lollipop was something of a mood ring for the girl, revealing her general mood. Ghosts don't have clothing, per se, but we can, with practice and effort, control our ghostly forms and what we appear to be wearing. In this case, that bright yellow lollipop meant Emily was curious.

So, baby-faced Emily, wide eyed and apparently curious, popped into my pacing path on the roof of that casino.

"Walter," she said, her voice airy, coming out as if she had been running. "Come quick. There's a case you've got to see."

Emily also has a lisp. Completely adorable and combined with her appearance made it hard to remember what an old ghost she was. So that last sentence was way more adorable in Emily-speak: "There'th a cathe you've got to thee."

But adorable wasn't enough for me. I said, "No," rather sharply, turned and paced the other direction.

"Walter! This is important," she said, putting the full force of four-year-old earnestness into the delivery.

Around us was the sprawl of Tucson. Low buildings, only a couple of stories tall at the most, roads and traffic and the endless noise of it. The sky was washed out, dingy with the dust the winds kicked up. To the north were the low craggy hills of Tucson Mountain Park. I might have been fooling myself, but I thought I could hear the comforting dinging of slot machines below us.

"No," I said again, continuing to pace.

I heard another "pop" and Emily was in front of me, her lollipop was edging away from yellow and towards an angry red, her little arms folded over her chest.

"Walter Anthony Anchor!" she yelled, stomping her foot on the duct. She was a ghost, so it didn't make any noise. This ghost happened to be my best friend, so her plea reached me.

I sighed—it was a thing full of resignation and defeat which makes one wonder why Emily kept hanging out with me. I would think that she could do better.

And, no, ghosts don't breathe, although we have a lot of flesh-and-blood habits left over with analogous effect.

"What is the case?" I asked.

Emily's green eyes lit up and she rushed up to me and took my arm. "Let me show you."

EMILY ALWAYS TANTALIZED ME WITH THE DETAILS OF A case. Usually something lurid. Like, "A true crime of passion, you've got to see this," or "The bum is smushed like a bug," or "This is a gruesome one, bub."

But not this time. She took my slightest agreement, grabbed my arm, and popped me to the scene of the crime.

"Popping" is what we call it when a ghost goes from one place to another, instantaneously. It has that name because of the sound it makes when the ghost leaves or appears. Not all ghosts can pop. Emily is very good at it. I've only managed it a couple of times in extreme situations. This means that it can be very difficult for me to get away from Emily if she's determined. Popping, for a ghost like Emily, extends to people as well as places.

The room we popped to was one I instantly recognized. How could I not? It was one of the treatment rooms of my former dental practice. It had been painted, obliterating the gorgeous mural I had on one wall. A picture of Marilyn Monroe from *The Seven Year Itch*, the one where she's in heels and a white dress standing on a grate in New York City, wind blowing the skirt up around her, a dazzling smile on her face. An iconic image that went with the name of my practice, "Hollywood Dental," and showed off Ms. Monroe's excellent teeth.

Before going to dental school, I made a go of being an

actor. Sarah Michele Gellar once vanquished me on *Buffy the Vampire Slayer*, and as a cowboy, I once died in the arms of Jane Seymour's *Dr. Quinn, Medicine Woman*. Those were my acting claims to fame, but I mostly worked as a grip in Hollywood and paid for dental school that way.

And I fell in love with an actress whose name you would recognize, married her, got divorced, and ran away from Hollywood back to my hometown, Tucson, Arizona. That "Hollywood Dental" on the door was my marketing ploy and an homage to the life I wished I had.

Yeah, I don't always make things easy on myself.

"Emily…" I began, confused.

This was the room where I died. The room where I "woke up" dead with a needle in my arm. This is the room where the world thought I died of a self-administered propofol overdose.

She had a guilty look on her round face and her lollipop had gone a dull yellow with swirls of red. She was worried and guilty, maybe a little bit angry. I had never seen the lollipop look like this, meaning that these were complicated emotions.

"What are we doing here?" I asked. I didn't have a mood-ring style tell on my ghostly form, but if I did it would also be a swirl of colors. Red for angry. Yellow for confused. Black for the dark mood that was creeping up the back of my neck.

As it was, I had on a trench coat and a fedora looking like a 1940's detective—Emily's idea—which would have fit in nicely with the picture of Monroe from 1954.

Her bottom lip quivered and she wouldn't meet my gaze.

"Emily!" I shouted and immediately regretted it as she jumped back like a scared animal. I squatted down to get to her level. "Honey. My case is cold. What are we doing here?"

She pursed her lips and her jaw set. "We need to solve your case," she said slowly. "So we are going to start over."

Emily had been directive with me. Sometimes very. Especially when I was a new ghost and didn't know anything. But she had never been this way about my own death.

I searched for the words. Something that would say that this was not only useless, this would probably be very bad for me. Seeing Sun, my ex-wife, had been as horrible as it was wonderful. It reminded me of what I had lost and now that I was dead, I could never have what I had wanted the most.

Hollywood Dental had kind of been my consolation prize. My way to make it in this world that wasn't acting and wasn't with Sun. I had trouble with gambling. And, yes, I had trouble with propofol making the whole "he overdosed" thing easy to believe. But I had gotten past my addictions. I had started to do better. My last day alive was an ordinary day at the office.

"No," I said, crossing my arms and mirroring her stance.

"Yes, we are," she said, her nose scrunching up comically in her seriousness.

"No, we are not," I said.

Let me tell you this, from long experience with Emily. Don't try to out four-year-old a four-year-old. Even one that's been dead for over eighty years. You can't. It won't work.

But I tried. The standoff continued for several minutes. I flew up to the roof and she popped me back to the room. I walked through the wall to the outside of the bland office building and she popped me back to the room. I yelled.

She yelled. It was childish and silly and she was not giving up.

"Why, Emily?" I finally asked, staring at the stupid mauve wall that used to have a classic Hollywood image on it. I was avoiding looking at the dental chair, where I died, and was fixated on how my partner had thrown away what was special about Hollywood Dental when he changed the name and painted the walls. "Why now? What good will it do?"

Emily let out a long sigh. "I miss you, Walter," she said quietly, her arms relaxing as she stared at her bare feet. "I miss when cases were fun, when you listened to me, when we were…"

She looked up and there were tears running down her cheek.

It was the pure unadulterated grief of a four-year-old. Big crocodile tears, quivery lip, runny nose, rosy cheeks.

"When we were what, Emily?" I asked. I had to know. That look dragged the words out of me. I was so stupid.

"When we were partners," she said with a sniff.

AND THERE IT IS. THE POWER OF EMILY TO LAY ME OUT emotionally. It's like this was a boxing match and that was the moment where the bell rings, the referee raises Emily's gloved hand into the air and shouts, "We have a winner by a knockout!"

Sun was the partner I had wanted. And she had been. We had been married. We were both struggling actors together. She got pregnant. And one rainy day on the LA freeways, an accident caused a miscarriage, and that was something our marriage could not recover from.

Emily wasn't my partner like that, not in a romantic

sense—and, yes, there are those kinds of relationships among ghosts, although it's not quite what you think—but we were partners. We spent significant time together. We solved murders. We brought people to justice. We shared a path and a purpose.

It wasn't the partnership I had wanted (that would be my beautiful Sun), but it was the partnership I needed. And despite my often foul mood, it was one I cherished.

My mouth moved as I struggled to speak and I let my gaze wander around the room. A counter with a sink and faux wood cabinets with a monitor and keyboard sitting on it. The blue dental chair with the long arm of the light hanging from the ceiling. A chair and a stool.

It was a small room, but one so familiar, the painting over of the mural the only change from when it had been mine.

I let myself look at the room, all of the room, and I tried not to bolt.

I hadn't been back here. I had told Emily about it, but I hadn't been in the room, and that brought with it a rush of memories. I felt my ghostly form changing and looked down and saw that I was wearing blue scrubs which I had spent so many years in.

This is my default ghostly form, the one I first had before taking on the 1940's detective look for Emily. It was how I looked in this office every day for five years. I felt vulnerable looking this way again, as if that trench coat and fedora had become armor for me, a shield against my past, and now that it was gone, I couldn't keep the past at bay anymore.

I looked at Emily's green eyes and there was compassion there but also a hardness. A dedication to this path she had dragged me on to.

"What do you want?" I asked.

She smiled, it was tentative and shy. Her brow furrowed and she licked her lips.

"There's something here," she said slowly. "Something we missed. I know it. I want you to walk me through your day, your last day here. Everything. One step at a time. Leave nothing out."

If I had had a body I would have been shaking. I would rather do anything but this. But Emily. For my partner. For my best friend.

I swallowed hard and nodded. Now that I was in scrubs, now that I was here, I knew it would be easy and so very hard. Easy to remember but so hard to relive it all.

I walked out of the former Monroe room and into the small reception area and nodded to the curved Formica counter and the computer sitting on the desk behind it.

"My day… my last day, started here," I said. "I was in early. I was on Yelp, looking at my reviews."

She raised her right eyebrow and gave me an encouraging nod.

The details came flooding back and I told her everything.

Well… almost everything.

Part One

LIVING

Chapter One

BEING A DENTIST IS NOT ALL THE GLAMOUR OF WIELDING a drill, hollowing out decayed parts of teeth while keeping your patient calm, and then stuffing in synthetic substances. Oh no.

And it's not all the fun of delicate injections into the gums or fitting crowns or root planning.

And yes, ladies and gentlemen, those *are* the fun parts. Perhaps now you know why the suicide rate for dentists is so high. And even though my death looked like a suicide, and I knew of no one in this world that wanted me dead— well, maybe a few patients who didn't have an optimal experience—it was most definitely *not* a suicide.

Much of a dental practice is accounting, marketing, and being your own HR department. That morning, my last morning as a living human being, I had gotten in early and looked at the books and then wandered the office. From the curved blue Formica of the reception area with the simple, comfortable armchairs in light pastel shades, to the three treatment rooms, each one with a mural on one of the walls. The Monroe room. The Casablanca room. And the Mary Poppins room for the kids.

I straightened up the magazines in the waiting area and ended up behind the reception desk on the computer looking at Yelp for new ratings and to ritualistically beat myself up about the one-star ratings:

"Has no personality, like a dead fish except smells worse."

"Talks too much. I don't care that the loser was on TV."

"Hit a nerve with that damn needle and I passed out and woke up in the ER. Thanks, Dr. Anchor, you almost sunk my ship."

My name is Walter Anchor, so I found the "sunk my ship" slight particularly galling. And that morning, there was a new 5-star rating that did catch my attention:

"I can't stand dentists or the drill, but Doc Anchor and his magic propofol made it all right!"

I smiled, because that's why I started with the propofol —to help patients. It's a bit of a tricky drug, though, a strong anesthetic and the dosages are hard to get right. But then I felt that smile turn into something that wasn't happiness at a job well done but longing for something that wasn't good for me.

I wanted to numb the pain. I wanted to have that brief high where you know there are issues, there are problems, but you just don't care anymore.

"Good morning, Walter," Midge, my office manager, said, a smile on her round Midwesterner's face, a frilly black sweater on over her scrubs that emphasized how her shoulder-length brown hair was starting to be invaded by grey.

I looked up, trying to wipe that embarrassing smile off my face, my eyes roaming towards the supply room and the locked cabinet that contained the glass vials of milky-white substance that I so wanted right then. The cabinet that I didn't have the key for, but Midge did.

"Everything all right, hon?" she asked, coming back behind the reception desk, her brow furrowed and her lips pursed in a most motherly fashion, her foofy perfume flowing after her like a cloud. At forty-one, I'm only about ten years younger than Midge, but she's a mother through and through, and the mother of this office.

My eyes refused to meet hers and I pointed lamely at the screen. "Just torturing myself with Yelp," I said with a shrug.

She smiled, one of those motherly smiles of pity, and shook her head. "Enough of that. Now shoo. Doctor Wheeler will be here any moment and you don't want him to see you moping. I'll get the coffee going, looks like you could use some, hon."

DOCTOR ELIAS WHEELER. MY YOUNGER, HANDSOMER, fitter practice mate. He had an endless parade of lovely women by his side and a thousand-watt smile. With his shaved head and his true salesman's heart, I brought him onboard three years earlier because he was the kind of guy that could sell heaters in Tucson in the summer. Of all the "not fun" parts of running this business, getting new clients in was the worst for me, and Doctor Wheeler loved it—a lot more than the drilling—and that just made him a weirdo to me.

Suffice to say that I needed Doctor Wheeler, but I didn't particularly like him. Midge said just the right thing. I definitely did not want him to see me moping.

So I got up and went into the supply room... because

that's what I do in the morning. Look at the schedule and make sure we have all we need for the procedures. And yes, I have staff to do that, but it was always a habit of mine to double-check. Not a good idea to get halfway through a procedure and find you don't have what you need to finish it. "Oh... sorry, Mrs. Evenington, but we're out of the material we create temporary crowns with. You'll have to survive for a day with that sharp stub of a tooth." Yeah, that will get you a big, fat one-star on Yelp.

But this morning, I went in there and stared at the locked steel-grey cabinet. The one with the enticing vials of milky-white liquid. The propofol. It was just a short metal cabinet with a cheap lock. It would take three seconds with a screwdriver to open it up, but it was the lock and the shame of everyone knowing that kept me from doing that.

Well, to be precise, the shame of Mother Midge seeing that cabinet and knowing what I had done was shame enough to stop me. She had found me, more than once, when she came in to open the office, passed out in a dental chair from a propofol session.

The cabinet was the compromise that got her to stay on the job. I had wanted to brush it off, she had wanted to get all the propofol out of the office. The cabinet was detente.

Right above the cabinet was a picture of my ex-wife Sun and me on the set of a movie she was acting in and I was working on as a grip. Behind us are some rolling California hills and Sun has her sunglasses on, her long black hair framing the smile on her beautiful face. She's got her arm around me and is flashing a big thumbs-up.

We're about three months married and this minor part in this major movie has made Sun very happy. We are both very happy, the honeymoon period still full in force.

My curly black hair is disheveled (kind of like always) and I look so damn happy. Like nothing could ever change, that we would always be that happy, be that hopeful, be that in love.

I put that picture there above that locked cabinet for a reason. And yes, it's a bit like Yelp in that it can be a form of self-torture, but I wanted an extra layer on top of the cheap lock and the promise I made to Midge. It's there to remind me of better times and a better me that didn't need the damn propofol (or poker for that matter) to be all right.

Except I wasn't all right.

"Good morning, Hollywood Dental," I heard Doctor Wheeler call. It was his usual, overly cheerful greeting when he came into the office every morning.

I groaned. I wasn't fond of the man.

"Good morning, Walter," Doctor Wheeler said with a jaunty nod a moment later as he strode into the room.

I turned away from the picture and went to the coffeepot and poured myself a cup. Hollywood Dental was not a big office, so the one room housed supplies and had a small fridge and coffeepot and served as the break room.

"Good morning, Doctor Wheeler," I said, trying to put a genuine smile on my face and ignoring for the thousandth time that he called me "Walter" and I called him "Doctor Wheeler." We were colleagues, yes, but not friends, not in the least, and he hadn't earned the right to call me by my first name.

He rubbed at his "Mr. Clean" shaved head in a gesture that made me wonder if he missed his hair. I ruffled my abundant curls, just to emphasize my thick hair.

"I've got two crowns coming in today and a root canal," he began as he put too much sugar into his coffee. "You?"

This was his game. I had brought him on because he

219

was good at sales, good at bringing in new patients, but he had a habit of rubbing it in.

Well, that day, I still considered that perhaps this was his egotistical way of making sure that I knew he was pulling his load—I was the boss, after all. Now, though, I know different. He just liked to rub my nose in the fact that he was doing more of the expensive procedures than I was.

"Oh, you know," I replied slowly as I took a noisy sip of coffee. "Saving the world one mouth at a time."

His brow furrowed, quite the show with his shaved head, the wrinkles rippling up past where his hairline should have been. And then he smiled, his teeth bleached so white they could almost blind you. "I like that, Walter. 'Saving the world one mouth at a time.' You know, maybe that should be our new motto. 'Hollywood Dental: Saving the World One Mouth at a Time.'" He said it like he was a radio announcer from the fifties.

He chuckled and clapped me on the back on his way out. I couldn't tell if he was making fun of me or not.

It might have been my last day living, but I didn't know that yet. It was just the start of another day at the office.

Chapter Two

I STARED AT EMILY FROM THE STOREROOM/BREAK ROOM of my former dental office. I had paced around the empty office and told her the story of my last day going to each place I spoke of, feeling the feelings, almost seeing what had happened.

"It was just another day," I said with a weak shrug, still getting used to my ghostly form being in scrubs again.

Her lollipop was yellow, both dull and bright swirling together. I think she was both worried and curious.

The storeroom still had a metal cabinet in it, although it was black instead of the dull grey it had been on that day, but the picture of Sun and me still hung above it.

Doctor Wheeler hadn't taken it down when he had transformed Hollywood Dental into Wheeler Dental, when he transformed it from a practice with personality to a generic dental practice.

"It's a nice picture," Emily said. "You look happy."

I nodded. "I was. We had no money and I had already shifted away from acting and was doing grip work to put myself through school. But Sun was starting to get gigs and her happiness was contagious."

"Kinda surprised that your bald compatriot didn't take it down," she said.

I shrugged. "He would have. He took down all of my Hollywood pictures that were hanging in the lobby, but Midge is still working here and Midge insisted."

"Sounds like that broad has some moxy," Emily said, slipping into 1920s speak. Slang can be strange with her. She's seen the language evolve over the decades and has picked up pieces of it here and there.

I smiled. "That she does. Mother Midge can be a force to be reckoned with." The smile evaporated as my mind traveled forward to after I had died, to when I was haunting the practice.

I looked at Emily. "Maybe we should skip ahead. Things are more interesting after I died."

She shook her head, her tight, blond curls bouncing around her young face. "One step at a time, bub. I want to hear it all."

I nodded. There was logic there. I had told Emily all about my last day, but being here, the memories were richer, they were right there at the edge of my consciousness like they wanted to come out.

But this wasn't a good feeling. It was like there was something in there that I didn't want to know. Something that would change how I lived my afterlife.

Chapter Three

HALEY CALCO HAD LONG BROWN HAIR, PALE BLUE EYES, and a shy smile. She was slim like many of the young ones are, her blue scrubs hanging off her a bit too loosely.

It was that last day, my death day, and we were in the Monroe room, the picture of Marilyn looking on as we worked. As I drilled into Mrs. Champon's mouth, I caught Haley staring at me several times, instead of watching the action.

She was new, substituting for Mary Paulson who was on maternity leave, and Haley had a crush on me.

At least I think she did.

And while I didn't really mind the attention, I was far too old for her. And while I used to be an actor, I am, by no means, Hollywood handsome. I'm just plain everyday handsome. My acting career, while I was still thinking of it as a "career," was headed strongly into character actor territory, not leading man. Sun, now she was Hollywood beautiful, and far out of my league, but her beauty has served her well in Hollywood.

Back behind the front desk there were a few of my

Hollywood pictures hanging. When I interviewed Haley for the temp position and she had the opportunity to ask me questions, she said, "So you know Sarah Michelle Gellar?"

I suppressed a smile and said, "We worked together for a couple of days. I can't say that I 'know' her."

"But Sarah Michelle Gellar. Buffy. That must have been…"

And then I had to smile. Haley was young and idealistic and somehow thought just because Sarah was famous, she didn't have the same human hang-ups and problems as the rest of us. Fame brings with it a host of opportunities for the enhancement of our human foibles.

"She was very nice," I said, because it felt like I needed to say something.

The memory would often resurface when I caught Haley staring at me. Part of what she was feeling had to do with the life I had briefly lived that looks to the world to be very glamorous, but most of the time is far from it.

"Suction," I said, releasing the trigger on the drill. "Almost there, Mrs. Champon. You're doing great."

The whole Hollywood thing I had going on here was, in part, a marketing ploy. Look, there I am with Sarah Michelle Gellar. Look, there I am with Jane Seymour, and here I am with Johnny Depp (just ignore the fact that my small part was cut out of the final film). I wasn't an overt salesman like Doctor Wheeler, but it helped patients feel comfortable with me. And, in some cases, it contributed to how some of my employees felt about me.

And as ashamed as I was of my failed marriage, of giving up on my dream and running back to Arizona to drill in people's teeth, I didn't want to forget the Hollywood days.

Yup. It's a bit like the Yelp ratings I was obsessed with. It could be torture, but it was a part of myself I wasn't willing to let go of. The bits of glamour that I did experience, the awe I felt at rubbing elbows with famous people. I was still drawn to it, still wanted it. And it was never going to happen.

"That's good," I said to Haley, and got back to drilling.

She nodded, pulled the suction tube out of Mrs. Champon's mouth, and didn't say anything. She acted shy, this Haley, but I could see a spark in her eyes from time to time. There was something there that made me curious.

And truth was, I was a lonely man. I had given up gambling, had locked away the propofol, but what else did I have besides this practice and Gambler's Anonymous meetings?

There. Haley was staring at me again and I had to smile underneath my mask. I shouldn't like the attention, but I did.

Chapter Four

"THAT HALEY?" EMILY ASKED HER EYEBROW ARCHED and her lips pursed.

"Yes," I said with a sigh. This time I was staring at the chair I had died in in the now bland treatment room. This had been my room, the room I worked in, the room that was my home for so many years. "Haley who we discovered murdered following the one lead we had in my case," I said. "Haley who I had pretended to like to keep her from losing herself to the bardo."

The bardo. Where do I start with that? Our community of ghosts, like any other, has words that are shortcuts to much bigger concepts. The bardo is the place those cliched slack-jawed ghosts are in. It's basically a hell of their own making where they are reliving their regrets. It's where I would have ended up without Emily.

This is the place Emily saved me from when she found me. And this is the place I saved Haley from by distracting her, pretending I had a thing for her.

"Well this explains a lot," Emily said, nodding her head, her curls bouncing around her face.

And it does. I had fallen for Haley when I "pretended" that I liked her, when we were both dead and age didn't matter, when I wanted to believe I was still attractive to the opposite sex even though I didn't have a body anymore.

I've already written about the train wreck that all turned into and won't be dragging that up further. Suffice it to say we were deep into a very uncomfortable part of my past.

"You liked her," Emily continued.

I shrugged again. "I guess. I mean, it felt weird because I was just about old enough to be her father, so I didn't let myself feel much of anything."

"But you liked her," Emily continued with a smile, acting the age she looked. "You were all googly-eyed thinking how pretty she was."

"Yes and no," I said, crossing my arms. "She was pretty, sure, but she wasn't Sun. She was too young. I was lonely."

She squinted her eyes and it seemed like she was looking into me, not at me, using her formidable ghostly intuition—all of us are more intuitive dead, but some more than others. She nodded slowly, apparently satisfied. "So you liked her," she said with a wicked smile, now more the eighty-year-old ghost.

"Yes, Emily," I said, sighing yet again. There was clearly going to be a lot of sighing going through my past at this resolution. "I liked her."

Emily nodded, a smile on her face. Clearly, she was enjoying this a lot more than me.

Chapter Five

_____

AT THE END OF MY LAST DAY AS A CORPOREAL BEING, Haley Calco was there in front of the reception desk dressed in jeans and a silky blue blouse that went well with her eyes.

I was tired, still dressed in my ever-present scrubs having just finished a root canal that almost went bad. I wanted a drink... no, what I wanted was a good card game, or better yet, a nice propofol session.

"Haley?" I asked. "Why are you still here?"

She smiled shyly looking down at her sandals. I had close to twenty years on her, and in this moment it showed. I looked around and the office was empty, the light filtering in the waiting room window a dusky orange.

"Well... I..." she stammered, her pale blue eyes briefly meeting mine before they wandered to the photo of my *Buffy the Vampire Slayer* episode.

My heart thudded in my chest and I felt like a teenager, much younger than the twenty-something Haley. She wasn't going to ask me out, was she? That would be so very inappropriate, but my lonely heart not-so-secretly hoped she would.

The sound of my breathing was way too loud and I tried putting my hands in the pockets of my scrubs so I could look relaxed, but the pockets weren't very deep and I just ended up looking dorky. I could smell her sweet perfume, and while she was not my type—my Korean American ex-wife Sun was my type—the loneliness and isolation of this life had made me desperate.

I'm not proud to say it. But if I'm going to look at my past this myopically, if I'm going to find my murderer, I need to be honest with myself.

She bit her lip and took a deep breath, her red lips parting—had she just put on lipstick? She had. Oh boy. Here it comes.

"So... Doctor Anchor..." she began.

"Yes, Haley? You can tell me anything, you know that, right?" That was a phrase straight out of the HR side of my job, but true enough.

She nodded and bit her lip again. "I was... I am..." She took a deep breath and squared her shoulders. "I am hoping that after Mary returns from maternity leave that there will still be a place for me here at Hollywood Dental."

She ended with a bright smile and my heart sank because this wasn't about her being attracted to me. This wasn't me finding out that women can still be attracted to me. Those glances earlier were about this. She was sizing me up. Figuring out what to say. Those words, once they came out, sounded decidedly practiced.

But I am an actor... or, at least, I used to be one. I put a bright smile on my face and said, "I hope we can work that out, Haley. We'll just have to see."

She nodded shyly and we exchanged a few pleasantries, but she got out of there quickly.

I didn't know it then, but it was the last time I would see Haley alive and the last time Haley would see me alive, but it wasn't the last time we would see each other.

After she left, the shame I had held back came flooding in, my cheeks burning hot. I marched into the supply room and stared at the steel-grey cabinet that held the propofol, wondering if I took it quickly enough if it would erase the memory of what had just happened.

I was just about old enough to be Haley's father. Of course, she was not interested in me. How stupid was I? If I wanted to date, I needed to get on one of those websites, but I just couldn't.

My eyes wandered up to the photo of Sun and me, so happy. What I wanted was Sun, and I could never have her.

I turned, walked out and slumped down into the chair behind the counter. No propofol. I was past that. No gambling. My financial life could not take it. And while my life was nothing great, I did have this practice and I wanted to keep it.

I tried to dig into the charting I had left to do, but I just didn't have the focus for it. I wiggled the mouse and went to Yelp. At least there was one unhealthy thing I wouldn't feel too guilty about doing.

———

AFTER HALEY LEFT, MOTHER MIDGE WANDERED IN AND saw me slumped behind the desk staring at Yelp, the one-star reviews sorted to the top. My face was slack and I kept looking at the door Haley had walked through.

I was feeling old and rather sorry for myself. Haley

hadn't been interested in me, just interested in keeping her job. Well... that's not true. She was interested in me in so far as I was the source of her job.

"You okay there, Walter?" Midge asked, her voice taking on that gentle "I'm worried you are going to use again" tone.

I turned, put on a smile, and nodded. "Of course. Haley was just pitching to keep her job after Mary comes back."

Midge cocked her head and looked closely at me. She knew when I was acting, and I had just been acting.

"She can be a handful," Midge said, an eyebrow arching. "She looks all pretty and young and innocent, but that girl has got a temper on her. Let me tell you."

I nodded absently. I hadn't seen it, but I believed it. There was something dangerous in those blue eyes of hers.

"But..." Midge continued, "we could probably work it out. She is good with the patients."

Now I was the one giving Midge the look. I expected her to tell me that when Mary was back from maternity leave we wouldn't need her, that I would have to let her go. "Really?"

Midge nodded cheerfully but wouldn't meet my eyes. Something was going on.

"I've got to get home, hon," she said, a slight blush of red invading her round cheeks. "Hal will gnaw his own foot off if I don't get him something to eat."

"Okay, Midge. Thanks for everything today." I knew there was something to get to the bottom of, but I just didn't have the energy.

She stopped at the door and turned back, her eyes finally meeting mine. "Go home, Walter. Get some rest." What she was really saying was, "Don't use, Walter."

I nodded my head and lied, "I'll do that."

After she was gone, all thoughts of self-torture via Yelp left me and I wandered through the office trying to figure it out. What were Midge and Haley up to? Why did Midge want to keep her around?

The two of them, they were keeping something from me.

It was a mystery and I was no detective. I was alone in my offices having no one to question. I could only move around, look around, and think about it.

Writing this, it was a strange prescient moment that outlined what my life—rather, afterlife—would soon be.

And that mystery, what Haley and Midge were up to, is a mystery I have solved, but not until after I was dead. I won't go into the details here but suffice to say that it was a twisty little mystery that involved Haley's murder and a bit of a smuggling operation going on in my office.

But it was a dead-end as to my own murder. I was ignorant of it when I was alive and wasn't a threat to the scheme because of that ignorance. There was no reason to kill me.

Back in the office, that night, my last night as a biological being, I walked and I searched through desks and filing cabinets and I worried until well after midnight.

I was tired, punch-drunk tired, but the mystery had derailed me from my trip to shame town, so using wasn't even on my mind.

I remember being frustrated and exhausted. I turned off the office lights and stumbled into the Monroe room and got into the dental chair. I needed a few minutes of rest before going home.

I lay down, took a deep breath in the darkness, enjoying the antiseptic tang in the air, and immediately fell asleep.

Chapter Six

I SAT ON THE FLOOR OF THE FORMER MONROE ROOM staring at the bland industrial carpet. It was vaguely blue, but up close there were enough colors in there that I wouldn't have called it blue. It had grey and off-white and teal, but nothing that was straight-up blue.

It's interesting that I always thought of it as blue, that I never looked close enough to see the constituent parts. That I had never understood the illusion of my carpet.

"I'm sorry, Walter," Emily said gently. She was sitting beside me staring at me, not the carpet. "That must have been a tough moment with Haley."

I have to wonder if she was starting to see the strands that made up me, the pieces of my last day. That maybe if she knew enough of my pieces that the illusion would dissolve and I wouldn't be who she thought I was. That she wouldn't want to spend time with me anymore.

I tried to smile, but I'm sure it came out all twisted and weird. I was too in it to pretend that it wasn't a bad moment. It was, but it was just a moment. Just a brief moment of shame on the long road of my life.

Try being an actor and going to endless auditions and being constantly rejected. This wasn't that big of a deal in the scheme of things.

"What is it, Walter?" Emily asked, putting her hand on my shoulder and doing it right so I felt that ghostly sense of touch, that barely there sensation. It's not like when you are alive, but touch is still important even when you aren't physical.

I sighed. "I…" I began, but looked away.

"What?" Emily asked.

"You know how we have such good memories?" I asked.

Emily nodded, her green eyes wide as she stared at me.

"Well… doing this. Being here. Telling it all to you…"

Her face melted into a compassionate smile. "You are remembering more things," she offered.

I nodded. "Things I hadn't wanted to remember," I said.

"Worse than Haley?" she asked.

"Much worse."

Chapter Seven

My phone rang, drilling into my brain like a nervous dentist in training. I didn't know where I was. The phone was buzzing against my chest and I reached into the pocket of my scrubs and pulled it out.

It said "Sun."

My heart thudded in my chest and I was suddenly sweating. I looked around in the dim light of nighttime Tucson shining in through the window and felt the faux leather underneath me and knew I had fallen asleep in the office. Again.

I briefly remembered the shame at thinking Haley had been attracted to me, that I had then wondered why Midge wanted to keep Haley and ended up searching the office late into the night, finally coming into the Monroe room to lie down for a few minutes on the dental chair before going home.

But it was Sun calling. It had been close to two years since we had talked. We were down to Christmas cards and the rare email. And the hour... It was almost 1:30 a.m. Something had to be wrong.

I sat up, flicked the screen to answer, and put the phone to my ear. "Sun? Is everything okay?"

"Hi, Walter," she said, her voice slightly slurred. She had been drinking. "It's good to hear your voice."

I blinked and nodded. She must be drunk if she was saying that. My heart beat harder. "It's good to hear your voice too, Sun. So… what's going on?"

"You were awake, right?" she asked, some surprise in her voice as if she had just realized the time. "I didn't wake you, did I?"

"No," I lied. "I'm still at the office. Catching up on paperwork."

She barked out a laugh. "Hard to imagine my Walter buried in paperwork and not carrying half his weight in gear rushing from setup to setup."

After the acting petered out, I worked as a grip and funded my dental training. I worked on Sun's first big commercial—it was how we met.

"Do you miss it?" she asked. And then I knew she was more than a little drunk. We never talked about my old life.

"Of course, Sun. I miss it. I miss—" I cut myself off. I was going to say, "I miss you," but she wasn't drunk enough for that. There was no drunk enough for that.

Sun and I had taken our shot and the accident and then our miscarriage had been the thing we couldn't get over. The thing that took us out. The thing you couldn't plan for or defend against. A goddamn accident that cost me what I cared about the most. Her pregnancy was a promise of our future together and after that accident, after we lost our child, that future was unobtainable.

"I miss you too, Walter," she whispered. "I do. I swear I do. But… You know…"

I nodded. We had been over this. Looking at me reminded her of the child we lost, of the life we almost had. "I know," I said. "It was just bad luck. A terrible day."

Sun sniffed loudly. Was she crying now? My heart, which had calmed down a bit, kicked back into high gear. What was going on?

"So, listen, Walter. I... I need to warn you about something."

"Warn me...?" I asked, the small room suddenly making me feel claustrophobic.

"The paparazzi, they... pictures, you know... probably on the internet already." She ended in a sigh. "I don't even know if it's going anywhere, but he's famous and..."

She wasn't being very clear, but the picture clicked into place. Sun had been photographed on a date and it was about to be tabloid fodder and all over social media.

I was never successful enough for anyone to take pictures of me and neither was Sun when we were together. This was one aspect of my failure as an actor that I was okay with. I never wanted to be famous, which may sound weird for an actor. I got off on the process, on the art, fame was a side effect, from my point of view, and not a desirable one.

My heart beat harder and I was sweating. I didn't want to see Sun glammed up and out with a Hollywood-handsome hunk. I didn't want to think about what my "not quite over Sun" brain would imagine. It had been years now, but Sun was still the love of my life. There wasn't really a time when I didn't want her back.

But I swallowed all of that because she *was* the love of my life and I wanted her to be happy.

"Is he good to you?" I asked quietly.

She sniffed again. "Yeah. He's... he's kind and thoughtful. Surprisingly so."

"Then don't worry about it, Sun," I said, forcing a

smile on my face that she couldn't see. "Focus on your life and forget about all that crap."

"But... I just didn't want you to be surprised. I... I worry about you, Walter."

And she had reason to. I had to borrow money from her to dig out of my gambling problem and she knew about my dance with propofol. I can't say we were close, but I kept tabs on her as she did on me.

"I'm fine," I lied. It had been a bad day with that Haley stupidity, the mystery I couldn't solve, and this was just making it worse. My background longing for propofol was quickly edging towards need. "Really. I'm glad you told me, Sun. I really do appreciate it."

"Yeah?" she asked.

"Yeah," I said, putting some punch in my voice that I wasn't feeling. "I am always happy to talk to my favorite actress. Quite the honor, really. I am your biggest fan."

"Shut up, Walter," she said.

"No, Sun. You are my favorite. By far. I snagged one of your season five posters. The one with you out front and center and the other four behind you in front of the LA skyline. 'Detectives: LA coming fall of 2010.'"

She groaned. "Yeah, I call that one the 'butt shot.' The men can face the camera head on, but the girls have to twist to the side and show their asses."

"Yeah. That one," I said. "It's why I like it so much."

"I bet." She chuckled but went silent for a few breaths. "Seriously, Walter. Are you okay with this? I do worry about you. You're a goddamn dentist. You could have stayed in Hollywood. You'd probably be directing by now."

Sun never understood the whole dentist thing. I mean, she must have intellectually. I promised my father that if I didn't make it in Hollywood after ten years, I would go get myself educated, find a career. But she had the drive it took to make it in Hollywood and I didn't. If you couldn't be an actor, being a grip wasn't a bad way to go, but watching actors all day and not being one was just too hard.

"I'm good. I really am," I said. "I have an annoying partner and the HR stuff drives me mad, but every day I get to use my acting skills to ease nervous patients and help them. It's a good life, Sun. I chose this life." It sounded like I meant it, and most of me did.

"Okay, okay," she said with a tiny chuckle. "You are clearly more emotionally mature than me. Because I would be a whiney baby if I couldn't spend my days acting."

"Oh, Sun, I act each and every day," I said with a chuckle. "I act like the calmest dentist on the planet. I act like a businessman who knows what he is doing." And sometimes I act like the person my ex-wife needs me to be, but I didn't say that part.

She laughed and it was a beautiful sound, a happy sound. It had been a very long time since I had made her laugh.

I lay back down in the chair and we talked for another twenty minutes, mostly her delivering day-to-day minutia about her life as a lead on a major network TV show.

I loved hearing about it and I was so happy for her, but I was sad for me. But I am a good enough actor and she had had enough to drink that she didn't notice.

After she hung up, I closed my eyes, squeezed them shut and didn't dare move. If I got up, I would head towards that grey cabinet and the propofol locked inside. If I searched for Sun on my phone and saw her with the Hollywood hunk she was seeing, I would rip my hair out and then go for the propofol.

And I wasn't going to go for the propofol.

I was not.

I made a decision then as the moments ticked by with excruciating slowness. No more propofol in the office. It was useful. It helped some patients. But this was my practice and I wasn't safe with it.

At least something good had come of this crappy day.

I took it one breath at a time until I fell asleep.

I have no memory of waking up until I was a ghost looking at my own dead body.

Chapter Eight

"WHAT IF I WASN'T MURDERED?" I ASKED EMILY. I spoke the words slowly, carefully, as if I were still corporeal and my mouth was filled with glass.

We were still sitting on the floor of what used to be the Monroe room, on that carpet that looked blue but was made up of all those other colors.

The room felt empty, too quiet. Outside the sun was setting, and while I could hear the rumble of the road, it felt distant. It felt like Emily and I were isolated and alone. I mean, we were. It was Saturday and no one was in the office, but more than that. Like this here, this story and her were my entire world.

Emily blinked, her green eyes wide. Her mouth moved and she fidgeted with her fingers. If any ghost knows how important being murdered is to me, it's Emily.

And I know that may sound strange, but think about it. If someone murdered me, then I have a mission as a ghost, something to do, unfinished business that points outward at my murderer. Then all this running around with Emily solving murders makes sense.

If I was an addict that slipped after a very bad day and overdosed, then not only was my life a mess, but my after-life no longer has meaning.

And living or dead, to have any sort of balance, you have to have meaning.

Emily's smooth brow furrowed, her mouth moved, and her eyes flicked away from me and I knew she had figured it all out.

"You were murdered," she said, standing up and straightening her shoulders. "You know me, Walter, I can smell a murder. And you were murdered."

It was sweet of her, it really was, but I didn't believe it.

"But if I am really a detective now…" I began. "If *we* are really detectives now, don't we have to look at the cold hard facts? Shouldn't we apply Occam's razor?"

Her lips pressed into a thin line. "Of course."

I shrugged weakly. "My last day wasn't a good one," I said. "That Haley thing was bad enough but… Sun. My Sun had called me after two years to tell me about the famous man she was seeing. I don't remember going for the propofol. I was fighting it as hard as I could. We sorted out the smuggling ring with Haley's murder and investi-gated Doctor Wheeler and there are no suspects. If we apply Occam's razor, we…" I couldn't continue.

She walked up to me, took my hand in her little hands, her green eyes wide and compassionate.

"Occam was a dick." She said it seriously without a trace of humor, her face close to full pout configuration.

I just waited, quite sure she wasn't trying to be funny, but not sure where she was going.

"The law of parsimony," she said, stating the more formal name of Occam's razor, "states that simpler solu-tions are more likely to be correct than complex ones. *More likely*, Walter."

I nodded weakly and she squeezed my hand. It was that super-weak ghostly touch, but I appreciated it. It helped.

She pulled me into a hug, her little body at the right height with me still sitting down. The hug almost made it worse. I wanted to cry. I wanted to rage at myself. I had been so stupid to use propofol in the first place, to keep it in the office, to not go get help for that particular addiction.

When she stepped back, her nose was wrinkled and she said, "You stink, Walter."

"What?" I was completely confused. Ghosts don't have a sense of smell so she couldn't possibly be smelling me.

"You stink bad." Her whole face scrunched up like she was smelling something terrible.

"Emily... I...?"

"You stink of murder," her eyes widened with a lust no four-year old could ever experience.

"Emily. Please... I..." I mumbled. I was teetering already, and this tact wasn't really helping. Was she trying to be funny?

"I'm serious, Walter. Which is the simplest explanation? That my murder sense is off for once or that you fell off the wagon? So it wasn't a peachy day, but it wasn't *that* bad of a day."

"I... you know, Emily, addictions are complicated. It's possible that it could have happened."

She nodded slowly. "But not probable. It's also not probable that my first impression of you was wrong. You stank of murder then and you stink of murder now."

I just sat there, my mind reeling. I thought it was brave of me to open up to the possibility of an overdose, but to have it so vehemently resisted, I didn't know what to say or what to do.

"So that was your last day," she said, crossing her arms. "You haunted the practice and Midge for—what? —months."

I nodded.

"So tell me about that," she continued. "There's a clue there. Something you haven't remembered. I know it."

Part Two

DEAD

Chapter Nine

FIRST OF ALL, I KNOW, DEATH BY PROPOFOL IS NOT A BAD way to go, the effects of the anesthesia can be quite pleasant. But dead is dead and when propofol is used as a murder weapon or is the instrument of an accidental overdose, it's not a pleasant thing.

When I "woke up" and saw the needle in my arm, the elastic band loose around it, my first thought was, "Shit, Walter. Not this. Not again."

I didn't know I was dead. I was in the Monroe room in the pale-blue dental chair, the sodium yellow glow of a Tucson night sneaking in through the window, the office lights off. I heard the sleepy hum of late-night Tucson outside and everything was quiet in my office.

My escape from Hollywood post-divorce had not been easy and I dealt with some serious depression. As I have explained, I turned to gambling and propofol.

Counseling and antidepressants would have been a much better choice, but, you know, that would require me to talk about myself and my past, which is something I'm getting better at now that I'm a ghost, but I was frankly terrible at as a corporeal being.

Human Self-Expression 101 was not a course they taught in college, and like many humans (looking at the gentlemen readers) I needed not only the 101 course, but the 202 and the 303 and the 404. I mean, I think I'm a decent human being, and I do try my best, but getting out words that even halfway describe how I'm feeling is usually worse than a root canal.

But I got through that, so as I stumbled out of the chair, still not having a single clue as to what had happened, but thinking I had relapsed, I was racking my brain trying to remember, trying to understand why I would do this to myself—not kill myself, I didn't know I was dead yet, but using propofol again.

I was having a perfectly understandable reaction. There was a needle stuck in my pale arm, a vial of milky-white propofol on the instrument table next to the dental chair, the office quiet and the lights off.

This was a scene I had repeated many times, waking up predawn from a blissfully quiet propofol-induced sleep. Waking up that way brought the fog of forgetting with it, and that was part of what I liked about it. Forgetting my failure as an actor, my failure as a husband. Forgetting how I had made it to middle age with a career, plenty of debt, and an epic amount of loneliness, but not much else.

I got up and stumbled out of the Monroe room into the hall and I felt so strange. I wasn't dizzy or anything, but I was oddly numb, like the anesthetic effect of the drug hadn't worn off. My body felt distant, indistinct, like it wasn't my own. But my eyes could see so well in the dark office with the scant light leaking in the windows. Was this some side effect of propofol I hadn't experienced yet? I looked down and the needle wasn't in my arm anymore and I had no memory of removing it. I shrugged and tried to stumble out of the room, but something was stopping me.

I looked right behind me and there was this glowing silver cord snaking back into the room. I had no idea what it was and I was so disoriented I wasn't curious. I just shrugged again and surged forth, meeting more resistance, so I just tried harder.

Not that I was aware of what I was "trying." I mean, I thought I was walking, but that is not what was going on. I didn't have a body and I had no idea about that yet. And didn't know it, but that silver cord was attaching my spirit to my body.

I was in this primal space and rather dumb and just tried to go forward again and heard a loud snapping sound and found myself in the hallway. I was glad to be free of the resistance, but uninterested in what it had been.

I went down the hallway into the supply room. There I blinked and shook my head. Below the picture of Sun and me, the short metal cabinet had been forced open, the grey door bent enough to bypass the cheap lock. The orderly assemblage of items in it looked like it had been hastily rifled through, the other vials of propofol lying on their sides in disarray.

But I didn't break into that cabinet, did I?

Memories of my last day came flooding back. So vivid. Haley. The mystery of Midge wanting to keep Haley. Talking to Sun for the first time in two years. I could remember every detail of the day, the sounds and smells and tastes, such as I had never experienced before.

And the present seemed strange and muted by comparison. Beyond my sensitivity to light, I found that I could hear very well but I couldn't smell. The break room, where I found the jimmied cabinet, didn't smell of stale coffee and microwaved burritos. The office didn't have that antiseptic tang that I, honestly, loved. And while I could see just fine, my hands and arms looked strange. In the dark they seemed to both glow and to be partially transparent. It didn't make sense. As I stood there staring at the picture of Sun and me, I realized I couldn't see my own nose.

Well, none of us actually *sees* our nose, not clearly, but it sits there in between our eyes, our brain often editing it out of what we see. But if you think about it, there's a shadow there in the lower center part of your vision. And your eyebrows and eyelashes, they sometimes impinge too.

I turned my head trying to see where my nose was. I tried to furrow my brow, but my sense of my own body was numb and indistinct, and I couldn't do it in a way that entered my visual field.

And then I tried to blink. Nothing. I tried to close my eyes. Again, nothing. What the hell?

Something was wrong. The propofol had really screwed me up. I panicked.

Well… yes, it was panic I was feeling, but it was more like the idea of panic, lacking the full body, hammering heart, sweating pits experience. It was indistinct too.

And that made the panic I could experience, the mental part, get even worse.

I surged out of the supply room and down the hall and past the treatment rooms. I had to get to a mirror. Turn a light on. See what had happened to me.

At the plain white bathroom door, my hand just went through the silver handle.

What?

I tried again and my hand flowed right through, this time my fingers disappearing into the door.

How screwed up was I?

I tried again, my reach off and my whole hand went through the door and the handle.

I did it over and over, like I was caught in some twisted nightmare. My hand reaching out and passing through the handle, through the door, through the wall as my swings got wider, as I got more desperate.

I heard a whimpering sound and stopped my vain attempts, looking for the source of the noise when I realized it was me doing the whimpering.

That stopped me. I stood there, for how long I can't say, my mind slipping, unable to process what I was experiencing.

I looked down and saw that I didn't have legs, not really. The lower half of my body was a vaguely blue shape that kind of looked like two legs in scrubs at my waist, but then became a diffuse mess around my feet.

I had no nose or eyebrows that I could see. I couldn't blink or close my eyes. My body was glowing and transparent. My feet looked like a dissipating cloud of blue.

A dream. This must be a dream. If I got back to the place this all started, maybe I would wake up.

I slowly turned around and went back down to the Monroe room and looked in.

There slumped on the dental chair was the body of a man with curly black hair and a needle sticking out of his arm. He looked like he was dead.

I screamed.

Chapter Ten

EMILY AND I WERE STANDING IN THE HALL OF WHAT WAS once Hollywood Dental staring into the first treatment room. The room where I died.

"I wish I had found you sooner," Emily said quietly.

I nodded. It still wouldn't have been good, but it would have been better.

The line between life and death is stark. Razor thin. I bet a lot of ghosts have said something like this as they tell their stories here at the SECI chamber, that typewriter for ghosts, but it's true.

I was alive and healthy one moment and then another moment—how much later, really—I was dead. Was the line a second? A millisecond. A nanosecond? Less?

How long did it take for the irreversible journey from alive to dead take? When my diaphragm stopped working because it was paralyzed by the propofol? When my heart stopped beating? When my brain died? When my soul, my ghostly form, separated from my body.

Maybe with old age or disease the line isn't so thin, isn't

so sharp and stark. Your life shrinks as your ability to function goes away until you are in a coma, until your life ends.

No. I don't buy that. The change is still abrupt. Very abrupt. Even if you were like my mother and spent a few days in hospice, slipped into a coma, that line was still sharp. Breathing one moment and not the next.

We stood there, two ghosts silent for a long time. As the light faded from the sky, as the sodium yellow glow of streetlights leaked into the room, as the traffic outside lessoned. As the living went on with their endless biological maintenance.

We were ghosts. Time was different for us.

"I'm sorry, Walter," Emily finally said.

I nodded my head, not understanding what she was sorry for. Maybe that I died. Maybe that she maneuvered me into reliving it all. Maybe for the fact that we all have to die.

I didn't want to know what she was sorry for. "It's okay," I mumbled.

"Can you continue?" she asked.

I thought about it, time slipping away from me again. I wanted to stop. I needed to stop. But I felt something pulling me forward. This wasn't about Emily and her wanting me back and basically forcing me into this. This was about me. About understanding how I got here to be this ghost detective who can't solve his own murder with Emily as a partner.

I had to continue, so I did.

Chapter Eleven

I STARED AT ME, AT THE CORPSE IN THE DENTAL CHAIR, for the longest time. What used to be me.

What I was experiencing was not a dream, but in many ways the way my mind was acting was like it was. Time slipped by, rapidly sometimes and at other times it crawled like molasses. My thought processes were strange and disconnected.

"Wow," I thought. "That guy looks just like me. Poor bastard, he overdosed. I wonder if he meant to do that?"

My excellent vision could see every wrinkle in the slack face of the man in the dental chair who looked just like me. He wasn't old, but he was getting there.

"You dye your hair, don't you?" I said, nodding, noticing the slightest splash of silver at some of his roots.

"Did you mean to overdose?" I asked him. "I guess I should call someone."

And then the needle sticking out of his arm caught my attention. I don't know why, but it seemed wrong for it to just be sticking there, a few drops of blood encrusted around it. "You mind if I take this out?" I asked the dead guy I wasn't accepting was me yet.

"Not very talkative, are you?" Suddenly in my mind the man wasn't dead, just sleeping it off, and I started to feel jealous.

I tried to pull the needle out, but my hand just went through it. "Okay, then, I guess you don't want me to take it out. I guess you don't like to share. Be that way."

I stood there for the longest time staring at the arm and the needle in the arm, and then looking at the vial of propofol on the instrument tray, and I felt like a starving man looking at a steaming plate of food that I couldn't reach.

"Got any other needles, bud? I mean, it looks like there is enough of that stuff to go around." I looked around, afraid someone else might be here, that Mother Midge might have heard, and then she would quit, and that would be me losing yet another person that was important to me, and there would go my practice.

I started moving around the room. What I wanted to do, what I was trying to do, was pace, but that wasn't quite possible with my vaporous legs and nonexistent feet.

I kept glancing at the propofoled guy in the dental chair who looked so damn familiar. I did this for a long time. I don't know how long. Every once in a while, I would stop, try to pull the needle out, ask if I could have some propofol, and then get mad at him and start "pacing."

It was like a weird dream. I was caught in a loop. I couldn't get out of it.

My mind would not accept what I was seeing.

That the person in the chair was me.

That I was dead.

That I was a ghost.

But it wasn't a dream, and the sun came up, and Midge came in to work.

"Walter," she called. "You here, hon? The door was unlocked, but the lights are off. What's going on?"

And then I was there with Midge at the entryway to Hollywood Dental as the lights came on. The waiting room was painted a calming pastel blue and festooned with framed pictures of old Hollywood stars. Greta Garbo in *Mata Hari*, Katherine Hepburn in *Morning Glory*, Humphrey Bogart decked out in his trench coat and fedora from *Casablanca*, and so many more.

She walked to the reception desk, her head swiveling around. "Walter?"

I didn't speak. I don't know why. I just followed Midge, curious. My mind wasn't right yet, I can't say that I was sane. But Midge, I knew her. Mother Midge, she would figure it out.

Worry blossomed on her face as the seconds passed, her furrowed brow making her look older.

From the waiting room, down the hall, you can see just a slice of the Monroe room… and the dental chair… and the body lying in the dental chair.

"You didn't sleep here again, did you, Walter?" she asked, but her voice was hushed, barely above a whisper. I noticed her hand shaking that clutched her brown purse to her chest.

What was she talking about? Why was she speaking so quietly? Was she trying not to wake the man in the chair?

And what was going on with her perfume? I couldn't smell it—and you could always smell Midge's perfume. It was like she took it as her mission to make the world a better smelling place. It was one of those smells I didn't actually like, but I found comforting because I associated it with Midge.

I was about to ask her about it when she swept forward. "Walter!" She was yelling now and running. She screamed my name when she got to the door and dropped her purse. She stood there shaking and huffing like she had just run a race.

"Walter…" she said, but this time quietly, mournfully.

I was so confused. I was standing right here. She had walked right by me.

She walked farther into the room, her steps slow and tentative, like a toddler just finding their feet. I couldn't see her anymore and I moved to the doorway.

There, Midge held two fingers to the neck of the body on the chair. "Oh, Walter," she said, this time with such sadness, I wanted to cry.

So the guy was dead. I guess that made sense, he had been lying there still since I woke up. But why was Midge so sad, and why was she telling me?

"Damn you!" Midge said, suddenly standing up straight. Even though "damn" is a very mild curse, it was an unusual thing for Midge to curse at all. "I shouldn't have agreed to that cabinet. I should have got that goddamn drug out of here. I should have…"

She bunched up like someone had just hit her in the stomach and started crying. Big heaving messy sobs. She fell to the floor and gasped out my name over and over while she cried.

I moved farther into the room and really looked at the body. I could see with just a little light, but now that there was full lighting, I could see everything. The drool dried at the corner of the man's mouth, the vacant look in his slitted eyes, the pale tone of his skin, and his face. I really looked at his face.

Time slipped past me again while I looked at the body's face and it slowly dawned on me that it was *my* face.

And the rest of what had happened suddenly made sense (sort of). My legs, my glowing and translucent arms, my hand going through things, not being able to see my nose.

"Yes, this is Midge Williams at Hollywood Dental on East Broadway. There's been an accident." She wasn't crying anymore, but still on the floor, her cell phone out. "There's been an overdose."

That was me in the dental chair with the needle sticking out of his arm… my arm.

I was looking at my own body, but how?

"His name is Walter Anchor. He…" her voice broke and the sobbing briefly came back. "He is dead."

Chapter Twelve

GUILT IS HEAVY.

It's like tying sandbags to yourself and trying to run a race. It slows you down. It changes your every moment. It slows your steps. It makes it hard to function normally.

Guilt feels so heavy. And there in what was once the Monroe room with Emily I felt like I was loaded down with the sandbags of guilt.

As a ghost, our sense of touch is very limited as is the sense of our ghostly form. We never feel heavy. In fact, there is a lightness that is endemic to being a ghost. It can make it hard to be grounded. It's why we walk and act as human as possible even when we don't have to.

But right then, after telling Emily about the moment I realized that I was a ghost and I was staring at my own corpse, I felt so heavy.

Emily had taken my hand and I hadn't even noticed.

"Maybe I was murdered," I said quietly to the dark room, "but it was my fault."

"What?" Emily asked, sounding surprised, as if she

had been stuck in the dream of my death and was just waking up. "What are you talking about, Walter?"

"The propofol. The addiction. That was me," I said. "If I hadn't kept it in the building then I couldn't have died that way."

I wasn't looking at Emily but staring at the damn dental chair, the place I died. It was the same one, I was sure of it. The wear pattern on the faux leather quite distinct. They hadn't replaced it.

"You were murdered," she said, her voice fierce. "If the propofol wasn't here, they would have found another way."

I turned and looked at her. She had the round face of youth, but it was sour like the old ghost she was. "How can you be sure?" I asked.

"I'm sure," she growled.

I love Emily, but she is not perfect. It's her imperfections that are the most loveable parts of her, really. I nodded, weakly, to acknowledge what she was saying, not to agree with her.

"Keep going, Walter," she said, her voice still half growl.

And I did.

Chapter Thirteen

THE BODY WAS GONE. MY BODY WAS GONE.

I stood there in the Monroe room of Hollywood Dental, my mind whirling. Half the time it was "the" body. The other half it was "my" body.

The ambulance had come and gone.

The police had come and gone.

The words "suicide" and "accidental overdose" were said boldly, clearly, no one hesitating.

Mother Midge sold me out and told them I had had a problem with propofol. That I had had problems with gambling. That I was divorced and depressed and childless. That I had once been an actor.

It was all true, but it sounded like an indictment of me despite her tears and sniffing and blubbering. Like all I was could be summed up as propofol addict, gambler, divorcee, and failed actor.

Like that is what should be etched in granite on my tombstone.

Here lies Walter Anchor. He loved to gamble, take propofol, and tell everyone he met of his small acting victories during the "good ole days" before his more talented wife divorced him.

The office was shut down for the day and I was soon alone, the emptiness and the bright Tucson sun outside making it feel ghostly somehow, abandoned. There should be people here. There should be the whir of drills, the slurp of suction, and the sharp smell of antiseptic.

Instead it was me wandering around, my mind slipping, my regret building, the bardo calling.

As I mentioned, the bardo is a term used around the graveyard for that place the "classic" moaning ghost is trapped. A hell of their own making where they relive their own regret over and over.

Hell indeed.

And oddly, sinking into the bardo is tempting. Just like when you are standing on a high precipice, peering over, and jumping is bizarrely tempting. Or maybe that's just me.

The bardo is a lot like addiction. It whispers into your ear that it is better, far better than what you are currently experiencing. But the bardo, just like addictions, is a damn liar.

And I think I would have fallen off that precipice into the bardo if not for Doctor Wheeler.

The next morning, he came into the office first—let me tell you, that had never happened before—whistling like some damn songbird on the first day of spring.

I'm pretty sure he was whistling "Don't Worry, Be Happy."

And that just made me mad.

And all of those scary ghost movies… the grain of truth in them is that ghosts can be pretty unpleasant when they are mad.

I'm not very good at the whole haunting thing. That

morning, my first morning as a ghost, when Doctor Wheeler came in whistling a happy tune, I attached to him.

I can't explain the mechanism, since I don't really know how it works, but for that day everywhere he went, I went. I was dragged along... everywhere... even to the bathroom where he took way too long on the toilet and poked at his damn phone the whole time.

I watched him wash his hands—he, thankfully, did a good job of that—and then make eye contact with himself in the mirror for far too long. He ended in a sly smile and a nod, and while I couldn't read his thoughts, I'm pretty sure it was some narcissistic egotistical self-promotion. Something like, "You got this, Wheeler!"

I was there with him when Mother Midge came in, her eyes red rimmed, her brown-going-to-grey hair flat and lifeless. I saw him consciously wipe the smile off his face before he rounded the corner and saw her. He held out his arms and she collapsed into his embrace.

"I... I didn't sleep," she said, sniffing. "Not for a minute. Poor Walter. I can't believe he..."

"There, there, Midge," he said, rocking her gently, his blue eyes bright now that she couldn't see him. "I know today is going to be tough. But we've got to get the patients rescheduled. Our hearts are heavy, but this is about them."

She sniffed and nodded her head while it was still buried in his chest.

"I know just what to do, Midge. I know just what to do."

And he did. As if he had thought this through. As if he was the one that put the needle in me and ended my life.

MY FIRST DAY AS A GHOST, IT WAS DOCTOR WHEELER

and his easeful transition into leading Hollywood Dental that had my full attention.

I was there as he and Midge worked side-by-side calling patients, telling them the sad news, rescheduling their appointments.

This was the first time Wheeler had picked up the phone to call a patient about scheduling, and yet he seemed to be perfectly comfortable with it.

While Midge was sniffing half the time, taking awkward gulps of air, Wheeler was cool and collected. It would go something like this.

"Yes, he was found dead in the office. No, I cannot comment further until the police have completed their investigation, but I can assure that it was nothing communicable and after the weekend we will be open and ready for patients. No, he didn't really have any family, but the authorities have contacted his ex-wife in LA."

I got close enough to listen to the other side of the conversation, but only at first. They left a lot of innocuous messages, but the spectrum of reactions to those they talked to directly was breathtaking. From "Oh my God, I can't believe it. Dr. Anchor was such a kind man," to "I can't reschedule, I have to get this tooth fixed before my vacation."

And there were business realities too that Wheeler seemed to have a grasp on what to do about. I owned Hollywood Dental, well... most of it anyway. I gave Wheeler a ten percent share as a signing bonus and Midge owned ten percent—an additional inducement to stay the last time one of my addictions got the better of me. But mostly it was the banks that owned it. There was some value in the practice, but not a ton.

My will, which I knew someone would get around to soon, left everything to Sun. But Sun didn't need the money or the hassle and Wheeler knew it. He didn't come out and say it, but I read between the lines as he and Midge talked after all the calls were over. He was going to buy it from her and he would get it for a song.

He placed his hand gently on Midge's, they were still both behind the counter, Midge slouched in exhaustion. "I know that was hard and I am sorry for that, but listen to me, Midge. I know what to do. I will keep the practice going. We will all still have jobs. Just trust me."

Midge looked at him with her tired brown eyes and he held her gaze with a gentle smile and a small nod of his head.

"What... we..." she mumbled. "Do we need a lawyer? Walter owned most of the company."

Wheeler kept nodding slowly. "I already talked to one. I know what to do."

"And... services, we need services, a memorial. Poor Walter." She almost devolved into tears again but sniffed and nodded.

"You will do a brilliant job with that, Midge. I know Walter relied on you for everything, that he would want you to do that."

She nodded slowly.

"And I know good old Walter would want us to soldier on. To keep helping patients too... what did he say to me that morning? He would want us to go on 'saving the world one mouth at a time.'"

He kept talking but I couldn't hear him anymore. I had said that phrase sarcastically, to ward him off. He was telling Midge what I would want, but he hardly knew me.

My world became tinged in red. I wanted to do nothing more than to hurt Doctor Elias Wheeler. To put my hands around his neck and squeeze.

And then it occurred to me that Wheeler had the most

to gain from my death. Here he was sliding right in as if he had been planning it all along.

Things got even redder and my vision started tunneling in.

Wheeler killed me. I just knew it, the propofol having erased my memory of it.

Maybe I wasn't alive anymore, maybe I didn't have hands to wring his neck, maybe I was a ghost, but there must be a way to hurt him.

I put my ghostly hands around his neck and "squeezed" wishing that he was dead, that I was killing him.

His eyes widened and he stopped in mid-sentence and cleared his throat.

I had done it. I had done something, at least.

"Where was I?" he asked Midge.

"You were asking about his will," she said, "whether I had ever met his ex-wife."

He nodded sharply. "Right. So…?"

That was it? I made him clear his throat with all my rage. What the hell?

If I had felt helpless when I was alive, I had been fooling myself. This was much worse.

I just stood there and listened while Wheeler outlined how he would take over my practice.

WHEELER DENTAL.

That was the crowning jewel of Doctor Wheeler's plan. Paint over the murals, take down the Hollywood pictures and rename the practice once he owned it.

Wheeler Dental.

He actually had the insensitive, narcissistic cojones to tell Mother Midge that the day after I had died.

I was apoplectic.

I screamed. I raged. The world went red-tinged. I gripped his throat over and over with my ghost hands and squeezed. I made him clear his throat. I made him cough.

And that was it.

And then he was gone and I was left alone watching Midge quietly cry back behind the counter of what would not much longer be Hollywood Dental.

Part of me was curious that I hadn't followed Wheeler. He had motive. He had opportunity. Maybe he drove past the office after midnight, saw that my car was still there and the lights were off. This was the opportunity he had been waiting for. He took the vial of propofol out of his glove box, put on a headlamp, snuck up, and dosed me before I could wake up. After I had stopped breathing, he jimmied the cabinet and left things looking like I had just overdosed.

"He did it, Midge," I whispered to her. "He killed me. We need to catch him. This is how we make it better."

She couldn't hear me, of course.

And while I believed it, I had no way to prove it and I had no way to tell anyone about it.

And then Midge blew her nose and shut all the lights off. She stood at the door gazing in with a look I can't really describe very well. Her eyes were red-rimmed, her round face was sad, but there were layers of other emotions on her face. Regret, for sure. Guilt, maybe.

"Goodbye, Walter," she whispered.

I stood there for a moment staring at her and then at the empty space where she had been. It was almost as if she knew I was here.

Or she was resigning herself to the fact that Wheeler

would be erasing me out of this place at his first opportunity.

I wanted to follow Midge, to listen to her talk to her husband about me. I wanted to know what was going on with her and Haley. I couldn't do anything here, but I couldn't leave either.

I tried. I floated to the door and couldn't go any farther. I was stuck in Hollywood Dental, which was now officially haunted. By me.

Chapter Fourteen

"THIS IS EXHAUSTING," I TOLD EMILY. WE WERE IN THE reception area and I had been pacing, telling her of my time haunting my own dental practice.

She nodded, a grim smile on her face.

I was walking carefully, like Emily had taught me. I was still back to my default ghostly form of scrubs, but that felt right somehow. I couldn't be bothered with niceties. I had all this energy now. All this anger.

Wheeler never cared about me. I was just an opportunity to him. My past was with me so strongly that I could almost hear them talking. I could remember what it was like being a new clueless ghost. I felt so useless, so powerless, so confused.

"Do you need a break, Walter?" she asked quietly.

"No," I snapped and kept walking. "I need to get through this. I need to be done with this."

Emily backed up a step into one of the armchairs. A very unusual faux pas for her. A dim part of me felt bad for scaring her, but this was her fault. She had started all of this. She had made me do this. Did she expect me to feel nothing, to just stumble onto the clue we had missed so we could happily go solve my own murder and get back to normal?

But we're dead, what the hell is normal anyway?

Is it normal to be a ghost? To be a ghost that solves murders? To be a ghost that types up our cases so justice can be served?

As I write this, I have a little more clarity on what was going on with me. I was getting close. I was almost there. Part of my mind knew what was coming, knew that it would be bad. And that energy was spilling out in unhealthy ways.

Emily set her jaw and stepped out of the chair. Her face was a stern mask that didn't match with her apparent age. "Then get on with it, Walter," she growled.

Chapter Fifteen

WHILE HAUNTING HOLLYWOOD DENTAL IN ITS FINAL days under that name, I learned a lot about people. I had nothing else to do but to follow and listen. All day. Every day.

I couldn't leave the practice, and every morning when someone came in, I was so glad for something else to do but to stew in my own regrets and wander the empty offices staring at the pictures of Hollywood icons and my brief life working there.

And let me tell you, on a Monday morning when someone came in after being a ghost alone in the offices all weekend, I didn't leave their side. Not for a moment. So starved I was for something, anything.

So I learned things.

Haley had a horrible habit of chewing her fingernails and she would sometimes be obsessive with running her fingers through her long brown hair, as if she were a Victorian lady with a prescription for how many times to brush her hair at night.

Wheeler had IBS or—and this would be much worse—

just liked to take breaks, long breaks, while sitting on the toilet fiddling with his phone. Lacking a sense of smell, it was hard for me to tell which. He was also the aforementioned narcissist, and while he was good at manipulating people, he couldn't even do simple math in his head.

Mary Paulson, once she got back from her maternity leave, had a terrible case of postpartum depression and would sneak into the bathroom and flick through the live streams of the cameras she had set up in her own home to see her baby and the woman she had hired to care for him. She seemed tired, strung out, and more than a little bit distracted.

Mary was about ten years older and a lot stouter than Haley and really disliked the younger woman. Haley was supposed to be gone, but she wasn't. Midge and Wheeler had kept her.

Midge was hiding desperate insecurities under her mother hen personality. I often caught her whispering affirmations to herself. "You can do this, Margaret." "You are strong and capable." "You make a difference."

She also had debt problems and was being hounded by creditors.

And on it went for each employee of the office, and even those that worked for the cleaning service that came in at night. I watched. I listened. I learned.

I was trapped there for months and had nothing else to do.

I didn't know it then, of course, but this was the training ground for becoming a ghost detective. Because watching and listening are our main tools.

And I slowly started to see patterns. There was something linking Wheeler and Haley and Midge. They passed packages around and spoke cryptically about them.

About three weeks into my haunting, Midge handed a

package to Haley and said, "You'll get this delivered today."

It wasn't a question. It was the end of the day, Haley out of her scrubs and into jeans and a pink blouse, Midge behind the counter, rising briefly to hand the package over and then going back to the computer.

It was out of the blue. No context whatsoever. The manila envelope plain but with a sticky note on it with an address.

Haley nodded, studied the address and then crunched it up and put it in the recycling bin.

And that was it.

Something was going on.

I tried to follow Haley, but just couldn't leave. It's not like there was a barrier or anything, I just couldn't do it. I would get to the door and couldn't go any farther.

And while I wouldn't solve the mystery of that package, not until I was with Emily and investigating Haley's murder, it did change something in me.

First there was a brush with cynicism. Seeing people more clearly, seeing them vulnerable (which happened a lot more than I thought), seeing their weakness and foibles and how everyone was looking out for themselves made me like them a lot less, made the world a darker place for a while.

But then I watched more. Midge used those affirmations so she could hold the rest of the practice up. She was building up everyone all the time and no one was doing it for her, so she had to do it for herself.

I felt so bad about that.

And then I started seeing how everyone in that office, to a person, was struggling on one level or another. I mean, I knew I was a mess most of the time, but somehow my ego hadn't let it dawn on me that *everyone* was a mess most of the time.

And they were all grieving on one level or another.

Wheeler, although he was eager for the reins of the practice, found it to be very overwhelming. The buck was stopping with him and that meant so many mind-numbing decisions, from raises, to how to discipline late employees, to questions of taxes and what vendors to use. His usually bright face started to sag after a few weeks of this.

Haley was moody and I got to see bright flashes of anger.

"You okay?" Mary asked Haley one day. Haley was in the break room, her shoulders hunched, sipping on coffee and staring at the picture of Sun and me still hanging on the wall. The old grey metal cabinet had been replaced with a new black one. It still held the propofol and I still wanted it.

Mary was a big-boned blond with round cheeks and kind brown eyes.

Haley nodded. "I miss him," she said quietly.

Mary looked around, and seeing that they were alone, said, "It's not the same here without him. I can't stand it that they are going to change the name, take all his pictures down."

Haley turned, her eyes wide. "Not this one, I hope."

Mary shook her head and smiled ruefully. "Not while Midge works here."

I was glad to see the two of them getting along, having something of a conversation. And then silence descended as they both stared at that happy picture of Sun and me.

And then Mary sniffed, turned away, her shoulders gently shaking.

"I know," Haley said, taking Mary into her arms. "I miss him too. It's... I don't..."

And then they were both crying.

I almost didn't stay. I honestly can't tell you which is

worse. Watching people grieve for you or watching people who don't seem to care at all that you are gone.

But something drew me close and I floated over and heard the women whispering.

"Doctor Wheeler is…" Haley began. "I don't…"

Mary nodded and squeezed her. "He didn't… did he?"

My nonexistent heart seized up. How had I not seen it, that the lovely young Haley was just the type that Wheeler always seemed to be dating. Which always puzzled me how the stocky, head-shaven older man got all these younger women.

Haley pushed away for a moment, smoldering anger in her eyes. She shook her head. "Let him try something. I'll…" and then her shoulders slumped and the anger bled out of her and she was holding Mary again. "No. It's just… I miss Walter."

Mary nodded and I could see her face. Tears flowed freely out of her brown eyes and she bit her lip before saying, "I know. I do too. Walter… he was special. He was…" Wracking sobs took hold of her and I would have left if I could. I felt like I should. Like this intimacy was something I shouldn't be watching, but it was about me.

After the crying subsided, Haley whispered right in Mary's ear, so low that no one else but a ghost could hear. "Did you… did you love him?"

My mind raced as Mary took a big shuddering breath and nodded her head slowly.

Mary who had just had a baby. Mary who had been my assistant since the beginning. She was my first hire, even before Midge. She had been by my side for years. Had been my friend. Had talked to me about her struggling marriage and how she hoped the surprise pregnancy would bring them together. I felt genuine affection for her, but I had never imagined that…

"Oh, shit," Wheeler said, strolling into the room, his head shaking. "Let me guess. The Walter Anchor Fan Club is in session."

The women fled. Wheeler pulled something from the supply cabinet and left. But I stayed there, my mind reeling. How could I not have known?

―――――

PATIENCE IS A GHOST'S BEST FRIEND. SOMETIMES YOUR only friend. The patience to stay with someone until you get the clue you need to break the case. The patience to continue haunting your old practice until something changes and you can leave. The patience to get through the lonely times where there is literally nothing to do until you get to your next spectral interaction.

I think that my failures in life, my addictions and attempted recovery from them, prepared me for my afterlife.

The bardo, while tempting, never took me. It came calling every day I haunted the office, most strongly at night when I was alone, but I knew addictions and I knew what they felt like, and the bardo felt like the worst kind of addiction. One that promises everything and delivers nothing.

But knowing that Mary... that she...

I can't even type it yet. Let me rephrase.

Knowing how Mary felt, that I had missed it, completely. That if I had known how she felt I might have made different choices... I might have...

Well, let me continue being honest. Mary wasn't my type. And I say that in the most shame-filled way I can. She was a big woman of Germanic descent, while my ex-wife was a slim Hollywood actress of Korean descent.

Mary could never live up to Sun in my mind. I'm sure she knew it. I'm sure this is why she never made her feelings clear.

But what drove me to consider the siren's call of the bardo, as I stood in the supply room/break room during one of the last days of Hollywood Dental, was wondering what if I had known.

What if Mary had poured her heart out to me, confessed her feelings, and I had very gently told her that I did love her, but as a friend and as a trusted peer.

That wouldn't have been good for her, but it would have been good for my delicate, Hollywood-trained, very human ego. My life might have been different, my life might have been better knowing that I was still lovable. Maybe, if she had done it soon enough, I might never have tried the propofol in the first place.

And even though I had never heard the term bardo yet, didn't quite know what the whispered call that promised escape from all of this was, in that break room, after Mary had told Haley that she had loved me, as the activity of the office swirled around me, I finally gave in.

The call of the bardo was the call of the propofol or of the green felt of the poker table. It promised to take me away from this, from knowing this small thing that could have made a huge difference in my life. If I had known this small thing, I would still be alive.

It wasn't a question in my mind. I "knew" it.

The room started to fade as I started to fall. This was the one thing I couldn't stand. Mary, my sweet, hardworking friend Mary had... she had loved me. And I, a man who was sure he was unloved and unlovable, had missed it.

I would have fallen, then. I would have become one of

those clichéd moaning ghosts and forever haunted the practice, or worse yet, Mary, but Midge saved me.

She was closing up the office and stopped in the break room and stood right in front of me staring at the picture. Midge was short and I could see over her, and her attention caught my attention, the tendrils of it that were still left.

"Okay, Walter. We're done for the day here," she said it quickly and turned to go, but then her shoulders slumped and she turned back to the picture. She sighed, it was long and full of pain. "If I could leave, if I could quit this damn job, I would. It's just not the same without you. I miss you, hon. See you on Monday."

Of course Midge wasn't for the transformation to "Wheeler Dental." Of course she hated it. I had been in my head too much and convinced myself otherwise.

Even though the bardo was still there, still calling, even though it started to whisper to me in Sun's voice saying, "I'm here, Walter. I am waiting for you," I followed Midge.

I didn't think about it when we reached the door and I floated right through it after her. I didn't think about getting in her blue Prius but was suddenly sitting in the passenger's seat beside her.

Midge missed me. Midge must have known how Mary felt.

Thoughts of my murder were gone and I was no longer haunting the practice but haunting Midge.

Chapter Sixteen

EMILY WAS STARING AT ME. MY ANGER HAD BEEN replaced by surprise. I had forgotten about this exchange. I had forgotten that Mary loved me. I had wanted to forget it again.

So even with the clarity of my ghostly memory, I had managed to shove it down, to let it go, to forget it. Until Emily dragged me here and made me walk through it step by step.

And I hadn't told Emily. What I just wrote was all of it, but the version I told Emily I had edited slightly. In it the girls had grieved for me, but Haley hadn't asked Mary if she loved me. I hadn't almost fallen into the bardo before attaching to Midge.

I didn't mean to lie.

It just came out that way.

But I couldn't tell her. I couldn't speak it. I couldn't let that possibility become any more real. The possibility that Mary had been involved in my death.

See... I still can't go there. Mary with her strained

marriage and her post-partum depression. Maybe she had killed me to…

That's where it gets tricky. Yes, Mary had served in the military and had more medical training then a normal dental assistant. Yes, Mary knew all about my propofol problem and would have known how to deliver an overdose.

But… I couldn't imagine it. I couldn't accept it. I still can't.

Then, my mind went to her husband. A big man and also a former soldier. A violent man who had hit Mary. Maybe he did it. Maybe he knew of Mary's feelings and was jealous.

"What's going on, Walter?" Emily asked quietly, a strange look on her face, her lollipop the palest of yellows. She was worried.

We were in the storage room and I was pacing—well, more floating—not even very aware of it. My ghostly form was diffuse, not as bad as when I was a new ghost, but not normal for me anymore.

I focused on it, took some deep breaths, and tightened it up like Emily had taught me.

"It… it was hard to see them cry like that," I said.

Emily's eyes narrowed and the lollipop on her T-shirt snapped back to a cheerful red. She knew I was keeping something from her and had decided to hide her feelings from me. "I bet it was," she said slowly.

I felt a distance between us, one that felt decidedly dangerous. My afterlife worked only because of Emily. But I couldn't tell her about Mary. I couldn't think about her being involved. About her betraying me.

"I… I just need to finish this," I said.

Emily nodded warily and I continued.

Chapter Seventeen

I had been to Midge's house over the years. An old, squat house made out of cinder blocks. A plain rectangle with a garage on one end painted a cheery blue. A simple house with a roomy backyard surrounded by other old cinder-block houses in an older Tucson neighborhood.

I had been there for Thanksgiving and Christmas Eve dinners. I had been there for Fourth of July barbecues. I had been there after Hal's heart attack helping out.

I say all of this to make it clear that I knew Midge and her house. I had been there many times. But when she got home, pulled her Prius into the driveway, I was shocked.

The yard was unkempt, far past the need for mowing. The blue paint was starting to peel off the facia and the Christmas lights were still up all these months later.

"What's going on, Midge?" I asked from the passenger's seat. I didn't expect her to hear me. I spoke out of reflex.

Midge was just sitting there, staring at the garage door,

blinking too much, her chin quivering like she was barely able to hold back the tears.

I saw a motion out of the corner of my eye and turned. A young woman was rollerblading over the faded black of the road. She caught my eye and waved at me.

And then I noticed she was a little bit transparent, which was puzzling. A pickup came up from behind her and she didn't notice. I shouted and the truck ran her over and…

No. She was still there. She waved again and skated off.

It took a minute for my mind to engage and realize what I had just seen. She was like me. She was a ghost.

Of course there were other ghosts, I just hadn't seen them since I had spent my entire time dead in my office.

As I wound back our drive in my mind, I remembered seeing way more people at the park we drove by than I expected, considering the heat out there this time of year. Some of them had looked odd. A bit transparent. Maybe floating.

I didn't have time to ponder it because Midge was out of the car and heading towards the house. "You've got this, Margaret," she muttered. "You can handle this."

As she opened the door, I was wishing I was still at the office. As I haunted the place, I got to know its inhabitants in a different way. Was I ready to do that with Midge in her own home?

But it wasn't like I had a choice. I floated in with her and…

Well, nothing really. Midge put her keys in a blue ceramic bowl on a narrow table in the entryway, kicked her shoes off, and said, "Hal. I'm home."

The house looked the same. It was neat and clean with shades of blue dominating. The powder-blue shag carpet was way past the need for replacing, but it had been that way as long as I could remember.

"Honey," Midge called. "How was your day?"

I could hear the muffled sound of metal clanging and a soft curse. "He's in the garage," I said.

Midge walked through the small two-bedroom house and then went to the garage where Hal had the hood up on an old Chevy pickup truck. "How was your day, dear?" she asked.

Hal had buzzed-cut grey hair that had receded a good long way from his forehead. He had a barrel chest and thick arms, a faded tattoo of a hula girl on his forearm that he got in the Navy and Midge hated.

"Too damn hot," Hal growled. "Got the McLaren's deck finished, but the truck sounds funny."

Hal was a contractor. After his heart attack he had scaled back and started taking smaller, simpler jobs.

"Dinner's at six," Midge said cheerfully. "And we're supposed to Skype with Rachel tonight."

Hal grunted his ascent and Midge went into the kitchen and started making meatloaf. Rachel is their daughter, a lovely young woman getting her master's in psychology in California.

I felt strange being away from the office. I worried about the other ghosts, like a puppy seeing a big dog for the first time. There had to be more. What would happen the first time I came face to face with another ghost?

Midge cooked and their evening wound down and I began to relax. I hadn't seen any other ghosts. The house needed some maintenance, but nothing horrible was going on here. I watched their call with Rachel. I enjoyed watching TV with them, an episode of one of the many *Law and Order* shows. Normally TV shows other than Sun's weren't my thing, but after being stuck in my head (this is pretty much the literal state of a ghost) for so long, I was happy to be entertained.

And then Hal went to bed.

And then Midge changed.

"It's okay, Margaret," she said, her hands clasped as she rocked in the living room's rocking chair. "We'll find a way. We always find a way."

I had found it odd that she had stayed in her scrubs all evening. Well, not that odd. I had often done it, but I had always thought I was the only one. Scrubs were comfortable. In many ways they were a piece of my post-actor identity. And that piece of identity was important.

After Hal went to bed, I found out why Midge stayed in her scrubs. And it was odd.

Midge had five one-hundred-dollar bills tucked into her bra, like some high-price stripper. Except Midge was short and round and over fifty.

She pulled them from their hiding place with gritted teeth and a long sigh. She went deep into the cabinet under the right-angle bend of her kitchen counter and pulled out a metal lockbox. It wasn't locked, but I can't imagine this was an area that Hal explored. She put the five hundred-dollar bills with a growing stack of money.

"This is the way, Margaret," she whispered. "I know you hate it, but this is the only way."

That night, while Mother Midge slept, I just watched and thought and pondered.

HAUNTING MIDGE WAS BORING FOR THE MOST PART.

Midge worked. Midge came home. Midge passed strange envelopes to Haley that she got on her breaks when she walked in a nearby park.

Midge would go and sit awkwardly on a bench, trying desperately to look casual, she just looked ridiculous, her hands roaming around strangely as if she didn't know what to do with them. The woman was not built to be a spy. She would grab an envelope taped to the underside of the park bench and rush away. In the envelope would be money, a sticky note with an address, and another envelope that never got opened. This is where Midge got the hundred-dollar bills. Midge put them in the lockbox after Hal went to bed. Midge worried and talked to herself a lot.

Wheeler was involved with it too. Sometimes he would come back with the envelope and hand it off to Midge. Sometimes Midge delivered the envelopes herself after work. Sometimes she handed the envelope off to Wheeler or Haley.

Whoever got it didn't deliver it, and they never really talked about it. It was just a handoff. Wheeler and Midge kept the cash, Haley got to pad her timecard.

I was there with Midge for every moment of every day, and while it was apparent something strange was going on, I didn't know what it was.

Was this why I was killed?

Had I ever really known Midge? Had I ever really known anyone?

After weeks of this, I don't really know how long it was, I was a wispy mess floating after Midge as she got up, as she took a shower, every time she went to the bathroom, to the office, her feet pounding across the carpeted floors, back home, making dinner, watching TV.

I remember her gathering all those hundred-dollar bills one night after Hal went to bed. She went to the little rolltop desk they had in the living room, got an envelope out, and counted all the money and added it up. She then took a stack of unpaid bills, including overdue mortgage statements, and added those up.

Sweat beaded on her forehead and her round face flushed red.

It was over twenty thousand dollars and I had to wonder how long they had been at this. Right under my nose.

Hal wasn't making the money he used to before the heart attack. Their bills had stacked up. Hal's medical bills. Rachel's college. And all the normal stuff. Midge managed the household funds and hadn't told him how bad it was.

"You did it, Margaret," she said with a satisfied nod. "You did it."

She stuffed all of it into her purse and in the morning, which was a Friday when the office was closed, she took it to the bank. She had cashier's checks made out in the amount of all her bills. She took them to the post office and filled out all the paperwork to send them registered mail. Her hands trembling as she filled out form after form.

"No more," she said when she got back to her car and started it, turning the air conditioner on high, the breeze it created playing with her shoulder-length brown and grey hair. "No more."

And then it was over. Or, at least it seemed to be.

Midge was lighter, happier, but the drone of her days as I was dragged along after her became so dull. Preparing and eating food and eliminating food. Taking care of the house and laundry. Work and shopping. A brief bit of TV in the evening with her husband. Days off where Midge was just as busy, but in the house instead of the office, her feet pounding over those carpeted floors.

Soon I started to filter it all out. I could make no sense of it. The packages. The money. All three of them delivering them. If I had been able to follow Haley, maybe I would have figured something out. But now that it was all over, there were no more clues.

I saw Doctor Wheeler, of course. He was happy. He was cheerful. His plans to take over my office taking shape. He was dating women far too young for him and going through them rapidly.

Every once in a while, I got up the energy to try to hurt him, wrapping my ghostly hands around his throat, but all I ever did was make him cough.

I was a decidedly inept ghost.

And then I just gave up and started filtering it all out. And the more I filtered out reality, the wispier I became. It was hard to tell that I was wearing scrubs anymore, my look edging towards that of a classic ghost, made of nothing more substantial than smoke.

I wasn't thinking about my murder. I wasn't pondering the mystery of Midge and the money. I could hear the bardo calling, promising me relief from all of this, but I didn't believe it. I wasn't quite here and I wasn't quite gone. Not yet.

It's not like you become a ghost and get it all figured out in a day. It's not like you tend to figure it out at all without some help. It's a bizarre experience. The bardo, filled with all your regrets, is waiting and much more tantalizing than facing the reality of your life and addressing your unfinished business. Or even more banal than that, the bardo is much more tantalizing than the boredom of watching the living and the endless treadmill they are on taking care of their biology.

Except as a new ghost you don't even know that you have unfinished business. You just don't know anything.

Without help, without a guide or a mentor, most ghosts fall into the bardo.

And I would have, but for the letter and Emily.

Midge found it in her mailbox one day. A plain white envelope with her address shakily written on it in blue.

She stood there in the heat blinking and staring at it like it was something dangerous.

There was no return address on the envelope.

There was no stamp.

Sweat formed at her hairline and her face flushed red. She grabbed it and shoved it under her scrubs and under her bra strap.

"Just breathe, Margaret," she whispered to herself. "Just breathe. You can do this."

Her use of affirmations had stopped after she got all her bills paid, so this woke me up a bit and I started paying attention.

She walked into the house and said a brief hello to Hal and her daughter Rachel who was visiting from school. They both stared at her as she whizzed by. This wasn't the kind of greeting they were used to.

She went to the bathroom, locked the door, and sat down on the toilet.

She opened the envelope with shaking hands. Inside on a plain white piece of paper written in blue in the same shaking script it said, "If you need to reach me again about your financial problems, drop a note at this address."

It was followed by an address that I knew was in a sketchy neighborhood.

Suddenly I wasn't so disengaged. I wasn't so gone. Here was something real. A clue. An address. A way to find out what all of the passing of envelopes and money with her and Haley and Wheeler was about. Maybe a way to find out who killed me.

Midge's hands shook as she slowly tore up the letter and flushed it down the toilet.

There was fear on her face, but guilt too. I felt a flash of anger, but I understood that circumstances had driven her to this, had made her do whatever it was she had been doing.

She was taking care of her household and her husband and her daughter.

Midge hiked down her scrub bottoms and went to the bathroom for real, her whole body still shaking.

My mind reeled. There was a lot of money here. Was this why I was killed? Was it because of what Midge and Haley and Wheeler were doing? Midge who was someone important to me. Midge who I loved and trusted. Midge who had done so much to make my life here as a dentist work as well as it had.

Had Midge done this to me? For money? So she could pay off her bills and keep her kid in college?

The empathy I had felt twisted back to anger and that twisted into a crushing depression.

I had failed as an actor. I had failed as a husband. I had failed as a dentist. What did any of this matter? My life had been a flop, who cares who killed me?

And then the bardo got loud and I was ready to be away from all this. I was ready to fall into the arms of addiction, to never come back.

The room faded and I could hear Sun laughing. I could see the scrubby hills outside of LA where that happy picture of Sun and I was taken, the one that hung in the storeroom of my dental practice.

"Come on, Walter," I could hear her saying, her voice distant but getting clearer. "Stop with the kissing. It's time to take a picture."

"But I like kissing you," I heard a distant me say. "It's all I want to do."

I knew it was a bait-and-switch, hearing those happy

voices. I knew it wasn't real. That it wouldn't last. I knew this thing was a worse deal than the propofol, but I just didn't care. I just needed to escape.

I was still in the bathroom aware of Midge shaking on the toilet, but I could also see the sun hanging in the clear blue sky above me, and I could smell the dry dust the breeze was kicking up at that shoot. The day was becoming real.

But then I heard another voice. A girl's voice. A little girl. She said, "Not cool, let the lady go to the bathroom in private. What kind of sicko are you?"

And then I wasn't in Southern California anymore and there was another person in the bathroom with Midge and me.

She was short, looking to be about four years old. She wore blue shorts and a white T-shirt with a large red lollipop printed on it. She had blond hair cascading around her round face in ringlets looking very much like Shirley Temple when she was a child actor back in the thirties.

I opened my mouth to speak and did a double take. Her feet weren't quite touching the ground and she was just a little bit transparent. She was a ghost but more substantial than any ghost I had seen. My mouth moved, but I couldn't speak. Sun's laughter faded from my consciousness and I missed it so much.

The little girl ghost put her balled up hands on her hips and said, "You heard me. Leave the lady alone. I mean it."

"I... What...?" I said, finally finding my voice.

"Christ on a stick, are you a bardo-brained perv or what?" she asked.

"Huh?" I said, not understanding what she was talking about. While I had been experiencing the bardo, I didn't

290

have a word for it, much less any idea what "bardo-brained" might mean.

"Did you die in here?" she asked, her voice getting loud like I was hard of hearing. "Are you going to spend the rest of eternity haunting people trying to relieve themselves?"

"No," I said, coming more into myself. "Of course not. I... I was murdered. She knows something, that letter she just read is a clue."

"Well then prove it," she said, turned on her heel, and walked through the bathroom door.

Something made me follow her. Part of it was that she was a different kind of a ghost, part of it was how articulate she was and how young she looked. She spoke with a bit of a lisp making her sound young, but her words were anything but.

I followed her into Midge's living room with its faded blue carpet and preponderance of blue knickknacks.

The girl squared her shoulders and turned to face me. "So, are you trying to be a gumshoe or something?"

I blinked. Not that it did me any good since I didn't have real eyes. I knew she was asking if I was a detective, the archaic slang adding to the mystery of her. "I just want to find out who killed me."

"And then what?" she asked, crossing her arms.

"I... well..." I hadn't thought that far.

She shook her head slowly, giving me a most disapproving look. "You don't know anything, do you?" She looked up and added, "Lord, why me? This fellow is so wet behind the ears he's about to drown." She sighed and looked back at me. "Come along. I guess you've won the lottery, big boy, because ole Emily here is going to show you the ropes."

"I need to stay here," I said. "I need to follow Midge. I need to find out who killed me."

She sighed again. "One-track mind. Can't say I mind that in a man, as long as the track his mind is on is one I like." She gave me a leering grin that was completely out of place on her young face with that lispy voice. "Look... What's your name?"

"Walter."

"Look, Walter. You stay here you will end up in the bardo, a lost cause, a waste of an afterlife. But if you really want to find your killer, come with me now. I'll teach you enough so you can be a proper ghost." With that she walked away from me, to the front door, and right through it.

Down the hall I heard the toilet flushing and then water running. Midge would be coming out. It might be interesting to find out how she acted toward her family.

But the girl ghost who didn't act like a girl said she would teach me. If I knew what the hell was going on, it might help. It might lead to my murderer.

I saw Midge come out of the bathroom and straighten her scrubs. Her lips were moving and I could hear her mumbled affirmations. "You did your best, Margaret. You did what you had to do. For Rachel. For Hal. No one got hurt. It's just another evening. You got this."

I could remember the address from the letter. I could go there any time. I didn't need Midge for that. She had paid off her bills and all the passing of envelopes had stopped at the office.

And then I heard Sun laughing again and could smell the dusty air and feel the sun from that long-ago shoot. The bardo was taunting me, tantalizing me.

But what I wanted wasn't here with Midge or back in the past with Sun. What I wanted was to go to that address and find out who killed me. What I needed was some help in figuring out this ghost thing.

The choice was clear, but it wasn't easy. I stood there, the moments ticking by until I had to move or else Midge would have walked right through me.

I took one step forward and then the next followed and I was outside the front door.

The little girl ghost was there, a wicked grin on her round face that was so out of sync with her apparent age. "Good choice, boy-o," she said. "My name is Emily and I died in 1931 of dysentery." She thrust out her hand.

I looked at it. I was a ghost. How could I shake hands?

"Come on," she said. "I don't bite… at least not that often. Take my hand, tell me your name and how you died."

"What…?" I asked.

"Death 101," Emily said. "You greet a new ghost by telling them your name and how you died. It's just good manners."

I nodded slowly, still trying to figure out how to actually shake hands.

"Come on…"

I put my hand in hers and… I felt something. The barest sense of touch as our hands joined. It surprised me, but in a good way. I had existed for all this time with just two senses, sight and sound, so touch was something of a revelation.

"My name is…" she prompted with a nod.

"My name is Walter Anchor and someone killed me by overdosing me with propofol and I'm going to find them."

She smiled. "Okay, okay. A bit more than asked for, but that was good." She let go of my hand and looked me up and down. "You may not be the brightest bulb but at least you're easy on the eyes."

My jaw hung there as I tried to process a four-year-old looking at me like she had just looked at me and with the lisp it sounded like "eathy on the eyeth." But then I remembered she said she had died in 1931 making her eighty years as a ghost. I could tell that this was going to be interesting.

"Can we go to that address?" I asked. "And look for clues?"

Emily narrowed her green eyes and looked at me closely. She leaned toward me and sniffed loudly. "Yeah... yeah... I can smell it. You were murdered, weren't you?"

"You can smell?" I asked. Probably not the most important question given what she had said, but I really missed smelling.

Her smooth brow furrowed. "Not literally, genius. I just have a sense about these things. And you..." She sniffed loudly again. "...something strange happened to you."

"Yeah," I said. "Someone stuck a goddamn needle in my arm and overdosed me."

"Language, young man!" she said, her eyes wide, stepping back from me and crossing her arms. "You will watch that language around me."

I was beginning to second-guess this decision. I mean, this strange little ghost clearly knew what she was doing, but maybe she was just too strange.

"Umm... sorry," I said.

She sighed. "Well, we best get you to the graveyard and start getting you a little less wet behind the ears."

"And then we'll go to the address?" I asked.

She nodded slowly. "Yes, mister one-track mind, we'll go to the address once you know how to be a ghost. But keep your panties on, it's going to take some time."

I looked back to Midge's plain cinder-block house with the peeling paint. I could hear the drone of the TV from inside as dusk deepened and the lights of the neighborhood flickered on.

My chest hurt and I looked down. My blue scrubs were clearly visible and I wasn't so wispy anymore. Why did my chest hurt? Maybe because since the moment I died I had been connected to the life I had been living. As a dentist at Hollywood Dental working with Midge and Haley and Mary and even Dr. Wheeler.

Emily, the little girl ghost who had been dead for decades was walking away, not looking back, but she was walking slowly. She was a complete unknown, but at least offered some hope for figuring out what happened to me, finding out who killed me.

I was so myopic then. I was a clueless new ghost. I wanted to find my murderer and then… I couldn't even conceive of something more than that. Emily was right, I did have a one-track mind.

Emily was halfway down the street and I still stood there looking back at the house, back at the past, and then looking toward the diminutive ghost and towards the future.

I chose the future.

"Wait!" I yelled and flew to Emily who was still walking.

She gave me a look like she had just eaten something sour. "Walk, Walter. Don't fly."

"What?" I asked. "Why wouldn't I want to fly?"

"Just do it," she growled.

So I did. There on Midge's street I tried to walk and… it wasn't easy. I had to think about every single movement. I had no muscles, so there was no muscle memory to guide me.

Emily was patient, slowly coaching me, and in about ten minutes I was doing a fairly scary impression of a human walking. My gait was rather spasmodic, my feet either not touching the pavement or landing inches below, but at least I was walking.

She grinned at me. "Feel better now, don't you?"

I nodded. Because I did. I felt more substantial. I felt more… real. And that one tiny lesson made it clear that I had no clue as to how to be a ghost.

As the night deepened, we kept walking, winding our way through quiet Tucson neighborhoods avoiding the living. My mind cleared and it felt kind of like a meditation.

"I've been thinking," Emily finally said.

I stopped and looked at her. Her mouth was slightly open and she looked like a kid anticipating Christmas morning and all the presents under the tree.

"I can sense murder, right?" she said. "It's how I found you in the bathroom watching that poor woman."

I nodded for her to continue. I really didn't want to talk about that part.

"I find new ghosts that way," she said, "and help them out when I can."

I didn't say anything, the wheels were clearly turning in her mind.

"And you want to be a gumshoe," she said.

"Well… I… I want to solve my own murder," I said slowly.

She nodded. "Yeah. So what if we do both? I find the murders and you solve them. I mean, you've got to learn a lot before we can even try it, but… you know…." her face lit up. "It might be a whole lotta fun."

Her smile was so bright I couldn't tell her that I didn't want to be a detective, that I just wanted to solve my own murder. I was a dentist, and before that an actor. I was not a detective.

But her joy was infectious so I said, "Yeah. That could be fun."

She clapped her hands and hopped up and down, her curls bouncing around her round face. She then got a very serious look on her face, stood up straight, and cleared her throat. "Listen up, everyone," she said to the quiet neighborhood with her lispy voice. "I want to introduce you to Walter Anchor, ghost detective!"

Epilogue

IT WAS DARK ON THE TUCSON STREET NOT FAR FROM
Midge's house. As my story had moved, Emily and I had
moved. From my old dental office to Midge's house, where
everyone was asleep, to the streets of the old neighborhood
with one-story cinder-block houses and large mature trees
where I first got to know Emily.

The strategy had been effective. The proximity
strengthening my already good ghostly memory.

I looked at Emily and she was staring at me, her
lollipop still a cheerful red, her face round and youthful,
but her expression mature and guarded.

She knew I had left something out.

Something important.

A lead on my cold case.

A clue I couldn't bear to follow.

And she had stopped reflecting her mood through her
lollipop T-shirt. She was anything but cheerful.

"You saved me, Emily," I said with my best smile. It's a
good smile too, it landed me some parts.

"I am glad, Walter," Emily said with a small nod and a grim tone that did not go with her words.

We were on the section of the street where she taught me to walk. Where she started turning me into a proper ghost. It made the distance between us feel even stranger, because even when we barely knew each other there was less distance.

"I don't know if I ever properly thanked you," I said, keeping up the faux cheerfulness. "I really am so grateful. I would be stuck in the bardo if not for you."

She nodded again and even with her bouncing curls it wasn't a happy thing. "I'm glad I could help you." She tried to smile, but she had too much four-year-old in her and it just looked like she was in pain.

"Look I—" I began.

"I think I—" Emily said at the same time.

"Go ahead," I said with a nod.

"I think I should go, Walter," she said. "I think I'm going to go pop over to Tokyo. It'll be light there. I need to take a walk by the ocean."

I blinked. Same reason you would have—surprise—but it did me no good. Just a stupid biological holdover. I don't have eyes. I can't close them. I had heard that Emily was into travel, and with her popping she could go wherever she wanted. But it was clear that I wasn't invited on this Tokyo stroll.

"Sure. Sure," I said. "Maybe I'll head over to the Midnight Circle. See what play Banquo and the ghosts are putting on."

Emily and I didn't know how to do this. How to talk and not mean what we were saying. How to have a rift between us.

"Sorry I dragged you through all of this," she said with a sheepish grin. "I was just so sure you'd find something."

Her eyebrow arched and it seemed like she was looking into me again, not at me.

She was giving me another chance to tell the truth, a chance to heal the rift before it became serious. I opened my mouth but couldn't find words. My actor's mask of cheerfulness fled me.

And then I felt my face tighten in anger. This was my death. My murder. My case. My secret to keep or to tell. I'm not perfect. I couldn't take this on right now. There was nothing wrong with me taking a step away from it. Giving me time to process it.

"Me too," I said, putting the smile back on my face.

Emily's frown deepened and she took a step down the street away from me.

"But…" I began and she stopped and turned, hope on her round face, her green eyes a little brighter. "I think I'll go to the SECI chamber instead," I continued. "Type all of this up. Maybe by going through it a second time, I'll find something."

Emily looked into me again. She was a skilled enough and wise enough ghost to know that I had found a clue and was just buying time. And she was enough of my friend to let me do that.

"That's a good idea," she said. "You do that. I'll talk to you soon."

With a small smile and a pop she was gone and I was left there alone on the quiet Tucson street wondering if Mary Paulson had killed me. Or her husband. Or both of them.

Or had I slipped after my very bad day and accidently overdosed?

Neither prospect was acceptable. Neither path led anywhere I wanted to go. Being murdered had been so important to my identity as a ghost, but if it had been

Mary, someone I truly cared about, that would further erode my perception of the life I had lived. And if I had done it myself... how was I to "live" with that?

If I tell Emily what I had remembered, we would be off investigating Mary and her husband. If I don't, the rift between us will grow.

Neither of these were acceptable.

I stared down the quiet street, the living sleeping, their porch lights on, their work done for the day. Not thinking about their lives, much less their afterlives.

I had no one to turn to, and without Emily, I felt so alone. I felt pulled west to Hollywood. I could go check on Sun. But what would I find? I could go to a casino and watch the living gamble, hoping that a bit of the old thrill would bleed through. I could go to the Midnight Circle and pretend everything was okay—I was a good enough actor for that, but I had no desire to be around other ghosts.

So I shrugged my shoulders and flew up into the night towards the SECI chamber. To write all of this for you.

What do you think I should do?

Because I still don't know.

A HOLLYWOOD KIND OF MURDER

A WALTER ANCHOR GHOST DETECTIVE STORY

ROBERT J. MCCARTER

AUTHOR OF *SHUFFLED OFF*

Chapter One

EMILY TOOK MY HAND AND DRAGGED ME AWAY FROM THE gathering ghosts. Her green eyes in her young face were sparkling and I knew it could mean only one thing. Murder.

A smile played on her lips and her head slowly nodded, her tight blond curls bouncing around her round face. She guided me quickly around the granite gravestones and the ghosts, the noonday sun hanging in the sky above us. A breeze was rattling the leaves of the tall trees that watched over the graveyard and the murmur of ghostly conversation was a pleasant white noise.

Every night at midnight in our Tucson, Arizona, graveyard we ghosts gather and tell stories or put on plays. It is at midnight that the dead feel most alive. We gather to hold our loneliness at bay and to affirm our shared humanity despite our lack of biology.

But lately, we have started to gather at noon, when we feel the weakest and just assemble into groups and talk. It's not a formal gathering like the Midnight Circle, but a natural confluence of need.

The world is starting to believe in us ghosts and that has caused a spectrum of reactions from joy to revulsion, and there have been mumblings among some ghosts that maybe all of this communication with the other side, as ghosts like me write their stories, is not a good thing. That the living should not be concerning themselves with the dead. That we should remain silent and invisible and focus on what we are here to do, namely taking care of our unfinished business.

We are the earth-bound spirits. We all have unfinished business. My name is Walter Anchor and I have more than most. Solving my own murder for starters.

I glanced down at Emily, there was a wicked look on her face. She died when she was four years old, and looks it, but that was eighty-one years ago and she often acts like it.

She is this strange dichotomy, this mixture of youthful enthusiasm and world-weary wisdom. She can be like an excited child one moment and like a wicked old lady the next. You never know which Emily you are going to get.

"What's going on, Emily?" I asked.

Her eyebrows shot up and she jerked her finger to her lips like a librarian scolding a restless boy in a library and kept dragging me forth.

And then I noticed she wasn't wearing her usual blue shorts and white T-shirt with a big red lollipop on it. She always wore that outfit, unless it was Christmas when she wore an awful red and white sweater. Emily was wearing a plain black dress that went just past her little knees and had a black ribbon in her hair corralling the blond ringlets.

She was jerking me along, weaving us in and out of the ghosts who were staring at us. I shook my head and focused on keeping up with her, keeping my legs going and not bumping into any other ghosts.

I could have flown, but Emily wouldn't have liked that. It wasn't how we conducted ourselves at the graveyard. We did our best to look and act like we did when we were alive.

Emily had saved my afterlife. She was my best dead friend. And we were ghost detectives, solving murders together, so I felt like I could give her the benefit of the doubt here.

Besides, novelty is always welcome. Since ghosts don't have to spend all that time maintaining their bodies (food, sleep, washing, work, elimination) we have a lot of time on our hands.

"Is it a murder?" I whispered. With Emily it usually is —the girl just loves murder.

Her eyes widened and her lips pursed, so much so that it looked rather comical on her four-year-old face. I chuckled and let her drag me along.

And that chuckle was really needed. I had recently delved deeply into my past and had to confront some uncomfortable realities about how I died. About how fixated I had been on finding my murderer and had blocked out a suspect that might have either done it or been a catalyst. Someone close to me that I didn't want to believe would hurt me.

And I hadn't told Emily because she would want to investigate and I just couldn't face it.

Even though she looked like she was a little girl, Emily was a wise old ghost and she must have known I was holding something back. Things had gotten kind of tense between us. But this was playful and different, so I welcomed it.

"Maybe we should branch out," I said as she dragged me along, getting into the playful spirit of it. "You know, do some spying for the government. 'The case of the missing beryllium' or 'The spatiotemporal anomaly' or some such madness. No. I got it. Let's go to the International Space Station and help with some experiments. They could boost up one of the new smaller SECI chambers and we could chat with them all day."

The SECI chamber is a high-tech typewriter for ghosts that lets me tell you my stories. I know they are working on a version three which won't be a chamber at all, but kind of a really chunky laptop.

Now Emily was just looking mad, her forehead furrowed and her lips forming a pout so I shut up. She wasn't being *that* playful.

But I am a detective now, not an actor or a dentist like I was when I was alive, so I started detecting.

First the unusual clothing. She looked like she could be dressed for a wedding or a funeral or church in the long-sleeved black dress. Her feet were bare, but they were always bare. For a ghost, shoes don't serve a functional purpose, especially if you died at the age of four in 1931.

Next was her being so mysterious. Why drag me through the graveyard when she could have just grabbed my hand and popped me away? "Popping" is what we call it when a ghost instantly goes from one place to another. It's an advanced skill that not all ghosts can do.

Did she want all the other ghosts to see us? Did she want me to wonder? Was this driven by a playful four-year-old or a wily ghost over eighty years dead?

Our last case had resolved nicely, no loose ends, so it couldn't be that.

When we were well away from the other ghosts but still in the graveyard, she stopped and let go of my hand and looked me up and down. I was a dentist when I died, and having spent most of the last ten years of my life in scrubs, that's what my ghostly form looked like. After we solved our first case, the murder of Haley, a dental assistant that had worked at my practice, Emily had talked me into changing my ghostly appearance into something more appropriate to our chosen line of work in the afterlife.

So she was looking at my trench coat and fedora, which looked just like Humphrey Bogart's in *Casablanca*. It worked for Emily because of her age and this is how she thought a detective should look. It worked for me because I had tried to make a go of it as an actor and loved those old movies. Besides, this outfit has a definite noir feel to it and that reflects my view of this afterlife.

"Change into something more appropriate," Emily said, pointing at her black dress.

Now this is not an easy thing to do. It took a lot of practicing to go from scrubs to a trench coat and hold it steadily. But I am an actor and I found that I have some affinity for "costume" changes when the need arises. I can't always hold them for very long, but I can do it.

It's been very useful when we have interviewed ghosts for our cases. Being "dressed" in a familiar way is essential if you want to talk to a new ghost. They are easily spooked.

Yeah, I know. That joke was kinda lame, but I gotta try. Can't let all this afterlife stuff get too heavy. Not all the time, at least.

"Why?" I asked, crossing my arms. This was all fun and games, but a costume change was still work and I didn't have a clue what was going on.

"Because," she said with a twist of her mouth, in full-on defiant four-year-old mode. She crossed her arms to match mine and copied my rather stiff posture.

Like I said, things had gotten rather tense between us because of the secret I wasn't sharing and we weren't talking about.

I sighed and nodded my head, letting the fedora

dissolve away revealing my curly black hair. I didn't wear the hat all the time—being up on my head it's hard to know if I have it right. So that was easy.

I looked down at my trench coat and turned it from tan to black. A small change that I could manage easily. "There," I said.

Her arms still crossed, she shook her head. I could do better and she knew it.

This wasn't fun anymore, but I felt guilty about how things were between us, so I kept going. I shortened the trench coat to just below my waist showing black slacks. I pulled in the lapels and made my tie plain and black.

It was a lot to hold, a lot to think about it, but I could maintain it as long as I didn't have to think about much else. Honestly, my little costume trick is linked to me being in a role. If I get into the head of being a butler, I can look like a butler. I had no role here, so it was hard and I was sticking close to my default form.

The trench coat was my default form since I had held it for so long, so if my concentration broke, it would pop back.

The coat wasn't quite right, it was still too baggy, the lapels still too big, but it wasn't half bad. I was rather pleased with the effort.

"I guess that'll do," Emily said, but she looked rather resigned.

I opened my mouth to ask her what was going on, but then closed it. She wasn't in the mood to tell me, but this whole outfit change led me to believe this was something important to her. Something personal. Something she didn't want to involve the rest of the graveyard in. Something sudden and unexpected.

She grabbed my arm and with a "pop" we were gone.

Chapter Two

THE DEAD ARE INTO ALL KINDS OF THINGS THAT HELP them pass the slow progression of time. Some spend their days at funerals, others spend their nights at clubs. Some are obsessed with weddings, others haunt hospitals and wait to greet the newly dead. Some know the TV schedule and which house usually has on the shows they like. Some haunt theatres and put on performances right next to the living and some are in the audience watching. Some travel and see the world.

Many end up haunting the ones they left behind or a place that was important to them and can't leave. I did both before Emily found me. And most of them end up trapped in a place filled with their own regrets we call the bardo. Emily saved me from the bardo.

No body means no job, no eating, no need for shelter, and nothing to buy. And all those things mean you have a lot of time. You have to fill it. The Midnight Circle is one way we ghosts do that. It's our social time where our community gathers.

And Emily, having been dead for over eighty years and

not fallen to the bardo, must have developed some great ways to pass the time. With us, though, it's always been solving murders.

It never occurred to me that Emily had another pastime. I mean, we weren't always together or anything. She was off doing things all the time. But I looked at her as the murder girl. The ghost that found me right before I fell into the bardo, who said she could smell murder even though ghosts have no sense of smell.

And that thought makes me feel guilty. Emily found me, trained me to be a proper ghost, helped me find something worth doing in this afterlife, and I didn't know nearly enough about her. Looking back and writing from where I am now, I feel terrible about this. I had let our relationship be all about me.

Sure, at the time, it felt like Emily was just dragging me from murder to murder because that was her thing, but I know better now. I know she was doing it for me, to keep me busy, to keep me from losing myself in my regrets and falling into the bardo. She was trying to help me do the thing I said I wanted to do the most. Find my own murderer. And here I was holding out on her.

But this is all hindsight. And this kind of rumination can quickly become unhealthy if you don't learn your lessons and move on—whether you are dead or alive.

And I'm here writing about all of this because I want to learn my lessons. I want to be a better ghost and a better friend. I want my afterlife to have purpose and meaning.

That day, though, Emily popped us to a funeral.

It was an open casket affair in a wood-paneled room that looked like it belonged to an upscale mortuary. The coffin was brightly polished wood with ostentatious flower arrangements flanking both sides. Behind it was a strip of stained glass with a prominent cross in the middle, bright light streaming in. The grieving widow was dressed all in black weeping in front of the coffin. She was in her fifties, but with a beautiful face, the crow's feet and laugh lines only serving to make her more appealing. She had blond hair and bright blue eyes.

I couldn't stop looking at her.

"Tony, Tony, Tony," she said, dabbing at her eyes carefully with her handkerchief. She had a thick Boston accent. "Why'd you go and do it? Why'd you take him on? You knew it would end with a bullet in your heart. You knew you'd leave me here alone. What? I wasn't pretty enough or young enough for you anymore?"

Something tickled at my brain about her. She was familiar. There was something about her little speech that was off, but I couldn't look away. In the casket was a handsome man in his sixties with a cleft chin and greying black hair dressed in a very expensive black suit, his skin grey.

The widow's upper lip trembled as she stared at the man, her face going from sad to angry in a heartbeat, her cheeks flushing red. "I knew about the affairs, Tony!" she spat. "Of course, I knew about the affairs. But I—"

"Cut!" another voice shouted and the woman stepped back and looked around, the anger draining from her lovely face. I looked around too.

We weren't in a funeral home, we were on a set, the façade of the funeral home only went back twelve feet. I looked down at Emily and she smiled, a wicked glint in her green eyes.

"Okay, Sheila," the voice said. It belonged to a thin man of about thirty with sandy blond hair and a lean athletic build. He had a beanie containing his hair and one of those annoying ultrashort beards. He looked like he belonged in Hollywood and I instantly disliked him. "That was perfect. We're going to pull the cameras in and do it all over and get some closeups."

Shelia… I did know the woman. She was Shelia Green and had been on a daytime soap for over twenty years. *The Wild and the Willing.*

I had worked with her on a play way back when. She was a diva if ever there was one.

My nonexistent stomach clenched. We were in Hollywood, where I had failed as an actor, where I had found the love of my life, married her, and then lost her before I went running back to Tucson to become a dentist.

I'd only been in Hollywood once since I died. I didn't want to be in Hollywood.

"What the hell are we doing here?" I asked Emily, my voice coming out harsher than I intended.

"Wait for it…" she said, her right eyebrow arched, her nose wiggling like she was sniffing something, completely oblivious to my tone. She was telling me that she "smelled" murder.

"How much longer, Alvin?" Shelia asked the young director, her Boston accent was gone and she looked bored. People swarmed the set and moved around equipment. They were the grips. This was the job I did after acting petered out and while I was working my way through college and dental school. "I've got a Pilates appointment I just can't miss."

"Not long," Alvin said with a smile. "We'll get you out of here on time."

Shelia rolled her eyes as soon as Alvin turned his back and leaned against the coffin. "You can move, you know," she said to the corpse. "Jesus Christ, Eddie, are you sleeping on the job?"

"Wait for it…" Emily whispered again.

The actress sighed and looked around at the organized

chaos. Lights were being moved, perched on tall stands. Cameras and cables and sound gear, too. At a glance it looked like madness, but each person knew what they were doing and moved swiftly and quietly. Time was money and the crew acted like it.

I liked being a grip. I liked still being in the action even if it did make my heart ache to always be on the wrong end of the camera.

Shelia turned back to the casket. "Enough, Eddie. Really!" She poked the man in the casket once and then twice and then she leaned close. "Eddie...?"

I glanced at Emily and she had on a huge thousand-watt smile. I looked back at the casket where Shelia was gently touching the man's face. "Oh... I.... You... your skin is cool." And then her voice rose into a shout. "Eddie! Oh my God, Eddie!"

Shelia Green screamed and all that activity stopped.

"He's dead?" I asked Emily quietly. Being back in Hollywood and popping onto a set that looked like a funeral home but was not with an actor that was really dead, not just faking it, was messing with my mind. I felt like I could barely think.

"He's dead," Emily repeated gleefully. "So dead."

"Murder?" I asked.

"Oh, yeah," she said.

I nodded and flew straight up. I had to get out of there. It was too much. Solving murders in Tucson was one thing, but here in the land of dreams where I had lost everything was... well, it was too much.

Chapter Three

EMILY DID THIS ONCE BEFORE. SHE FOUND A DEAD BRIDE alone in a bridal suite who looked a lot like my ex-wife. She thought I would love it. I lost it.

It's the nature of Emily, sometimes she miscalculates things like this. Badly. She was four when she died. She learned most all of what she knows about the living while dead. She learned by observing the living, not actually living.

And that is not to say that she isn't pretty shrewd about the human experience at times, it's just kind of hit and miss.

And this was a huge miss for me.

I paced the massive curved roof of the soundstage on the Warner Brothers lot. The hum of the Ventura Freeway was to the north of me and the bushy Mount Sinai rose to the east and the Hollywood hills to the south. The sky was clear, a washed-out blue, and the sun hung right above me, not providing me with the warmth or comfort it did when I was alive.

I had been on this lot. I had worked in the soundstage

below me on both sides of the camera. I had lived with my ex-wife Sun a few miles to the west of here.

I was upset, but I didn't fly away. I just paced. And I did it right. One step at a time, with intent. Trying to act as if I was living, like I had a body, trying to calm myself down and keep my ghostly form firm.

The roof was a dirty grey and showing its age. The grunge of it hiding the glossy illusions made right below it. Except the guy in the coffin was really dead. That was no illusion.

This was my old world and my new world colliding. The acting life I had, that I wanted so much, but couldn't keep. And the afterlife I was living with Emily trying to solve murders. Trying to solve my own murder.

It didn't take long, Emily popped in with a sheepish look on her face.

"What are we doing here, Emily?" I asked.

"What we always do, Walter," she said quietly. "Solving a murder."

"He had a heart attack," I snapped. "He died of natural causes." I just blurted it out, but it made sense. And could be right, ghosts are more than a little bit intuitive.

Emily pointed at her nose and shook her head. "No. I mean, he may have had a heart attack, but if so, someone helped him along."

I stopped and crossed my arms. "Why are we here, Emily? Here. Why not New York or Chicago or London. There are murders everywhere. Why are we *here?*"

Emily licked her lips and nodded, sitting down on the flat strip at the crest of the roof. She was back in her blue shorts and lollipop print T-shirt and I realized I was back in my trench coat. I had lost my focus and my form had reverted, but I didn't care.

I paced some more, and she just sat there placidly

looking out over the city. She was waiting for me to calm down, to sit down. I sighed and sat, but I was anything but calm.

"Ever since you wrote about your last day alive—" she began, taking my hand.

"I've been a miserable bastard," I finished.

She nodded.

Here it was, the moment where I should tell about the lead I had and we could pop off and go investigate my murder again, except... It was too much. I was tired of confronting my past and seeing that it wasn't really what I thought it was. It's like the life I thought I had was crumbling, eroding away every time I looked, and soon it would be nothing that I would even want to remember. For me hindsight and all that twenty-twenty business was just a bitch.

"I'm sorry, Emily," I said. "I... It was a lot harder than I thought reliving all of that."

She nodded and squeezed my hand. She did it right so I felt that ghostly, barely-there sense of touch you can experience as a ghost. "I bet. But I know you aren't telling me something."

I opened up my mouth to speak, but she held up her hand.

"And you get to have your secrets," she continued. "I've got secrets, Walter. Things about my past I'll probably never tell anyone. It's okay. But..." She trailed off, staring up at the pale blue sky and then her green eyes found mine and her round face pulled down into a frown.

It was times like this that I wished Emily looked her age, that it was an old woman sitting across from me. As much time as I've spent with her and as well as I know her, when I look at her my mind still tells me she's a kid.

She shook her head as if clearing her thoughts and

changed her tact. "I think you should stay here, Walter. This was your dream. This was what you wanted. You may not be alive anymore, but you can stay here, you can investigate that death." She nodded down to the roof and the set below us. "You can find a way to do something useful here."

I tried to gather my thoughts. Staying here didn't feel right to me. And I was so curious as to what she had been about to tell me with that "but" and how we all have secrets.

"I know you think I goofed in bringing you here," she said, standing up and brushing her shorts off. The gesture was a lot like Emily. It was a normal thing to do, but only if you had a body and sitting on a roof could actually get you dirty. Emily maintained the illusion of being alive because it helps you feel stable as a ghost. But she went the extra mile with it. Maybe that's one of the reasons why she's managed to be dead for so long and has not fallen into the bardo.

"I didn't goof," she said, standing up straight, her head just above mine since I was still sitting. "I didn't. Looking at your past really socked you, but good. Like a hard smack to the kisser. But you were looking at the past you didn't want, the dentist. Maybe you are meant to be here, a ghost among the actors. You could solve murders or... I don't know... start a gossip column telling all the secrets of the stars, or... something."

She leaned down so we were eye to eye, her green eyes intense. "I just want you to be happy, Walter. Maybe you can find a way to be happy here."

She stood, gave me a wistful smile, and with a "pop" was gone.

Chapter Four

THE SET WAS CHAOS, MORE CHAOTIC THAN ITS USUAL norm, and that was saying something.

Shelia Green was crying as she hauntingly told the police about finding the body, her hand shaking as she pointed back to the set and the coffin. She made it sound like this was the worst thing that had ever happened to her, but I wasn't sure I was buying it.

What I was sure of is that there was some acting involved. Her emotional display was being manipulated, but I couldn't tell how. I was a good enough actor, had done it myself enough, that I could tell she was acting. Now, someone like Meryl Streep, forget it, I would never know. But Shelia Green, yeah, I could tell she was faking this to some degree.

Two paramedics had pulled the corpse out of the coffin, but they were moving slow since there wasn't a life to save. Blue uniformed security guards were doing crowd control, shooing away curious cast and crew. And I hovered over it all. Watching. Listening.

Not because I wanted to. Not because I thought there

was an afterlife for me in Hollywood, but because… Well, I don't really know why.

After Emily popped away, I sat on the roof, my mind not in gear. I was half convinced Emily knew exactly what I was keeping from her. I mean, she got that the end of my life in Tucson had been a failure and it had become more of a failure by going back and remembering it all and reliving it all.

Why didn't I want to follow the lead and see if I could find my murderer? Why? I was scared of confronting more of the reality of my life. Terrified, actually, to see it any clearer. What kind of coward was I?

My life was a shambles those years as a dentist. The gambling problem. The propofol problem. The not moving on from my ex-wife problem. But it was the work that got me through my days. I genuinely liked dentistry. I liked working with my staff—even though there were illegal activities and so much other stuff going on right under my nose that I was clueless about.

And that was why I was hovering over the set, watching the humans swirl, listening to the combined cacophony of all the voices as I hovered above them. I enjoyed my work in the afterlife too. Sure, I would be grumpy every time Emily dragged me away and presented me with a new corpse and a new mystery, but I did like solving cases. Just like with dentistry, it felt like I was doing something good, doing something important.

The clue I found reliving my last day and the haunting of my dental practice was a person. Someone close to me. Someone that might have murdered me or been catalytic in my murder. That was the reality that I couldn't face. That someone I cared about could have done it.

And, yes, I've been a detective long enough to know that is how it usually goes. Most murders are done by someone the victim knows. But that is a dry fact. Facing that reality was something I wasn't ready for.

"Oh no. Oh hell no!" a voice close to me said.

I looked around and found another ghost floating near me. It was a plump woman with bright red hair and brighter lipstick. She had glasses hanging from a chain around her neck and wore a blue pants suit.

"Get on out of here," she said, making a shooing motion with her hands. I noticed that the fingernails were also a bright red. "Darla doesn't need any help. This is my crime scene. My case. Get your trench-coated ass outta my soundstage."

She had red high heels on with her business attire which just struck me as funny given we were floating twenty feet above the floor.

"Hi," I said, extending my hand. "My name is Walter Anchor and I died when someone overdosed me with propofol."

It was the ritual, how a ghost greeted another ghost back in Tucson with our name and how we died. I had done it many times, but this time it felt strange. I wasn't in Tucson and this ghost didn't seem to care.

"I know who you are," she said. "Darla was a big reader when she was alive. Darla read through all your cases, you and the little one that looks like Shirley Temple but is a wicked old thing. But you just go now. This here is my case. I don't need no Walter Anchor to help me out. I don't need no schooling from you."

She flapped her hands at me and my jaw just dropped.

She knew who I was. She didn't want me here. And how did she know about the murder? I looked at the scene below, all the emergency personnel, and saw a policeman on his radio. She had probably been somewhere listening to the police band.

She was glaring at me, her sharp blue eyes embedded in her round face. "Cat got your tongue?" she asked. "Big, strong man afraid of Darla? You run out of murders in Arizona?"

I just stared. I mean, the afterlife has all sorts, but I had never met a big, red-headed, high-heeled woman that speaks of herself in the third person and seems to care more about securing her territory than actually investigating the murder.

I nodded slowly and pointed down at the sniffling Shelia Green. "If this was a murder, I would look into her." Darla opened her mouth to speak, but I held up my hand and stopped her just like Emily had just done with me. "I've worked with her, and right now she's acting. Those tears aren't real." I turned and pointed at the corpse. "The paramedics suspect a heart attack, but Emily was sure this was a murder. Maybe he was poisoned so it will look like a heart attack. If you have anyone that helps you, I would have someone stick with the body so you can get those details."

I smiled at her, as genuinely as my acting skill would allow, and floated up towards the roof. "Nice meeting you, Darla," I called back. "Good luck solving the murder."

Chapter Five

THE TRUTH IS, I WAS FINE WITH SOMEONE ELSE
investigating the murder, if that's what it was. It seemed all
too Hollywood to me. An actor found dead in a coffin
while filming a funeral scene. People could say, "Well, at
least he died with his boots on, doing what he loved."

But I didn't fly east back to Tucson when I got outside.
I looked over the rows of huge soundstages with their
humped roofs and over to Stars Hollow, the bucolic town
square just to the east, and New York Street not far from it,
and the iconic Warner Brothers water tower.

This was where the living made illusions seem real.
This was where I had hoped to spend my life working. And
then it hit me, this combination of excitement and fear
right in the gut. My ex-wife Sun might be here. Right now.
Today. Her police procedural drama was set in LA, and
they sometimes shot on this set.

Sun and I had reconciled, as much as the living and the
dead can, after the case with the ghost bride. I had written
her a few times via the SECI chamber, but I hadn't seen
her again.

There was a lot about the Hollywood life out here that I hated. The constant competition and backstabbing, the vast gulf between the haves and the have-nots, the homeless people and the drug use, the constant traffic. But there was one thing out here I could never get enough of. Sun.

I flew, and I flew fast through the soundstages and I quickly found one of their sets, the interior of a police station, the detectives' room with cramped desks and one of them with a name plate that said "Melissa Lee." The lights were off and it was nearly pitch black, but that doesn't matter to a ghost.

I had been on set with Sun before. We met when she was in an orange juice commercial and I was working on the crew. But I had never been on the set of her TV show, never seen her working since she hit it big.

I sat in the chair behind her beat-up metal desk and looked slowly around the room. I had seen every episode of her show. I had found a man in Tucson that watched it religiously, even the reruns, and would show up there on Thursday nights and watch it with him.

So I knew this room well. The whiteboard they were always putting pictures of their suspects on and drawing theories. The narrow table with the coffeepot and refrigerator below it where they would have crucial conversations to move the plot forward. The stained beige walls that looked like they hadn't been painted in decades. The grubby linoleum floor where Melissa Lee nearly bled out the time the gang took over the precinct.

But my view now was of a room without a roof and with only three sides. The illusion of this being a real room with real detectives was quickly eroding. I mean, I used to work in rooms like this, I know how the Hollywood sausage is made. I know the realities of making illusions seem real. And still it bothered me.

Of course, I saw Sun every time I saw Melissa Lee, but after seven seasons, the character was a different person in my mind than the actress.

When I flew down here, I had thought it would be fun to see Sun work, but I turned to go, no longer wanting to erode any more of my illusions. I didn't want to follow the lead to my murderer, which involved someone close to me, and I didn't want to see Sun dressed like Melissa Lee and out of character.

I had shattered enough illusions lately. I needed a break.

I got up and walked out of the set and saw the new ghost, Darla, standing in front of a director's chair.

She had a sheepish look on her face, her red lips pursed. She held out her hand. "I'm sorry I was such an ass over there," she said, nodding towards the other sound-stage. "I'm new to this and… well… I was just intimidated. You're *the* Walter Anchor."

Now there's some irony for you. I appear to be more famous as a ghost detective than I was as an actor. "Not a problem," I said, trying to put on my best boyish grin. "This is your case."

"I'm not good at apologies," she said, "but I could sure use a hand."

I smiled and nodded. A distraction was just what I needed and I really didn't care much what it was.

Chapter Six

DARLA ASSIGNED ME CORPSE DUTY. I WAS USED TO running the show and this was the kind of thing I would hand off to one of Anchor's Irregulars, like Blinky or Fredrick. I would let them tag along and learn from the medical examiner and then come report to me.

After we flew out of the soundstage and were hovering above the one that Emily popped us to, Darla pointed below to the paramedics wheeling the body to the ambulance. "You stick with the stiff, like you said. Okay? Darla will follow the hoity-toity actress."

I just stared at her.

"Please," she added and smiled. She looked a lot nicer when she smiled.

I nodded. If Emily was here, she'd laugh at me and say this was "bassakwards." But when I had been working in Hollywood, I had spent a lot more time behind the camera than in front of it, so it was no big deal. Maybe Emily was right, and this was what I needed. To be doing something useful, but maybe it would be better to do it here in Hollywood and to have less responsibility.

"Sure," I said with a smile I actually meant. "This is your case, Darla. I'm happy to help."

She was taking a deep breath to argue with me and then her eyes got wide. "Really?" she asked.

I shrugged. "Yeah. Really. I bet you could teach me a thing or two."

She blinked and then stared at me hard, her blue eyes drilling into me. Maybe I had laid it on too thick.

"It's been a bad few weeks," I said with a sigh. "I welcome the distraction."

She smiled and nodded knowingly, and I flew down just in time to go in the ambulance with the corpse. Not much to see, he was zipped into a black body bag. The two paramedics, both young men, looked bored and chatted about fantasy football as the ambulance driver headed us toward the morgue.

Ghosts have shuffled off their biology and that changes a lot of things. No need for food or water or a bathroom break, and that can make you really patient. Except you know how your mind can just go crazy sometimes? Well, as a ghost you don't have any of that biology to interrupt your mind, so it can go really crazy.

The dead are great at physical patience, but not necessarily mental patience.

Which is to say, I didn't pay much attention to what was going on. I hovered just inside the roof of the ambulance, my mind spinning away.

About my past and my potential murderer. After I died, I discovered that my long-time dental assistant Mary Paulson had a huge crush on me. She also had a struggling marriage and a new baby and was devastated by my death. She, or her husband, had motive. Mary could have done it to try to preserve her marriage and her new family. Her husband could have done it in a fit of jealousy.

Not pretty, but the motivations for murder are never pretty.

That was the lead I couldn't bear to follow. And it was embarrassing in many ways, because even with my excellent ghostly memory, I had blocked it out and focused on the odd goings on at the office which led to my first case but had nothing to do with my murder.

I had loved Mary, but like a friend. I had relied on her every day at work. I just couldn't bear the thought of her being a part of my death. I couldn't handle the reality of my life being even less than I thought it was.

It's not only Hollywood that manufactures the illusions we consume.

And then there was Emily and the friction between us because I hadn't shared this with her. So much so, that she had thought I was pining for my Hollywood life and hunted for a murder out here for me to investigate.

My mind raced as the ambulance navigated the busy streets of LA and got us to the morgue where the body was unloaded, wheeled in, and transferred to a stainless-steel table.

I wasn't doing a very good job for Darla. I should have been listening carefully. You never know how these mysteries are going to twist on you—but the good ones usually do.

Once in the morgue, I remembered the actor's name. It was Edward Lincoln. He had also been on *The Wild and the Willing* for a few decades. I didn't watch the show, but I don't think this was the first time his character had died on it, but it definitely would be the last.

The morgue was pretty standard, in the basement of the building, short windows at the tops of the wall letting in some natural light. There was the obligatory wall of stainless-steel doors that held refrigerated corpses, two stainless-steel tables, sinks, and cabinets full of medical equipment.

After an hour, a young man with freckles and curly reddish-brown hair came in. He had "Dr. Tomas" embroidered on his white lab coat.

Okay, time for the autopsy, this was going to get good now. But that is not what happened. He undressed the body, examined it, drew some blood, shoved a thermometer in Lincoln's liver to gauge the time of death, and shoved him into one of the drawers.

With a yawn and a glance at his watch, he closed up the morgue and left, taking the blood with him.

It was late afternoon. I doubted that murder was even suspected. Nothing was going to happen until the morning, but I couldn't be sure of that. I had to stay here, watch the body, and stew in my own dilemma overnight.

That's a lot of dilemma stewing. I groaned and regretted agreeing to help Darla. She sure hadn't done me any favors by putting me on morgue duty.

And, yes, I had done that many times with Anchor's Irregulars, the ghosts that help us out with cases back in Tucson. A ghost who goes by Blinky often did it. He claimed to love it, but as I experienced it, I had to wonder if he really did. Maybe I should mix things up more with the team.

But I didn't have a team. I was alone working with a new strange ghost with nothing to do but stew.

So that's what I did.

Chapter Seven

THE HOURS SLOWLY TICKED AWAY AS THE SUN SET outside and I just paced the linoleum floor of the morgue.

My choice was to hang out in an empty morgue or...

Or what?

I could leave and go try to find Emily. It would take me a few hours to fly back to Tucson, but that sounded a whole lot more pleasant than my other choice.

Except I'm not built that way. It's probably why I've turned out to be a decent detective. Mysteries seem to infect me, like a virus, and I just have to know.

Even if I couldn't write my stories and get the authorities the facts they need to make arrests, I think I would still do it.

When I was alive, I finished plenty of mediocre books just because I had to know what the ending was. The same goes for TV shows. I get hooked and I can't step away.

It's like the external puzzle gets internalized and I'm incomplete until it is solved. If the mystery, once it infects me, is like a virus, drilling into my cells and changing me, then solving the mystery is the only cure, the only way to make me better.

And, yes, I am the guy that was addicted to gambling and propofol when I was alive, and now I am addicted to solving mysteries. My body is gone, but much remains the same.

I paced the bland off-white floor of the morgue pondering all of this.

Morning takes a long time to get here for a ghost alone in a morgue. After an hour of pacing, I was wishing that Edward Lincoln had some unfinished business and his soul would separate from his body and his ghost could tell me how he died.

If he knew, that is. Take it from me, just because you are a ghost, it doesn't mean you know how it all ended.

After another hour, I poked my head in all the corpse drawers and found a young man and an old woman. I was soon wishing either one of them would have ghosts attached. While dealing with brand-new ghosts is rarely easy and never fun, I was that bored.

After another hour, my mind fell back to wondering about Mary Paulson and her husband. About what happened my last night alive during the bits of it I can't remember because of the propofol I was overdosed with.

After the sun set and the city started to quiet, I began to doubt myself more and more. Despite Emily's insistence that I was murdered, what if it had just been an accidental overdose? What if I had done this to myself?

I've built my afterlife on the idea that I was murdered. If I wasn't... well, that's the kind of thing that can send a ghost careening toward the bardo.

And as I contemplated it, as I paced in the dark morgue, I finally understood why I hadn't told Emily about it. Telling her would lead us to investigate Mary and her husband. This long past my death, it would be hard to find anything, but ghosts can be patient.

The result of the investigation, which would likely take a long time, months even, would be one of three things.

If Mary killed me, it would be a betrayal of someone close to me, someone I cared about.

If it was her jealous husband, then that would kinda be on me for not seeing how Mary felt, not dealing with it appropriately, and not being a good friend to Mary who had confided in me how her and her husband fought. How he sometimes hit her.

And if we found nothing, then the only logical conclusion would be that I had done this to myself.

As I paced, I discarded the jealous husband theory. He would have to know about propofol and how to administer an injection. He was a former soldier and a construction worker, so that made no sense.

That left either Mary did it or I did it, and neither was acceptable.

I know, I know, you're probably thinking, "Suck it up, Walter. Face the reality and deal with it." Well… maybe you are not saying it to me, but as I type this, I am yelling it at my past self. At the top of my non-existent lungs.

Except I couldn't face it. Even though I'm dead, I'm still human, and there are just some things I can't deal with.

All of this is to say that it was a very long night, and when in the morning a middle-aged woman walked in the door, I was never so happy in my life to witness an autopsy.

UNLIKE A WELL-DONE TV SHOW, THE DAY-TO-DAY LIFE of a medical examiner involves a lot of paperwork, a lot of safety protocols when you are dealing with human tissue, and a lot of slow, methodical work.

That's why they always cut to the scene where the intelligent but quirky medical examiner delivers just the facts needed to the diligent detectives.

But for me, after the night I had had, I was happy for the paperwork and the slow prep and the safety measures. But I'll do you the favor of cutting to the crucial bits.

Dr. Prescott was a thin woman approaching sixty, with long black hair streaked with grey pulled into a ponytail, dressed in pale pink scrubs and a white lab coat. She was methodical, but efficient, pulling more tissues samples early on and sending them off to the lab.

She was assisted by a short young woman with dark skin named Alison who appeared to be quite nervous through it all while she followed instructions, took notes, and helped pull Edward Lincoln apart a piece at a time.

I watched them moving the body from the drawer onto a table. Examining his skin for wounds. And then sawing through his sternum and exposing his organs.

Yeah, Edward Lincoln had died for the last time on *The Wild and the Willing*. A bone-saw ripping you open is an undeniable curtain call.

And while I won't give you all of the details, I loved it. I took a gross anatomy class in dental school where we carved up a smelly cadaver over the course of a semester, but this was something else entirely. It was fresh, it was fast, it was real.

Kind of made me wish I had gone to medical school, but that would have taken even longer than becoming a dentist.

So, Edward Lincoln did have what Prescott termed a "cardiac event" as I first guessed with Emily. He also had two stints and fairly clogged arteries. Not to mention his greying liver, and the damage to his lungs from decades of smoking.

Lincoln may have looked good on the outside, but he was in terrible shape under the hood.

The heart, though, was fascinating. The decaying heart had a grey section on the dark red from a previous myocardial infarction, a heart attack. But that is not what killed him, according to Dr. Prescott.

There were two wires in his heart, one that went to the right atrium and the other to the right ventricle. The tiny wires led through a vein to a roundish metal disk about an inch and a half across that had been implanted under his skin. A pacemaker.

She pulled it out and rinsed it off and showed it to her assistant, Alison.

"I'll bet you lunch that this did it," she said, a grim smile playing on her thin lips.

"How do you know?" Alison asked.

"He had this thing because his heart didn't always know how to beat right. Beyond the cholesterol blocking his arteries, he had electrical problems with his heart. If this stopped working, his heart rate could plummet and he would just pass out and…"

"Look like he was sleeping," Alison finished.

"Right. And he was an actor acting like a corpse when this happened. No one would have noticed."

"But…" Alison began, her gloved hands touching the device, "wouldn't that be a rare event? The batteries shouldn't just fail."

Prescott smiled a quirky smile that lit up her hazel eyes. "So is it a bet?"

Alison shook her head and smiled.

Chapter Eight

SO HERE IS SOMETHING I DIDN'T KNOW, BUT MODERN pacemakers can be accessed and adjusted wirelessly just like hearing aids.

There are security protocols and the equipment to do it is regulated, but maybe someone just turned off Edward Lincoln's heart while he lay there in that casket. Maybe someone murdered him via remote control.

This mystery was now in my blood, in my cells (even though I possessed neither). It was part of me. I had to see it through. I had to know if that was it and who did it.

In most cases, the murderer was someone close to the victim and I wasn't part of that, being stuck here with the dead guy. It was starting to itch at me like a mosquito bite. I wanted to investigate his life, find out if he was married, had any lovers on the side, a psychotic ex-wife or two, or disgruntled children. One of them that was technically inclined.

While my mind churned with all these details, Dr. Prescott called for a CSI technician and they got back to the autopsy, but I wasn't that interested in the details anymore. I knew how Edward Lincoln died, and I knew he was murdered.

I watched, just in case something else relevant came up, but I really needed Darla to come by, to check in and find out what I know, to take me to the frontlines of this case that had infected me so.

THE WHEELS MOVE SLOWLY IN A BUREAUCRACY, AND after the autopsy was finished, I stuck with Dr. Prescott as she drafted the report, went to lunch at a nearby restaurant with Alison, and then did another autopsy and drafted another report.

No technician came to look at the pacemaker. No diligent detectives came by to check on the results. No Darla. No other ghosts. And I found myself alone for another night in a dark morgue pacing over the plain industrial linoleum floor.

The truth is being a ghost detective in Hollywood isn't any more glamorous than being a ghost detective in Tucson. I can't interview witnesses. I can only follow and observe. It's slow, boring work. It can give you a lot of time to think, but I would usually have Emily with me and boredom was never a problem when she was in her four-year-old mode.

That night, I really missed her. I also came to grips with how dependent I had become on her. She had saved me. She had tutored me along as a ghost until I was functional. She had been with me for each murder I had been involved in solving.

And while it hurt, while part of me was angry at her for dumping me out here like this, I was also grateful for the clarity.

To put this night in perspective for the living, you know those nights when you lie awake and can't shut your mind off and it keeps going around and around but not getting anywhere? Well, that is just another night for a lot of ghosts.

It's why we gather at midnight at the graveyard and share stories or put on plays in the Midnight Circle. It's why we socialize a lot, because without it there is only your mind going in circles. And that night it was my mind spinning around all of this while I paced.

I thought of flying back to the graveyard for the Midnight Circle, but this case was so weird and had so infected me, I couldn't take the chance of missing something.

So I paced and I stewed and I paced and stewed some more. And then I couldn't stand doing that, so I started flying through the old building investigating every nook and cranny, every office, every lab, every storeroom.

And then I started flying around the outside of the building for some variety. Around and around, faster and faster. I don't have an inner ear anymore, so no issues with getting dizzy.

I swirled around the building under the sodium glow of the Los Angeles metro area, cars buzzing by on the I-5 all night long.

I made it a game. How fast could I go, how close could I come to the building without touching it. How sharply could I turn the corners.

A silly game, a childish game, but it was something to do. You living always have something to do because of your biology. It demands so much attention. The dead have to come up with other things to do.

The top of the building had steeply pitched roofs

A Hollywood Kind of Murder

coming together in an eight-sided construction that looked
something like a bell tower.

This building clearly had history. It was made of red
bricks and ornate, but not like a church. Maybe it was origi-
nally a courthouse or something. I was over five hundred laps
around the building—yes, I was counting and, yes, I was that
bored—when I saw a little girl with blond ringlets standing
on the tiptop of the tower. She was a tad transparent dressed
in blue shorts and a white T-shirt with a red lollipop print on
it, her hands on her hips, her lips pressed tightly together.

"Emily!" I yelled, flying to her.

I landed on the curved roof of the tower down a bit
from her so we were eye to eye.

She looked me up and down and did a tsk-tsk.

I looked and saw that my form was wispy, the ends of
my trench coat diffuse, my ghostly form a lot more transparent than hers.

A ghost's appearance often reflects their mental/emo-
tional state and I was a bit out of it. I took a deep ghostly
breath and stared into Emily's green eyes and calmed
myself like she taught me. Being dead, we don't actually
breathe, but acting like we are alive has a physical
analogue in the afterlife. So I calmed down. My form
firmed up. My trench coat came into focus.

Flying, while it can be a lot of fun, is not something the
living can do so it is not good afterlife hygiene. We don't
have bodies to maintain, but our ghostly forms take focus.

"Better," she said with a nod and a smile. It hadn't
taken me long. I wasn't the newbie ghost she had found
haunting my former dental office manager in her bathroom anymore.

"This case is fascinating," I said, the words rushing out.
"There's another ghost. Darla. She claimed the case and I

agreed to help out. I followed the dead guy, Edward Lincoln. They did the autopsy today. It's his pacemaker. I think someone turned it off and he died in that casket on the set. You were right, it is a murder. I'm so glad you are back. God, I really missed you, Emily. And I could really use your help finding Darla. She hasn't checked in on me. She knows about us, by the way. Read some of our cases while she was alive. I think it's why she's doing this. I…"

I finally stopped when I realized how long I had been babbling on and the frown on Emily's young, round face fully registered.

"What's wrong?" I asked. Something had to be wrong. This was the kind of weird case that Emily just lived for.

"I'm happy for you, Walter," she said, but her frown stayed in place.

My mind slipped for a moment trying to figure it out. This couldn't be the four-year-old Emily, she'd be excited about the gory details. This was the eighty-year-dead Emily watching her protégé excited about something after being so grumpy.

The color of the lollipop on her T-shirt changes color to reflect her mood. It's something of a mood ring and the lollipop had swirled into a deep, sad blue.

And then the picture clicked into place.

"I don't want to do this without you," I said.

Her smooth brow furrowed. "You don't?"

I shook my head. "No. I'm stuck here. I can't pop. I have no idea where Darla is. There's nothing to do and…"

Her eyes hardened and she crossed her arms in front of her, pursing her lips again, some angry red invading the blue of the lollipop.

I shook my head. My words were coming out too fast again. "It's you, Emily. I miss you. I miss doing this together," I said, trying to correct my mistake. I made it sound like I just needed her because I can't pop. "I miss your delight in the gory details. You would have loved this autopsy. You could actually see the damage on his heart from his previous myocardial infarction. And the liver... whew, I bet they could smell the alcohol. I..."

I looked away to the cars buzzing by on the highway. This wasn't what Emily needed to hear. I needed to treat her like my friend, like my teacher.

"I'm sorry I haven't told you what I found out when I wrote about my last day," I said. "I figured it out though, why I haven't said anything." There was a burger joint across the street, it must have been close to 2 a.m., but there were still cars lined up at the drive-through, the living needing to feed their biology and often not being choosy about what they shove in.

"I just can't face it, " I continued. "It's embarrassing, but I can't. It's more than I can handle. I want to tell you and I'm sure I'll tell you someday but..." I ended in a weak shrug, still not looking at my friend.

"Do you want to stay here?" she asked quietly.

I didn't know what level she was asking the question, but I guessed it wasn't just about this building, but this town. "This was never an easy town to live in," I said, looking back at her. "I mean, you were right, part of me loved it so much. It was my dream to be a working actor here. But now...? I think if I stayed here, I would end up haunting Sun and that wouldn't be fair to her."

It was true, I knew it was. I would fight it, hard, but I'd soon have a bad enough day and her house would be only a few minutes flight away and I would go there. I would see her and I would never want to leave. Sun would be my addiction, not gambling or propofol. I would lose myself again.

"But that is my old life," I said quietly. "You are my afterlife, Emily."

Emily nodded slowly, her eyes tearing up. There are some ghosts at the graveyard that are "romantic" and what I was professing here was not that kind of thing. Emily was my best dead friend. She was what made my afterlife worth living and I loved her.

But I didn't say any of that. I could feel my cheeks redden, echoing the actions of a biology long gone. And while I hadn't told her about Mary Paulson, at least I had told her why I wasn't telling her.

"Where's the stiff now?" she asked, a grin forming on her face, the lollipop on her T-shirt swirling into a happy red with bits of curious yellow. "You wanna show me and walk me through it?"

I nodded and smiled so big. Emily was back and I couldn't be happier. But that didn't mean this was going to be easy.

Chapter Nine

As soon as we got into the morgue and I pointed out the drawer that contained Edward Lincoln, Emily walked in. His corpse was covered in a sheet so we couldn't see the Frankenstein style stitching that held his chest together, but there was enough light leakage for her to see his face and hands and feet.

We stood there and I went over everything I knew. I told her about the autopsy in gruesome detail. I showed her the office where the pacemaker was sitting on the cheap wooden desk.

"Are you sure?" she asked, touching the roundish pace-maker with her ghostly finger. She couldn't actually touch it, of course. It's not at all easy for the dead to interact with the living, and even harder with inanimate objects.

"That's what Dr. Prescott said when she was explaining the device to her assistant," I said. "If they can be adjusted wirelessly, then it stands to reason that they can be turned off wirelessly."

Emily looked at me, her green eyes wide while she bit on her lip. "But... JJ did those things, he... Oh crap..."

She stared off into space for a moment and then grabbed my hand. "We have to go."

With a pop we were standing on top of a rock spire with the Grand Canyon all around us. The gibbous moon illuminated the formations and the layers of rock in ghostly shades of grey, like we were in the middle of a frothing sea at night made of rock. We were on top of one of the temples in the middle of the canyon, and we were not alone.

JJ Lynch was there staring off to the north. His form was firm, jeans and a long-sleeved black T-shirt, and he glowed with his own light. He was a ghost. The first ghost to use the SECI chamber and write about the afterlife. He turned, a smile on his boyishly handsome face.

"Emily. Walter," he said with a nod.

"Sorry to bother you, JJ," Emily said. "We are working on a case and have a quick question for you."

He smiled, but there was something a bit strained about it. I had heard that this was his retreat spot, where he came when he wanted to be alone. Maybe that reluctant smile was about that. "Ask away," he said.

Emily flapped her hand at me and said, "Tell him about the thingy and the remote control part that could... you know."

"The pacemaker?" I asked.

She nodded. "Tell him how it works."

"Okay..." I said, not quite sure where this was going. "It monitors your heart rate and when it gets too low, it kind of substitutes your body's own electrical signals to keep it beating. Modern pacemakers can be adjusted wirelessly."

Emily nodded, her curls bouncing. "How hard would it be for a ghost to fry one of those?"

I stood there blinking, my mind catching up to the leap

Emily had made. Maybe it wasn't shut off wirelessly, maybe a ghost did it. And if a ghost could do that… well, I didn't want to finish that thought.

"For me?" JJ asked with a grim smile.

Emily nodded.

"Not hard if the person wasn't moving," he said. "But if you've never messed with electricity?" He shrugged. "Well, that would take some doing."

When JJ was a new ghost haunting those responsible for his death, he had learned how to turn light switches on and off. He had eventually done a lot more than that. He knew more about manipulating electricity than any other ghost I had heard of.

"Thank you," Emily said. "I'm sorry to have disturbed you here."

"No problem," he said with a grin. "I hope you solve the case."

She took my hand, and my mind still reeling, she popped us back to the morgue's office. She pointed at the pacemaker. "So our suspect list just got a lot bigger. A whole lot bigger."

Chapter Ten

EMILY POPPED US TO DARLA. IT WAS THE NEXT MOVE. And now that I think back on it, it's a wonder how easily Emily and I just got back into the rhythm of things. Maybe her dumping me here had been a test. Maybe she had been desperate to shake me out of my depression. Maybe I don't fully understand the complexity of my best ghost friend who died when she was four but has existed for over eighty years as a ghost.

The last part is undoubtedly true, but what was clear is that Emily and Walter were back. The case had infected us both and we just had to know.

And yes, I can see that this "infection" I've been talking about sounds a lot like what happens when you shoot up with propofol or when a gambling addict sits down to a game of Texas Hold'em. And you could even say we were addicted to solving murders.

I will admit that there is clearly something in it for us, but unlike propofol and gambling (or alcohol or meth) we were doing something useful. We were bringing criminals to justice. We were adding to society, not taking away.

That is what makes it different than those other addictions.

And, yes, we were enjoying it.

So, Emily popped us to Darla.

But it wasn't what we expected.

Actually, given the woman I had met briefly, I didn't know what to expect, but this wasn't it.

She was immersed in a large, bubbling hot tub with Sheila Green, the actress that had been playing the grieving wife to her husband played by Edward Lincoln on *The Wild and the Willing*.

Shelia was nude, a glass of champagne in her hand, tears running down her face and her mascara running.

Darla was in the water next to her, her large ghostly form also looking nude as she drank and cried and carried on right next to Shelia Green.

My jaw hung open. I had never seen a naked ghost before, but I guess it could make sense. I appear to be wearing a long trench coat and a fedora because I practiced that after Emily and I solved our first murder—she thought it was befitting of the role. But before that, I had been in blue scrubs because that is what I identified with.

Maybe Darla had been a nudist. Maybe this was her default form.

It didn't really matter, though, it was just surprising. As was the crying and the drinking of faux champagne. Ghosts can't drink and the champagne glass had to be an extension of her ghostly form.

"I loved the narcissistic bastard," Shelia said, her voice slurred. The hot tub was in a lovely courtyard surrounded by tall trees and well-tended gardens. "To Eddie, my Eddie, the only Eddie I ever loved." She took a sip, tilting the glass too far and pouring champagne over her chest and she giggled.

"Darla loved the narcissistic bastard," Darla said, her voice matching that of Shelia Green. She took a sip from her glass, which now that I looked at it was empty. "To Eddie, my Eddie, the only Eddie Darla ever loved."

"Is that her?" Emily hissed, her chin jabbing out at Darla.

I nodded and sighed.

Shelia muttered more about Eddie and Darla copied it except this time I heard it differently. Darla was amplifying Shelia's tone, parodying it a little, almost like she was trying to reflect it back to the grieving woman.

"I don't think she knows what she's doing," Emily whispered.

"Darla heard that!" Darla said, rising up out of the water. She wasn't wet, of course, her red hair dry but wild around her, glasses still hanging around her neck by a chain.

I averted my gaze. No biology means that nudity doesn't hold a charge anymore, but it was just the way I was raised.

Darla floated out of the pool and stood in front of us. I stared at her bare feet on the courtyard's flagstone, her nails painted a bright red.

"Hi, I'm Emily," Emily said, extending her hand to Darla, "and I died in 1931 of dysentery."

"Darla knows who you are," she said, "and Darla will not be fooled by your cutesy appearance. Darla knows those adorable curls hide a wicked old woman."

In the hot tub, Shelia kept babbling on about Eddie and how much she loved him and how much she hated him, interspersed with drunken laughter and splashing.

I could feel Emily's mood change. Her lollipop edged into the dangerous spectrum of red and I saw her throw her shoulders back and straighten her spine. "Walter here has some interesting updates for you," Emily said, all business. "And we were wondering what you found in your investigation."

"Something wrong there, Mr. Anchor?" Darla asked me. "You got a problem with what a real woman looks like? Did you never find yourself in the presence of a goddess, or did you only spend your time with too-skinny-to-be-healthy actresses?"

Now she was making me mad and I was beginning to wonder if Darla had multiple personalities. The brash and insulting Darla I had first met that always spoke of herself in the third person, and the reasonable Darla that had asked for my help.

I raised my head and met her blue eyes. "Emily and I are going to leave now. When you find yourself wishing to have a civil discussion, we'll be on the roof of the Los Angeles County Morgue. I trust you know where that is."

I gave Darla my best smile and took Emily's hand.

"Darla doesn't need you two to solve this murder. Darla has it figured out, you know. So many suspects. So much motive and opportunity. You two will be sitting there waiting for Darla for a very long time. Darla is just fine without—"

Emily popped us away and I was very grateful.

Chapter Eleven

EMILY DID POP US BACK TO THE MORGUE, BUT WE DIDN'T
stay long. It was still dark and nothing would be happening
here until morning. After we had given a reasonable
amount of time for Darla to get sane and fly over here, she
popped us back to the soundstage on the Warner Brothers
lot where Edward Lincoln had died.

The main lights were all off, but there was still enough
light for us to see. The set was blocked with yellow police
tape but otherwise it was untouched. The cameras were
halfway moved to do the close-ups, cables snaking over the
floor, some of them not hooked up yet. The casket was
open in the middle of it all with the faux funeral home
walls behind it with unlit stained glass that looked eerie in
the darkness.

"What do you know about him?" Emily asked, nodding
toward the casket.

I shrugged. I mean, it was a reasonable question, I used
to be an actor, and even after I stopped, I worked in Hollywood for a while and paid attention. "He was in his late

sixties and had been on this show for over twenty years. He had been married and divorced three times, had four kids along the way. I had heard rumors he could be kinda grabby."

Emily started pacing back and forth in front of the ornate casket. We weren't here because we expected to find anything, we were here for a change of scenery that might help us think of something that would get us closer to solving this one.

She stopped and looked at me. "I guess we should start with the wives and then move on to the children."

I nodded.

"So," Emily began. "First wife. What was her name? What did she look like?"

If I had still been alive, I wouldn't have been able to tell you, but somehow our memories get better without all the flesh. I had absorbed a ton of Hollywood trivia that I could recall easily now that I was dead.

"Helen Lincoln," I said. "Former model with green eyes and long black hair. Played a Bond girl once and didn't act much after that. She had two children with Edward and they were married for eight years. They've been divorced for thirty-one years."

Emily took my hand and her face constricted in concentration. Emily was good at popping, but this was asking a lot. I summoned Helen Lincoln into my mind, visualized her as strongly as I could, but my memories of her appearance were from several decades ago.

It took a minute, but with a pop, we were gone.

HELLEN LINCOLN WAS LIVING IN NEW YORK CITY AND

was up for a sunrise breakfast. She was an elegant sixty-something with a few more pounds and wrinkles than her early days, but her black hair was still long and luxurious and her blue eyes were sharp and clear.

She had a corner apartment with floor-to-ceiling windows overlooking Central Park. She was alone dressed in a dark blue robe drinking coffee, eating papaya, and reading the paper.

"Does she look like a remote-control murderer?" I asked once we had searched the apartment—which was all high ceilings and abstract artwork and Zen elegance—and found nothing of interest.

Emily shrugged and stared as Hellen dug into the soft yellow/orange flesh of the papaya and took a delicate bite.

I so miss eating. The feel of a piece of steak in my mouth as I bite down, saliva flowing, the stomach grumbling happily. The simplest of things, the most basic thing, and yet so precious when you don't have it anymore.

The newspaper rattled as Hellen changed the page and took a quiet sip of coffee. She was calm and relaxed. She wasn't acting like the father of her children had just died, so either she didn't know or she was a psychopath and quite capable of murder.

"We have to stay, don't we?" I asked Emily.

She turned and smiled at me. "You have to stay, Walter. Tell me about the second wife and I'll go visit her."

I sighed and told her about Melany Tabor, who had been a director on *The Wild and the Willing* during Lincoln's early years there. She was a brunette with generous curves and a scar on her chin.

Emily popped away and I was left watching Hellen Lincoln eat breakfast while the sun rose over Central Park.

I had been to New York once, for a dental convention. I caught a show on Broadway and really enjoyed that, but I can't say that I understood the city. It was so dense, so many people when I was used to the urban sprawl of California and Arizona.

After breakfast, she took a shower so I wandered the sparsely furnished apartment and looked at all the family photos, a few of them featuring a young Edward Lincoln, many of them featuring their two children, a boy and a girl, now grown with children of their own. They were both tall with black hair like their parents and it looked like one of their grandchildren had recently gotten married.

This wasn't that big of a family, but if we had to follow each of them until we saw something that let us know if they were or weren't involved, this could take forever. We would need help.

There was something odd about the apartment. The generic artwork. The sparse furnishing. The single bedroom. The family pictures in frames on the furniture, none of them hanging on the wall. And then I remembered that I had read in *Variety* that Hellen liked doing a show on Broadway every few years.

That nearly ruled her out. She would have had to have flown to LA, somehow got the equipment to turn Edward Lincoln's heart off, and flown back without being noticed. On top of that, she would have had to know enough about the shooting schedule of Edward's soap opera to know when the funeral scene was being shot.

Not likely. Not likely at all.

I heard crying from the bedroom and found Hellen balled up on the floor slumped against her bed, a pale green towel wrapped around her wet body. She was staring at her phone, a text message that read, "Sorry to tell you this, doll, but Eddie is gone. Died on set like the bastard would have wanted."

There are lots of ways that people cry. The way they

cry in public is way different than the way they cry in private. Hellen didn't know I was there so what I was seeing wasn't a show. Her weeping was controlled but intense, tears running down her cheeks, but she wasn't making that much noise.

She clicked on the link that came with the text that sent her to some cheesy entertainment site and a silly article that had a picture of the set with the yellow police tape and another picture of Shelia Green talking to the police with tears running down her cheeks.

The article talked about Edward Lincoln, his acting career, his three wives and four children, his long stint on *The Wild and the Willing*. It was a simple article likely compiled from Lincoln's Wikipedia page. Just crappy click-bait designed to foist a few ads on the reader.

Hellen's demeanor changed when she saw Shelia Green. Her nostrils flared and her lips pursed. "Bitch," she said under her breath.

I stayed with her while she googled and cried and looked at old pictures of the two of them that she found on the internet. She did this for about half an hour before she shakily rose to her feet, put the phone down on the bedstand, and went back into the bathroom.

She was grieving her long-divorced husband and the father of her children. Add that to her being in New York and I didn't think she did it.

I gave her privacy and went back into the living room and watched Central Park wake up and wondered how my ex-wife Sun reacted when she got the news of my death, when they told her it was a suicide and that I had over-dosed on propofol.

Seeing Hellen Lincoln like that stirred something in me. I wasn't quite ready to go there, but I knew I would have to follow the clue I had to my own murder.

A death is never isolated, it affects those that love us. Maybe I wouldn't like the truth once I found it, but it would have the virtue of at least being the truth.

Chapter Twelve

"MELANY TABOR IS A BUST," EMILY SAID WHEN SHE popped back to me. Helen Lincoln was still in her bedroom and I was still watching New York wake up and pondering my own death and how it affected those that loved me.

While I waited, I stood here and stared at Central Park enough that I thought I almost understood New York City, at least a little bit. You had the tall buildings crowding it on all sides, full of people and their problems and their drama, but in the park, you had grass and trees and water and nature.

It was controlled and a bit contrived, but it was abundant nature and very accessible to people living on this island. So you could enjoy the people and the city and all the many activities, but you could easily escape if you wanted and be reminded of nature, smell fresh air, gaze at the water, walk for miles.

Arizona was full of open land, and cities like Tucson had some excellent parks, but the sprawl and the heat kept people away. How many people lived within a twenty-minute walk of Central Park? You couldn't match that in any western city.

Emily was standing quietly next to me staring at the park. Maybe sensing my mood. Maybe just enjoying the view.

She had dumped me in Hollywood and that had woken me up some, and now I had to wonder what it would be like to be a ghost in New York City. How many ghosts does a city like this have? And there must be plenty of murders to investigate, that's for sure.

I took a deep ghostly breath and softened my sense of vision as I looked at the tiny people below in the park. Not having eyes, it was different than you might think, but what I was trying to do was the equivalent of focusing on my peripheral vision.

I didn't focus on individual figures far below but on all of them that I could see moving in the park. Runners. Bikers. Walkers. The homeless starting their day.

And then I saw it. Some of them weren't moving quite normally. Some of them seemed a little brighter and a little bit transparent. A lot of them. Actually, most of them.

"Ghosts," I whispered. "There are so many ghosts."

The thought was both exciting and terrifying. So many dead. So much unfinished business. So many suffering in the bardo or haunting their loved ones or those they blamed for their deaths.

"Oh, yeah," Emily said. "City's like this, they're just rotten with ghosts."

"Where do they all go?" I asked. In Tucson we mostly called the graveyard home, but here? In a city this big and this old. Just do the math, there could be thousands and thousands of ghosts.

It made my experience in Tucson seem quaint.

"Everywhere," Emily said with a shrug. "There are

tons at the graveyards, lots on the roofs, others here and there. Not that different, just more in a smaller space. Same as the living."

I shook my head, shaking off the thought. Something to contemplate, but we had a strange murder to solve. I turned to Emily and focused on her, letting my view of the ghost-filled Central Park go.

"What did you find?" I asked.

Emily's face twisted into a sour configuration as if she had just bit into a lemon. "Alzheimer's. She's in a facility. Not pretty."

I stared at her, not sure what to say, my head still full of thoughts of the New York ghost population. Before I could come up with something, she asked, "What about this one?"

I shook my head. "She just found out and is grieving. For real."

Emily pursed her lips and nodded. "Third wife?"

"Amanda York," I said, staring back out at the city, my eyes now easily finding the ghosts, a few flying from a high-rise apartment down toward the park like they had just woken up and were going for their morning flight around the hood. "She was thirty-one years younger than him. Rumor has it she was pregnant when they got married, but the marriage only lasted a year or so. She was his assistant and that's how they met. I only read about it, so I'm not sure what she looks like."

Emily crossed her arms and sighed dramatically, her cheeks puffing out and her lips flapping briefly. "That's not enough."

We stood in silence watching the sun brighten the trees below, the pedestrians looking like ants and the cars like toys, the ghosts interspersed among the living.

"The kids?" I asked Emily. "We've got pictures here of them."

Emily shrugged, her eyes distant. I couldn't tell if she was watching the scene below or somewhere else completely. But I had to agree with her indifference. This didn't feel like a kid thing, much more like a wife thing or a lover thing.

But we didn't have a way to find Amanda York and we had no idea where Edward Lincoln had lived, so we couldn't search for clues there. It's not like we can google it.

And then something tickled in my mind. I had missed something. Something obvious.

Helen had called Shelia a bitch. Shelia had been truly grieving when she was alone in the hot tub with Darla. "Shelia Green and Edward Lincoln were together," I said.

"Really?" Emily asked. She's not good at these kinds of things, having never experienced the full power of hormones while alive.

"There had been rumors over the years," I said, "that Lincoln cheated on his wives a lot and with her specifically and repeatedly. That she was the reason his marriage with Helen ended. But he wasn't married when he died, hadn't been for a few years. I was wrong about Shelia's reaction on the set, there was something genuine there."

Emily was staring at me, her eyes wide. While she didn't understand these hormone driven things, she was fascinated by them. "Does that give her a motive?"

"Maybe," I said. "If he was cheating on her, but…"

"But what?" Emily asked, her voice eager.

"She seemed destroyed in the hot tub. There's something else… I just can't quite get it. Something we're missing."

Emily just stared at me as I racked my brain. Well, not my brain, specifically. I didn't have any grey matter, but you get my meaning. My mind, however, it was possible that I had one, worked much like it had worked with all that grey matter. I had a better memory but the mysteries of the subconscious seemed to survive death fully intact.

"Can you pop us to Shelia Green?" I asked. "Let's see what she's doing."

"But that... woman," Emily spat out, undoubtedly referring to Darla who was in the hot tub with Shelia Green last time we saw her.

"We won't stay long if she's there," I said.

Emily nodded and grabbed my arm, and with a "pop" we were gone.

Chapter Thirteen

We found Shelia Green naked and unconscious in bed on top of her satin green comforter in her spacious bedroom, a nearly empty bottle of vodka and a spilled bottle of sleeping pills on the bedstand beside her.

I rushed to her and leaned my head down to her chest and could hear her heartbeat, but it was slow, maybe forty beats per minute. She was bradycardic. She was dying.

The bedroom was large, with plush carpet, a big TV hanging on the wall, a beautiful antique armoire, and a chaise lounge. Expensive knickknacks were placed with care, like a green oriental vase and a marble sculpture of a reclining woman. Decorating the walls were elegantly framed posters from Shelia's career, some of the movies and plays she had been in. In other words, it was just what I would have expected from a diva like Shelia Green.

Darla was there, her arms crossed as she stared at the unconscious woman. She was back in her blue business suit, a sneer on her face.

"She's dying," I shouted.

Darla just smiled.

I ignored the red-haired woman, grabbed Emily's hand, and flew us out of the house.

"What are we doing, Walter?" she asked.

"Getting the address," I said. "It's 911 time."

Shelia Green's house was up in the Hollywood hills. Not a big place, but gated and lovely. We got the address, Emily popped us to the hidden SECI chamber that I and a few other ghosts used. And I typed and typed fast.

"911. Shelia Green has overdosed in her home and needs immediate medical attention."

And then I left her address.

"911" is not the actual code, it's longer than that. After the first time I wrote about the code, every ghost that died after reading that story was using it when they made it to the SECI chamber. They all wanted to get a message to their loved ones right away. And all those 911s were waking up Tamara Watson, the woman that runs Afterlife Communications. She wasn't getting any sleep, so the code is no longer 911, and there is a system in place so she's not always the one fielding them.

So all of you thinking of 911ing your SECI communications after you die. Don't. It won't work. I'm also not going to say one thing about this hidden SECI chamber either. If the word ever got out, I would never be able to get these cases written up.

Emily popped us back to Shelia Green and we did what we could until the ambulance arrived.

If you read my first case, about Haley, you know what a dedicated ghost can do to hurt the living. You know what Haley and I did to her murderer. Well, there is a much less dramatic way a ghost can help the living. It's called, quite simply, "the warmth."

I can't say that I understand it, but ghosts can tap into a benevolent source of energy and channel it into the living. It's called "the warmth" because that is what it feels like. And, yes, warmth is a rare kind of sensation for a ghost, so if you feel it then you know when you are doing it right.

And that can be tricky because it is a subtle skill. Like much about being a ghost, it is about intent, but after that it is all about letting go. Not forcing it. Detaching.

Emily and I didn't talk, we walked into the bed, put our hands on Shelia Green, and let the warmth flow.

Darla glowered at us from next to the chaise lounge but didn't say anything.

"It's helping," I said after a few minutes when I could hear Shelia's heart rate increase just a touch. She was pale and her breathing was still very shallow, but it looked like we might be able to save her.

And that made all of this Hollywood madness worth it. Sure Shelia Green was a diva and was far too fond of herself, but she was a good actress and years ago when we had worked on that play, I had seen her be genuinely kind and I knew she did a lot for animal welfare charities.

And on a personal level, I didn't want the world thinking she had died of a suicide, just like the world thought I had. Not that many people had noticed my death.

But none of that really mattered, either. Emily and I were helping her because it was the right thing to do. Sure, I know without a doubt that there is an afterlife, but that doesn't make life any less precious or any less worth preserving.

"Darla doesn't like that you are doing that," Darla said, taking a step towards us, her face stuck in a deep frown, her eyes narrow. I had to wonder if we had found yet another one of her personalities.

But I was with the warmth and that wondering wasn't

something I was serious about, so I just let it go. And then the tickling in my mind that I was missing something came back.

Darla took another step toward us, the edges of her form starting to flicker red. Emily has her lollipop T-shirt that quite artfully reflects her mood, but a ghost experiencing extreme emotion and not in complete control of their form will sometimes have a visible aura around their form. Darla's was red. She was furious.

But why? I was missing something about Darla.

She had been so strange, so different, every time we met.

The big woman took another step toward us.

"I got this," Emily growled, stepping away from Shelia, and I heard her heart slow down again.

Emily had way more experience at this than I did. She was a much more capable ghost. I didn't want to leave the warmth, but I wasn't the one that Shelia needed.

"Stay, Emily," I said. "Please. You are better at this. I'll deal with Darla."

Emily gave me a worried nod and stepped back in as I stepped out, my relaxed mind suddenly seeing what I had missed.

The article that Helen Lincoln had read listed all of Edward Lincoln's ex-wives. The article said, "...had been married three times to Helen R. Lincoln, Melany A. Taylor, and Amanda D. York."

It had used middle initials.

Amanda D. York.

I remembered back in the morgue when Emily had been worried that a ghost might have done this. I remembered Darla telling us how much she read, that she had read about Emily and me, and she must have read about JJ and what he did with electricity.

Amanda Darla York.

Sheila Green had been the reason for Edward and Darla's divorce. Darla had killed Edward, had shorted out his pacemaker while he was in that casket for that shoot. He had passed out. No one had noticed and he had died.

The murderer was a ghost.

Darla had been in the hot tub amplifying Shelia's grief to drive her to this point, to this overdose.

"You know," I said as I stepped toward Darla and extended my hand, "we never met properly. Let's start over. My name is Walter Anchor and I died when someone overdosed me with propofol."

I was at the end of the bed, a furious Darla in front of me. The edges of her ghostly form were a bright, flickering red, her long red hair starting to form around her like she was in the presence of a massive amount of static electricity.

"Get out of my way," she said, her tone low and dangerous.

"Let me try for you," I said. "Your name is Amanda Darla York, and you died... let me guess, you died of a broken heart after Edward went back to Shelia, leaving you with his baby."

Darla's blue eyes found mine and beneath the fury there was pain. Her jaw moved as if she was struggling to find words and then she spoke. "Look at me," she said, slapping her chest. "Darla is not the kind of woman he wanted, or you for that matter. You want your Hollywood girls and not a real woman with a real body and a real heart."

That hurt because she was kinda right. Sun was the only woman for me. I hadn't even noticed Mary Paulson's quite obvious interest in me because she wasn't Sun and she didn't look like Sun.

But she was also wrong. Sun had plenty of heart and was plenty real. I will admit to some typical shallowness when it comes to the kind of packages I am attracted to. But heart always mattered to me. It wouldn't have worked with Sun if she hadn't had a heart and a mind to go along with her appearance.

Darla backed up a step, tears forming in her eyes, the red flickering around her ghostly forming dying down. "Eddie wasn't used to someone really caring for him, really loving him. We... we had our time, and it was... it was sweet." The tears were rolling down her cheeks. "But then he went back to that *woman*. While I was pregnant. With his child. I fought for him. So hard. I fought for our family, but he kept going bat to *her*. I—"

The red flared back to life and she charged, her face contorted in rage, her red hair swaying around her as if it had a life of its own, and she surged forward.

I didn't think. I braced myself and caught her and flew her up out of the house into the predawn LA sky.

Because of Emily, I know how to touch as a ghost. I know how to modulate my frequency to match another ghost's so we just don't go through each other. I hadn't had to think about it. I held her and flew straight up.

I was mad, her emotional state leaking into me through our contact. I was mad at myself for being so cowardly about facing all the facts of my own death. I was mad at the world for that accident that caused Sun's miscarriage and led to the crumbling of our marriage and my life with her. I was mad at myself for not making it in Hollywood, for letting my dreams go. And I was furious with myself for my retreat into addiction when I went back to Tucson and not getting proper help for it.

"Let me go!" Darla shouted.

I ignored her and flew straight up.

"Why the hell did you have me help, have me follow the body?" I asked.

She snorted. I could feel her struggling, feel her changing her frequency, but I kept matching mine to hers. "Darla knew the mighty Walter Anchor wouldn't let it go. Best to get him out of the way while Darla did what needed to be done."

That just made me laugh, because she was so wrong. I wouldn't have stayed, wouldn't have investigated but for her asking. I laughed because she had called me "mighty" when I couldn't even face the reality of my own death and find out the truth. I wasn't mighty. I was just trying to get by, to survive this afterlife, to do something worth doing while I'm here.

And with Darla up in the sky, I was doing what needed to be done, faking it and hoping it worked. I had no idea what to do with a murdering ghost that was intent on being a serial killer.

I know it's a very actorly thing, but I kind of think everyone should do a little improv. It was a fairly big part of my training as an actor and has served me well in this life… and afterlife. You take what you get, you improvise, you try to turn it into something good. You do it over and over until it starts to come naturally.

"Let Darla go!" she shouted. I could feel her rage intensifying and she was switching her frequency faster and faster, our forms going diffuse and then firming up. If this got much worse, I wouldn't be able to hold her.

And then she suddenly gave up and stopped struggling, but we weren't going up anymore, we started drifting down. She was trying to fly down while I was trying to fly up. I felt her wrap her big arms around me and she grunted with effort and we started going down faster.

I had never fought a ghost before, not "physically." I

was like some kid on the playground getting in his first fight, not having a clue as to what to do, and flailing around awkwardly.

I increased my efforts and slowed us down, but I wasn't strong enough to stop our descent.

The horizon to the east was starting to lighten as the day dawned. I could see the Ventura Freeway in the distance and the Warner Brothers lot where this all started. I could see the Hollywood sign perched on the craggy hill lit up and declaring for all to see where we were and how grand it must be.

I used to love this town and I used to hate this town. I loved the job, the creation of illusions for entertainment purposes. I hated the town with all the crime and poverty and far too many egos.

Darla was laboring under the illusion that revenge would help. It wouldn't. It would probably lead to the bardo, and from what Banquo once told me back when Haley was trying to exact her revenge, it could lead to an even darker place.

And if I cared enough to try to save Shelia Green's life despite her flaws, shouldn't I try to save Darla's afterlife despite her flaws?

What does one do with a murdering ghost?

I didn't know, so I used my training and improvised.

"Darla, listen to me," I said, whispering to her, hoping that would get her attention. "You can stop now. Eddie is dead and Shelia is ruined. She'll never be the same after this. The shame of her suicide attempt will haunt her for the rest of her life."

"Good," Darla grunted. "She ruined my life."

"Don't kill her, Darla," I said. "You don't really want to kill her."

"Oh, no. Darla does want to kill her." She grunted again and we descended faster.

"Eddie's not a ghost," I said, "but I know that Shelia will be if she dies like this. You pushed her over the edge, she won't move on."

"Darla wanted Eddie to be a ghost," she said with a sniff, our descent halting briefly. "To be her ghost. To start over with Darla again."

She hadn't just wanted to kill him, she wanted him to be with her in the afterlife. The thought almost derailed me. I almost let her go. At first the thought felt so foreign and then I thought about Sun being a ghost and how we could be together again and I understood.

The idea was a siren, the same kind as gambling or propofol used to be. An empty promise that would bring only pain and ruin.

Darla would not have gotten what she wanted if Edward Lincoln had not moved on and become a ghost. It would have made things worse. And I won't get what I want if I haunt Sun waiting for the day she dies and can join me.

The thought was a quick storm in my mind and I came back to myself and renewed my grip on her.

"I'm sorry about that, Darla," I said. "But listen to me. If Shelia becomes a ghost, she will haunt you."

"What!?" she asked, and we were rising again. Below us I could hear the warble of a siren bouncing off the hills as an ambulance rushed to Shelia Green's house.

"Imagine your afterlife, Darla," I said, still whispering to her. "Imagine every day like this, like you and me struggling, like right now. She will know you killed Eddie. She will know you drove her to suicide. She will haunt you. She will follow you. She will not give you a moment of peace."

Our ascent got quicker, Darla barely trying to fly us down anymore, the city growing smaller beneath us again.

"She'll tell you of her passion with Eddie," I whispered. "How they made love, where they made love, how she had loved him the longest and the best. She'll tell you about Eddie and the night he left you for her and what it felt like, what they did, in excruciating detail."

And yes, I was being a real asshole right then. I needed to paint a picture so revolting that Darla would give this up. And while it was only one possible outcome here, it was certainly possible.

"No! Darla doesn't want that."

"How he used to love to come up behind her, pull her lovely hair aside, and kiss her neck," I whispered. "She'll tell you exactly how that felt, how that stood up the hairs on the back of her neck, how that—"

"No! Eddie used to kiss Darla's neck. No! No! No!" Darla intoned and we were flying up twice as fast as before. Darla was flying up too.

"She'll be a ghost," I said. "She'll be able to remember everything perfectly. She'll tell you about it until you beg her to stop and then she'll tell you about it some more."

"Go... go save her," Darla said. She was crying now. "Darla begs you to save her. Darla will leave this awful town. Darla will find a nice quiet place. Darla will be good."

I let her go up there high above Los Angeles. We were high enough that the ocean was just visible to the southwest and the sun was just peaking up above the distant horizon.

Darla stared at me, the fury in her face still clear, but fear too.

"You belong with that wicked old woman that looks

like a little girl," Darla spat. "Darla thinks you are wicked too and that Emily is perfect for you."

The accusation stung because there was some truth to it. But I did what I had to do to save a life.

Darla looked down at the city below us and shook her head, her lip curling into a sneer. She looked up at me and shouted. "Go! Go save the horrible Shelia Green. Let her live without Eddie. Darla thinks now that that is punishment enough."

With that she flew to the north and I flew down to do as she asked.

Chapter Fourteen

THAT WAS THE LAST WE SAW OF AMANDA DARLA YORK. I asked Tamara to look into her and a quick google search revealed that Darla had overdosed on... you guessed it, vodka and sleeping pills. I don't quite understand it, but Darla had figured out how to infect Shelia Green with her own depression, had tried to give Shelia her own death.

Darla and Eddie's baby was now with Darla's parents. He was only twenty months old, so maybe with their love and the support of Eddie's estate the kid would have a decent life.

We stayed with Shelia Green for three more days, pumping her full of warmth. It wasn't pretty, those days in the ICU. She almost died two times. We're talking a crash cart, and shocking her heart, and all that mayhem.

It got so I had to wonder if we were doing the right thing, if her biology was damaged enough that we should just let her go. And there is no easy answer here. I guess it got kind of personal for me. I didn't want her overdose, influenced by Darla like it was, to turn into what looked like a suicide.

It may seem like a silly distinction. Dead is dead, right? But it's not for the people that loved her. It matters. And while I was no longer sure that my own death was a murder, it could have been an accidental suicide, I knew without a doubt that Shelia Green was under the influence of Darla, and what happened wasn't really her choice.

So we stayed and we fought for her survival.

I think it was a little bit healing for Emily and me, too. Being in the flow of the warmth that long, constantly letting go, coming back to that lovely sensation was just what we needed.

We didn't talk much, we just kept our hands on her and let the warmth flow. It was like a meditation retreat… except for all the nurses and doctors and beeping machines and IV bags.

When Shelia woke up, when it was clear that she was going to be okay, we only stayed a little longer. Long enough to hear her daughter tell her what happened and promise that she'd be there for her. She had support and that's important whether you're alive or dead.

Emily took my hand and we walked out of the hospital into a bright LA day, an ambulance rushing up with its sirens blaring.

It occurred to me that this could be a valid way to be dead. Hanging out at hospitals and trying to help the living survive whatever kind of trauma had befallen them. Spending your days in the flow of the warmth.

But it wasn't for me.

"Are you okay, Walter?" Emily asked. The lollipop on her shirt was red, but it was a pale red. We were both exhausted and needed to fade, go into that dreamless "sleep" ghosts do from time to time when they are really tired.

I nodded and we kept walking. Something so basic

while you are alive, but pure artifice when you die. But still, walking helps ground you, helps you feel more human. "Are you okay, Emily?"

She smiled, but it wasn't a youthful smile, it was a world-weary smile on her young, round face. "I guess."

Emily had found me this murder, had left me here thinking that this might be what I needed. But it wasn't. Tucson and our graveyard was my home now.

"Um... I..." I began, the words hard to find.

Emily stopped and hopped up onto a low wall that bordered a cheerful flower bed in front of the hulking hospital. She sat down and patted next to her.

I sat down and stared at the cars on the street. "I know I need to follow up on the lead I found, but... I can't. Not yet. I need time."

"You don't have to do it for me, Walter," she said, her lisp a little thicker than usual, another sign of fatigue. "You have to do it for you."

I nodded. "Thank you."

We sat there for a while watching the living flow in and out of the building. Some in wheelchairs, some limping, some clearly injured, and then others walking quickly in scrubs, or concerned family members with worry written on their faces.

"I was wondering something, Emily," I said.

She nodded for me to continue.

"What do you do when we are not... you know..." I nodded towards the hospital. "Dealing with all the murder and mayhem."

She shrugged and cocked her head, her green eyes intense, the lollipop on her T-shirt swirling into a bright yellow. "Why, I like to travel, Walter. Why do you ask?"

I suppressed a laugh. The phrasing of it was so innocent on the surface, but it was very clear she liked this avenue of questioning. "Because," I began. "Maybe you and I can do something besides murder. You know, for a change of pace. Something that you like to do."

She smiled and nodded enthusiastically, her blond ringlets bouncing. She hopped off the wall and held out her hand. "I would like that, Walter."

I stood and took her hand and we kept walking. We needed to fade, but we still needed to ground a little more. So we walked away from the hospital and down the busy street, seeing a few homeless people, some joggers, and some pedestrians. Behind us was the hospital with the sick and the dying and here it was just another day in Hollywood.

"Edward Lincoln's funeral is today," Emily said, a mischievous look on her face. "I know we are both tired, but maybe it would help."

It seems strange that we were so tired but still looking for something to do. For the living, this would be needing something calm and normal to do after a particularly harrowing and exhausting day. Like flopping down on the couch and watching a show or two. Something normal. Something fairly mindless. Then you'll be able to go to sleep.

Well, for ghosts, there is little more normal than a funeral.

I nodded and with a "pop" we were in a cemetery, a large crowd gathered, most of the living in black. Behind and above the arrayed living, many of them actors and actresses I recognized, were ghosts. Hundreds of ghosts. Young, old. Short, tall. Slim, fat. Dressed in everything from nightgowns, to modern suits, to clothing that are clearly over a century old.

There were wispy moaning bardoed ghosts that are the cliched version of what the living think of ghosts. There were well-practiced ghosts that were barely transparent, and clearly newbie ghosts that were having trouble keeping their forms solid.

Tall trees surround the granite-filled grassy area, and six pallbearers carried a rather plain wooden coffin on their shoulders.

Emily, still holding my hand, pulled me in line right behind the pallbearers, as if we had an important place in all of this. I saw nods and looks of recognition from the other ghosts as they saw Emily, but the ghosts were as silent as the humans, some sniffing coming from both the living and the dead.

Emily had clearly been here before. In her over eighty years dead, she's probably been everywhere.

I looked down and caught her eye and she gave me a tight smile and a nod.

It gave me hope. It made me think that the two of us were going to be okay. And maybe by asking her to do something else with me besides murder, she wanted to open up, wanted to show me this whole other community of ghosts.

We followed the somber procession through the hundreds of living and hundreds of dead until we got to the gravesite and the casket was placed on the metal frame that will lower it into the ground and take the remains of Edward Lincoln six feet under.

We stood there while a Catholic priest, dressed in white, spoke, while ghost after ghost walked up to the casket, reached in to touch Edward Lincoln's corpse and whispered their goodbyes.

And I recognized some of these ghosts. The faces you see during the Oscar's In Memoriam segment. I was starstruck in the presence of some of them. Oscar winners and some of my acting heroes long gone.

Not to mention the living. There were a slew of Emmy winners and a few Oscar winners among them. I had been in Hollywood a while and never been around this density of stars.

I caught Emily's eyes after a very famous actress, dead ten years now, said her very tearful goodbyes. Emily threw me a brief grin and squeezed my hand, and in that moment I realized something.

I don't deserve Emily. How could I? She could be anywhere hanging out with any ghosts she wanted. The former rich and the former famous. Or the brilliant and insightful. Or the most interesting storytellers this world's earthbound spirits has to offer. But she chooses to hang out with me. Over and over.

I don't deserve her.

I opened my mouth to speak, to say something about this realization, but Emily put her finger to her young lips and whispered, "Wait for it."

I looked around. What could be coming?

The priest was finishing the service saying something in Latin that sounded quite regal. A prayer, many heads, both living and dead, bowed.

When he snapped his bible shut, there was a collective intake of breath from the dead.

A spirit was rising out of Edward Lincoln's coffin. A ghost. A Hollywood handsome man in his sixties with salt and pepper hair and a cleft chin. The spirit was "dressed" in an expensive three-piece suit.

"What?" I asked.

Emily shrugged. "Sometimes it takes a while for the soul to separate. Sometimes a long time."

I smiled and shook my head. This was what Darla wanted, but she missed it. I watched as the new ghost of Edward Lincoln was welcomed into his new community.

Gently. Slowly. Each ghost taking their time, trying not to shock him into the bardo.

It takes a village to raise a ghost properly and this group of ghosts knew what they were doing. They got him moving. Got him talking. Distracted him from the living and the coffin being lowered into the ground.

After the living wandered off, the dead really started the party. I met ghost after ghost and found their greeting ritual is the same as ours back in Tucson.

"Hello, my name is Walter Anchor and I died when someone overdosed me with propofol."

I met stars and fellow grips and plenty of regular old people. All like me with unfinished business. All in search of an afterlife worth living.

Hours later, Emily and I were finally alone again.

"Thank you," I said.

"Sure," she said with a nod. "Lots of your people here."

I shook my head. "No, Emily. My people are in Tucson." She opened her mouth to speak, but I continued. "Don't get me wrong. This has been great, and I'd love to hang out here some, but my home is with you and Blinky and Anna-Marie and Fredrick and... even Banquo."

She swiped her forehead dramatically, pantomiming great relief. "Glad you got that figured out."

This whole thing had been her trying to help me. I didn't deserve her, but I was dedicated to doing better.

But it was a strange dichotomy. I needed to get the courage up to follow the lead, find out if my former dental assistant was involved in my death *and* I needed to pay more attention to the needs of my friends and not make this afterlife all about solving murders... especially mine.

My life had been a strange dichotomy, actor and then dentist, so why not my afterlife?

"You know," I said with a smile. "*Annie* is playing on Broadway. Maybe New York would be fun. We could see some shows."

Emily smiled broadly and I caught a wicked glint in those green eyes of hers. "And maybe," she said, "we'll just stumble onto a murder and..." She ended with an exaggerated shrug.

I had to laugh. Emily so loves murder.

THE RED ARROW MURDERS

MURDERS

A WALTER ANCHOR
GHOST DETECTIVE STORY

ROBERT J. MCCARTER
AUTHOR OF *SHUFFLED OFF*

Chapter One

EVERY MURDER MYSTERY HAS TO BEGIN WITH A LIFE ending. By definition.

I don't know about you, but when I was alive, I always loved the predictability of watching murder mysteries, that the bad guy would get caught in the end. There was some comfort in that. But that someone had to die to catalyze that experience, it eventually began to wear on me.

There has to be injustice, of course, for justice to be served. I get that. But does someone have to die every damn week?

"Well, Walter?" Emily asked, looking at our next injustice to right, our next corpse. "What do you think?"

This was standard for Emily. She would find an interesting murder, drag me to it, and try to entice me into solving the case. The weirder the better for her. After all, what are a couple of ghosts supposed to do with their afterlife?

Emily was all smiles, her eyebrows raised expectantly, looking like the four-year-old she was when she died over eighty years ago. She had shoulder-length, curly blond hair, like Shirley Temple, rosy cheeks, shorts, and her usual lollipop-print T-shirt.

She had the enthusiasm of a four-year-old and the jaded love of death of an eighty-year-old ghost.

Since ghostly forms are not fixed and Emily was an advanced ghost with a child's heart, the color of the lollipop was something of a mood ring for her. It was a curious and hopeful yellow. She wanted to engage me in what we both enjoyed doing. How could I turn that down?

I sighed, looking at the mangled body lying on the forest floor. A young man lying facedown, probably in his early twenties. He had been hacked up with a machete or a sword or something like that. Lots of small, precise cuts through his jeans and black T-shirt into his flesh. Slashes on the back of his head through his short brown hair. So many cuts. His blood had stained the dried pine needles red. His arms were splayed out behind him.

Emily had taken us far afield for this one. We were a few hundred miles north of Tucson in the forest just south of Flagstaff, Arizona. This body was by itself with no trail or forest service road in sight.

Someone had hiked out here with him, gone batshit crazy on him with a sharp edge of some sort, and left him to die a slow, horrible death.

There were marks in the pine-needle covered ground, showing him crawling about a dozen feet, leaving a trail of blood while he slowly died.

It seemed like my afterlife was becoming like one of those TV shows. Except Emily with her love of murder could find dead bodies more often than once a week. As often as I let her, really.

"There's no ghost," I said, turning back to the way-too-enthusiastic Emily. "After this, you'd think there'd be a ghost."

She rolled her eyes, her lips twitching into a pout. "Oh, those cases are boring, Walter. We talk to the ghost. Find out who did it. You go type it out at the SECI chamber. The cops arrest them. They go to jail. Blah, blah, blah."

To top it all off, Emily speaks with an adorable lisp turning "cases" into "catheth" and making the incongruity of her young appearance against her love of murder sometimes hard to take. A ghost that looked and sounded like an adorable little girl loving murder so very much.

The SECI chamber is that typewriter for ghosts that was invented at the University of Arizona in Tucson. It is what I am typing on right now. It is the piece of technology that lets ghosts be detectives and bring people to justice. Otherwise we'd be solving murders and not being able to do anything about it, and that would just suck.

I sighed and nodded. She was right, of course, a ghost could sometimes make cases so easy it was boring, but I didn't have to like it. And I didn't have to like wading into another screwed-up human circumstance either.

I think this has become a bit of a ritual for us. Joyful Emily finds a murder so bizarre it makes my head hurt. I get grumpy and protest too much. Emily launches a charm offensive that eventually wins me over and we take on the case. Blah, blah, blah.

I was tired of that happening every "week" too.

So I decided to mix it up.

"Wow!" I said, my voice actually containing some energy. "This is wonderfully strange, Emily. You did good, kid, finding this poor boy. Let's get to work and find the murderer and bring them to justice!"

I was trying to be enthusiastic, but it came out a little bit weird. Well, a lot weird. I used to be an actor, I could have done it convincingly, but I didn't. It came out stilted and awful.

"What is wrong with you, Walter?" Emily asked, her head cocked to one side and her fists on her hips.

"Nothing, honey," I said, digging in deeper with the faux enthusiasm. "I just want to solve this murder. Let's get to it!"

I turned around, slowly taking in our surroundings. Which was trees. So many trees. And pine needles. And downed branches. And pinecones, from new nut-brown cones to grey rotting cones. And volcanic rocks with pale grey lichen on them. The body was in the middle of a small clearing of trees.

Flagstaff is in the middle of the largest ponderosa pine forest in the world. It's a massive forest where almost all the trees are ponderosas. There are some scattered oaks, most of them pretty scraggly, and aspen and fir at higher elevations, but around here it's all pine trees. Endless damn pine trees. One part of the forest looking much like another part if there are no landmarks visible.

I flew straight up about two hundred feet and rotated around again. I could see highway 89A cutting through a valley to the east. It goes from Flagstaff to Sedona. The land was undulating and rough, the result of uneven erosion in the rocky land. The earth here is all volcanic, the San Francisco Peaks, which I could see to the north, was once a massive volcano and built up the north country.

"Walter?" Emily called from down below.

She didn't fly up but stayed on the ground. As the saying went around the graveyard in Tucson, "If you act like you're alive, you feel more like you are alive." And I get that. It's good hygiene for ghosts, helps you stay stable without a body. But who wants to be a ghost and not fly around sometimes?

"What are you doing, Walter?" she called.

"Just getting the lay of the land," I said. "Why the hell would anyone ever come out here?"

"You know… to hike," Emily said in a very youthful and condescending tone. "Fresh air. Exercise. Stuff like that."

A groan escaped me despite trying to stay cheerful about this. I was never much of a hiker. When I was an actor, keeping in shape was part of the job description, and even afterward as a dentist I kept it up. But at a gym. Where things are civilized. Away from bugs and snakes and bears. Where pine needles and pinecones can't poke you.

My ex-wife Sun did like to hike, but in exotic locations with beautiful views. I'd doggedly hike with her since the view when she was in front of me was always a good one.

But thoughts of Sun just soured my mood. It hadn't been easy, but Sun and I had repaired things a lot while Emily and I were investigating the death of the ghost bride. But Sun was the one that got away and it was not like we could have much of a relationship now. I am not a haunter. Definitely not one of those ghosts.

"So where's the trail?" I asked Emily. "I don't see any trail. There's a dirt road about half a mile away, but that's it."

Emily sighed, loudly and petulantly. "Please come get me, Walter. I want to see."

Emily and I were not quite at our best. I had been digging around my past a lot lately and it just made me grumpy… well, "grumpier." I'm not one of those ghosts having a good time in their afterlife. I feel like I have a job to do, that "unfinished business" and all. And I figure that my unfinished business is my own murder, but the leads ran out a while ago, and recently… well, let's just say it's gotten complicated.

I slowly lowered myself to the ground, putting in some

effort so my long trench coat flared out around me like I was really passing through the air. A little drama that made it take longer than it needed to.

Emily raised one eyebrow and shook her head. If anybody knew me, it was Emily. And she knew this was my little passive aggressive version of a fit.

Four-year-olds are really better at them. They don't hold back or pretend it's not happening, they just let loose and you know what they are upset about.

Adults? Not so much.

"You ready to tell me what's going on?" Emily asked when I got to the ground.

"Nope," I said. And I wasn't.

I reached down and picked her up. So ghosts can see and hear, really well. But they can't smell, they can't taste, and touch... well, it's barely there and you have to do it right. And I did. I matched the frequency of my ghostly form to Emily's—basically making my form neater and less transparent—and took her in my arms.

The ghostly sense of touch is a barely there, almost numb feeling, but it is actually very important. I can live without the sense of smell and taste—yeah, I get grumpy about that too—but touch is essential to being human. It really is. Touch is the sensation that lets you know you are not alone in this world.

And maybe that is what Emily was doing, in part, by having me fly her up. She's a wily old ghost and well skilled. She knows what it takes to survive as a ghost and she does a lot of little things to keep me stable.

Like have me help her solve murders.

All the time.

I took her slowly up into the clear blue sky. That's the one thing I'll say about the high country, the air is clean and the sky is so blue it almost doesn't look real.

I took us up about two hundred feet and Emily said, "I thought so." She was looking straight down at the victim.

"What?" I asked.

She pointed. "See the arrow, Walter?"

And I did. The kid had dragged himself bleeding across the forest floor making a long red stain and his hands were back behind him at about 45-degree angles turning his body and the blood stain into an arrow.

The arrow pointed to the northeast, towards Flagstaff. But...

"That can't mean anything," I said.

"Why not?" Emily asked, her pale blue eyes full of challenge.

"Well... we're far enough away from Flagstaff that he would have to be a human compass or something to point to anything. And even if he was, the whole of Flagstaff is mostly in that direction. How would we know what he's pointing at?"

She pursed her lips. "Well, then you explain it, Mr. Smartypants." It came out as "Thmartypanth," taking a bit of the sting out.

I opened my mouth, but didn't speak right away. My faux cheerfulness was gone, and probably for the better, but I couldn't believe she was even asking me this.

"He was dying, Em. He used his last bits of energy trying to get to help. His arms just ended up that way."

She sighed and nodded. "But it's a lead, Walter. While it might not be anything, it could be something."

I just stared at her.

"Come on," she said, putting some punch in her young voice. "You're Walter Anchor, ghost detective. You can't let a mystery like this go."

This was not looking like a very fun case to me.

Chapter Two

WE DIDN'T GO FOLLOW THE ARROW. NOT YET. I FLEW US much higher, several thousand feet up, so we could get a better sense of where the arrow pointed and look for any other anomalies.

The blood had turned rather dark and flies were all over the corpse, so we knew the death wasn't fresh. Which was a bit unlike Emily. She often got us to murders shortly after they happened. She had a sixth sense for these kinds of things.

I sometimes wished she could sense murders before they happened. But that's not the kind of thing I ever said to her. She would take it like a four-year-old and it wouldn't go well. And we have the talents we have, after all.

She's good at finding murders. I'm good at being grumpy.

We didn't find anything interesting up high, so I flew us back down and we started taking a closer look at the crime scene.

"Where's his backpack?" I asked, slowly walking around the scene. Being ghosts we didn't have to worry about contaminating evidence or stepping in the blood or smelling the corpse, which must be starting to get ripe right about now.

Emily shrugged.

"He wouldn't be out here without a water bottle, at least, right?" I asked. Not being much of a hiker, it really was a question.

Emily shrugged again. What would a girl who died at the age of four really know about hiking anyway? Did people even call it "hiking" eighty-some years ago?

"And the shoes," I said, pointing. They were black canvas sneakers. Not hiking boots. Crappy tread. "Those aren't hiking boots."

Another shrug.

Crap. The silent treatment. I had told her I had discovered something in my past but wasn't ready to talk about it. That had been a good step, but I hadn't told her about it yet and it was still this barrier between us.

I much preferred her loud and angry than quiet and sulky.

I sighed and just ignored Emily, squatting low and looking closely at the body. This is an area where we were way better than humans. Great eyesight. No creaky knees. No getting barfy because we can't smell.

The pants were plain old blue jeans but were very worn with a few holes in them and they looked super dirty, like they hadn't been washed in way too long. I glanced at the face and from what I could see from the side, confirmed that he was in his early twenties. The T-shirt had holes in it too and, given the coolness of early fall, he was way underdressed. The shirt was black fading to charcoal from too many trips through the washer and there was some faded silk screening on the front that I couldn't see enough of to even hazard a guess.

Emily seemed to have gotten bored with giving me the silent treatment and was doing the same thing I was. Getting close. Looking hard. Mentally cataloging details.

She really does love murder. She might be mad at me, but she was still driven to solve this case. Any case, really. The living are driven by their biology to get out there and do things. You have to. The biology can't be ignored for too long.

The dead have to find other ways to keep active, because being active is essential to being sane.

"How did he get out here?" I asked. "I don't think he walked all the way here."

Emily's green eyes darkened and narrowed as she studied me. She straightened up on the other side of the corpse and folded her little arms across her chest. "I don't think I want to solve a murder today."

I shrugged, pretending not to understand what she was getting at. "Okay. I bet he'll be here tomorrow. What do you have in mind?"

Her nostrils flared and she shook her head. While she knew I had found something in my past, and while she had told me it was okay to have secrets, that we all had secrets, this one had started to fester and I knew it. But still I couldn't do anything about it.

This wasn't me just being grumpy. She didn't have any problem with that. In fact, I think she liked it. She could counteract the grumpy Walter with the exuberant Emily. I think she liked it like that, it gave her an excuse to be so exuberant.

Maybe she thought I owed her the truth here—she had

saved me, after all. I had been a dentist. Murdered in one of my own dental chairs with an overdose of propofol, a drug I had some unfortunate recreational experience with, so it was ruled a suicide. I had ended up haunting my old practice, unable to leave, and then haunting my office manager, Midge. Emily had found me, barely holding on, in the bathroom with poor Midge. I was desperate. I thought Midge was the key to my murder. I didn't leave her side until Emily came along and taught me how to be a proper ghost.

Ghosts who don't find something to do, don't find a way to be in balance, end up slipping into their regrets and reliving all their mistakes in a place the ghosts in Tucson call the bardo.

And yes, Emily saved me. And yes, I owed her. And so I remade myself into a detective, with a trench coat and a fedora no less, and have been learning to solve murders.

And part of it had been selfish, thinking that if I got good enough at this, I'd be able to solve my own murder, finish my unfinished business and "move on."

But I had a lead, I had a suspect, and I had enough experience now to figure it out. But I couldn't do anything about it. I couldn't see my past erode even further like it had every time I had gone looking at it.

I was a ghost and I was the one being haunted, by how I died, by the life I had lived, by all the things I had missed while I was alive.

Emily was staring at me, her arms still crossed, her eyes narrow, watching my face, probably picking up half of what I was feeling. With the density of flesh gone, ghosts are more than a little intuitive. But they aren't mind readers. Emily knew something was up with me but didn't know what.

"Yeah, I'm not feeling it today," she said, her voice the growl of an old woman.

With a pop, she was gone and I was left there in the middle of the forest with a dead body and the trail of blood behind it forming something of an arrow pointing toward Flagstaff.

Chapter Three

I KEPT INVESTIGATING.

This was becoming something of a pattern for us. She had found the Hollywood murder case and left me there, thinking that since I had wanted to be an actor, maybe I was better off in Hollywood.

She had found this one with her usual exuberance and I had just gotten weird with my false enthusiasm and driven her away.

And this was a bizarre murder case, just the kind of thing Emily likes the best, so I knew it was bad.

I couldn't "pop" like Emily and go instantly from place to place. I had to fly and I wasn't in the mood to fly back to Tucson and try to find Emily and try to make it right. She might not be there. She could be anywhere in the world.

And I was more than a little bit worried about her. About us. She loves solving cases more than anything. Which meant something serious was going on. This growing pattern was not a good thing.

It wasn't much of a decision on my part, I just pretended Emily had gone off to get us help or something and kept looking. I followed the bloody trail back to its origin and found an area where feet had scuffed through the layers of dead pine needles and crunched some fallen pinecones. There had been a fight of some sort. There were also small splats of blood on the ground a few feet away.

So the victim and the assailant had struggled. Maybe the edged weapon hadn't come out at first.

I flew up a few feet and looked down, trying to see if I could detect a pattern in the markings.

The forest floor was thick with dead pine needles, so it takes a lot to disturb them. Just walking across them won't do much. There were a few spots where their feet dug all the way to the ground.

I flew up a little higher and it became clearer. The scuffs radiated out in an irregular wandering pattern. There had been shoving. Close to a pine tree was smaller scuff. Someone had fallen and their feet had dug in when they levered themselves up.

So either hard shoves or punches were thrown.

I flew down to the ground and looked over the area closely, hoping to find something that was dropped. And sure enough under a scuff of pine needles was an open penknife.

I couldn't move it, of course, but I could sink into the ground and get my head close to it. I don't cast a shadow and don't actually have eyes, so I could get close enough that it was like I had a magnifying glass.

The knife was old, the edge a bit mangled by someone who really didn't know how to sharpen it. It was a cheap knife with a faux wood plastic handle, the blade about three and a half inches long. The blade was clean, not a bit of blood, and my heart sank.

If there had been blood, that would have probably

been from the perp and the police could take it from here and I could leave this poor dead kid with a good conscience.

But no blood. No easy answers. And no Emily's endless enthusiasm.

I sighed and kept looking.

I TRACED BACK FROM THE SCUFFED AREA. WHILE walking doesn't do much to the thick layer of pine needles deposited over many seasons, it does do something. I spend hours studying the forest floor and getting a feel for the normal variations and then going back to the scuffed area trying to see if I could tell which way they came from.

No trails here. No roads closer than half a mile. If they were the only ones to walk here, I should be able to find it.

But finding the trail was not some romantic, look here's a broken twig, and over there is a bent branch or a bit of cloth like you might see in the movies. This was slow and arduous and very boring, but slight, smaller scuffs were there. I could only pick them up occasionally, but I could find them.

It was this strange, nearly meditative state. The forest floor was all there was to me. The natural variants, the animal trails that disturbed in a thin line, the small volcanic rocks with pale green lichen clinging to it, the scuffs from our perp and vic.

The arrow was pointing to the northeast, so I expected the trail to go to the southwest, deeper into the forest, but it didn't. It quickly curved around and headed east. To the dirt road.

This took the rest of the day. I kept slipping out of my zen state and worrying about Emily, wondering how I would even survive my afterlife without her, but being terrified to tell her my secret. And then I would lose the trail and it would take me time to get my mind in the right state and I would have to backtrack.

Under the robin's-egg blue sky in the thick forest, it was a long and awful day. I kept expecting Emily to come back, but she didn't.

We had had our misunderstandings, of course we had. But it was often the four-year-old that got hurt and that was easy enough to rectify. This time it was the eighty-year-old ghost that was hurt, and this wasn't going to be simple and it wasn't going to be easy.

And I was quite sure that I was going to have to tell her my secret and that would just make things worse.

As the sun was edging close to the horizon, I tracked the perp and vic back to the dirt road and found some fresh tire tracks.

The perp had driven him out here, marched him through the forest, fought him, and then cut him time and time again until he slowly bled out while dragging himself across the forest floor and leaving his arms arranged like an arrow with his dying breath.

Yeah. I don't think so.

I have been doing this long enough to know that when you hit something in a case that just doesn't make sense then you are missing a piece of data or have made a wrong assumption.

There are exceptions, of course. Humans are far less rational than we like to pretend we are, but I had something wrong here, something very wrong.

I WALKED BACK TO THE BODY, ALONG THE COURSE I HAD

tracked, just in case I might have missed something. I went to the scuffed area and tried to recreate the fight, but it was chaotic enough that I couldn't say it was much more than a fight. But I walked through it anyway in case some details fell out.

I felt silly referring to them as "perp" and "vic" so I gave them names—Paul and Vince—as I thought it through.

So Paul and Vince walked out here for some reason heading mostly west and then shortly after they turned to the northeast they started fighting. Shoving, shouting. Maybe they were fighting over a girl or a job or a bet. Anyway, just shoving at first. And then Paul shoved Vince too far and he stumbled back and landed by the tree. He was losing, being the weaker of the two, and pulled out his penknife and threatened Paul with it.

Paul, not being a dummy, picked up one of the many branches lying around and hit Vince's arm with it, knocking the knife away. The fight escalated then to blows and then... Paul pulled a sharp-edged weapon and started slicing Vince up with vicious precision?

Yeah, that makes no sense. None at all. How does a scuffle escalate into a cruel killing? A stabbing, sure. Someone falling and smashing their head on one of the many rocks around here, absolutely. But delivering dozens and dozens of shallow cuts, no way.

The sun was down by now, but that didn't matter to me. I could see just fine in low light and I kept going.

I decided to assume the fight was staged or incidental. In other words, I no longer believed the fight was a catalyst to the murder, and if it wasn't, then...?

Then the murder had been premeditated. Paul had brought Vince out here to kill him. Maybe the fight had been a defensive one initiated by Vince.

I went back to the body. Something about it was really bugging me. I looked at the arms and they were straight, palms up, and back from his body forming a perfect arrowhead.

And then it hit me.

Vince didn't put his arms that way with his dying breath—Paul had arranged them that way.

Paul had arranged the whole thing. Bringing Vince out here. Cutting him and arranging his arms so he looked like an arrow, especially from above. Somehow getting Vince to crawl in a straight line while he bled out.

A chill ran through me although I lacked a body, and I looked around, suddenly afraid I was being watched. This murder had been premeditated and cruel, designed to leave Vince looking exactly like he does. Like a big red arrow in the forest pointing towards Flagstaff.

If I had had a stomach I would have thrown up.

This was not like the other murders we had solved. This was not like anything we'd seen. And this case went beyond the little squabble Emily and I were having.

I flew up into the sky, because I couldn't stand being next to the corpse anymore, but then I could see the dark red blood trail edging towards black in the quickly darkening night. I turned away and looked south towards Tucson and did the only thing I could think of doing.

"Emily!" I screamed. "I need you, Emily. I need you right now!"

Chapter Four

EARLIER I MENTIONED THAT GHOSTS ARE MORE intuitive once the flesh is gone—like Emily and her sixth sense about bizarre murders. As ghosts spend a lot of time together, just like when people spend a lot of time together, they can have intuitive incidents, somehow knowing something about the other that doesn't involve the five senses.

Well, ghosts with their enhanced intuition are even more so. Emily always seemed to know when I was in trouble, when I was teetering on the edge. When I really, really needed her.

That's what I was doing six hundred feet above the corpse arranged as an arrow pointing towards Flagstaff, Arizona. I was hoping that Emily wasn't too mad to pay attention to her intuition. I needed help on this case and I needed it now.

And my own ghostly intuition was telling me... well, it wasn't actually telling me anything coherent, I was just freaked out and paranoid and worried that the killer was watching me.

Ignore for a moment the fact that the killer was alive

and I was not and couldn't possibly be watching me. I "felt" like he was. It felt dangerous. I felt vulnerable.

So I screamed for Emily. Not "at the top of my lungs" because I didn't have any lungs. I also didn't have any vocal cords to get worn out so I just threw a fit and screamed and screamed and screamed.

Unbecoming, yes, I know. Looking at Emily and me, you would assume that I was the parent in the relationship. After all, I look to be in my forties and she looks to be around four. But Emily has had consciousness for over eighty-five years and I knew that her feelings towards me tended toward the maternal.

All that said, I screamed. A lot. "Emily. I need you. I need you now! Emily!"

But she didn't reply, so I changed my tune. "I'm sorry, okay. Do you hear me, Emily? I'm sorry. I've been keeping something from you, something big. I know you know this, I told you as much in Hollywood, but what you don't know is that I have a good reason for not sharing it. It would change everything and I…" I wasn't shouting anymore, just talking. It wasn't the volume that counted as much as the emotion. "I don't know that I want things to change.

"Emily. Please. Something terrible happened to this boy and I can't do this on my own. I can't do this without you."

Still nothing. Just the buzz of cars going down 89A and the glow of Flagstaff beating away the growing darkness as the stars popped out above me.

Screw it then.

I would do this without her. I would fly back to the graveyard and grab some of the ghosts that help us with tough cases who Emily has named "Anchor's Irregulars." The reference to Sherlock Holmes and his "Baker Street Irregulars" was more than a little bit embarrassing to me. I was no Holmes. I was just a washed-out actor who became a dentist and only started on this detective thing to solve my own murder.

And there's the rub. My own murder.

At Emily's encouragement, I recently went and wrote all about my last days alive, all that was happening, all that I remembered. Ghosts have fantastic memories and the act of writing can really pull details out. There had been a lot I had been ignoring, clues I hadn't remembered. But writing about my last day and about haunting my practice brought it all back.

I was pretty sure I knew who killed me.

I just had to prove it.

And once I did, once I finished my proverbial "unfinished business" I could "move on."

Just like the living, us ghosts aren't real sure what is next, but it seems to be a pleasant thing from all reports.

"Emily," I said softly. "Please, you've got to understand. I think I know who killed me. I might know why. And if we prove it, I'll... I'll..."

I couldn't finish, but I didn't have to.

With a "pop" Emily was there hovering over the dark forest, tears streaming down her round face, her green eyes wide.

Emily and I are a strange match, but we had found something unusual living or dead, a working and loving partnership. I was having trouble conceiving of my existence without her, but I truly did not like being a ghost. I wanted to move on even though what was next was a big mystery. My life felt like it had been a bit like I was being tossed around in a dryer. My afterlife had been wading into the darker side of humanity. And while I loved Emily, I was ready for a more peaceful existence, and "moving on" felt like it was that.

Emily sniffed, still studying my face. Had she heard me? Maybe she had been close enough all along. Was her finely tuned intuition enough that she got the essential details now that I had spoken them? It didn't matter, it was clear from her stricken face that she knew.

And then her lips formed a thin line and she took a deep breath, her face slowly hardening.

It only took a few seconds, but it was a bit frightening. The four-year-old who wears her emotions on her sleeve was subsumed by the eighty-year-old ghost that had seen way the hell too much. The hard look of the eighty-year-old ghost on her four-year-old face was so incongruous as to be disturbing.

"What did you find out about him?" she asked, her chin pointing down to the corpse, a dark spot in the darkening night that pointed towards Flagstaff.

Chapter Five

BECAUSE EMILY DIED AT THE AGE OF FOUR, SHE NEVER lost the child in her, even through all the decades dead. It was what made her so unique and special… and often baffling and infuriating.

It was what was most essential about her, that tug of war between her vastly different selves. Sometimes as crotchety as can be and a few seconds later a joyful little imp.

But that was not the Emily that went to work with me that day. She still looked like a four-year-old with her blond Shirley Temple curls and white T-shirt with big lollipop print, but there was no child in her manner and a growl in her voice.

The traditionally cheerful lollipop on her T-shirt, which was a reflection of her mood, was a dark, dingy purple. I had never seen that color before. I wasn't sure what it reflected other than a dark mood.

She was focused on the murder and it was abundantly clear that she did not want to discuss my own murder and the prospect of me moving on.

And you might think that would have been fine by me, after all, I had been the one keeping it a secret, but now that the proverbial cat was out of the bag and I knew it couldn't be stuffed back in, I wanted to talk about it.

I followed Emily down to the forest floor. It was fully dark and the moon wasn't up, but starlight still works fine for ghosts. Our eyeless sight is remarkably adaptable. It's not like we could see as well as in full daylight, but we could still see.

I showed her the carefully arranged arms, palms up at just the right angle. I showed her where they scuffled and the fallen knife. I took her along their path back to the road and showed her the recent tire tracks.

She was quiet the whole time, asking questions with as few syllables as needed. Her face a grim mask of determination that was incongruous with her adorable four-year-old form.

"Conclusions?" she asked after I had shown it all and we had walked back to the body.

This, too, was unusual behavior. Emily generally acted as the catalyst in cases, letting me take the lead, although I often suspected that she knew a lot more than she was letting on, allowing me to go through the motions as a way to teach me and to keep me busy. That single-word question was like Holmes querying Watson to make sure he had followed the clues properly.

"The murder was premeditated," I said. "The goal was to leave the corpse looking like this, like an arrow, especially from above so that..." I trailed off.

"Continue," she said, her hands on her hips, her jaw set.

"The arrow is meant to be seen from above." I turned to the northeast, the direction the arrow was pointing. "The airport is over there. Maybe planes fly over this land, maybe it was meant to be spotted by them, but…"

She sighed. "But what?"

I didn't like this new Emily. Not a bit.

"I… I just have a feeling. I think we were meant to find this. I think someone did this, arranged this body for you and me."

Her jaw dropped open and her green eyes went wide and she suddenly looked like a terrified four-year-old. Her head snapped around looking at the tall, dark trees that seemed ominous now in the dark.

"Walter…" she began, her voice almost shaking. "But that… I…"

I nodded. "I know, honey. That means someone has been reading my stories. Just like that ghost we came across on the Hollywood case. I think what we have been doing is influencing the living. Someone believes my stories. And that someone is now toying with us and they took a life to get our attention."

She swallowed hard and shook her head. "But that is a big leap. A giant leap. People on the ground would notice he was arranged as an arrow."

I nodded. She was right. "One good rain or even a little snow and this doesn't look nearly as much like an arrow. The ravens have been at the body, but once the coyotes find it, it won't be an arrow anymore. And how long before someone stumbles upon this body? No trail, no close roads. We are in the middle of a huge forest."

She bit her lip and nodded.

"I might be wrong about this," I said. "Maybe this whole thing is just creeping me out. But how about we assume we were meant to find this? That the murderer knows your ability to find bizarre murders and that you and I are running around trying to solve them."

"Yeah… okay." She took a deep breath, her face hardening again. "You stay here, I'll get the Irregulars and we'll have one of them watch the body and—"

"Two," I said, interrupting her. "Two of them watching the body. I don't want to leave anyone out here alone for long."

She nodded. "Two to watch the body, and then I'll take you to the SECI chamber and you can type up enough to get law enforcement out here and then…" she trailed off.

I sighed. "And then we follow the clue left for us, we follow the arrow and try to figure out what it is pointing at."

The wind whipped up, rattling the branches around us and Emily happily popped away to get help and I shoved my fears down and kept an eye on our victim Vince.

Chapter Six

_____

IT WAS ONE THING BEING A GHOST, BEING INVISIBLE TO
the living world and going around and solving murders. It
was something completely different knowing that there are
living people doing things _because_ you are dead and solving
murders.

This boy, "Vince," might have been killed just to get
our attention. And let me tell you, that will mess with your
mind, living or dead.

While we got a tiny taste of this with the Hollywood
case, this was something else entirely.

I was hoping Emily would be gone for a minute or two,
that she would pop back with a couple of other ghosts and
I could get the hell out of here. But it wasn't quick. Emily
was honest, she told them what we thought we were up
against and, well... who really wants to volunteer for that?
To go from an invulnerable ghost to...

There was so much I didn't know and my mind just
went wild. If our perp, "Paul," was doing this to get our
attention, that meant he had read my stories, studied my
methods, thought this through and planned it. But what

was the goal? To try to outsmart the ghost detectives or to do something a lot more sinister.

My creeped-out factor said Paul was trying to do both.

If I didn't think much of the forest before, I really hated it now, all dark and foreboding. Trees groaning in the wind. Branches snapping and falling. Clouds rolling in to cover the stars and blot out the little light we had.

After an hour of this, I shook it off and stopped just standing around. It wasn't good for me, not at all. My biology was gone, what could the living possibly do to me?

I started examining the body again, even though the light was getting worse. I sank into the ground so I was eye-level with him and looked at every square inch of our victim. It took longer in the near darkness, but I could still do it. And I found some things.

His right palm had a fresh scrape which lined up with the scuffed-up pine needles and the dropped knife.

His head was turned to the right and I saw a slight bruise on his right cheek. Again, the fight was looking more and more real.

And then I found a needle mark on his right arm.

At first, I thought maybe he was a drug user, that might explain his unkempt appearance, but there was only one and it was recent.

Maybe he had a recent blood test, but it looked like the needle gage was too small for that.

Or maybe Paul injected Vince with something. Before the fight? After the fight? Before they even came out here?

I could only guess, but it certainly complicated the picture.

If we assume that the injection was part of what happened here, what could the murderer possibly gain? Whatever it was, it couldn't be good.

The distraction had been good, but now I was even more creeped out than ever.

―――――――

I GO TO THE SECI CHAMBER AND WRITE UP THESE CASES for a couple of reasons. The first is so the police have something to go on and can arrest the killer. The second is because I need to write these cases. Call it therapy. I am still quite human, despite the lack of biology, and these experiences take some sorting through.

I understand that Tamara Watson and Jin Shi, who run Afterlife Communications, have been publishing our stories, making money off of them to fund what they are doing. And I never had a problem with that, but now...?

If this killing was done to get our attention, that feels like a violation, like someone is using what they know against me, like they know things they shouldn't, private things.

And I guess this blurring of the line between the living and the dead was inevitable with what Tamara and Jin are doing. And in some ways that is the whole point. If you know that death is not the end, does that change how you live?

If I am right, that did indeed change how our perp, Paul, has lived. It has channeled his murderous tendencies in my direction. Not exactly the kind of reaction you are hoping for when you imagine how the assurance of an afterlife will affect the living.

I had way too much time to think about all of this while the clouds sped above and the wind blew and the trees creaked and the night crawled on.

After I had examined the body, I just paced in a slow circle around it, trying to keep my emotions in check.

When Emily popped back in, I jumped, so lost I was in my own thoughts. She had Anna-Maria with her, a young Hispanic woman with long black hair arranged in a braid, a round face, and an easy smile. She wore a leather jacket, jeans, and tall black boots like she was ready to jump onto a Harley.

"Where's Fredrick? Where's Blinky?" I asked. They were the other two that were regularly part of the Irregulars.

Emily pursed her lips and shook her head.

"I don't know what they are scared of," Anna-Maria said loudly, louder than she needed to. "Is this the stiff?" She took a step towards "Vince" and her lips puckered into a sour expression.

I nodded. "What happened?" I asked Emily.

She shrugged. "Things, in general, have gotten wonky lately with more and more of the living believing in us. First all the lookie-loos at the graveyard and then the protests at the Afterlife Communications offices." She sighed. "Folks are a bit spooked. I talked to Fredrick first and he begged off, saying he needed to stay at the grave-yard, and then I couldn't find Blinky."

I could imagine it. Emily telling Fredrick what we suspected that there was a murder committed just to get our attention. You've never seen a grapevine where word travels as fast as a graveyard and I bet Blinky got word and got lost.

"Wimps," Anna-Maria said with a jab of her chin. "I ain't afraid of the living."

I sighed. I really hadn't wanted to leave someone here alone. As I could attest, this idea could really worm its way around your head and get to you.

"Thank you, Anna-Maria," I said. "I really appreciate it. We won't be long."

She shrugged and it looked casual but her brown eyes were a bit too wide. I can't pop, and with the delay we had already had, I wanted to get to the SECI chamber and write this up. I would send Emily, but she is the world's slowest typer and she would be at it for hours.

Anna-Maria died while rock climbing. She used to ride motorcycles and had gotten herself arrested protesting on the border. She was young and brash and as tough as they come, but I was worried about leaving her out here alone.

I shook my head trying to clear it. I had just spooked myself. The living were no threat to us.

"Let's go," I said to Emily, and she grabbed my arm and popped us away.

Chapter Seven

I SHOULD HAVE SENT EMILY BACK TO BE WITH ANNA-Maria while I typed but I didn't want Emily out there either. Her looking like a cute four-year-old still messes with my mind because she's old and tough and probably the most skilled ghost around the graveyard.

But she didn't volunteer either, which was telling.

She popped us to the 2.0 version of the SECI chamber. They are getting ready with a portable 3.0 version, but this one is reserved for me and a few other ghosts and is in a secret location.

There are a lot of ghosts out there that want to be heard, and even though not all of them can manage to type on these, the well-known SECI chambers tend to be crowded.

The SECI chamber works on the principle that ghosts emanate high-frequency electromagnetic (EM) radiation. The chamber is a bit larger than a phone booth and shielded from external EM radiation and has a big keyboard on the wall with a monitor above it. The keys detect ghostly EM radiation when you poke your finger through and the monitor displays what you are writing.

The hard part is that that high-frequency EM radiation that it detects is a much lower frequency than is natural for us ghosts. That's why it's hard to do and takes so much concentration.

As Emily watched, I got to it, typing out the basics of what we had found.

"So... you know who your murderer is," Emily said quietly once I was about a paragraph in.

Her tone was calm. Even. Not the joyfully inquisitive tone of a four-year-old or the growl of a jaded eighty-year-old.

"Yes... well, maybe," I said, trying to stay focused on my task. It was clear now that Emily didn't pop back to Anna-Maria not because she was afraid but because she wanted to talk to me. "I've got motive and opportunity."

She nodded and sighed. The chamber was not big so she was right next to me.

"And when did you figure this out?" she asked, again her tone neutral.

I didn't answer her right away. I kept on typing for a while. It was clear this was going to be a thing, a big thing, but this murder was more than a little disturbing and we needed help.

"A couple of months," I finally said when I was almost done.

"When you went and wrote about your last days?" she asked.

She already knew this. I had told her as much on the Hollywood case. Things had been getting tense between us and I felt I needed to explain my shift in mood.

I nodded and kept typing, the tension in the small space nearly palpable.

"After you were done," she said, her voice still calm, "you told me you didn't find any new leads."

I nodded. "I'm sorry, Emily. I just couldn't face it."

It wasn't enough. Expression of sorrow always seems to be so hollow when you've hurt someone you care about.

"I understand," she said, but I knew she didn't. She couldn't. I hadn't bothered to explain it.

"It was... I..." I stammered, staring down at Emily, her face slack. I opened my mouth to say more but she raised her hand and cut me off.

"I need some air," she said quietly and walked through the SECI chamber wall.

A ghost never needs air.

I bit my lip and got back to my typing.

Chapter Eight

IT TOOK LONGER THAN I HAD HOPED TO TYPE UP THINGS
at the SECI chamber. Emily distracted me with her questions. I was still spooked by the murder, my paranoia going
so far as to wondering if they knew about this location, if
they were watching us here.

Not that they could watch us. We were ghosts. The fact
that the SECI chamber could detect our EM radiation
enough to let us type things like this was something of a
miracle.

But what if someone had figured it out, how to
broaden that technology and learned how to detect the
super high-frequency EM radiation that ghosts emitted?
Then a ghost would be visible.

My head just wasn't on right. I stood alone in the SECI
chamber after I was done, after I had typed the secret
"911" code at the end of the document to get Tamara's
attention so she could pass it on to law enforcement. I just
stood there, my mind racing.

It had been a joy to most of us to be able to communicate from beyond our biological existences, but the world was changing because of it. It had to. This murder, if my paranoia was right, being one of many changes.

I also paused because I didn't want to deal with Emily. With the secret I had kept. With her disappointment in me. It was all just too much.

I wasn't even a detective. I mean, I was living my afterlife as one, but I had no real training, although my time as an actor made me comfortable with improvisation and faking my way through things.

But I couldn't fake my way through my friendship with Emily, and the murder we were dealing with deserved better than that too.

I shook my head and tried to shove all of that down. There was no time for this, not for any of this.

Emily was no nonsense when I walked out of the chamber and I was grateful. She grabbed my arm and popped us back to Anna-Maria without a word.

The clouds had thickened and the night had grown darker. We popped in about a dozen feet from the corpse and I saw several figures hunched over it.

Several.

At first, I thought that the body had been found, but these people glowed with a light of their own and were slightly transparent. Ghosts.

And then I realized that Anna-Maria was not there. All three figures were men.

Emily, who still had a hold of my arm, must have noticed the same thing. She squeezed. It was the numb, barely there sensation of a ghost, but the meaning was still the same.

When I was alive, I was a dentist. The boss of my office. I was not used to people messing with my things, and after the shock wore off, I got angry.

"What's going on here?" I asked, sounding like nothing other than a parent talking to their children.

"Ah…" one of them began, standing up. "If it isn't Casablanca Walter and little baby Emily."

He went by Galt and he had small grey eyes and his quirking smile revealed crooked teeth. His stringy black hair was shoulder length and he was dressed all in black, simple pants and a long-sleeved shirt looking rather goth-ish. He was flanked by two other young male ghosts dressed about the same.

We were not friends, to say the least. Back on my first case, he had been the one who taught Haley to hurt the living. She almost killed her murderer with what Galt taught her. I still missed Haley who was up in Utah at another graveyard where things are a lot quieter and a lot simpler than they are in Tucson.

His Casablanca reference was to my trench coat and fedora. It was at the end of that first case that Emily in her enthusiasm had talked me into changing my ghostly form so I looked like a 1940s-era detective.

"Mind telling me what you boys are doing here?" I asked, keeping my tone even.

Emily gave my arm another squeeze. "Where is Anna-Maria?" she asked, her tone was not nearly as even as mine.

Galt took a couple of steps forward and crouched down a bit like one might do when talking to a real four-year-old. "I'm sorry that your friend had to go. Poor girl scares easily."

There was laughter from his two sidekicks.

There is a dark side to being a ghost. Those bad movies Hollywood makes about ghosts are inspired by folks like Galt and his gang that mess with the living for spite and fun and can do a lot worse when they want to.

"You better not have hurt her," I said.

He stood up straight and took another step forward until we were nearly nose to nose. "Whatcha ya gonna do about it, Walter? Are you ready to 'destroy' me now?"

I had been mad the first time I had confronted Galt. The case with Haley had gotten complicated. I had formed feelings for the girl and Galt's pushing her toward the darker parts of the afterlife had caused her to cross lines, do things that couldn't be undone, which had destabilized her. In my anger, I had threatened to "destroy" him.

"Leave," I said.

"Why should we?" he asked, and his companions chuckled.

"Because if you don't," I said calmly, "I'm going to let Emily do to you guys what I made her promise to never do again."

Before I was a dentist, I was an actor. Played a couple of bit parts on TV shows in the late nineties. I had enough skill to sell it.

Emily chuckled next to me. It was half growl, and Galt stepped back and everyone was silent as the wind blew and the trees creaked and a few pine needles swirled around us. In the distance I could hear the traffic on 89A and the warbling of a siren coming this way.

What I said was something of a bluff, but I honestly didn't know how much. Emily, despite her appearances, was one of the most experienced ghosts around. She was formidable. Did she actually have the skills to hurt another ghost? I didn't know, but they didn't either.

Galt smiled a smug little smile and slowly nodded his head. "We'll move on… this time. There's nothing much to see here anyway. Just a dead guy. Boring." He took a few slow steps backwards.

"Where is Anna-Maria?" I asked.

He shrugged and when he got to his companions, he took their arms and they all popped away.

Chapter Nine

IT'S A SILLY THING, BUT FOR THE MOST PART I JUST WANT to solve murders without interference and without an audience. With the ghosts I trust. With my friends.

We were a clique as were Galt and his goth boys. I knew this. It's how societies form, living and dead.

But what we were doing was important. This time more important than usual. I didn't even have to wonder about how they knew about the murder. That graveyard grapevine had done its job.

After they left, I turned to Emily and said, "I'll stay here, you go pop to Anna-Maria."

That's the thing. A ghost like Emily can pop not only to a location but to a person.

"I could have torn them up, you know," she said, her voice a growl again.

"I know, honey," I said with a grim smile, trying to ban the image of little Emily with her cute blond curls laying into those boys like a rabid squirrel. It made me wonder what paths her eighty-year afterlife had led her down, what things she didn't talk about.

I had fought another ghost on the Hollywood case, but it felt like (and probably looked like) a couple of kids who didn't know what the hell they were doing. We aren't physical, we are energy, and I don't really know what a proper ghost fight is like, but that is probably a clue right there.

Our graveyard in Tucson is a congenial and peaceful place. I had only ever heard of one other fight, one JJ Lynch had gotten in with some ghosts in Globe, Arizona, something he wrote about in his first memoir.

I took a step forward to make sure that nothing had changed with the body when I realized that Emily was still here.

I turned and her face was squeezed in concentration. This wasn't right.

She looked at me, her eyes wide. "I can't… she's not…"

I looked around, not that that would help. I felt paranoid again. Had something happened to Anna-Maria?

"She's not what?" I asked, keeping my voice as calm as I could. The warble of the sirens was getting closer.

"She's not where I can find her," Emily said slowly.

I nodded. There were only two possibilities. She had answered the call and moved on, which seemed highly unlikely, or she had "faded."

Faded is what we call the state of an exhausted ghost. If you are in the presence of one while they are doing it, they quite literally fade away. We don't have unlimited energy, we need to rest, and if we don't rest for long enough, we have to fade.

And no one knows where we are when we fade. We are just gone. Completely. And when we come back, it's like waking up from the deepest sleep you can imagine. No dreams. No memories.

How long you are faded is also variable depending on how depleted you were.

An anger stirred in me and all I wanted to do was to destroy Galt. Anna-Maria was no pushover. When these ghosts had come here, she would have asked them to leave and wouldn't have taken no for an answer. She does not scare easily. Galt and his boys had done this.

I looked at Emily and saw the anger in her face. This had been a day so far. First a body and our conclusion that this corpse had been put here to get our attention. Emily and I not exactly getting along. And now Galt and his gang had messed with one of our own.

"Could they have hurt her? Permanently?" I asked.

She shook her head, but the movement was a bit too tentative for my liking. "Not physically," she said. "She'll be fine when she comes back, but…"

"But what?"

Her eyes narrowed and she studied my face with an intensity that made me want to turn and run. "Being a ghost is all a mental game. You know this. We all have unfinished business. If they pushed the right buttons, she might not be a-okay when she is done fading."

I nodded and bit my lip. The sirens were closer, but their approach had slowed. This was definitely about us. Tamara must have called it in, and the dirt roads were slowing down the emergency vehicles.

"There's going to be a reckoning when this is all over," Emily growled, and I knew she wasn't talking just about Galt and his boys.

Chapter Ten

WE WERE IN THE COUNTRY, SO IT WAS TWO SUVs FROM
the sheriff's office that came first and secured the scene.
The Flagstaff Police Department came next, and then the
meat wagon from the county medical examiner.

The dark night was now lit up with harsh white lights
and flashing blues and reds strobing against the tall pine
trees.

This is what we wanted. This is what we needed. But it
was a grim business and it took the rest of the night.

The scene was secured. The evidence was collected.
Pictures were taken. And Emily and I were with them all
of the way, seeing what they saw, remembering what they
said.

They found the knife. They photographed the scuffed-
up area where "Vince" and "Paul" had fought. They
photographed the tire tracks on the dirt road, and finally
they got to the body.

There were whispers and eyes a bit wider than they
needed to be. Officers looking behind them more than they
might have. This world was beginning to believe in ghosts,

to believe in the afterlife, and they knew that ghosts had found this body.

The medical examiner was a woman of about forty with short brown hair and deep frown lines and dark circles under her eyes. She had on blue slacks and a green fleece jacket. She had her blue latex gloves on and was slowly examining the body. She reached into his back pockets, which were exposed and readily accessible.

"No ID," she said. A square-jawed young man with brown hair and a short beard behind her scribbled notes on a clipboard. He was also dressed in civilian clothing.

"Here's the needle site *they* mentioned," she said, shining a bright flashlight on Vince's right arm at the crease. There was something about the way she said "they." As if she was surprised to find the information good. "I... I concur, this was definitely an injection."

She went to his face which was turned to the right and pulled open one of his eyes. "Brown eyes, pupils dilated. Likely drugged. We'll need to check the blood to be sure."

Emily stepped closer and so did I. This was what we were waiting for. This was what we couldn't do.

"Now on to the cuts," she said with a sigh as she gently opened up a slice in his black T-shirt to examine one of them. "This one is about four inches long, but the cut is only a few millimeters deep." She dabbed at the spot with some gauze and gently opened it with her gloved fingers. "It went through the dermis and the hypodermis and into the muscle, but only barely. Whatever did this was extremely sharp and whoever did it was careful. With something this sharp they could have gone very deep. The cut is extremely straight and it looks like it was done quickly."

Could a sword or machete do a cut that controlled? I didn't think so. What the hell happened here?

The night dragged on and I was wishing that I could fade and just escape all of this, sink into blessed unconsciousness, have a few moments free from the horror of it all.

The medical examiner, her name was Wendy, and her assistant slowly cataloged all the wounds on the back of the body, some sixty-two of them, and then some sheriff's deputies helped them turn the body over.

It was the same on the front, sixty-two precise cuts that went through the skin and just into the muscle. On his legs, his torso, and his face. No single wound life-threatening, but all of them together turning into something mortal.

The T-shirt was a faded concert T-shirt of the Rolling Stones. That didn't seem to be a clue. The kid had no identification on him and nothing in his pockets. And that was strange too.

As the sun was just starting to lighten the eastern horizon in a gentle predawn glow, they zipped the corpse up into a body bag and loaded it into the back of the medical examiner's SUV.

All the living were moving around sluggishly despite the coffee many of them had been drinking. Eyes were too wide and conversations were quiet and stilted.

Flagstaff is a small town. You don't see this kind of thing around here. Hell, I hope that this is the kind of thing that no one sees anywhere.

"Should I go try to get help again?" Emily asked. We were standing on top of a sheriff's SUV just watching quietly. And we needed help. We needed someone to stay with the body while we tried to figure out where the arrow pointed.

I rolled it over. We had Galt and his goth ghosts likely to harass whoever volunteered, so we needed someone they were afraid of. "Yeah," I said with a smile. "See if you can get Banquo to help us."

Emily looked puzzled at first. I wasn't a big fan of Banquo's, for lots of reasons. He wasn't a bad guy, not at all, it was just… well, Emily had a huge crush on him and he was the leader of all the plays that were put on at the graveyard. It might be a bit—or a lot—petty, but that had kept me from really getting to know him. Oh, that and the fact that he was always in teacher mode and always pontificating, which got on my nerves.

And then Emily looked excited as the "crush" part of this kicked in. I was glad to see a glimmer of something besides angst and worry and disgust.

"We need a ghost Galt won't mess with," I said. "Now, go."

With a pop she was gone, and I flew up and watched the scene from a few hundred feet up, which helped. The living looked much smaller which gave the illusion that the challenge we were facing was just a bit smaller too.

It was a trick, I know, but right then I needed anything I could get.

Chapter Eleven

"THANK YOU FOR HELPING," I SAID TO BANQUO AFTER they popped back. We were all hovering over the scene, the meat wagon was just pulling out slowly over the rocky land, and the horizon had lightened just a touch.

Banquo was older, looking to be in his sixties, with a bald head and a thin strip of grey hair. He was short with a large belly and his form was very crisp and barely transparent. He wore dark slacks and a long-sleeve button-down shirt.

"Of course, my boy," Banquo said with a grim smile, his voice deep and resonant. "'Desperate times breed desperate measures,' as the bard said."

Banquo was always quoting Shakespeare. That was another thing I wasn't fond of. I mean, Shakespeare and his plays are amazing, but as a modern actor, I would prefer some more modern plays. How about a nice Sam Shepard play? Maybe "Fool for Love."

But in this case, I loved the quote. Not because it was accurate, which it very much was, but because it was Banquo making a subtle dig at me, saying that I must be desperate if I had wanted his help. Which meant that maybe I annoyed him some too, and…

Yeah, yeah, I know. It was a petty line of thinking and it wouldn't seem like we had time for subtle jabs, but it was honestly just what I needed. Knowing that Banquo was maybe a bit jealous of me and my friendship with Emily was like a shot of espresso waking me up.

"Indeed," I said to Banquo. "We need all the help we can get on this one."

"Then I best be to it," he said, flying down to the meat wagon.

"What now?" Emily asked, her eyes a bit wide and on Banquo. I honestly didn't know if Banquo was unaware of the crush or just ignoring it. Whatever the case was, this was yet another thing I didn't like about him. Emily deserved better.

I gave her a grim smile and said, "Now, we follow the arrow."

Below us the dark red stain where the body had been was still on the ground and still clearly marked the direction.

A SINGLE ARROW SUCKS AS A CLUE. WE WERE ASSUMING that it indicated direction, that it was precisely placed by the murderer. And even if we assumed they had GPS and a great compass, it was executed by a dying man crawling over the forest floor and couldn't be 100 percent accurate.

This was the very definition of a long shot.

Just the kind of thing Emily and I tended to take on.

And I would have been happy—well, let's be honest, and say less grumpy—to explore it as the sun came up over the mountain town and the clouds started to break from the storm that didn't quite materialize last night.

But it wasn't that simple. Our working theory was that this young man had been murdered to get our attention, and that changed everything.

But we worked it, nevertheless.

Emily stayed behind the arrow and acted as spotter as I flew forward. She had discarded the need to be carried. There was no getting around flying for this. I flew out slowly and she guided my path with small adjustments until I had a landmark to follow, which were towers on the east side of Mount Elden.

Elden is the low, rocky mountain that hangs over the east part of Flagstaff. It rises about 2,300 feet from the surrounding town and is covered in ponderosa pine trees, except for the eastern portion which had a devastating forest fire in the seventies that land is still recovering from. There are towers on that side of the mountain and that seemed to be just about perfect.

I flew slowly and listened carefully as Emily guided me.

She used her fine popping abilities and would pop from the arrow, close enough for me to hear her, and adjust my course if needed, and then she would pop back.

We were high enough so there was a clear line of sight, and ghostly vision being free of biology is pretty fantastic so she could see me from a long ways away.

My path took me first over 89A, a two-lane road that cut through the thick forest. Then over the golf courses and large homes of the gated community called Forest Highlands. Then over a working-class community called Kachina Village. Then over I-17, a divided highway running north/south, then the Flagstaff Airport, some more homes, and finally to twirling on-ramps and off-ramps where the east/west I-40 met the I-17.

I made sure I had my landmark fixed and stopped.

This had taken a good hour. We went slowly. We looked for anything below us that might stand out over the entire way. But there was already too much ground to cover, too much to search. And as soon as we crossed the highways we would be into the university and the main part of Flagstaff.

"This is useless," I said when Emily noticed I had stopped and popped to me.

She nodded, her green eyes looking a shade darker than usual. "We're missing something."

I nodded. "We have to be. Either the arrow isn't the clue we thought it was or we don't have enough information. The arrow gives us a direction, not a distance."

Emily shrugged. "So we search all of Flagstaff."

I nodded. "Looking for what? A sign that says, 'I am the red arrow murderer, come arrest me, you damn clever ghosts'?"

Emily pursed her lips and narrowed her eyes. She and I had unfinished business and my grumpiness level was going up and no one was having any fun.

"Sorry," I said. "I'm… I'm just a bit freaked out about this."

She nodded. "Pretend you're not having a little fit, what would you do?"

Ouch. I sighed and let the "little fit" part go. I took some deep breaths and tried to calm my mind. As I've explained before, ghosts most definitely do not breathe, but the more we act like the living the more we feel like the living, so those "deep breaths" have an analogous effect on ghosts.

I stared at the traffic whirling below us. Even though it was early there were cars on the road and even more semis. I-40 runs nearly the entire width of the country.

The patterns were lulling, the drone of the engines and the hum of the tires soothed my stressed mind as I "breathed."

So we had direction not distance. We had a body around here somewhere with the medical examiner working on it and Banquo watching them. We had a murder that was theoretically done to get our attention. And if the murderer wanted to get our attention, they wouldn't just give us one clue and then leave us hanging.

The murderer was playing a game with us. A sick game, but a game nevertheless.

"Sixty-two," I said slowly. "The victim had sixty-two cuts on his front and his back."

"And that has to be on purpose," Emily said with a wicked smile, her green eyes sparking.

I nodded. "One hundred twenty-four in total."

"So is that distance?" she asked, "to go along with direction?"

"Maybe, but are we talking meters, kilometers, or miles?" I asked. "And was it sixty-two on both sides to get our attention or to make up 124?"

"And we're ghosts," Emily said. "Sure, we can follow a direction, but we can't measure distance accurately."

"So what then?" I asked. "A house number? A street address?"

"Maybe," Emily said, and her cheerful expression let me know that while we had our unfinished business to deal with, she was back on the case. "Let's fly back. You stay up high and I'll search for sixty-two or 124 below."

I nodded. It was a long shot, but at least we had a theory and a plan.

Emily's grim smile melted from her face and her eyes defocused and she swiveled in the air and looked to the southeast.

I didn't say anything. I knew better. She wasn't alive, so it wasn't like she was having a stroke or something. I had only seen her do this a couple of times, but I knew what it was. It was her murder radar, or whatever you want to call it. Someone else had died.

"Oh, no," she said, her eyes wide and focusing on me.

"What?"

"There's been another murder," she said slowly, her smooth forehead furrowing. "Walter, I think we have a serial killer on our hands."

Chapter Twelve

When you think of Flagstaff, you think of the forest. The tall ponderosa pine trees with their brown bark and their dark green needles in bundles of three. They are everywhere. The early settlers came to harvest the trees and had to beat them back to make room for humans.

When Emily popped us to the murder she had just sensed, we were back in the forest in another area where the density of trees was relatively low and the rocky ground was covered in dried, tawny pine needles with a scattering of pinecones. Another body lay on the ground, a streak of dark red blood behind it.

"Shit!" I said.

We were sooner this time. The body still had spots of red blood while the tail of the arrow was a dark ochre red. It was a young woman, the ends of her long blond hair thick with blood and sticking to the sweatshirt she was wearing. She had tights and running shoes. And she had precise cut after cut all over her body. She was lying face-down and the arms were arranged to turn her into a perfect arrow. She was pointed north-ish.

I grabbed Emily and flew us up high and fast. I needed to know where we were. I needed to see if we could spot a vehicle moving away. I needed to get away from that corpse.

I cursed as I flew us, and Emily didn't even say a word, didn't tell me to mind my language, didn't tell me to get my "mitts" off of her.

Solving a murder once it's done can certainly be stressful. Solving murders that are being committed because of you, was a whole different thing.

"This is about us," I said between curses.

"No shit, Sherlock," Emily growled. I don't think I had ever heard her curse. This was serious.

The body was in the forest east of I-17 and south of town. There were dirt roads ambling around it, but none close and no trails. To the east was Lake Mary Road which headed out southeast from Flagstaff.

The terrain was flatter, but otherwise the same as where we found the other body.

Except this one pointed almost due north towards Northern Arizona University (NAU). Just like the other arrow. We had found our missing clue.

There were two arrows and together they pointed to a single spot.

Dammit!

"No cars," I muttered, studying the dirt roads.

"Don't bother," Emily said. "Our perp has medical training. They left themselves enough time to get away before the victim died. Before I would notice."

She was right. Shit!

I nodded. "The precise cuts reinforce that assessment," I said. "I'm beginning to think the murder weapon is a scalpel."

I flew us back down to the body and sure enough there

was a small puncture in the fold of the right arm.

"So the perp drugs the victims," I said, pointing out the needle mark, "slices them up, and coaxes them to crawl in a line as they bleed."

"And then is long gone before they actually die," Emily added.

"And no ghost," I said. "Not with either of them. A ghost could ID the murderer."

Emily glanced down at the body. "Too soon to tell."

I shook my head. I knew there wouldn't be a ghost, that the murderer had chosen carefully to find people that weren't full of regret. Had used drugs to mask the trauma of their passage. This was part of their plan too.

Although the sun was crawling above the horizon and the day was lightening, I felt a darkness bearing down on me. Despite being in the forest, I felt claustrophobic like the trees were closing in.

These murders were my fault.

If I hadn't been writing about these cases, about Emily and her ability to sense murders, these people would still be alive. And yeah, I get that I wasn't the sicko murderer, but my writing, my therapy, had been used to fuel these acts. Even if you are being charitable it's clear that I am the catalyst in all of this.

Me. Thinking I was so clever to catch these murderers. Going to the SECI chamber and writing about my life to help me come to terms with it.

I had done this.

"...what do you think, Walter?" Emily was saying, her voice sounding distant.

I felt the need to escape more strongly than I had since I was alive. Since I kicked my gambling addiction, since I stopped shooting myself up with propofol from my dental practice, since right before Emily found me when I was haunting my office manager and out of clues.

I was staring at the body. The woman was thin and from what I could see of her face, maybe twenty years old. She wasn't some washed-up actor with a failed marriage and a career he liked but didn't love. She wasn't depressed and lonely and desperate. She had her whole life in front of her, at least until I came along.

"Walter!" Emily was shouting now and I could hear the urgency in her voice but I couldn't pay attention to her. I could only stare at the girl and watch the blood slowly dry.

Part of me knew what was happening. I was sinking into that ghostly state that we call the bardo. A place where you are trapped by your regrets. All those wispy moaning ghosts that are a part of how the living view the dead, those ghosts are in the bardo, trapped in their own hell, unable to escape their regrets.

And the part of me that knew I was sinking into the bardo knew without a doubt that I deserved to be there.

I had failed at acting, the thing that I had loved so.

I had failed my wife and our unborn child and watched my marriage crumble.

I had failed to create a life worth living in Tucson.

And I had failed to know that someone wanted to murder me and let them use my known propofol addiction against me. I had died in one of my dental chairs, the needle still in my arm, the milky white bottle of propofol close by. My death had been ruled a suicide.

And I had new leads on who killed me and I screwed that up too. I hadn't told Emily and I had let that killer get away with it.

I wasn't even a very good detective.

I deserved to be in the Bardo.

"Walter!" Emily screamed as she slapped my face.

It wasn't just that numb, barely there ghostly touch. What Emily did to me was something different. She put her energy and her intent into it. She flew up so our heads were even and let me have it.

I felt an electric shock flow through me and the darkness that had almost swallowed me receded a bit.

She slapped me again.

"But... this is... I..." I mumbled.

Another slap.

I had heard of several techniques for helping a ghost slipping into the bardo, and none of them ever involved slapping. Leave it to Emily.

"You don't get to do this, Walter," she said, hysteria edging into her voice. "You don't get to leave me. Not you." She slapped me again, harder, a zap of energy flowing through my body akin to rubbing your feet on the carpet and touching something metal.

For a ghost it was an extreme sensation.

She slapped me again and again, but I didn't want to come back. I had screwed up my life and I had screwed up my afterlife. Emily was still talking, but I wasn't listening to her, the darkness coming back despite the energy she was pumping into me.

And then I could hear it, the bardo. It was calling to me, not using words, but something deeper and more primal. It was promising me relief from all of my suffering, an end to all this running around and trying to solve murders or the painful process of closure with my ex-wife, and an end to all the loneliness.

It was sweet and insistent, the call of the bardo, but not pure. It wasn't sound or taste or any particular sense, more like the irresistible tug of gravity. I was going, nothing could stop me. The bardo just had to be better than this afterlife.

Part of me knew that was a lie. That the bardo wasn't about escaping your mistakes but endlessly reliving the worst of them. The bardo played the same music and held the same promise as my addictions had. It was like the gambling and the propofol, promising escape but actually making things worse, much worse. But the part of me that knew that wasn't in control.

The forest darkened further like the darkest of nights and I was almost gone when I heard crying.

Not the quiet tears of an adult but the desperate wailing of a child, hurt and inconsolable. The unfettered crying of youth before they started bottling up their emotions to be an adult.

It was louder than the call of the bardo and it pulled at my heart.

And then I knew who was crying. Emily. It was the kind of crying that leaves your eyes red-rimmed and snot running down your face. It was the cry of a child that had lost what it cared about the most.

And even I, with all my self-loathing, could not let that be. I had to go to that cry. I had to help.

It took every ounce of will I had, but I turned from the bardo and towards the crying child, towards Emily.

The world came back to me and I took her in my arms as she wailed. "I've got you, honey," I said. "I won't leave you. I promise I won't leave you."

Emily's crying slowed until she was making less noise but her chest was still heaving with emotion. "Don't... don't make promises you... you can't keep, Walter," she managed to get out and then the wailing took her again.

And this was part of what was between us that we didn't talk about.

I had been trying to move on from this afterlife since I got here. The bardo wasn't the right way, I knew that now that I was rational again, but there was something beyond this life as an earth-bound spirit and I was determined to get there. As soon as I solved my own murder. Which I had enough information to go try to do now.

I held her as tightly as I could and gently rocked her there in the early morning in the forest south of Flagstaff next to our serial killer's bloody second victim.

"I won't leave you, Emily," I said, my voice thick with emotion. "Not until we catch the bastard that did this."

Chapter Thirteen

EMILY CAME BACK TO HERSELF FAIRLY QUICKLY, WIPED the snot off her face and said, "Get your hands off me, you perv." But there wasn't much energy behind it and her eyes remained red rimmed, although as a ghost there was no reason for that.

I put her down.

"We need help," I said, slowly. I was ashamed. I knew we needed to talk more, but the corpse and trail of blood laid out like a red arrow had to be the priority. There would be time enough for all that shame and all that talking later.

She nodded.

"I know where we are well enough to describe it," I said. "Can you pop me to the SECI chamber so we can get the authorities out here?"

She nodded again, wiping more snot off her face.

"And then you need to find someone to stay with the body while we go follow the arrows."

"Who?" she asked. "Fredrick was making excuses last night and Blinky faded to avoid me, and Anna-Maria..."

She trailed off. Anna-Maria was an issue, but we had more pressing ones. I bit my lip and nodded, hoping Anna-Maria was just faded. I racked my brain. We needed someone fearless, someone who wouldn't care that the living were stalking the dead. No. We needed someone who would be pissed that the living were stalking the dead.

"JJ," I said. "We need JJ."

JJ Lynch knew Tamara and Jin when he was alive. He helped them build the first SECI chamber and was the first ghost to use it. He had written two long memoirs in it and once entered the bardo of his own free will to rescue someone he didn't know.

"He ain't afraid of no living," Emily said, a smile cracking through her grief like the sun lancing through the clouds after a violent storm.

"Think he'll help?" I asked.

Emily smiled coyly. "Oh... I think he likes me."

I laughed, it was strained and short lived, but I was grateful for it.

"Good," I said. "We have a plan. But before we go, we need to do some counting." I took a deep breath and looked at the body and all the cuts through the clothing and into the skin.

Emily's jaw set and she nodded and we got down to it.

JJ FOR ALL HIS DARING DO, IS A KIND AND GENTLE BEING. He's medium height and medium build with brown hair buzzed short and intense blue-grey eyes. He looked to be about thirty years old and was dressed simply in jeans and a long-sleeved black T-shirt.

As soon as I was done at the SECI chamber, Emily was

there with JJ and she popped us all back to the forest. She was showing him the body and all that we had found.

"And here is the injection sight," she said, pointing at the needle mark on the right arm. "We believe some kind of drug was used to make the victim docile."

JJ nodded, looking closely where she pointed.

"She has sixty-two cuts on her back, just like the last victim," Emily continued. "And if our perp is true to form, there will be sixty-two cuts on her front."

"Why would they do that?" JJ asked.

Emily shrugged her tiny shoulders. "We haven't figured that out, but we think it's a clue."

Emily went on walking JJ through what we had found, but I wasn't listening. He had said, "Why would *they* do that." They. I'm sure he just chose a gender-neutral pronoun and English being bad at that had chosen "they." But what if earlier when I had chosen to call the perpetrator "Paul" I had biased my thinking in two ways. In thinking a man did it and thinking a single person did it.

We had no evidence of either.

Emily was done and they were both looking at me, so I shook it off. "I really appreciate this, JJ," I said.

He gave me a short nod.

"I would expect Galt and his boys to show up," I added. "Not sure why, but they seem to be interested in this one."

JJ shrugged.

"They messed with Anna-Maria," Emily said with a bit of a growl.

He smiled at the girl and shrugged casually again. "They show up," he said, "I will nicely ask them to leave. They don't leave, maybe they're ready to answer the call."

Emily blinked, her jaw wide and I could see her crush get that much more crushing. There was the paradoxical combination of humility and confidence to him and apparently Emily couldn't get enough of it.

Some ghosts have specialties. Emily can pop. Blinky, the absent member of our team, specializes in looking like inanimate objects—which is quite tricky to do with the "more you act like the living the better you feel" thing. And JJ, he can summon the call... and not say yes to it, somehow.

I've never experienced the call, but I hear it is like hearing the most beautiful music that you just can't describe. Unlike how the bardo calls to you, "the call" is full of nurturing energy and the promise of a better existence. It is the reward I have been striving toward, the reason I turned myself into a detective, it is my escape from this existence as an earth-bound spirit.

It's a one-way trip, so we don't know what's on the other side of the call. Except as ghosts we know for sure that there is an afterlife so there must be something there when you "move on."

It was only a moment, my mind churned through all of that and I found myself looking into JJ's kind eyes. "Umm... Can you... I..." I stammered looking a lot sillier than Emily with her crush. I took a deep breath. "I might need your help," I said. "After this is all over."

His eyes widened as he comprehended what I was saying. "That would be my honor, Walter."

I stood there for a moment more, my eyes locked with JJ's. I just couldn't look away. JJ, being Banquo's apprentice, wasn't someone I had spent a lot of time with and I was regretting that. I was regretting my jealousy towards Banquo too.

"Thank you," I finally said, looking at Emily who was staring at me. "We better get going."

JJ smiled. "You guys are so brave. Go find who did this. Stop these murders. I got this."

I picked Emily up and floated us up several hundred feet so we could orient on this arrow.

"You've got a crush on JJ Lynch," Emily hissed in my ear.

"I do not," I said. "You have the crush."

Her cheeks flushed red and she said loudly, "I do not, you do."

"I do not," I said. "I am heterosexual."

She snorted. "As if that matters anymore, it's not like you have a ding-dong or anything."

"Emily!"

The embarrassing part of all this was, that ghostly hearing being as good as it is, JJ probably heard every damn word.

Chapter Fourteen

IT TOOK TIME. FOR EMILY AND ME TO GET BACK INTO the game after my brush with the bardo and our time with JJ. For us to get oriented on this bloody arrow and for me to fly forward with Emily spotting like with the last arrow. And more time to go back and redo that arrow.

We checked and double-checked. We triangulated. We stayed focused and we ended up floating above a large building on the south campus of NAU.

The building was comprised of two large square sections, the bottom right edge of one almost touching the top left corner of the other. Bridging the two was a third square section offset at 45 degrees and joining the other two.

The main square sections had pitched roofs that peaked in the center of the building making them look like two large Xs from above.

I cursed.

A lot.

I knew this was the spot. The murderer was playing with us and knowing the arrows would be a bit imprecise, the goddamn location for us to find was marked by huge Xs.

Emily just stared at me, her face gone pale. I was holding her on my hip since we were together and she preferred not to fly.

"Well…" I began, not really having words for any of this.

"Oh boy," Emily sighed. "What have we gotten…? Oh boy."

Fear doesn't leave you when you're dead, not at all. But the fear of someone hurting you physically does because you are not physical anymore. But what I was feeling hovering over those two giant Xs was that kind of fear. Like someone was out to hurt me and it was personal.

"We… we should go search," I said, remembering how JJ had just called us brave and feeling anything but.

"Yes, we should," Emily said, her voice eerily calm.

We just hovered there.

A minute ticked by and we both just stared.

"I'm sorry," I finally said.

Emily's green eyes found mine. "What for?"

I sighed. "For not telling you right away about the clues I found when I wrote about my last days. For typing all these cases up and fueling the madness of the psycho that did this. For being a general grump and not being nearly good enough for you, Em."

Her eyes widened and she stared at me for a moment, and then floating above NAU, she pulled me into a fierce hug. "I love you too, Walter," she whispered with a sniff.

And then I was crying. God, how many emotions can I have in one damn day?

I do love Emily. Not in the crushing way of romance but in a deeply unique way. It was like she was both my mother and my daughter at the same time. I loved her as the person that saved my afterlife and as my best dead friend.

There were tears on her face when the hug ended. "One more case after this one, Walter," she said slowly. "And then you can move on." Her face clouded and the slow trickle of tears threatened to turn into a raging river, but she sniffed and her face hardened. "You should move on if you want to. Don't you dare stay for me."

I nodded.

"Do you hear me?" she said, loudly this time, pushing away from me and floating on her own there up in the air. "I don't need you to stay for me." Her nostrils flared and she put her little fists on her hips.

My own tears threatened torrential proportions and all I could do was nod, and I loved this strange tough little ghost all that much more.

"Now let's do this," she said her lip curling comically in a four-year-old's version of defiance.

I nodded and we both started flying down when there was a pop and Banquo was there.

His round face was white and his grey eyes were wide. "Wait," he said. "There's something you have to know."

Chapter Fifteen

I DIED OF AN OVERDOSE OF PROPOFOL. THE DRUG IS AN anesthetic, a tricky one to administer, and an easy one to overdose on. It doesn't really take pain away, but it leaves you just not caring about the pain. It allows you to disconnect from it in this most amazing way.

It can also wipe your short-term memory, which can be quite useful sometimes.

Propofol is not as regulated as some other drugs and not that hard to get, especially if you are running a dental practice.

I loved propofol. I knew my problems weren't gone, but when I was high on it, I could float along in a cloud of "I just don't care." It was the relief I craved, but it wasn't earned. It wasn't real.

And I hate propofol, because I wasted all that time with it and it ended my life.

My afterlife was built on the foundation of "I was murdered." It gave me purpose. It gave me ambition. It gave me my unfinished business.

When I was writing the story of how I died, I was

forced to confront the fact that since I have no memory of it, that I might have done it myself. I might have overdosed, although Emily insists that she can smell murder and I stink of it (this despite the fact that ghosts have no sense of smell).

I tell you all this so you'll understand how what Banquo said hit me.

He popped in looking half-terrified, and let me tell you, this is not Banquo's normal demeanor. He's the rock of the graveyard, the one who is always helping other ghosts.

"Propofol," he said with a gasp. "They found propofol in the victim's blood."

Before I had believed these murders were about me. Now I knew.

I couldn't hear the sound of the cars on the highway just to our south or the birds greeting the fall morning anymore. The darkness of the bardo was calling again, but I paid it no mind. I felt a rage spark deep in me and I wanted to hurt someone. Badly. I wanted to find who did this and yank them across the veil, make them a ghost, and then I wanted to take my ghostly hands and figure out how to beat them senseless.

This was more than personal on the part of the murderer (or murderers). This was cruelness at a level I don't think I had ever experienced.

It was fight or flight time again, and unlike before when I was falling towards the flight of the bardo, I wanted to fight. I was ready to fight. I needed to fight.

"Thank you," I said to Banquo, my voice sounding strangely calm and oddly distant. "Did they find anything else or just propofol?"

Banquo's eyes narrowed and his focus seemed like he was looking through me. Into me. "They think there may be more," he said, "but they haven't identified them yet."

I nodded. Emily was right, we needed to solve this case. That was the only thing that mattered. We needed to stop whoever was doing this.

"Are you okay, Walter?" Banquo asked.

I smiled. I know it looked stiff and weird, but it was the best I could manage. "I will be once we solve this case." I turned to Emily. "Are you ready?"

She was staring at me too. They both knew my past, they must have had a clue how this hit me. I think they were expecting more of a reaction.

And I was having one, but I was keeping it inside, letting the fire slowly grow, waiting for when I could unleash it.

I didn't wait, I flew down to the huge two Xs to find the next clue the killer had left us.

Chapter Sixteen

The building was a student union called the Du Bois Center. I think it used to be two separate buildings and they built the diagonal piece to join the two large squares. It had tiled floors and comfortable sitting areas and places to eat. It had a ballroom and conference rooms, and this early in the morning there was only a janitor there mopping the floor.

It didn't take long to find the clue, and when I did the spark inside of me threatened to go nuclear.

Along one of the winding hallways on the main level there was a desk that said "NAU Box Office." They sold tickets to events on campus. On the wall were two glassed-in frames that held posters of upcoming events.

The first poster was of an upcoming production of "A Midsummer Night's Dream." More Shakespeare. I almost groaned.

The next poster wasn't right. It took a moment for it to register it was so not right. My mind slipped a gear. I recognized it, of course. I used to have this same poster hanging in my living room as a form of torture, as a reminder of the past that I had lost.

Central to the poster was a beautiful woman of Korean descent standing at an angle to the camera, her head turned to face it. She had high cheekbones and was Hollywood beautiful with full lips and a perfectly symmetrical face. She wore a dark blue pantsuit and her long, silky black hair was pulled back into a ponytail. On her hip was clipped a brass police badge.

To her left and right, fading into the distance where four other figures, three men and another woman, all of them standing up straight, some with their arms crossed. They were all standing on aged and cracked blacktop and in the background was the Los Angeles skyline.

The top read "Detectives: LA — coming fall of 2010." And right below it "Season Five."

This was no NAU event. Someone had put that there for me to find. That woman was Sun Parker. My ex-wife. The love of my life. For season five of the show they made what they called "hero" posters with each one of the five leads taking the center for one of them.

This was Sun's hero poster.

Sun's huge success and this series had come a while after our divorce. I had looked at that poster every day after I had gotten it. They were promotional only, not for sale, but I still had plenty of Hollywood friends.

I loved that poster and I hated that poster.

On one hand, I was so proud of Sun, she had made it. On the other hand, it was a reminder of what I had and what I lost. I am not Hollywood beautiful, more character actor material, and somehow I had ended up with that amazing woman. We had been in love. For real. I've already written about all of this, so I won't repeat myself here, but suffice it to say if the killer wanted to sucker punch me, this was the perfect thing.

"Walter…?" Emily gasped when she saw the poster. "That's… it's…"

I nodded. I couldn't speak. I felt like the wind had been knocked out of me.

"Is this the clue?" Emily asked.

"Yes," I said, before even thinking about it. "The killer used propofol on their victims." My voice was droning and flat. "The red arrows pointed to the X. The X holds a poster of Sun. The killer has pointed us at Sun and took two lives doing it."

Emily gasped, her hand flying to her mouth. "I… we… Oh, God," she mumbled.

If not for the spark, if not for that seed of anger, I think the bardo would have taken me. It called to me of escape, but I understood how it lied. The same way propofol lied to me, except the bardo never let you forget, not for a moment.

The killer wanted to hurt me, as badly as possible. Sun was the way to do that, especially now that we had had some closure and healing.

The spark exploded in me and I felt a rage like I had never felt before. I had once promised to destroy Galt, but now I knew I would destroy whoever did this. I would do whatever it took. I would pay any price.

"Take me to Sun," I said, still staring at the poster and not looking at Emily.

The red arrows had just been the first act. The search was the second act. Now it was time for the climax, for the killer's third act, and I was determined that it would not end well for them.

"Walter, I don't think we should…"

"Take. Me. To. Sun." I said the words slowly, keeping

my tone even. I didn't want to scream at Emily, but it was taking everything I had not to.

I turned and met her eyes and she took a step back. "No, Walter. Not when you're like this."

Haley was like this when she found her killer, she was a fury right out of Greek mythology. She attached herself to her killer and did everything in her power to destroy him. And she was a brand-new ghost that was just operating on instinct. I had been this way a while. I knew I could do better. If I was willing to lose myself while doing it.

"Fine," I said and turned back to the poster focusing on the image of Sun, on her lovely brown eyes, making her my entire world like she once was when I was alive and young.

I knew the theory behind popping. You had to visualize something so strongly that it became real and then you were there with it.

I had popped once before, during the ghost bride case, because I needed to see Sun. I did then because I was desperate. I was desperate now.

I stared at her face on the poster. Sun's face I knew better than my own. This poster was a few years old so there were a few more delicate lines around her eyes and her smile lines were a tad deeper, but she was still the luminous beauty she always was.

And I had this fire burning in me and I had a mission, I had a purpose, and that brought me focus.

I made her my world until with a "pop" I was with her.

Chapter Seventeen

WHEN I POPPED TO HER, SUN'S BEAUTY WAS PRESENT, but it was diminished by her left eye being swollen halfway shut, the bruising around it an angry red edging towards purple. Her hair was a bit disheveled and she wore jeans, hiking boots, and a flannel shirt. There was a rip in her jeans, a bloody wound underneath. The left shoulder of her shirt was ripped showing the strap of her black bra.

Someone had hurt her. That someone would pay.

I looked around and did a double take. I was in a small travel trailer while Sun sat on a couch, a steaming cup of tea on the small glass table next to her. She was focused on her phone, flipping casually. She didn't appear to be in distress although she looked tired.

Next to her was a script flipped open and some lines highlighted in yellow.

Wait a minute.

I got close and could see the artifice behind the damaged eye. Makeup. She was on set. If I had a heart, I think it would have beaten its way out of my chest by then.

Being on set has this feel to it. I did it more as a grip,

which has a very different vibe, but I did it enough as an actor to know the rhythm.

Long days and sometimes nights. Lots of waiting for the setups. And then you are on, so on, and have to throw everything you have into the scene.

It runs hot and cold. But when it's hot, it's scalding hot. It's everything you've got. It's whipsawed emotions and bright lights and dozens of crew staring at you and money being spent by the minute so you have to get it right.

It's adrenalized and high stakes when you are on, and I loved it.

It's boring and tedious when you're not, and you have to structure your day so you don't go mad. You can study lines, rehearse, take care of business, or just goof off. But you best have a plan to get through the psychotic nature of a day on set.

Or night.

It was early morning and the fatigue written on her face despite the makeup she wore was probably from shooting all night. I took a moment and flew through the trailer. It was just her. I looked out the window and saw tall green-needled pine trees.

She was fine. She was working. Thank God.

But she could easily be in Flagstaff and that worried me.

With a "pop," Emily appeared, her eyes going wide and her mouth opening when she saw Sun.

"It's makeup," I said, trying to keep my voice calm. "I think she just did a night shoot."

Emily looked at me and her brow furrowed as her eyes took me in. "Are you okay, Walter?"

"No!" I said, my voice loud. "I am most definitely not okay. I am furious. Look at those trees. We are probably still in the Flagstaff area. This is so not over. If something happens to Sun, I'll—"

My words were choked off by a knock on the door. My anger had twisted into fear by seeing what looked like a beaten Sun, even though I knew it wasn't real.

Sun put her phone down and stifled a yawn. It was still early, but honestly since I became a ghost it was hard for me to judge the time. It was somewhere around 7 a.m.

I looked around, my head snapping back and forth. I had forgotten something. I just knew it. I should have done more than just stare at Sun when I got here. She wasn't safe. I wasn't doing what needed to be done. I wasn't protecting her.

Sun opened the door, a smile lighting up her face, and suddenly she didn't look tired anymore. "You must be Mary," Sun said, stepping aside and letting another woman walk in.

A woman I knew.

A woman I knew well.

Mary Paulson used to be my dental assistant. My first hire when I started the dental practice. She was a big woman with brown eyes and round cheeks. Her blond hair was cut shorter than when I had seen her last, something of a pixie cut, and she looked older. A lot older.

It wasn't anything specific. She would be in her mid-thirties now, but the dark circles under her eyes and her slightly sallow complexion made her look older. The Mary I knew was a woman that smiled a lot and had the smile lines to prove it. On this older woman they looked like frown lines.

After going to the SECI chamber and writing about my death by propofol, I had remembered that Mary had a crush on me and I had never seen it. I had known that her marriage was troubled, that she was hoping her unplanned pregnancy would bring her and her husband closer. She had confided in me a lot. We had been friends, but I had never imagined anything else.

She had.

She was an army medic in Afghanistan before training to be a dental assistant. She knew all about propofol and the secret I hadn't told Emily was that I suspected she was involved in my murder.

I had played the scenarios out in my mind. Mary telling her husband about her feelings for me just after their baby had come. Him sneaking into the practice, confronting me, and overpowering me and shooting me up with propofol.

But that didn't work. He was a construction worker and before that a soldier. He wouldn't have the knowledge of propofol or the skill with a needle. There would have been a fight and my body showed no signs of one.

That left me with Mary as my murderer. She knew my problems with the drug, everyone in the office did, and knew exactly how to use a needle. But I couldn't face it.

Being dead and reflecting on my life, especially when I went back and relived my last day and my haunting of my dental practice, had slowly eroded my view of the life I had lived. The hindsight of a ghost, with our spectacular memories, changed it. Withered it. Left me with my mistakes and my grief and made my life something I didn't quite recognize.

You might be thinking that this is the work of an earth-bound spirit. To look at their lives and finish up their unfinished business. And it is. But it can be so very hard.

When I found the Mary clue, I turned away from it. I just couldn't handle it. She was my colleague and friend. Someone I worked with and relied on. Someone I confided in. If she was the one that killed me, that would erode the view of my life even further. Too far.

I just couldn't face it. So I avoided it. Refused to believe it.

But as I saw her standing awkwardly just inside the trailer, brushing at her short blond hair, her down jacket still on, I knew that I had been a fool.

I had been afraid to see it.

I had been unable to accept it.

Mary was my killer.

Mary was the red arrow murderer.

Mary was here to kill Sun.

Chapter Eighteen

I COULDN'T MOVE. I COULD HARDLY THINK. AND thankfully I didn't need to breathe. Emily had taken a hold of my arm, like she didn't want me to be able slip away again. She was looking at the two women, a puzzled look on her face.

"Don't worry about the eye," Sun said with a chuckle. "It's just makeup."

"Thank you for seeing me," Mary said, looking down and not meeting Sun's eyes. Mary was wearing jeans and a blue down jacket zipped all the way up. It was early fall and the mornings get cold, but it seemed like she was over-dressed.

"Of course," Sun said motioning towards the couch. "Would you like to sit? Can I get you some tea? I'm afraid I can't keep coffee around anymore... I used to drink way too much of it."

Mary looked up, smiled briefly and shook her head. "I'm okay. And I... I think I need to stand. I'm just so nervous." She shifted a large brown purse that was on her shoulder.

"That's fine," Sun said, grabbing her tea and taking a sip, but staying standing. "So, you worked for Walter?"

Mary nodded. "I… I feel so bad about what happened to him and I…" She took a deep breath. "Do you mind if we talk about something different? Just until… you know… I…" She brushed at her hair again with her left hand and I noticed she wasn't wearing a wedding ring anymore and wondered if that was part of the reason behind all of this.

Sun smiled and nodded. "Sure. What did you have in mind?"

She looked around, eyeing the trees just out the window. "What are you guys doing in Flagstaff? I thought your show took place in LA."

Emily looked at me, her eyes wide as she chewed on her lower lip. "It's her…? From your practice?" she whispered, even though the living couldn't hear us.

I just nodded.

"Oh, it does," Sun said. "This is the climax of a long storyline my character, Melissa Lee, is part of. Abusive relationship." She pointed at her eye. "But don't worry, the bastard gets his own in the end."

"Really?" Mary asked, suddenly seeming more normal. "Melissa Lee is such a confident, strong woman, how did she get caught up in this kind of thing?"

"The usual way these things happen," Sun said. "One small step at a time. One tiny abuse after another until…" she shrugged her shoulders.

"Have you…?" Mary asked, her eyes down again, but I could hear something hopeful in her tone.

"Me?" Sun asked, shaking her head. "No. Walter is a good man and I was lucky before him and I've been very careful since. But… I know women. We all know women." She was eying Mary, she caught it too. Mary had been abused in some way.

I remember Mary telling me of fights she and her husband would have where they would shout at each other, but she never mentioned anything physical and she never came to work with any visible wounds.

Mary nodded, her brow furrowed. "You said 'is.'"

"Excuse me?" Sun asked.

"You said Walter 'is' a good man. Not 'was.'"

Sun smile, it was a small wistful thing. "Well…" she began and looked around. "I've had a long night. Can we please sit?"

Mary nodded shyly and sat in an armchair and Sun sank into the couch with a sigh. "God, I hate night shoots. I think I'm just about too old for it."

Mary smiled but didn't say anything.

Sun leaned forward toward Mary, her elbows on her knees. "Walter is still a good man because he is out there, even as a ghost, helping people," she said. "I play a detective, but he has really become one."

"You are proud of him," Mary said. It wasn't a question.

Sun sat up and nodded. "Walter wanted this," Sun said, gesturing at the small trailer and all it implied. "He was good enough. He worked hard enough. He just wasn't lucky enough. I'm glad he's getting a second chance to do something…" Sun broke into a broad smile. "Well… something more important than all of this."

There was a weariness in Sun's voice that I wasn't used to. She had wanted the acting career even more than I had, had been even more driven and even better at her craft. Maybe it was all the years on the same show that had worn her down.

There was a knock on the door and a young man entered the trailer. "We're ready for you, Ms. Parker."

464

Sun nodded and smiled at Mary. "This shouldn't take too long. Wait for me?"

Mary smiled. "Of course."

And then Sun was gone and I would have followed her but for Mary.

"I know you are here," she said, her voice just above a whisper, her tone sharp, her lip curling a bit when she said "you."

Emily looked at me, her eyes wide again, her grip on my arm tightening, but neither of us spoke, like we were children hiding from our parents.

"Listen to me, Walter. You too, Emily." She opened up her purse and pulled out a gun. "You could fly off and go get the police, but if I hear a siren approaching, I'm going out there and I'll start shooting. I'm an excellent shot. Sun will die first."

I didn't know where we were. I hadn't left the trailer. I hadn't seen much but trees out the window and door. But from what she was saying we had to be fairly isolated. But that didn't mean law enforcement couldn't approach quietly.

"Don't leave, Walter," she said, slowly getting up. "You really don't want any more of the living involved in this." She unzipped her jacket and underneath was a vest with blocks of this grey play-doh-looking substance with wires and a single red light. "If this thing starts going the way I don't want it to… boom."

She said it dispassionately, without emphasis, and that made it all the more scary.

Emily squeezed my arm harder and I knew she must have so many questions, but neither of us spoke, terrified we might miss something.

"There's nails in the vest," she said. "A lot of people will be hurt. But look on the bright side, you might end up with some new ghost friends to help you go solve murders."

She zipped up her jacket and slowly smiled, looking all around the room. "Now, I need you to prove to me you are here. Flash the lights twice or something. If you don't, I'll go end this right now."

But I couldn't flip the lights on and off. It was within the realm of possibility, some ghosts could do it, but I couldn't. I had never tried.

She looked at her watch. "You've got two minutes."

"Can you?" I asked Emily, panic edging into my voice.

Emily shook her head. "JJ can," she said.

"Go get him! Go get Banquo. We need all the help we can get."

She nodded. "What are you going to do, Walter?" She was eyeing me like she thought I might try to do something crazy. And I might, but my mind was still too disorganized to even come up with a crazy idea.

"Better get a move on," Mary said.

"Please!" I said to Emily, and she popped away, leaving me alone with the killer.

Chapter Nineteen

I KNEW HOW JJ LYNCH HAD MANAGED TO TURN ON lights. He had lowered the frequency of his ghostly form in just the right way, put his hand into the light switch, and bridged the gap. That had allowed electricity to flow.

JJ had done a lot of crazy things with electricity. He had accidentally killed a man that was about to kill his best friend. He had spent the early part of his afterlife figuring this stuff out. I had less than two minutes.

It wasn't going to work.

And then I thought about the SECI chamber, this typewriter for ghosts. I have to lower my frequency and keep it lowered so it can detect my presence. Manipulating electricity was the same thing, lowering your frequency, albeit at a greater degree.

I had to try. What else was I going to do?

Ghosts emanate high-frequency electromagnetic radiation. It's how we see each other. That frequency is so high that the living can't see it. The SECI chamber has the best detectors they can get, but there is still quite a distance between our natural frequency and that. And even more to affect electricity.

"Ninety seconds," Mary said dryly.

Being an actor was all about faking things convincingly. I had acted my way into being a detective. Back at the university, I had had enough focus to pop. And doing things as a ghost is all about willpower, all about believing you can do something.

So I started acting like I knew what I was doing. I took my right hand and lowered its frequency to what the SECI chamber required. It's a feeling, not one I can really explain, because the biology of the living makes something this subtle hard to understand.

It's unnatural, it's difficult, it takes focus and you feel... I don't know, a quieting in your being. A slowing. So I took my hand down to SECI levels and just kept going.

I moved to the small kitchenette. It had a light above the sink that wasn't on. I lowered the frequency of my hand some more, slowed it down some more. Not my whole form, that would be too hard, just the hand.

"Sixty seconds," Mary said.

Where was Emily with JJ? He could do this easily. I felt my progress falter and then reverse some and I shook it off. If JJ got here, he could do something, but he wasn't here.

For Sun. I could do this for Sun.

To save her from this murderer.

The spark reignited and I used that energy to slow my hand down, to lower the frequency, to make it do what I needed it to do.

I stuck my hand in the switch and... nothing.

"Thirty seconds," she said. "Come on, Walter, surely you can figure this out."

I ignored her and focused. This was a mental game. This was willpower. I had a font of anger and desperation to fuel me. I was an actor and was used to pretending I knew what I was doing, which was effective a lot more than you think it would be.

I lowered my frequency more until my hand started to feel more solid, more substantial.

I tried again… nothing, but I almost felt something, a whisper of a sensation so dim I can't even describe it.

Frequency is so important as a ghost. If one ghost is to touch another they must be at similar frequencies or else they would just go through each other.

Frequency matters to the SECI chamber.

Frequency matters to electricity, which is another form of electromagnetic energy, just like I am.

It clicked in my mind and I suddenly wasn't faking it anymore. I really understood what I was doing. I just had to find the right frequency just like I did naturally now when I picked Emily up, but it was so hard at first.

"Ten seconds," Mary said, but her voice had changed. There was this sadness there, this tone of defeat.

That didn't matter. I tried again and… I definitely felt something, like the zing of a nine-volt battery on your tongue. I liked the feeling. I felt more alert.

I kept going. I knew how to do this. I just had to put enough energy into it, and for Sun I would do anything.

"Five… four…"

I tried again, the zing was stronger, almost too strong, but nothing.

"Three… two… one…"

I tried one more time… and the light flickered on and I felt a jolt run through me that was like… oh God, it was uncomfortable and horrible and so energizing. I loved it. I wasn't into cocaine or meth, but I have to imagine it was something like this. The addict in me woke up and smiled.

I removed my hand and the light went off and I missed

the jolt of energy. I put my hand back in and it went back on.

Mary was talking but I was so distracted by this feeling that I almost missed it. "…I'm so relieved. Oh, thank God, Walter, I was so afraid that I did all this and you weren't really here. That I was fooling myself with the odd tone I heard on the police scanners last night, and it wasn't you and Emily that found the body."

She sank into the chair, tears flowing down her cheeks.

Her hands were shaking and she rubbed at her face. Not thinking, I pulled my hand away from the switch and the light went out. I missed the feeling of the electricity, but this was more important.

"What are you talking about, Mary?" I asked, even though I knew she couldn't hear me. The electricity running through me was kind of like an extreme caffeine buzz and it fed the anger and the rage. "What the hell are you talking about!"

"I mean," Mary went on, "it wasn't easy finding that girl and getting her out there this morning, setting the second arrow up for you. Breaking into the union and putting the poster up. All in conjunction with Sun being here for this shoot. It all had to go perfectly. I… I can't believe that it did." She was looking around the trailer, her eyes trying to find me, but I wasn't visible to her.

She was babbling now, in between her tears. She wasn't right. She wasn't stable. She had done all of this to get me here, to be with her.

"I moved up here, to Flagstaff, after you died," she said. "I know you don't remember that night… the propofol took the memory away… and I… I guess that was for the best. I'd be in jail otherwise. I wouldn't be here now with you."

She dug into her right sleeve and pulled out a small

black switch about the size of a roll of quarters and held it in her hand. "I'm glad you're here with me, Walter. Today's the day that I join you on the other side. It's only right that you are here."

She took a deep breath and pressed the red switch on top and… nothing. Just a small click, and I realized what it was. A dead man's switch. This was far from over.

And then slowly, haltingly, she told me how I died.

Chapter Twenty

"I WAS IN LOVE WITH YOU," MARY SNIFFED AS SHE PACED the trailer, occasionally looking out the windows, which I was doing too.

The travel trailer was parked in a large lot that had a few other trailers set up, a semi, and a few cars. There was a small rustic-looking building fifty yards away and beyond that pine trees with some aspen groves. After a few looks, I recognized it as the cross-country ski area. We were outside of Flagstaff a ways, on the road that went to the Grand Canyon and was quite isolated.

I could see some white tents set up in the woods a couple hundred yards away, but there was no movement near us.

"And you never noticed," Mary continued. "Sun, Sun, Sun. It was always Sun. You thought of nothing but the past."

She walked to the door and peered out and then turned around, leaning against the door with a sigh.

"Look at me, Walter," she said, slapping her free hand against her chest. She was sweating and had unzipped her jacket showing a bit of the C4 strapped to her chest. "How's a girl like me supposed to compete with her? With the memory of her? With the perfect life you think you would have had but for that traffic accident."

Mary's tone was shrill, her eyes a bit too wide, her movements sudden and unpredictable. I had seen many sides of Mary in the five years we worked together, but not this side. I had seen depressed Mary and elated Mary and sad Mary, but not manic Mary.

"The truth is, Walter, you needed me. I wanted you, because you were a kind, handsome man in an unkind world. Because you really cared for your patients. Because you were so gentle. But you were so lost. I may not be skinny. I may not be beautiful, not like her, but all I wanted was to love you, to be with you, and you… goddamnit, Walter, you were so damn dense you couldn't take a hint."

Tears rolled slowly down her cheeks. "I gave up on you, after three years, I gave up. I met Ian and I was so glad to have a man interested in me that I didn't see how wounded he was."

She nodded her head slowly. "I know you want me to tell you what happened that night, fill in the blanks of how you died. Because I'm your unfinished business. I'm what's standing between you and your blissful afterlife. But isn't this perfect, Walter? When I was alive, I would tell you all my problems and you would kindly listen and try to help and I would fall a little more in love with you and you wouldn't even notice.

"Sixty-two months, Walter. That's how long we worked together. Sixty-two months. And you never really saw me, saw what I felt, not even once."

She had cut her victims sixty-two times on each side to commemorate each month she had loved me and each month I had missed it.

I wanted to leave. I didn't like seeing Mary like this. I didn't want to know how I died anymore. I just wanted to escape her, but I couldn't.

I had been stupid and obsessed with Sun. All those years after our divorce, I could hardly see another woman. I tried dating, every once in a while I would try, but it was always horrible and my heart was never in it.

Sun was my dream woman and acting was my dream job and I had treated my life after that as a consolation prize, as a defeat, as a reminder that I had almost had it all.

My profession. My practice. My life. All of it was a consolation prize.

"And now I die and Sun dies with me," Mary said, zipping her jacket back up and sitting on the couch so she could see the door. The knuckles of her right hand went white as she gripped the dead man's switch and a bead of sweat trickled down her forehead.

And now Mary was going to kill Sun and I was a ghost and I could do nothing to stop it.

Chapter Twenty-One

MARY WAS SO SHY WHEN I FIRST MET HER. SHE CAME TO her interview at the newly rented, but not yet furnished, offices of Hollywood Dental dressed in a tan skirt and a green blouse buttoned all the way to her neck.

She didn't look comfortable, not at all. She didn't make a lot of eye contact, but she knew her stuff. She had fought in Afghanistan and had more medical experience than the other candidates I had seen. She graduated at the top of her class, and if she survived being an army medic, she could handle a root canal.

But none of that is why I hired her. Well, I did hire her for all of those reasons, but that wasn't the deciding factor.

The deciding factor was that she wasn't my type. At all.

She was pretty in her own way and gentle when I had her examine my own mouth. She spoke thoughtfully and articulated herself clearly, but I wanted to avoid the possibility of falling for any of the women I hired.

I still held out hope for Sun even though it had been over two years since our divorce.

And while Mary and I were friends, while I would

listen to anything she wanted to talk about, I never fully opened up to her. I couldn't. She was an employee.

There was another candidate that was better than Mary, but she was thin with long black hair and brown eyes and quite beautiful. I couldn't have someone with me every day that reminded me of Sun, that I would try to make into a new Sun, so I hired Mary and shoved her so firmly into the little sister zone that I was blind to what was going on.

"So I married Ian," Mary went on, much of the energy out of her voice now. "He had served in Iraq. He knew what kind of nightmares I had because he had them too. We understood each other, but we couldn't help each other." She leaned forward, putting her head in her free hand. "But you know all of this, Walter. He was an angry drunk and he started getting drunk more and more. We fought. He wanted me, but we were not good for each other."

I did know all of this, she had confided in me over the years and I had been sad for her, I had tried to tell her she deserved better, but it hadn't been enough.

"He hit me," she said, her voice barely above a whisper now. "That's the part I didn't tell you. Not anywhere people would see, but he hit me... almost from the beginning."

She was crying. "After I got pregnant, he changed, for a little while, he changed. I thought it was going to work, but..."

The seconds flowed by and she sniffed. I was afraid for what was coming next. I didn't know what it was going to be, but I knew it was going to be bad.

When she raised her head, her eyes were hard and her nostrils were flaring. "But I couldn't stop thinking about you, Walter. It's you I wanted in bed with me, a kind, gentle man. It's your baby I wanted to have. You were so happy and so damn supportive when I told you I was pregnant. I knew you had wanted to be a father so badly. I became more and more convinced that I had the wrong husband and that I was having the wrong man's baby."

She sighed and leaned back on the couch. As she talked, I kept looking out the windows, seeing if there was any movement close. What if her thumb slipped off the dead man's switch? Sun would be coming back after the shoot was done. What then?

"But you were kind and supportive and didn't have one damn clue as to how I felt." She dug in her pocket and pulled out her phone and swiped a few times and held it up. On it was a baby, maybe a year old, with thin brown hair and chubby, happy cheeks. "I never told you, but his middle name is Walter."

I stepped back and heard the whisper of the bardo. It told me this was going to get worse, a whole lot worse, and if I just let go, if I just sank into it, I would never have to know.

"But... he's not mine anymore," she said, her voice shaking. "After you died... I wasn't okay." She barked out an awkward laugh. "I guess it was that, but not *just* that. You had died and I... I had helped you." She shook her head. "Even after I did it, did what you asked, you still couldn't see me."

The call of the bardo got louder. She wasn't clear in what she was saying, but it was clear that it was going to be bad for me.

"That night, Ian and I had a big fight. Over you. He had finally figured it out, proving himself to be at least a little less dense than you when it came to me." She got up and started pacing, gesturing with her hands. I began hoping that her finger would slip, that she would kill herself before Sun got back, while no one else was close enough to get hurt.

"So I left little Walter and drove to the office. You were still there. I told you everything, and you…" she stopped pacing and by some twist of fate she stopped right in front of me and was looking right at me. "And you lost your shit, Walter." She barked out another laugh. "I had no idea you were as wounded as the rest of us. I thought you were the one person who actually had it together. You had given up gambling and propofol. The practice was doing good. But no, it turns out you were just acting."

She shook her head. "And the damnedest thing is that it just made me love you more. You muttered stuff about me being your little sister, how you could never look at me that way, how I would have to find another job."

She started pacing again. "I still had my baby weight and was heavier than normal. I thought that was it, that if I was just skinny, that if I dyed my hair black, that you would love me. I promised you I would change. I begged you to think about it. I kissed you and you acted like the touch of my lips was poison. And then… I got mad."

The bardo sang to me loudly and this time I knew what it was offering wasn't a complete lie, but I ignored it. I couldn't look away now. I had to know.

She went back over to the couch and slumped down. "But you know what, Walter? The propofol was your idea. You told me, 'I have to forget, Mary. I have to forget. If you really love me, you'll help me forget.'

"It was stupid. You weren't making sense. But then you were in the supply room jimmying open the cabinet, your hands shaking like damn leaves. You kept muttering about Haley, about how you were so stupid, about how you didn't know anything. You told me you had just talked to Sun, that she was with some Hollywood guy and you couldn't stand it. You took a vial and a syringe into the room with the big mural of Marilyn Monroe with her white skirt flaring up over the grate. You got in the chair, but your hands were shaking too bad, so you asked me to do it."

She took a deep shuddering breath. "You asked me, Walter. You asked me to help you forget what I had said when I bared my soul to you. You asked me to help you." She shook her head. "And I did, Walter. I helped you."

Chapter Twenty-Two

WHAT MARY SAID DIDN'T BRING BACK THE MEMORY, NOT exactly, but I could see it in my mind. I could see her so scared and vulnerable, dressed in sweats just a month into her new life as a mother pouring her heart out to me.

I didn't like it, but I could imagine my reaction that day. Mary was important to me. She worked with me day after day and I had badly missed her when she had been gone. I cared for her and I knew she cared for me, although I had put that tightly in the sibling column and had from the beginning.

It had been a hard day. My misinterpretation of what Haley wanted from me, the call from Sun about her relationship. And then Mary on top of that broke me enough that my addiction took over.

Looking at it without biology and all the chemicals that come with it, I don't have as much empathy for myself as I might. But I do understand. Addictions, just like the bardo, can get to a point where you just can't say no. It's about resisting in small ways frequently, not one big act of willpower.

"'Please,' you said from the pale blue dental chair," Mary said, "your brown eyes so freaked out. You had managed to load the syringe but you could barely hold it. 'My hands are shaking too much, you do it.' I should have said no, but I didn't. You told me how much propofol to use, but it sounded like way too much, I argued you down to half."

Tears started running down her cheeks. "I asked you what happened with Haley and you told me you thought the little bitch had a crush on you, but it turns out she only wanted to keep her job. You told me that you knew Sun was gone for good and it was too much to bear. And..." She paused, her chest heaving, her head in her free hand, but hardly a sound coming out of her. "I was so mad, Walter. So mad."

With her free hand she beat on the couch, dust puffing out in ghostly plumes. She didn't do it once or twice, but over and over.

"I came there offering you what you wanted most, Walter. I came offering you love from someone you already cared about, from someone you already loved on some level. I came offering you a lifelong companion." She continued to beat on the couch rhythmically. "I came offering you me... and... and... you could only grieve the loss of your wife, the perfect Sun, and your misunderstanding with the skinny, way too young for you, Haley."

She stopped, hunched over, panting.

I realized that this was a confession. Mary was confessing her sin to me, explaining it to me. This was Mary's last confession. She had no intention of living. And that made her very, very dangerous.

"So I pushed the amount of propofol you asked me to," she said, sitting up, her voice low and quiet. "I saw your face relax when it hit you, that little moment of ecstasy. And do you know what you did then?"

I didn't know and I didn't want to know, but it was too late to turn away. Too much was at stake.

"You said, 'Thank you, Mary. Thank you. I do love you, you know. I love you like the sister I never had.'"

Mary slapped the couch once, a plume of dust rising into the air. "You told me that like it made it all right. Like being loved like a sister when I clearly had much more complex feelings for you would be enough to make me feel better, so I…"

She bit her lip, her eyelids fluttering rapidly. She swallowed hard and said, "So I pushed the whole damn syringe without even really thinking about it. You smiled, so big you smiled, the words 'thank you' on your lips, and then you passed out. And then you stopped breathing. And then you…"

The room was suddenly silent, too silent.

When I had resolved to find my murderer to deal with my unfinished business, I thought it would be something clean, something simple, something understandable. Not this mess of bad luck and human frailty. Not this unintended moment where Mary just did a little more than I asked.

And that's the key here. I asked for it.

Emily, with her murder sense, hadn't been wrong about me. The act of another person had caused my death. But it wasn't that simple. I had fallen to my addiction. I had convinced Mary to help me use again. I had done this.

In that moment, I knew that I had been wrong about why I was an earth-bound spirit. I thought my unfinished business was solving my own murder. It wasn't. It never had been.

My unfinished business is about me, about the choices I

made and how I lived my life after it fell apart, looking back, not looking forward. It's not about being the victim of one terrible moment in Mary's life.

"I wasn't all right after you died," she said, her voice slow and her words thick. "After I killed you. I tried, I tried so hard to put it behind me. To find a way to be okay with Ian and baby Walter. To move on. But it was too much for me. I kept having dreams about that last smile on your face. You see, it wasn't a good smile, not a smile of a happy person. It was a smile of relief, of addiction, of forgetting.

"And I couldn't forget." She paused and took a deep breath. "I lost my job at first—Dr. Wheeler liked Haley better anyway. I lost my baby next. I wasn't stable. I did things. Ian left me, took the baby, got full custody.

"I did what you asked me to do, Walter, and I lost everything. There is nothing in this world for me anymore. But you, Walter. You didn't stay dead. You started writing, and I knew when I started reading your words that it was you. That it was real. That there was life beyond this." She slapped her chest, sweat trickling down her forehead. She must be hot in that jacket this long.

"So I read everything you ghosts were writing. I plotted and I planned and I..." Her voice broke and what came out was something of a cackle. "And I did some really bad things, but here you are, Walter. It worked. I'm so relieved it actually worked."

She stood up, a smile on her face, and I had to imagine that it was as disturbing as my last smile. It was the smile of a mad woman that was about to get what she wanted.

"And now, Walter," Mary said, looking out the window behind the couch where in the distance I could see movement. "Now Sun and I will be joining you in the afterlife and we can all sort this out there together."

Chapter Twenty-Three

I SCREAMED FOR EMILY. I NEEDED HELP. I HAD NO IDEA what was keeping them. It seemed like it had been hours since she had left, but it couldn't have been more than fifteen or twenty minutes. But that was long, too long. Had something happened to Emily?

Mary was still talking, going back over what she had already said, but I didn't care anymore. I knew the truth. I knew the huge part I had played in all of this when I was alive and since I've been dead.

There was guilt, tons of it, but that had to wait on the sidelines. It wasn't quite time for its big scene. We were at Mary's endgame and I had to stop her from killing anyone else.

I flew fast through the trailers around me and found them all to be empty. I flew out to the tents, out where they were shooting, and I saw Sun standing over the fallen body of a man in an aspen grove, the green leaves making a pleasant sound in the morning breeze.

The man was on his stomach, splayed out on the ground on top of layers of decomposing aspen leaves.

That was an actor, he would get up when the scene was over, but the similarity to the bodies that brought me here was striking and bizarre.

Sun looked disheveled and hurt, but resolute, her brown eyes narrowed as she looked into the distance.

Behind her, the sun was just coming up over the grey hump of Humphreys Peak, the yellow light spiking down and warming her face. They had three cameras on her from different angles back about twenty yards and two drones buzzing overhead. You had one chance a day to get a shot like this and they weren't taking any chances.

This was a hero shot, showing Sun's character, Melissa Lee, after the trauma that had befallen her, leaving the viewers with hope that she would find a way and would eventually get over this and be okay.

If only it was like that.

Her show was a good one, they would have some follow-up on her difficulties coping, but it would still make it seem easy when it wasn't.

But that moment, looking at a worn but still strong Sun, filled me up. It was Hollywood fakery, but it was just what I needed.

This thing wasn't a movie or a TV show. This was life and death. Behind me I had Mary wanting to die and in front of me I had Sun still vibrant and strong, the morning sun shining on her tired face as she looked towards the future.

I knew what I had to do. It was terrible, but it was clear.

Chapter Twenty-Four

MARY PAULSON WAS SICK. THAT WAS THE ONLY WAY I could look at it. I knew her, she wasn't a bad person, but she had broken. Her time in Afghanistan, her postpartum depression, and me… basically talking her into killing me. All that had broken her.

My death wasn't a suicide, that was not my intent. It wasn't a murder, that wasn't Mary's intent, not really. It was just a terrible moment as this world frequently creates.

And now to salvage this mess, I had to create another terrible moment. One I didn't know I could recover from, but I was determined that no one else die today. No one else besides Mary, that is.

"That's a wrap!" the director called, a middle-aged man with greying hair. "Great job, Sun!"

Sun sighed, her shoulders falling and the fatigue returning to her face in full. The body below her stirred, a Hollywood-handsome man I didn't recognize grinned up and Sun and said, "Glad that's over—being dead is so boring."

If I had the time, I would have snorted at that, death

had been anything but boring for me. But time was what I didn't have. I flew fast back toward Mary, back toward the trailer, and halfway there, I heard a "pop" and Emily was there.

Her eyes were wide and her usually perfect blond curls were disheveled. "Sorry, Walter. I'm..." she looked around the forest realizing we weren't in the trailer with Mary. "Galt and his boys were harassing JJ and it got serious and..." Her eyes narrowed as she studied me. "What's going on, Walter?"

My mind reeled. I knew if I told Emily what I meant to do that she would try to stop me, but there was no other way. "We don't have much time," I said. "Sun is back there. Stay with her. If she comes this way try to stop her."

"How?" Emily asked, her brow furrowing.

"I don't know! Just do something. We don't have much time. Please, Emily. Please stay with Sun for me. She..." I felt tears coming and I could have stopped them, but I didn't and they rolled down my cheeks. I needed Emily to listen to me. I needed her to stay away, because while I was sure a human wouldn't survive what was about to happen, I had no idea what it would do to a ghost, and I couldn't have this day ending with Emily hurt or worse.

From her disheveled appearance there was clearly a story about her and JJ and Galt and his boys, but I didn't have time for it. I didn't have time for anything. Sun was already walking this way.

"Okay," she said slowly. "I'll... I'll think of something."

I flew back towards the trailer and quietly said, "I love you, Emily." I knew that Emily with her excellent ghostly hearing could hear it. I knew it would make her wonder and doubt. But I was done not saying the things that needed to be said.

Chapter Twenty-Five

MARY WAS LOOKING OUT THE WINDOW AT THE PEOPLE slowly walking towards the trailers when I got back. Her face was red and her hand holding the dead man's switch was white knuckled.

"…all your fault, Walter," she was saying. "You know that, don't you? If you had just blown me off like a normal person and not freaked out and gone for the propofol." She shook her head. "When you got the screwdriver and went to the locker, I told you that Midge would quit. That you would lose everything. And you looked at me and I remember your eyes. Not the soft lovely brown they usually were, but your pupils were dilated like you were terrified, and you said, 'I'll replace it. She'll never know.'"

Mary sank back down onto the couch and sighed. "You should have just told me you met someone, Walter. Or lied and said you once had feelings for me but buried them away when I met Ian. Or…" she trailed off with a sigh.

She was mad. She was ranting. She was blaming it all on me and I had to agree with her on that one. I stopped listening. I went back to the light switch above the little sink and started lowering the frequency of my hand like I had before to switch on the light.

I took it down to SECI chamber level and kept going. I felt my body slowing down, like it was thickening. I did my best to not think about the minute or two I had before Sun would be too close. I tried to tune out Mary's babbling and blaming. I tried to not think about Emily and what would happen if she got too curious about what I was up to. And I tried to not worry about what would happen to me.

A ghost's form is this localized emanation of very high-frequency EM energy. What is a ghost beyond that? I don't know. A faded ghost is just gone, like when Emily couldn't pop to Anna-Maria. But what would happen to a ghost that was in the middle of an explosion when those forces ripped through the localized emanation of EM energy that is a ghost?

It was those thoughts that I tried to let go of. Tried to not worry about. An explosion was going to go off, I was just trying to make it happen before any of the living or any other dead were here.

I put my hand into the light switch and... nothing. Damn it!

I could hear voices as the cast and crew approached.

Mary was crying. It was this half-hysterical, half-mani-acal sound and it was getting to me. It was speaking to me, or maybe it was the bardo. It was telling me that this was my doing. That I had pushed her over the edge. That I was responsible for all of this.

I shook it off. I refocused. I ignored the voices getting closer. I lowered my right hand's frequency and put it in the switch and... the light flickered on.

"What..." Mary mumbled between the tears. "Walter? Are... are you trying to say something?"

I pulled my hand away and the light went out. Mary

got up and slowly walked to the kitchenette, her eyes red rimmed and her round cheeks stained with tears. "Maybe you just want me to know that you are here. That we will soon be together."

She stood in front of the sink and waved her free arm around and it passed through me and I felt a slight tingle. Mary had an electromagnetic field, just like I did. A much denser one, and I felt it. But I didn't want her touch. I didn't want anything to do with her.

"Not long now," she said, nodding out the window where Sun was striding over the forest floor towards us, maybe thirty yards away. I could see Emily walking next to her, looking up and shouting. "And you'll be able to tell me yourself."

I was out of time.

I looked at the woman next to me and it wasn't Mary Paulson anymore. It wasn't the woman I knew who was working next to me all those years. It couldn't be her. If it was, I couldn't do what I needed to do. This woman, her name was Mary, but she was someone so different I could barely recognize her.

I looked at my slowed down hand, it didn't really look any different, but it felt different. I bit my lip and I put my hand into the dead man's switch Mary was holding and… nothing.

Damnit!

I could hear Emily's voice getting closer, her shouting and pleading with Sun. I could hear the chatter of the rest of the cast and crew as they shook off the manic energy of a night shoot.

What was wrong? My hand was at the right frequency. I stuck it back in the light switch and the light flickered on.

"What is it, Walter?" Mary asked. "If you are trying to

convince me not to do this, it won't work. I am going to do this. Not much longer now."

I didn't look out. I stared at the switch in her hand. She held the button on the top down and that stopped electricity from flowing, that broke the connection. I didn't understand the electronics inside, but I tried. The switch was spring loaded, and if it popped up, a small piece of metal would complete the circuit. Below it two wires traveled to the switch. If I tore it apart, stripped the wires and joined them, then it would go off.

But this wasn't high-voltage AC electricity like the light switch. This was low-voltage DC electricity, battery powered. Maybe that was it. My frequency was good for AC but not for DC.

But what should I do then? Go up or go down with my frequency?

I had no idea, but I put my hand inside of hers so it encompassed the whole switch. I stopped thinking about it and tried to feel. When I was getting close with the light switch, I could feel the slight buzz of electricity.

Mary was babbling, her eyes far too wide, her knuckles white and sweat trickling down her face.

I could hear the people getting closer. I should have looked, but I couldn't. However close Sun was, it had to be better if the explosion went off in the trailer with her outside. I focused on the switch. I varied my frequency. I searched for the slightest feeling.

"I love you, Walter," Mary said, her voice suddenly calm. "Since the day we met, I have loved you."

It didn't matter. Nothing she said mattered. I went with the feeling and... there was a bright flash of light and I knew nothing.

Chapter Twenty-Six

I FEAR FOR THE FUTURE. ONE WHERE THE LIVING DO things to get the attention of the dead and where the dead are forced to do things to the living. Terrible things.

Mary Paulson died instantly when I completed the circuit and the C4 strapped to her exploded. The travel trailer didn't contain the explosion or all the bits of metal that flew out, but it got some of it, it slowed it down.

The fireball reached an adjacent trailer and several pine trees ignited. Bits of metal and wood whizzed out into the forest and the parking lot.

Sun Parker was fifteen yards away, tired and desperate for some rest. The flash of light startled her and then the concussion of the blast knocked her down, bits of debris flying right over her.

Emily was buffeted by it and shouted out my name. While it weakened her greatly, it had no other effect.

A production assistant by the name of Alan took a bit of metal in his chest, and an actress named Sally got a pretty serious head laceration.

And it ripped through my ghostly form and destroyed it.

And I was gone.

I can't tell you where I was because I don't know, but I believe it was the same place we go when we fade. It is a state where we know nothing. Complete unconsciousness.

It was only the tiniest of moments as the light flashed and the unleashed energy ripped through my ghost form, but I felt the darkness coming and I was glad. I was ready for the comfort of the void. I was happy to not be.

But I didn't stay gone.

Eight days, twenty-three hours, and five minutes later I came back. To the same exact place I had been, except I was hovering several feet over charred ground in the morning looking at the burned-out bit of forest.

"I'm so glad you are okay," Emily said, a worried look on her round face. She was sitting on the charred ground close by. Waiting for me.

Being faded for nearly nine days is a long time. There was good reason for her to wonder whether I was coming back.

"What... what happened?" I asked. At first the nothingness of being faded clung to me like a warm blanket until the cold winds of memory ripped it away. "Oh..." I gasped. "I... Sun. Is Sun okay?"

Emily nodded. "She's fine. They took her to the hospital and held her for observation overnight, but she's fine. Some minor hearing loss, but it could have been a lot worse."

I floated to the ground and gingerly walked over to Emily. My steps were careful and tentative. I wanted to act as human as possible after what I had done. I didn't want to go fast at all.

The lollipop on her T-shirt was its usually cheery red,

but that didn't match with the serious face I was confronted with. She wasn't showing her emotions and had it locked to its default color. Not a good sign.

"I love you, Emily," I said. I had said it right before I blew Mary up and I figured she had heard it, but it wasn't the right way to say it and it needed to be said.

She stood up and smiled, but it was low-wattage and tentative. Something wasn't right.

"Is JJ okay?" I asked. "Anna-Maria? What happened with Galt and them?"

Emily shrugged and it was a lazy thing as if she barely had the energy to move, which was never the case with a ghost. "JJ's fine. He was faded for a few days, but that's it. He ended up summoning the call and Galt lost one of his boys to it. Things are..." her face darkened and she shook her head.

I squatted down in front of her and reached for her hand but she took a step back.

"Mary?" I asked. It was just one word, but it held a lot. I was asking her if Mary had moved on or if Mary was a ghost.

Emily shrugged. "No one has seen her, but..."

I nodded. I had been faded almost nine days, who knows what the explosion would have done to a brand-new ghost.

"Then what?" I asked.

Emily shook her head, her blond curls bouncing, but even that seemed low energy. "After all of this," she began looking around the charred ground and trees, "there is a group of ghosts that want to shut down the SECI chambers. They want it to go back to the way it was. There are living that feel the same. Factions are forming. Equipment has been malfunctioning at Afterlife Communications."

I tried to take it all in, but my mind wasn't quite all

here yet. There are always those that resist change. It's natural. There are some that do so violently. And new technology always brings unintended consequences—like what Mary did to get my attention.

"And what do you think, Emily?" I asked, suddenly understanding a little bit of her mood.

"I don't know, Walter," she said, slowly, like she had to think about each word. "I think we were doing some good, but…" She shrugged and looked around again.

Ghosts fighting each other. A human murdering to get a ghost's attention. Factions forming among the dead over the SECI chamber. Equipment being sabotaged at Afterlife Communications. And Mary's status still unknown.

It was a lot.

But it wasn't enough to explain how restrained Emily was, how missing the four-year-old was despite her ever-present lisp.

"What else, Emily?" I asked.

She hugged her chest, her green eyes hard and searching me. "I'm mad at you, Walter, and I'm afraid for you."

My mouth opened but I couldn't find any words. Her delivery was so flat and devoid of emotion that I suddenly understood that she wasn't just mad, she was furious.

"You should have told me what you were going to do," she said.

"But…" I began, "you would have stopped me. You would have—"

She held her hand up, cutting me off. "No, Walter, I would have helped you. I would have shared the burden with you and…" she looked down at the ground and kicked at the dirt that her ghostly foot couldn't move.

"But I didn't know what the explosion would do to a ghost, I…"

She met my eyes again and hers were fierce. "I did know what would happen, Walter. And I thought you, of all the people here, wouldn't be treating me like a child when things got bad. Wouldn't be making decisions for me. Wouldn't be trying to take care of me." She sighed.

I suddenly felt hollow. I had treated her like a child. If it had been JJ, I would have probably told him what I was going to do and asked him to stay away. But I didn't do that with Emily. I misdirected her. I let her appearance dictate how I treated her.

"I'm so sorry, Emily," I said

She nodded. "Thank you, Walter."

"What now?" I asked.

She smiled but it looked painful. "Now I'm leaving, Walter. For a long time, I think."

The reality of it tumbled down on me. "She" was leaving, not "we." No more Emily who loves murder so much and Walter who just wants to complete his unfinished business running around solving murders. No more Walter and Emily.

"Where are you going?" I asked.

She shrugged. "I think I'll start with Paris and see where it leads me."

"I really am sorry, Emily," I said. "I really am."

She gave me another one of those painful smiles. "I know you are. You were doing your best in a very difficult situation, I just…"

"What?"

She sighed and shook her head. "I can't explain it, what it's like looking like this and being dead for so long. I can't explain what it feels like when everyone treats you the way you look, the way they think someone that looks like me should be treated. I…" Her eyes roamed around the damage of the explosion and then found mine again. "I just need to leave."

I nodded slowly. "Okay, Emily. I'm... I hope you find what you are looking for."

She smiled and this time it was a little more real. "I hope you do too. JJ said to tell you that if you are ready for the call, he's happy to help."

With a "pop" she was gone and I was left amongst the damage alone.

Epilogue

EVEN THOUGH I FOUND OUT WHO KILLED ME, MY unfinished business is not finished. In fact, I was so wrong about what it even was. It wasn't about dying from a propofol overdose in my dental chair, it's about how I lived my life after I lost Sun and my acting career, including how I participated in that overdose. It's about how I lived my afterlife always looking for a way out. It's about the conflict happening now in our world among the living and the dead and what that means when the SECI chamber pierces the veil. And it's now about how I lost my best friend Emily by treating her like the four-year-old she looked like and not like the accomplished, experienced ghost she is. By treating her like a child and not my partner and best friend.

I have a lot of work to do. I never took up JJ on his offer of summoning the call for me. I am not ready.

"What do you think?" I asked Anna-Maria as I paced around the corpse.

We were in downtown Tucson almost three months after Emily left, the yellowish sodium glow of the streetlights filtering into the dark downtown alley. The young man looked out of place. A tourist with flip-flops and a crisp new concert T-shirt. He was slumped against a dinged-up dumpster, a trickle of dried blood on his chin.

Anna-Maria had come back from her encounter with Galt and his boys more than a little angry. They had fought, although her passionate explanation hasn't made it clear what exactly had happened, but she ended up fading and came back angry and she needed something to do besides trying to get back at Galt. So, with Emily gone, I have been working with Anchor's Irregulars, doing my best to turn them into detectives in their own right.

Which seems kind of ridiculous. It's not like anyone ever trained me. Well, that's not true. Emily trained me to be what she called a "proper ghost" and channeled all the twisted emotions I was feeling when she found me into something useful.

Anna-Maria needed something to keep her busy, something to do, and so did I. So it was time for more ghost detectives running around solving murders.

She was dressed in her tight jeans and leather jacket, her raven's wing black hair pulled back into a ponytail, a look of concentration on her youthful face.

"No obvious wounds, just this bit of blood on his chin," she said, stooping down and examining him closely. "The concert let out two hours ago—this kid shouldn't have been down here."

The young man was Anna-Maria's age, so her calling him "kid" just made me smile. But, then again, Anna-Maria had lived a lot of life in her twenty years.

I could feel his soul stirring in the flesh that used to contain him. This was likely to be an easy case, at least in terms of how he died and who killed him.

"You got this?" I asked.

She looked up from the pavement where she was squatting, an uncharacteristic look of timidity on her face. She composed herself and nodded. "Of course, Boss. I got this. I'll go grab Blinky if I need backup. I know you've got a tough one up in Phoenix."

I nodded, but studied her a bit more wondering if this was what Emily had been like with me. Seeing if I had enough of a challenge to keep me engaged but not too much of a challenge that I would be overwhelmed.

Anna-Maria was not nearly as wet behind the ears as I was back then, but she tended towards overconfidence and brashness and that could just get you into trouble. I wanted her to be focused and challenged, but I didn't want her getting anywhere near the bardo.

Things are changing. Everyone knows it. The little ghost detective thing I'm running is, in part, to give the living a good impression of the dead, to show that we can contribute to society, that it is important to hear our voices and not shut them off.

That's right. I am now involved in a kind of a "ghosts are great" PR campaign. As I had been for the first few stories I wrote, even though I didn't know it then. I wrote these cases up and Tamara and Jin published them. People read them. They thought about death differently. They thought about the afterlife differently.

Solving the murders has always been the focus, but telling these stories is important too. It's not lost on me what happened with Mary. That some might do bad things based on what I write. I still wrestle with it, but I think the good outweighs the bad here. I have to think that the world will be better if the living know, without a shadow of a doubt, that death is not the end.

I want to go after Emily. I have been practicing popping and I can pop to Sun reliably, and the rest of the

Irregulars I can pop to occasionally. I figure Emily is important enough that I can pop to her too. But Banquo told me to let her be, to give her time. This is how she deals with being dead so long, she withdraws completely, isolates, and eventually comes back.

But how long will that take? A year? A decade? Longer?

Emily feels like my most important piece of unfinished business. I no longer think that a ghost's unfinished business is one thing. My view on this afterlife has changed dramatically. I now think we are ghosts so that we can become better people before we "move on."

And solving murders and mentoring Anna-Maria is part of that, but I miss Emily so very much.

"I got this," Anna-Maria said with a grim smile. "Really, Walter. You can go."

I nodded, giving the corpse one last look. The ghost would be separating soon and then she would have to start mentoring a brand-new ghost. I looked into her brown eyes and smiled. I could feel it. She was ready.

"Thank you," I said and flew off into the night.

There was another murder to investigate and a whole lot of unfinished business to attend to.

More Mystery?

WHAT COMES NEXT FOR WALTER AND EMILY IS currently a mystery to me. If you'd like to find out news on them or my other writing, join my email newsletter and never miss a thing.

In the mean time you might want to check out *The Blood of Carterville*, the first book in my new mystery series.

The Blood of Carterville

Carterville, AZ. Population: 286. People with powers: 198

Just a sleepy former mining town turned tourist haven in the mountains of Northern Arizona until the "incident." The meteorite that gave everyone in the town powers, but only while near Carterville.

Some people think that the

blood of Carterville bestows
powers, but when a tourist stabs police Chief Henry
Carter's best friend, everything changes.

Henry will do the unthinkable to save his friend. But
when the crime gets complicated, can Henry find the
culprit and save his town, much less survive?

From Robert J. McCarter, long-time Arizona resident
and the author of *Shuffled Off: A Ghost's Memoir*, comes a
mystery and a town you will never forget.

Get The Blood of Carterville now!

Afterword

Now that we're at the end of the book, I can talk more about the story (that's a spoiler alert, you'all).

You might be wondering what comes next for Walter and Emily. I know I am. And the short answer is, I don't know. The longer answer is below, but in the meantime, the best way to stay in the loop and find out what happens next is to sign up for my newsletter at RobertJMcCarter.com/newsletter.

I am what you would call a discovery writer, which means I don't do a lot of planning up front and I "discover" the story as I write it. It's this fascinating, organic process that has me writing much like a reader reads. So that explains why I don't know what happens next to Walter and Emily but looking at what has already happened, there are a couple of really exciting things that came out in these stories:

- The ghost world is changing. Humans and ghosts are acting differently now that the living are believing in the dead. From solving crimes

together, to ghosts committing crimes, or
humans doing strange things to get ghosts
attention. And ghosts are divided about
whether they should be interacting with the
living at all. There is a huge amount of
fascinating stories to explore here. Some might
be with Walter Anchor stories or I might end
up telling them through novels in the main
ghost series. I'm just not sure yet. We'll see.

- Walter now knows what his unfinished business
really is and there are plenty more stories of his
to tell. My creative mind is currently mulling
over a full-length Walter Anchor novel where
he tries to clean up the mess between him and
Emily and really get to his unfinished business
all while taking on a really complicated case.

So those are things that stand out to me and will likely
feed into future efforts.

I hope you all enjoyed the adventure. Keep your eyes
open for more books from me. While I don't have any
more Walter Anchor stories in the queue (yet) I've got some
fun stuff coming out very soon.

Acknowledgments

This series took a long time to complete. It started in 2012 and here we are in 2020, so there are plenty of people that helped along the way, so here we go.

Big thanks Doctor Olivas who was such a great dentist that not only did he make up for a lot of not so great dentists, he inspired me to make Walter a former dentist.

To Kevin J. Anderson for his steadfast support of writers and for the inspiration of *Dan Shambles, Zombie PI*.

Huge thanks to my stalwart band of beta readers: Roni Hornstein and Peter Klein; my proofreader Diana Cox; and my publishing assistant Elizabeth Fitzekam. I can't explain to you what a relief it is to have other eyes on these stories before they make it to you.

And a huge hug and thanks to my most amazing wife Aleia N. O'Reilly. She's my first listener (I read these stories to her before anyone else sees them) and the key to me being a writer. If you love these stories, you can thank her. They literally would not exist without her.

And thank you so much for spending your precious

time reading these stories. I hope you enjoyed the adventure!

About the Author

Robert J. McCarter is the author of seven novels, three novellas, and dozens of short stories. He is a finalist for the *Writers of the Future* contest and his stories have appeared or are forthcoming in *The Saturday Evening Post, Pulphouse Fiction Magazine, Fiction River, Andromeda Spaceways Inflight Magazine,* and numerous anthologies.

His latest effort is a serialized novel called *Woody and June Versus the Apocalypse*, a story of adventure and love and taking things (even the apocalypse) in stride. Of his novel, *Seeing Forever*, Kirkus Reviews says, "Sci-fi as it should be: engaging, moving, and grand in scope."

He lives in the mountains of Arizona with his amazing wife and his ridiculously adorable dogs.

Find out more at:
robertjmccarter.com